For Gail, with love

Also by David George Clarke

The Dust of Centuries

Quincentenarian

The Delusion Gambit

Fatal Consequences

The Cotton and Silk Thrillers

Irrefutable Evidence

Remorseless

The Cambroni Vendetta

An Imperfect Revenge

Non-Fiction

Hong Kong Under The Microscope

A History of the Hong Kong Government Laboratory 1879–2004

AN IMPERFECT REVENGE

DAVID GEORGE CLARKE

AN IMPERFECT REVENGE

clarkeFiction

The best laid schemes of mice and men
Go oft awry,
And leave us nought but grief and pain,
For promised joy!

Robert Burns

Part One

Chapter One

2016

"Posso aiutarti?" *Can I help you?*

The accent was strong; the words slurred, hardly comprehensible.

Jane Bawley felt a jolt of panic surge through her body. Who the hell was this powerfully built man with hideous, twisted features who had appeared in front of her, blocking her way? Where had he come from? A moment ago there had only been dense forest either side of a narrow, ill-defined trail winding its way through thickets of bramble and tangled creeper, the same trail she had taken two hours earlier when she was looking for the abandoned villa. But now, without any warning, the nightmare she had long banished into the darkest recesses of her memory had once again burst into life.

Or so it seemed, and she wasn't about to take any chances.

Her grip on the torch in her right hand tightened, its rigid plastic frame giving her a flicker of reassurance. To think she had almost left it at the abandoned villa for when she returned later.

"What do you want?" gasped Jane in Italian as she took a sharp step backwards. She had almost walked into him. Was that what he had intended?

"Aiutarti?" slurred the man, the movement of his mouth

restricted by a thick, twisted rope of scar tissue running up from his jawline, across his left eye socket and disappearing into a mass of unkempt black curls. His right hand reached out to grab her shoulder.

"Keep away!" screamed Jane, this time in English. "Don't touch me!"

As she tried to retreat farther, her heel caught in a root and she tumbled awkwardly onto her back, the sharp contact with the uneven ground winding her.

The man shook his head rapidly, wild eyes darting across her body.

He stepped forward and knelt in front of her, positioning his right knee between her spread-eagled legs.

"No!" she screamed, as his right hand grabbed her left wrist, pinning it to the ground.

His face was now inches from hers. She twisted her head to one side to avoid the ragged, panting breath from his looming mouth and the coarse stubble on a chin not shaved for several days.

"Aiutarti?" he repeated, the saliva now dripping from his moist lips.

Jane's mind raced back to the awful night on Wimbledon Common four years before when another man had appeared out of nowhere, like this one had. He was also strong and had pinned her down, like this one had. On that occasion she had been more than a little tipsy, heading home late after a summer office party, a short skirt making the man's job even easier for him.

It had been the beginning of months of degradation, starting with the medical examination, the morning-after pill, the tests to make sure she hadn't been infected with an STD. And then the trial when they caught him, the smart defence lawyer making it sound all her fault. She'd provoked him; she'd encouraged him, that happily married man with two young children, while she was single with a string of dubious boyfriends and lovers in her history, married men among them. The jury found him not guilty. She'd been raped, injured, debased, and they had blamed her.

It wasn't going to happen again. This time she was sober and wearing jeans, and this time she had a weapon. Jane firmed her grip on the torch and swung it hard in the direction of the man's head, slamming it into his left temple with all the force she could summon.

But it wasn't enough to knock him out. He yelled with pain and surprise, his free hand reaching for his head as he slumped to one side, releasing his grip on Jane's wrist.

She rolled away from him and sprung to her feet, the torch still grasped in her hand. She looked down at the man. He was struggling to sit up, one hand clamped to the side of his head. He lifted his eyes to hers, his bewilderment evident, but the snarl forced on his features by the scar was hard to read, and Jane wasn't prepared to risk anything.

She lifted the torch, as if to strike him again. He recoiled, his arms shooting up to protect his head. He screamed something incomprehensible, something angry, the sound chilling Jane in her agitated state.

"Bastard!" she screamed. "Fucking bastard!"

She looked around in desperation. She needed to get away, but it was more than two kilometres to Villa Brocanti. Her attacker was young and tall and he looked fit and strong; if he recovered and chased after her, he would certainly catch her. At thirty-nine, she was hardly old, but she wasn't tall or strong, and she certainly wasn't fit. And a second time, he would probably be more forceful. No, two kilometres was way too far.

On the other hand, the abandoned villa was much closer. It was a no-brainer; she turned and ran.

Earlier, after finding that the bolts fastening the hinges of a well-hidden cellar door to the wall were loose and needed little persuasion to be removed, she had entered the villa and started to explore. The many elaborately painted walls and ceilings she found were no surprise — she knew about them; that was why she was there. It was what she found in addition that had shocked her to the core, sending her racing in terror from the villa for help. Yet even with the horror of what she had seen, thoughts of being attacked in this tranquil forest couldn't have been further from her mind.

But now she was running back along the trail, back to those dark rooms and corridors, running for her life, hoping to outwit the deranged man crashing through the undergrowth about a hundred metres behind her.

She charged through the cellar door, her torch beam slicing into the darkness beyond. Not pausing for breath, she sprinted to the stairs at the far end that led up to the ground floor and the labyrinth beyond. As she took them two at a time, she heard the man pounding through the cellar behind her, his steps getting ever closer.

<hr>

Chapter Two

Evie Lorrigan glared at the empty desk in front of her, as if radiating her displeasure would conjure up a receptionist. Where was everybody? This was a hotel, for Christ's sake! Or an agriturismo, as they preferred to call it. So where were the staff? It wasn't as if they weren't expecting her; the arrangements were all in place. They needed her review; they were desperate for it. She could make a difference; she *would* make a difference. As a senior travel writer with the prestigious online magazine WanderFever, with years of experience under her belt and a substantial following, Evie Lorrigan always did. In Evie's opinion, the byline of her interwoven initials was a hallmark for cutting-edge travel writing.

She shuffled off her backpack — camouflage-patterned like her trademark cargo pants — and slammed her open palm onto a call bell at one corner of the desk.

"Anybody here?" she yelled, not even trying to keep the edge from her voice. "Hello? Buongiorno?"

No response. The small reception area of Villa Brocanti remained eerily quiet, an aura of abandonment hanging in the air. She had sensed it as soon as she stepped from the taxi, the silence enveloping her as the cab disappeared down the gravelled drive, the crunch of tyres on stones fading to nothing.

Evie sighed in exasperation in the stillness of the lobby. She wanted the shower and swim she'd been promising herself throughout the drive from Perugia, the Umbrian city where she'd spent a frustrating hour searching for the office of the local agent of WanderFever. And what did she discover once she'd found it and made herself understood to the totally unhelpful secretary made up like she was about to audition for a porn movie?

"Ronaldo not 'ere, signora," she'd been informed with dismissive indifference.

"Well, if he's not here, where is he?"

"Out of town." The secretary's shrug, accompanied by a long-perfected pout, was designed to close the conversation.

Out of town! Couldn't someone in head office in London have told her that before she wasted her time?

The damn taxi driver the secretary reluctantly summoned for her hadn't helped either. Swarthy and smelling of sweat, he was full of elaborate shrugs and hand gestures when she'd asked for the air con to be turned on. From the torrent of excited Italian that followed and the many heavy thumps of the man's fist onto the dashboard, she deduced that the air con must be broken. She had wound down the windows and slumped into the rear seat, wafting her hand under her wrinkled nose whenever the driver looked at her in his mirror and launched into another outburst of what she assumed were excuses.

The drive with the windows open had been hot and dusty, especially the last few kilometres on potholed roads that had escaped local-authority attention after the previous winter's snow and ice. And the moist, sticky air, unseasonal for early June, only added to the discomfort — a total contrast to the chilly Essex Evie had left behind that morning at Stansted Airport. And to arrive at what? The Marie Celeste of agriturismos!

Then she saw the notice. Handwritten on a single sheet of paper, it had blown from the desk and was lying on the floor, half-hidden by a chair. Two languages: Italian and English; the English clumsy.

'Villa Brocanti reception closed for two hours 13.00–15.00 because all staff at a funeral. We apologise for any inconveniences.'

Evie checked her watch. 1.20. She pulled a face. Shit. She needed a shower and she needed it now, not in two hours' time.

Grinding her teeth, she tossed the notice onto the desk, trapping it with the call bell as an afterthought. "They couldn't leave one person on duty?" she snapped.

She was about to make herself comfortable by sprawling out on one of the three sofas in the reception area when she noticed a poster advertising Villa Brocanti that showed a large pool.

"I'd forgotten there was a pool," she said, addressing the poster. "Certainly looks good, let's see if the reality lives up to the photos. Think I'll take a dip and make a few notes. Perhaps there'll be some other punters there."

She looked around for directions to the pool, but could see none. Shaking her head, she turned again to the poster, her tone now loaded with sarcasm.

"Signage isn't up to much, Villa Brocanti. Little helpful hints like 'Bar', 'Restaurant', or 'Pool' might be an idea, don't you think?"

Picking up her backpack, she strode towards a door at the rear of the reception area. "Time to explore," she announced. "Let's hope this doesn't lead into the kitchens."

She pushed open the door and immediately grunted her disapproval. "Bar and restaurant. Not much use when there's no one to serve … wait, there are some French doors over there that seem to lead onto some sort of garden. Maybe I'm in luck."

Marching out onto the terrace, she noted one more negative: the low box hedges decorating and defining the substantial formal garden were in poor condition, either from neglect or, more likely, from a blight. She'd read about it somewhere online: an infestation that killed off hedges and cypress trees was working its way through the area, the only long-term solution being to rip them out, disinfect the ground and start again with disease-resistant strains. It was tragic; these gardens didn't exactly grow quickly.

She followed the main path through the centre towards a gate in a stone wall at the far side of the garden. A wooden board with the word 'Piscina' carved into it was attached to the gate.

"Perfect," she said. "Time to find the swimwear."

Turning to push open the gate with her backside, she pulled her backpack around in front of her, unfastened the main flap and fished inside for her bikini. Looking up as a light breeze teased a few wisps that had escaped the clip holding up her bleached hair, her anticipation of cooling off was replaced with irritated disappointment that rapidly transformed into anger. Instead of the expected crystal clarity of a chlorinated pool, the water was a vivid, semi-opaque green.

"Shit! I don't believe it! This is supposed to be a fully operational agriturismo, not some half-completed dump on the Costa Brava."

She walked to the poolside where a rope hung loosely across the bars of the steps, a laminated computer-printed notice dangling from it. The English part read 'Pool closed for maintenance. Do not swim for your health. All inconveniences are regretted'.

"Regretted!" shouted Evie at the pool's emerald surface. "Regretted my arse. It's totally unacceptable!"

She reached into the front pocket of her backpack to retrieve her phone. Her photographer wasn't arriving until the next day, but just in case everything changed, she wanted a record of this particular disaster right now.

Back in reception, Evie decided she would check her booking on the villa's computer, find which room she had been allocated and take the key. If she couldn't swim, she could at least take a shower. Except there wasn't a computer to be seen, nor were there any keys. And if there was a ledger, it too was hidden away somewhere.

She tossed her backpack onto a sofa opposite the reception desk and plonked herself down next to it.

"I'm trapped in a hellhole devoid of life where nothing works," she moaned in frustration as she snatched an energy bar from her bag and took a huge bite from it. "Why the hell didn't I rent a car?"

The answer to her question was the result of her own planning. She knew that the photographer — what was his name? Joe something? — was picking up a car at Perugia airport the next day and driving directly to the villa. They didn't need two cars and anyway she hated driving on the wrong side of the road. He could ferry them around while she fumed at the sheer number of homicidal Italian drivers trying to kill her.

She checked her watch again. She couldn't sit around for another hour and a half doing nothing; she was meant to be working, interviewing the manager and other staff. Her work ethic was strong even if she did have a short fuse. But first she'd call Jane Bawley, her managing editor, give her a piece of her mind for sending her on a wild goose chase.

Jane had soft-soaped her with sweet talk of her wanting a star-filled review of the place from her top writer, the one the readers really listened to. The owners were old family friends, Jane said. She wanted to help them to drum up quality trade.

Evie pulled her phone from her backpack and hit the home button. As the screen jumped into life, she took one look at the display and her jaw immediately clenched.

"Of course," she said, her tone loaded with sarcasm. "What else would you expect?"

She thrust the phone back into her bag with a snarl.

"No service."

Chapter Three

Evie stood up, her eyes roaming the reception area. She knew from her research that there was more to Villa Brocanti than just the main building, the boutique agriturismo with a dozen en-suite rooms that advertised itself as 'a relaxing retreat, a haven away from the bustle of the city where you can regenerate your inner peace'. There were also extensive vineyards and olive groves, and beyond those, a substantial area of forest offering, according to the website, 'a succession of delightful glades, a treasure trove of shaded hideaways, halcyon sanctuaries of peace'. She remembered thinking the punctuation needed attention.

She took a deep breath in an attempt to restore her fragile equilibrium.

"I didn't anticipate exploring just yet," she muttered, turning towards the beaded curtain of the entrance door. "But hey, there's no time like the present. Let's turn the problems here in reception into an opportunity. It's always good to have a look around when no one's watching, get the famous Evie Lorrigan warts-and-all perspective. And the woods certainly sound appealing from the blurb. Yep, a voyage of discovery is called for. Maybe there'll even be a shaded stream for me to cool off in."

.   .   .

Thirty minutes later, Evie was following a path through woodland more than a kilometre from the main house. She had taken a cursory glance at the immaculate vineyards and extensive olive groves closer to the villa, row upon row of lovingly tended trees and pristine vines curving gently over the rolling terrain, but the afternoon sun was strong and she wanted shade. She had considered leaving a curtly worded note addressed to Monica Lieti, the 'direttrice', as she called herself, a note leaving little doubt how unimpressed she was with her lack of reception. However, when she remembered that in her exchange of emails with the direttrice she had mentioned her meeting in Perugia and told her not to expect her before 5 p.m., she decided to put her criticisms on hold. She would chastise the woman to her face when she saw her.

She had also thought of leaving her backpack behind the reception desk, but it occurred to her that if she had been able to walk in unchallenged and unobserved, anyone could, and a backpack would be more than tempting. Given that it contained her professional and personal lifeblood of smartphone, laptop, Kindle, ear buds and her personal items, losing it would be a catastrophe. No, she'd take it with her; after all, it wasn't heavy. She prided herself on travelling light, any trip of up to two weeks was invariably hand luggage only. As far as Evie was concerned, people who took half their house with them for a weekend, or even stays of considerably longer, were bonkers. With her assortment of devices, she had all the entertainment, communication and reading she needed. Couple those with one or two changes of clothes and a wash bag of basic essentials, what else could she possibly want?

The first part of the wood was disappointing. The trees were sparser than she'd expected, offering only intermittent shade.

"I'm still looking for the 'delightful glades'," she said, glaring accusingly at the nearest stand of trees, as if expecting them to bend and indicate the way. "Not much here so far that fits the description of 'halcyon' on the website."

She shook her head. Had they really used the word 'halcyon'?

However, as the path began to descend, the trees became

denser and within the space of a few metres, the temperature had dropped several degrees. Almost without notice, woodland had become forest.

Still hopeful for a stream, Evie strode on, but there was only the path, now less well defined and increasingly overrun with brambles. After carefully making her way around a substantial thicket full of sharp spines, she found herself at a gate in a two-metre-high wooden fence that disappeared from either side of the gateposts into the trees. Another of the villa's notices hung from the top bar of the gate, this one professionally printed on a sturdy plastic sheet.

'Divieto d'accesso. Zona pericolosa. Entry forbidden. Dangerous area.'

"Doesn't look very dangerous," she muttered as she peered beyond the gate. "Looks like more of the same to me: trees and more trees, plenty of brambles, a bit of heather and — what's that stuff with the yellow flowers? Broom, that's it. How dangerous is that?"

She pulled a dismissive face. It was just a neglected area, denser certainly, but basically abandoned and ignored. And, although high, the ageing fence clearly wasn't the boundary fence for the property; that would surely be far more substantial if the one by the main gate she'd driven through in the taxi was anything to go by.

She checked the time. It was nearly three; the hotel staff would soon return from the funeral. But they could wait; her interest had been piqued. What was so dangerous? The gate had no lock on it, and what were gates for except to open and walk through?

The path beyond the gate soon petered out, its surface now indistinguishable from the surrounding tangle of creepers, bushes, grasses and brambles. Apart from the occasional flattened stretches, highways created by passing deer or wild boar and their families, it was hard going. However, Evie was now on a mission. Was the danger tangible or simply a ruse to keep out unwanted intruders? And if so, from what?

Before long, the effort of making progress was outweighing the cool offered by the dense shade. She was hot, the sweat gathering under her hairline trickling down the back of her neck and soaking into her white T-shirt, its trademark interlinked EL initials printed in large pink letters on the front.

She was beginning to think she was wasting her time. Back at the villa, even if a swim was out of the question she could be showering and berating the management.

Stopping to take a packet of tissues from her backpack, she pulled one out to wipe her forehead.

"They call this halcyon!" she sneered. "It's more like the jungles of Borneo than the idyll of Tuscany. I need water and something to eat."

She smiled triumphantly as she reached into her backpack for the half-litre bottle of water she had stowed there on the plane. She had demanded it from the cabin attendant to replace the one she'd been forced to relinquish at Stansted by some fascist in security. Did they honestly think that firstly she was a terrorist and secondly she would bring an explosive dissolved in water onto an aeroplane? She'd offered to drink some to prove it was harmless, but the humourless uniformed barrier to her progress was immoveable. Rules were rules however arbitrary and illogical they may seem.

She took a swig of the tepid water, after which she poured some over her upturned face. But instead of feeling relieved, she suddenly shivered and sneezed violently.

"Shit," she snorted, as she grabbed another tissue. "I hope I haven't caught that snot-infested family's germs."

Evie was paranoid about air travel and germs, convinced that two hours spent breathing recycled air full of other people's bugs could only end badly. She normally wore a face mask, but this time she'd forgotten to bring it with her, and of course, she had been sitting next to young parents and their eighteen-month-old, all three of them coughing and sneezing throughout the journey. Typical!

She screwed the cap back on the bottle and rummaged in her bag for an energy bar. Evie had a metabolism that rivalled a humming bird's, burning up calories almost as fast as she could consume them. She was always hungry and always eating, and yet, to the envy of her friends, pencil thin. No matter how much she ate, her slight, five-foot-one frame never gained weight. She would always carry enough energy bars to last her through the day, but the frustrations of this particular day had seen her eating more than usual.

"Is that really the last one?" she moaned as she peered into the depths of the pack. "I started out with loads."

She pulled off the foil, shrugging as she wolfed down the bar. "I'll get some more in the restaurant. I won't be that long out here in the enchanted forest."

Closing her backpack, she tried to put thoughts of infectious diseases and dwindling supplies behind her as she peered ahead. The trees were dense, but she sensed there was something there, something more than trees. Something substantial.

The first indication that she was approaching a building was when she glimpsed dappled sunlight playing on part of a large wooden shutter tightly closed against a stone wall. It had once been varnished, but most of the surface was now grey wood, only flimsy curls of the decaying remnants of its former protection remaining.

Moving closer, she could see that the building was a large villa, possibly as big as Villa Brocanti, but, from the look of the stonework, in poor repair. Every window and door appeared to be shuttered, many of the shutters with extra boards nailed across them as reinforcement, some even with two layers, the second layers of boards nailed directly into the walls, forming large crosses.

Looking upwards, she could see three rows of windows — six on each of the first two floors and three on the top floor — and the edge of a roof that appeared to be typically old Tuscan: almost half-cylinder tiles of terracotta interlocking with each other. Even at this restricted angle, it was clear that some of the tiles were broken or missing, and a number had fallen to the ground, lying in the vegetation close to the villa wall.

"There's your 'dangerous'," she said. "Probably best to avoid standing too close. No peering into windows, if that's even possible through those shutters."

.   .   .

As Evie's eyes moved from one shuttered window to the next, it became clear that she was looking at one end of the building; the villa was even bigger than she first thought. She took off in a clockwise direction, walked to the corner and round to what quickly became obvious as the front. Here there had once been a landscaped and gravelled forecourt, although it was now very overgrown. She made her way into a relatively clear part, much of it shaded by the trees behind, and focussed her attention on the front of the villa.

"Impressive," she said, nodding to herself. "Palatial even. Must be about fifty metres wide. A small-scale stately home if it weren't falling apart."

Looking more closely, she noticed a number of cracks in the stonework. "Hmm," she said, pursing her lips. "From the state of that wall it looks as if the dangerous bit is more than just falling roof tiles. What a shame; it could be gorgeous. Look at that entrance!"

She walked towards a pair of stone stairways curving their way up and around a broken statue of a lion and leading to a pair of heavy wooden doors. Like the windows, the doors were shuttered with extra planks fixed across them, turning what could have been a welcoming if formal entrance into something far more forbidding.

Undaunted, she ran her hands over the stonework.

"This place is a treasure," she said, nodding as she made a decision. "Evie Lorrigan, you *have* to look inside. There's got to be a way in somewhere."

She marched off along the front of the villa, continuing her clockwise route.

"They obviously didn't want anyone getting in," she said, as she risked coming close to the walls and reached up in an attempt to rattle one of the boards. "Probably worried about squatters."

At the far end, she climbed a flight of wide steps set into an embankment that led up to a path running towards the rear. But while she could now reach the windows, to her disappointment, their shutters were very secure. Turning the corner to the back of the villa, she could see the remains of a formal garden leading off a large stone terrace that reminded her of the one at Villa Brocanti.

"This must have been magical once upon a time," she mused. "Why the hell didn't Jane Bawley mention it? It would make an interesting added attraction to the place, crumbling stonework notwithstanding. I must get the photographer over here tomorrow."

About twenty metres along the terrace, a single-storey building projected about fifteen metres from the villa into the formal garden, separating it from whatever gardens there were beyond. Two doors without reinforcing boards and several windows with less substantial shutters than those on the main house immediately drew Evie's attention.

"Now those doors *do* look promising," she said, striding towards them.

The first door proved to be more resistant to her shaking than it looked. The second, however, rattled encouragingly.

She stood back to survey it. "Perhaps my Kung Fu training might come in useful," she said, narrowing her eyes and cracking her knuckles.

She spun around and directed a foot at a spot on the door about a metre from the ground, snapping her leg straight. Her aim was good but the lock held fast and she tumbled backwards.

"Shit!" she cried, landing awkwardly as she tried to avoid flattening her backpack. She stood up and inspected the lock.

"Right, you bugger, one more kick should show you who's boss."

The next kick was equally on target and the weakened lock gave up the fight. The door flew open.

"Yes!" exclaimed Evie.

Chapter Four

Peering into the gloom beyond the doorway, Evie could just make out three walls lined with wooden shelves, and, of greater interest, a door to the right, on the villa side of the room.

She dug into her backpack, pulled out her phone and switched on its torch. Taking two steps into the room, she reached for the door handle and to her delight, the door opened away from her into another room. A rapid inspection with her torch showed it to be a store for garden tools — spades of various shapes and sizes hung alongside forks, rakes, hoes, a pickaxe and three scythes, together with several implements she didn't recognise. All were clearly very old. However, more than the tools, what immediately caught her attention was another door in the wall opposite the one she had just come through. This would lead her even closer to the main villa. But it was locked and firmly resisted her attempts to rattle it.

With thoughts of more karate, she tapped at the wood with her knuckles, but it sounded thick and heavy, like the door from the outer storeroom. She shook her head: attempts at kicking it down would only result in a damaged foot.

Walking back outside, she worked out from her new knowledge of the low building's interior that the two windows closest to the main house would be in a third room beyond the inner door barring her way. The windows were shuttered, but there were no extra boards and there was a convenient gap under the shutters.

Looking around for something she could use as a lever, she remembered the shelves in the storerooms. At more than a centimetre in thickness, they should be strong enough. She went back to the first room and pulled at the shelves until she found a loose one. Ripping it from its fittings, she banged it against the floor and nodded her satisfaction.

Evie pushed one end of the board under the shutter of the window nearer to the house, and, once it was firmly in place, she pulled hard downwards. The shutter burst open, revealing a wooden-framed window. She considered smashing the glass, but then thought of checking it first. As she pushed on the frame, the window opened inwards.

"Getting there," she said with a smile as she dropped her backpack through the window, hauled herself onto the sill and climbed into the room.

As she slipped her arms through her backpack, she took a look around. The room was yet another store about the same size as the outer two, but this one had a waist-high free-standing unit in addition to wall shelves, and more importantly, there was a door in one wall that from its position must lead directly into the villa. Better still, the door was ajar, opening away from the storeroom into whatever room was beyond.

Rubbing her hands together in glee, Evie hurried over to the partly open door and pushed it. But it wouldn't move. She frowned, pushing harder and banging on the door panels.

"That's not wood," she said, the surprise sounding in her voice as she ran her hand over the surface. "It's … it's stone. But that's crazy. A stone door with all the features and mouldings of a wooden door. Why?"

As her hands reached the edge of the door, instead of her fingers finding their way to the other side and allowing her to grip it, she discovered that there was no edge, The apparent gap between the door and the doorframe wasn't a gap at all.

"This isn't a door," said Evie incredulously as she shone her phone's torch at it, "it's a bloody painting of a door, a painting on the wall. The whole thing's solid."

Frowning, she took a step back, her cool feeling of confidence now replaced with one of uncertainty. She reached out to touch it again, firstly not believing her eyes and then, finally, working it out.

"It's a … what do you call them? It's a trompe l'oeil, a painting that looks like it's in three dimensions but isn't, it's in two. It's a fake, an illusion. But why put it here? This is just a storeroom. What's a painting of this quality doing on a wall in here?"

She stepped closer to the wall again to run her hands over its surface. About a metre from the corner of the room, she found a slight indentation in the wall's surface running vertically up from the floor. Following the indentation with her fingers, she found she was tracing the outline of what could be a hidden door. When she tapped it, it sounded more like wood than stone.

"It's a door!" she exclaimed. "That's totally weird. We have a painting of a fake door a few feet away, while the real door is hidden right here. But where's the handle?"

She pushed against the door, but it was solid and tightly in place. There was no movement. "It goes right up to the corner of the room," she muttered to herself while she worked out the dimensions of the door.

Moving her attention to the side wall, she studied the bricks, which she was pleased to find were real. Was there a loose one? She pushed and teased at each of them, her fingers exploring the edges. Finding one that moved very slightly, she let her nails feed down both ends to get a purchase, and slowly she eased the brick from its place. After tossing it aside, she peered into the space, using her phone torch to illuminate it, and there it was: a slim metal bar projecting from a hole in the inner brickwork. She pulled it and the door swung open into the space behind it.

"Magic!" she cried, gloating at her success. "The intrepid Evie Lorrigan strikes again. Move over Indiana Jones, I'm heading in!"

Chapter Five

The space into which the door opened was pitch black. Evie shone her phone torch around and found she was in a narrow, low-ceilinged passageway running left from the opening for some three metres towards a wooden door.

"Painted or real?" she wondered out loud.

She had taken only three steps along the corridor when she heard a swish from behind her. She turned in time to see the door she had come through closing back into place. There was a faint click as its internal mechanism secured it.

"Shit," she said, nervously. "That wasn't in the script."

She rushed back to bang on the door, but it was sealed tight, without even a trace of movement as she thumped it. And, as with the other side, there was no handle.

"OK," she said, trying to boost a level of confidence she certainly wasn't feeling, "I wanted to go this way, anyway."

She hurried along the corridor, waving the torch beam up and down the wooden door at the end.

"Looks real," she muttered, "but so did the other one."

Reaching out to touch the door, she was relieved to find that not only was it made of wood but also its metal handle was real. She turned the handle and pulled. Nothing; the door didn't move.

"Take deep breaths," she said, her jaw clenched. "Stay calm; there's an answer to this."

She shone the torch at the door's edge and immediately snorted derisively. "Duh!" she cried, smacking the palm of her hand on her forehead before reaching out again for the handle. This time she pushed as she turned the handle and the door opened away from her.

Ahead, a short distance beyond the open door, hung a large and heavy dark-blue curtain falling into deep folds. Evie walked towards it, one hand aiming her torch, the other out ahead of her to move the curtain aside. But instead of grasping the curtain, her fingers scraped against a wall. The curtain was a painting, another illusion.

"This gets worse," she muttered and reached back to grab the door. She didn't want this one closing behind her as well. Reassured that at least this door had remained open, she leaned back against it and waved the torchlight around, only to see that the curtain covered not one but two walls.

"Why?" she said. "What's the point?"

She reached out in anger to slap the second curtain and her hand disappeared into its folds. This part of the curtain was real.

Springing forward, she pulled at the heavy material, first to the left and then to the right. But the curtain wasn't supported on runners. She could see by the torchlight that it went behind the wall of the short corridor she had come along, so she pushed her way along, swishing the curtain away from the wall until finally she found the end and stumbled into a large room.

"OK," she said, relieved to be out of the confining space of the corridor. "At least I now appear to be in the main house."

She shone the torch around, raising her eyebrows in surprise as the beam picked out one detail after another. The walls were decorated with a large number of ornately framed paintings, while above, at a height of about three metres, were elaborate cornices. A large fireplace formed the centrepiece of the wall to her left and there were huge curtains covering the windows on the wall over to her right. She stopped, puzzled. That didn't seem right.

She waved her arms around, trying to orient herself according to how she thought she'd reached the room.

"No, it's too close," she said. "That can't possibly be an outside wall."

Making her way to the curtained wall, she flashed the beam around so as not to walk into any furniture, which was when she realised there was none. As she moved closer to the wall, she could see that she was right: the wall wasn't an outside one at all, but more puzzling still, the curtains were not real, they were part of a huge painting that covered the entire wall.

She ran to the other walls, shining her torch up them to check the picture frames.

"Everything's fake!" she cried, the sound of her voice echoing through the room. "The frames, the paintings and the mouldings around the room, along with these curtains; they're all painted on flat walls. The fireplace too. This room is a box with plain walls giving the illusion of being sumptuous, but none of it is real."

She stood still to examine the walls. "I have to admit, though, the paintings are brilliant. Totally convincing. Even the ceiling. Christ! It's mind-blowing."

Looking up, she had seen what looked like a wooden balustrade bordering the room above the cornice, and above that, a sky that needed a torch beam shone on it to be seen.

"The whole thing's fake," she said, her voice now very quiet. "The ceiling is just a ceiling, totally flat."

She took several long, slow breaths in an attempt to calm herself. There had to be a door other than the one through which she had entered. Maybe it was disguised like the one in the storeroom.

Turning to the wall with a real curtain, the one she had walked behind to enter the room, she saw that it was longer than she'd thought, extending far beyond the opening to the corridor she'd come through. She tore at it angrily and it started to rip high up near the ceiling where it was fastened. She pulled harder and the fabric gave way, falling in a large pile in front of her.

With a yelp of delight, Evie rushed to the far corner of the room where an ornate wooden door, previously hidden by the curtain, was now visible.

She reached out to grasp the handle, relieved that it was real as her hand closed around it. She turned it gingerly and to her relief, the door opened towards her.

However, the relief was once again short-lived as she shone her torch through the doorway.

"What the …?"

Instead of another room her torch beam hit a black-painted wall a metre beyond the doorway. To the left was another black wall but to the right, a short corridor ran into the darkness. Stepping into the corridor, she could see yet another wall ahead of her, but before it, there was a turn in the corridor to the right that should take her in a direction running behind the wall painted with the fireplace in the room behind her.

Turning right into what she thought would be another corridor, she was surprised to find her torch beam picking out a flight of stone stairs leading upwards.

She peered up into the gloom, her torch beam not reaching the top. Clutching at any thought that might be positive, she calculated that the stairs must go to the floor above where perhaps there were real windows. After all, there were plenty of shutters on the outside walls.

She started to climb the stairs, wondering again why Jane Bawley had made no mention of this villa to her. She claimed to be a friend of the Brocanti family, surely they would have told her something about it, even if it was only to keep clear of it. Why would that be? Was it hiding something?

As she neared the top of the stairs, Evie could see by her torch beam that they led onto another corridor. But this one was reassuringly different. It was about three times as wide as the stairway itself, extending both ahead of her and behind. The walls were elaborately decorated with a succession of framed still-life studies, while dark-red oriental rugs covered the wooden floor.

The stairway had narrowed as it rose to the next floor, arriving to the right side of the corridor. Feeling increasingly claustrophobic, Evie turned left after mounting the top stair, wanting more space. She took a step and walked straight into the wall, yelping in surprise as she banged her head. The extra width of the corridor was an illusion.

"Bugger!" she yelled, sitting down on the top step with a thump.

As she rubbed her forehead, she played the torch beam onto the corridor wall. Now she was sitting still and now she knew what appeared to be in front of her wasn't real, she could see it for what it was. She reached out to touch what she had thought was space beyond the wooden balustrade at the top of the stairs, and found that as well as the balustrade, everything that appeared to be behind it was painted on the wall.

"Incredible," she said. "I was totally taken in. This corridor is actually bloody narrow. Rather too narrow for my liking."

Reaching out to touch the rugs, she discovered they too were painted on a floor of terracotta tiles.

"This would make a great ride in a theme park if it weren't quite so spooky," she said, exploring the paintings with her hands as she tried to ignore the increasing tide of uneasiness threatening to swamp her. "As it is, I think there would be a few people freaking out."

She gulped, realising that she was jabbering rubbish, but still she couldn't help adding, "Not for people of a 'nervous disposition'."

Returning her attention to the corridor, she directed the torch beam along it to where she could see several doors. "Please let those be real," she said, standing up.

As she walked along the corridor, she was uncomfortably aware it was getting narrower the farther she went. And when she stopped by the first two doors she came to, she saw they were the *only* two doors; the others farther along and the rest of the corridor itself all part of another trompe l'oeil. The two facing doors she was standing in front of marked the corridor's end.

She reached for the handle of the door to her left. To her relief it turned and the door pushed open into a room.

She was so delighted not to be forced to retrace her steps that it took a couple of seconds for her to realise she could see clearly into the room: the outside shutters on one of the large windows on the far side were open and daylight was filtering in. She frowned as her attention focussed on the window: she didn't remember seeing any open shutters when she'd looked at the building from the garden.

Her eyes still raised, she scanned the three walls she could see from the doorway. Each was even more ornately decorated than the room downstairs. Romanesque columns framed bucolic scenes with nymphs and shepherds, round arches bordered the window spaces, including the one with its shutters open. Looking up farther, she could see the ceiling rising into a magnificent vault.

Although from her experiences on the ground floor, she knew that everything she was looking at was false, that she was really in a room with four plain walls and a flat ceiling, she still couldn't take her eyes off the paintings.

Soaking up every detail of the walls and ceiling, Evie stepped into the room. She wanted to get even closer to the walls to examine them minutely. She wanted to touch them. She was also keen to know what was on the fourth wall, the one now behind her.

She took two more steps and was surprised to feel the floor give slightly under her left foot, the movement accompanied by a creaking sound. She looked down and screamed as she shuddered to a halt, wobbling on her feet. She had been so taken in by the stunning paintings on the walls and ceiling, the almost cathedral-like effect of the trompe l'oeil, she had failed to look down. And now as she did, her stomach took several leaps. Most of the floor had collapsed into the room below, a sitting room with much of its furniture clearly visible through the hole. And apart from a layer of dust from the time when the ceiling had crashed down on it, it appeared to be in remarkably good condition.

"Shit, that was close," she gasped.

She took a step back and knelt, leaning forward gingerly in case any more of the floor felt inclined to collapse. As her hand pushed on the board she had stood on, the board rrrsqueaked again, making her jump. "Whoa!" she cried as she scrambled backwards. She stared into the hole again, taking in the detail. Something wasn't right. Moving her head from side to side, she quickly understood.

Standing, Evie took a tentative step forwards, and then another until it appeared she was standing on thin air. Her mouth puckered in recognition of her gullibility. She had been completely duped. The floor was solid, the appearance of collapse a fiction.

"That is … mind boggling," she said, narrowing her eyes. "I'll bet the bastard who painted it is laughing his head off."

She turned to examine the fourth wall. It was equally elaborate in its decoration, with the exception of a panel to the right of the door where a stone stairway appeared to lead up and to the right of the room, tempting her to try it.

"You must be joking," said Evie. "I'm getting used to these tricks. I wonder what's in the room on the other side of the corridor, assuming the door to it is real; I forgot to check."

In spite of her newfound scepticism, she walked over to the wall and touched the steps to satisfy herself they were painted and didn't lead anywhere.

"Up yours," she said, sneering at them.

She turned and sneezed even more violently than she had in the woods. This time the accompanying shiver was stronger, and somewhere behind her eyes she could feel the building blocks of a headache starting to construct themselves into a wall of pain. She shook her head. Did she have any paracetamol in her wash bag? She couldn't remember.

"Bloody germs," she spat. "I do not need this. Sodding family shouldn't have been allowed on the plane."

Chapter Six

The door on the opposite side of the corridor was as real as its partner. And like its partner, it too opened into a room with an unshuttered window that cast enough light for the interior of the room to be visible. The first thing Evie checked was the floor, which looked solid enough but was it? She was no longer sure about anything she was seeing.

Unlike the room across the corridor, this one was furnished as a sitting room. Two large sofas faced each other on either side of a fireplace, with two armchairs near them. Closer to the window a writing desk stood alongside a chaise longue.

Still not trusting what she was seeing, Evie reached out and grabbed one of three upright chairs standing near the door and lifted it. She gasped; it was heavier than it looked. With a loud grunt, she pushed her arms straight and hurled the chair into the middle of the room where it bounced on the floor and skidded to a halt.

Satisfied that the furniture and floor were solid enough, Evie made her way to the middle of the room where she looked up at the wall around the fireplace to take in another series of trompe l'oeil paintings. But rather than the bucolic scenes of the previous room, the wall in front of her was packed with what she assumed must be family portraits. Severe-looking men in a variety of fashions from the past two or three hundred years gazed haughtily down on her, while family groups with varying numbers of children were hardly less austere. However, unlike similar groups of portraits assembled over the centuries she had seen on visits to National Trust houses and the like in England, these were not individual paintings mounted in frames. Every part of them from fake canvas to frames was painted directly on the walls. The shading of the frames was perfect, giving each the effect of having substantial relief. It was only when Evie drew close and shone her torch directly at them that she could see the reality of the flat walls.

She turned to view the wall that included the doorway through which she had entered. She was surprised to see it was filled with bookshelves reaching almost to the ceiling, each packed with leather-bound volumes. But again, as she walked towards them, it became clear that they were no more real than the portraits on the fireplace wall.

It occurred to Evie that her path through the house so far had led her onwards and upwards, with no indication of a way out. What she had seen of the ground floor hadn't included the inside of the main entrance, nor had there been any rooms leading directly onto what was farther along the rear of the villa. A main terrace, perhaps? Her experience had been limited to one end of the house. Where was she now? She looked over to the large window with the open shutters; she was no longer even sure which side of the house it would look out on.

"Let's find out where we are," she said.

Feeling confident that if nothing else, this window would offer her a way out, even if it was on the first floor, she strode over towards the chaise longue. The bottom of the window was just above her eye level, and even on tiptoes she couldn't see much. She climbed onto the chaise and peered through the lower panes.

"That's not the garden I walked through," she exclaimed in surprise. "It's far too pristine. Where are all the weeds and brambles?"

She was looking out on a formal garden, larger than the one she'd seen at Villa Brocanti, and this one had beautifully shaped box hedges in perfect condition; not a hint of disease in sight. And sitting on a bench seat with her back to the house was a young woman in clothing from a bygone era: a high-necked lacy white blouse and a full, ankle-length, dark-blue skirt. The young woman's almost black hair was drawn up into a tight bun on the top of her head, but neither her face nor her profile was visible as she leaned forward, reading a book she was holding in her lap.

As she stared in confusion at the view through the window, Evie started to notice details of the shadows and the trees beyond. She frowned, the view making no sense. She had spent quite some time exploring — it must be closer to five o'clock than four, she thought — and yet the shadows outside were short, as if on this side of the house it was no later than about one in the afternoon. Furthermore, there was absolutely no movement in the trees.

"It's another bloody painting!" she gasped. "It's no more real than the walls of this room."

"But how …?" she added, as she remembered the light.

Straining her neck to look up to the top of the window, she could see the limit of the painting and she realised that she was looking out through real glass onto the inside of a tall, expertly painted box, the far side of which was only about a metre away. High up, she could see that the top of the box was also glassed and above that, the sides mirrored so light would reflect into the room from above, as if from a skylight but with the direction of the light altered.

"No wonder I didn't see an open shutter from the outside," she said, "there wasn't one. It's not smoke and mirrors; it's windows and cleverly angled mirrors. I wonder how much of what I saw on the outside of the building is real, and how much is painted on."

She studied the edges of the window frame, looking in vain for a way to open it. It had the look of a sash construction, but it was another illusion. The only way through the window would be to smash the glass, and there was nothing to hand she could use, the chairs being far too heavy.

She climbed down from the chaise. "When I get back outside, I'll make a closer inspection," she said, trying to boost her sagging confidence. But a growing feeling that she was anything but in control was gnawing at her morale.

"If I can find the way out," she mumbled uncertainly.

Her eyes fell on the writing desk. "Anything interesting here?" she said, trying again to raise her mood. "A few bills perhaps, billets-doux from the odd ardent admirer?"

She took a couple of steps and reached for one of the brass handles. There were six: four in a row on shallow drawers below the green-leather-covered writing surface and two others on deeper drawers at either end. Except there weren't. There were no handles, only another illusion. The entire surface of the desk was painted to make it look ornate whereas in reality it was plain.

"Damn!" she cried, banging her fist down on the leather-that-wasn't-leather top. "I've got to get out of this place."

As she marched angrily away from the desk, she noticed a large curtain in the corner on the wall opposite the door through which she'd entered, similar to the one in the ground floor room she had come from. Her first inclination was to dismiss it as yet another clever painting, but was it? She needed to know; there had to be a way through to the rest of the villa.

Grabbing at one end of the curtain, she was ecstatic when it folded into her hand. It was real!

"Brilliant!" she cried, yanking at the curtain and expecting it to collapse like the one on the ground floor. But instead of falling, it swished along the long wooden pole it was hanging from. Behind was another door, a real one, she could tell. She was getting better at spotting the difference.

"Right," she said, rubbing her hands in anticipation as she pulled open the door. But her exhilaration was short-lived.

"Shit! Another black hole."

She turned on her phone torch and shone the beam into the darkness beyond the doorway, lighting up a narrow corridor running for a couple of metres before disappearing to the right.

The right turn was genuine: she didn't bang her nose again when she turned in the corridor, although she had a hand out as a probe, just in case. The corridor continued, wider now, and the handles of three doors glinted in her torch beam. Were they all real? The first two she passed were both locked, but the third one wasn't. As she pushed open the door, she glanced to either side of its frame. The wall had the appearance of stone stairs leading upwards, joining beyond the top of the doorframe, while through the open door was another set of real stone stairs, also leading upwards.

She stood back, uncertain whether to take this latest flight of stairs or whether to explore elsewhere. As her eyes moved from the painted stairs to the real ones, she found it hard to see where the transition was: the painting was so good that it appeared to blend seamlessly into place with the stairs she knew were real.

Sighing in resignation, Evie shone the torch upwards and the beam disappeared into the blackness. "Looks straight enough. Bit dark though, and long, too."

Playing the torch onto the walls, she was shocked to find that while the paintings here were still trompe l'oeil, they were more sinister. Mythological beasts and serpents ran and slithered upwards through a backdrop of dense jungle, while on the stairs themselves, roots and vines conspired to guide her upwards, dragging her on to whatever was at the top.

Just as the darkness seemed absolute, she reached another door.

"This has to be the top floor, doesn't it?" she said, pulling a face. She was far from certain.

She reached out for the handle, turned it and pushed. The heavy door swung open away from her, soft creaks emerging from hinges unused to moving.

Stepping through the doorway, she found herself in a room about eight metres wide but barely three metres deep. And unlike the elaborately painted walls in the rooms below, these walls were rough stone with no rendering.

Or were they? She shone her torch on the wall opposite the door and saw a centrally placed large wooden door mounted in a stone frame. Was that real? She was no longer sure about anything.

Before venturing into the room, she examined more of it from the doorway. Shining her torch beam upwards, she could see the ceiling was angled, forming part of an eave.

"This room is the weirdest shape," she said. "I wonder why it's so shallow. It's like part of a room that's been divided into two."

Returning her attention to the walls and the painting of the wooden door facing her, she walked forward, reaching out to feel them with her hands.

"And to add to the weirdness," she continued, reassured by the sound of her own voice in an otherwise silent building, "these walls aren't rough stone at all, they are plastered and then painted to look like stone. I don't get it. There's a real door behind me, a fake one in front. Painted walls all around the room and no windows, not even paintings of windows."

She moved her hand farther along the wall, looking for a hidden door like the one on the ground floor. As she focussed her attention on the detail, she heard the softest of creaks behind her. She spun around in time to see the door from the stairs shutting.

"Bugger!" she shrieked, diving for the doorway, but she was too late. She stared at the closed door in frustrated disbelief.

"There's no bloody handle on this side," she yelled, kicking angrily at the door.

Realising she would now be in total darkness were it not for the phone's torch beam, she went back to her exploration of the far wall, convinced there was some sort of release to be found. She traced the wall, as she had in the storeroom, feeling for every possible crack or indentation, hopeful for a loose stone or brick. But there were no stones or bricks; the surface was a painting.

"Damn!" she cried, thumping the wall with the fist of her free hand. "What the hell is going on? This is no longer funny."

She took a step back and aimed her right foot. "Bastard!" she screamed, kicking the wall at floor level, immediately next to the corner. To her surprise, she felt a movement in the wall where the toe of her cross-trainer had connected, followed by a soft swish from her right.

"Bloody hell!" she cried, turning her phone's torch in the direction of the sound. "It's a real door after all, and not only that, there's light coming from beyond it."

She walked gingerly through the doorway and looked up. Some five metres above her head was a filthy skylight. It was far too high to reach but it didn't matter: she could at least see without the phone's torch. Wary of the door closing, she slipped off her backpack and leaned it against the door before turning to look around the room. It was about the same size as the one she'd come through, possibly slightly deeper. She was right: the two rooms had originally been one. Why had they been divided?

Unlike the outer room, this one wasn't empty. There was a small wooden table and chair close to her, a lattice of ancient cobwebs threading across them. Farther into the corner, in a recess in the far wall and shielded from the dim light coming from above, she could just make out a second chair. She shone the torch towards it and screamed, jumping back in fright and colliding with the wall behind her. Her phone fell from her hand as she stumbled and half-slid down the wall. She reached for her backpack, snatching it from the floor and clasping it to her chest for protection. Her eyes hardly able to leave the corner, she felt for her phone. As her hand folded around it, she aimed the torch beam at the chair.

"It's a body," she whispered. "And it's ancient, skeletal."

Slouched in the chair was the shrivelled figure of a man wearing a heavy coat from another era. His head was tilted upwards, leaning against the high chair back, wisps of black hair clinging to fragmented remains of skin. There were no eyes, and the flesh had receded from his mouth and gums, the teeth prominent in a deathly grin.

Evie could feel her heart pounding against her chest. She pulled the backpack to her more tightly and turned to the open door. But there was no open door. In her horror and preoccupation with the body in the chair, she hadn't heard it close.

She felt instinctively that this was the final room in the trail of rooms she had followed through the villa. She knew it in her heart. She was at the highest point in the building; there was nowhere else to go. Everything had slowly led her to this room, and now she was trapped with the body of a man who had died here a long time ago. Also trapped.

Chapter Seven

Joe Oliver skidded the basic Fiat 500 rental to a halt on the gravel outside Villa Brocanti and unpeeled his cramped frame from the driver's seat, cursing himself for not paying extra for an upgrade. At five foot ten, he didn't regard himself as tall, but this car was made for people like his new girlfriend Jan, who was five foot three in heels. He certainly didn't relish the thought of touring half of Tuscany and Umbria for the next two weeks in the car's more-than-confined spaces with a journalist whose reputation was attitude. He'd never met Evie Lorrigan, but he'd heard plenty of tales. He half expected her to be waiting at the villa's entrance, arms folded and ready for a showdown.

She wasn't, and thoughts of the journalist were quickly forgotten as his photographer's eye began to assess the elegant stonework, decorative lintels and chestnut window frames and shutters for the best angles to show off the villa. A huge and ancient two-wheeled wooden cart outside the main door, complete with crumbling paintwork, together with a vast collection of assorted planters bursting with geraniums, would add dimension and interest to the shots he was instinctively planning.

According to WanderFever's Jane Bawley, who had employed Joe for the job, Villa Brocanti was well over a hundred years old. Not particularly ancient for villas of its size in the area, but the architect had clearly maintained all the Tuscan style and tradition when he designed it.

Joe shouldered his two backpacks, the larger and considerably heavier one containing his camera equipment, the smaller his personal stuff, and, brushing aside bead curtains, strolled through the double entrance doors into the villa's reception area.

"Buongiorno!" he called to the thirty-something woman standing behind the desk, noting her tall, slim figure and luxuriant black, shoulder-length hair framing an oval, olive-skinned face, her classical Tuscan beauty instantly capturing his imagination.

"Buongiorno, signore," she replied, smiling softly as she tilted her head in greeting. Breaking into English, she added, "I hope you have had a pleasant journey; the weather is a little hot for the time of year."

Joe dropped his bags at his feet as he stopped by the desk.

"Thank you, yes, it was an easy drive. But I'm puzzled; how did you know I was English?"

Monica Lieti's eyes darted up and down his clothing, an assessment taking perhaps a microsecond, before moving to his face and hair. The faintest smile of amusement flitted across her face. What was blindingly obvious to her was that, complexion aside, none of her countrymen would look like this man even if they were wearing the same clothes, their natural way of carrying themselves being altogether different. This man might as well have been wearing a Union Jack T-shirt. And, of course, there was his accent.

"You have a booking, I think. You are Signor Oliver, are you not?"

"Oh, yes, of course," said Joe sheepishly. He was rather proud of his few words of Italian. Antonella, an Italian ex-girlfriend from a couple of years ago, a waitress at the time in 'Luigi's Pizza' down the road from where he lived in Brixton, had complimented him on his accent; told him he sounded rather Roman. Maybe that was the problem: he was in Tuscany.

The woman held out her hand. "I am Monica Lieti, direttrice of Villa Brocanti. If you like, Signor Oliver, we could speak Italian. I want the stay of you and your companion to be as comfortable as possible."

Suspecting his Italian would get a battering if he agreed, and given that the direttrice was clearly comfortable with English, Joe gave what he hoped was a nonchalant shrug. "Perhaps later, if that's OK. I think English would be better for now."

"Of course," said Monica, as she pushed a registration form towards him. "If I could take a copy of your passport, Signor Oliver, we can complete the formalities."

"Talking of my companion," said Joe as he filled in the boxes marked with a faint cross, "is she around? I need to let her know I'm here."

"She is not with you?" Frowning, Monica glanced past him towards the entrance door, as if expecting Evie to appear.

"With me? No. She was supposed to get here yesterday."

"That is what I was expecting, signore, but she did not arrive. I assumed that since you were coming today, she had changed her plans and decided to accompany you. She did not tell you anything?"

Joe shook his head. "I haven't had any contact with her; our assignment was arranged by WanderFever, the magazine she works for. I'm a freelance photographer. Jane Bawley, Evie's boss, contacted me directly. I've never met Evie Lorrigan."

Monica nodded. "I know of Signora Bawley, of course, she is a friend of Anna Riccardi, wife of Ernesto Brocanti, the owner of Villa Brocanti."

"Isn't he a marquis or something?" said Joe. "Sounds important."

Monica smiled. "He is a marchese, yes. It is an old title, more symbolic these days than important."

"Sorry," said Joe, "you were talking about Jane."

"I was, yes. She visited Villa Brocanti about two years ago when it first opened as an agriturismo. It was a little before I started to work here. I believe the reason you are here now is that she agreed to help Anna Riccardi by reviewing our agriturismo in her magazine once it had been established for some time."

She paused, picking up the registration form and placing it in a box file at one end of the desk.

"Which is why," she continued, "it is strange that Signora

Lorrigan is not here. The timetable was carefully worked out. In her email, she told me she had a busy two weeks scheduled and that she hoped to complete her interviews with me and others on the staff today and tomorrow. I have made sure everyone is available."

Joe shook his head. "I don't know what to say. Look, I'll call Jane in London, see if she knows what's going on." He held up his mobile.

Monica Lieti shook her head. "I am afraid that will not be possible, Signor Oliver, not from your cellular phone. We are in the countryside and some distance from any transmission masts. The signal here is terrible." She shrugged. "This is Italy."

"It's the same in England," said Joe, with a resigned shrug. "It drives people crazy. But that doesn't mean I'm out of contact, does it?"

"Of course not, signore, we have a good landline. There is a phone in your room you can call with, or, if you prefer, you can use our Wi-Fi and make a call on Skype."

"Of course," said Joe, nodding. "What's the password for the Wi-Fi?"

"We do not have one, signore. We are a long way from our nearest neighbours. Our Wi-Fi range is short so there is not much chance of someone outside the hotel using it."

"Then I'll call from my room once I've sorted my stuff." He pulled at his T-shirt, which was sticking to him. "What I really fancy right now, after I've had a shower, is a swim. Which way is the pool?"

Monica pointed to her right.

"It is through that door to the dining room and then out beyond the terrace. But I am sorry to tell you that we've had a problem with the filter. It is almost fixed; the technician is returning in one hour to make a final check. If you could wait until then, signore …"

"These things happen," said Joe, with a shrug. "I'll make do with just a shower to cool down, then call London."

. . .

"Jane, hi, it's Joe Oliver."

"Hello, Joe. You sound as if you're at the bottom of a bucket of water."

"Chance would be a fine thing. The pool's out of commission and it's really hot here."

"Oh dear, not a good omen for Villa Brocanti, especially with someone as critical as Evie on their case. What can I do for you?"

"It's Evie I'm calling about. I was wondering if you'd heard from her, because she didn't show up yesterday as expected, and she hasn't today, either."

"Really? That's strange. Have you tried her mobile number?"

"I don't have it."

"OK, hang on a sec, I'll call her now on another phone."

There was a pause while Joe listened to a lot of Skype static, after which Jane came back on the line.

"I'm getting a 'caller unobtainable' message; her phone must either be turned off or it's out of battery. Where the hell is she? This won't sit well with the managing editor."

"Why's that?"

"I shouldn't really discuss the full-time staff, but Evie's become a bit unreliable lately, going off at a tangent, doing her own thing, which in addition to her inflated sense of self-importance and intolerant personality is all a bit much. I mean, it's all very well when she's researching something, but when arrangements have been made, people like you brought in, money spent, it smacks of irresponsibility. Between you and me, she's on her third warning. If there's no good explanation, she won't be working for WanderFever for much longer."

Joe pulled a face, rather taken aback by Jane's unprofessional remarks. But he had to respond.

"Bit of a bugger. I thought she was one of your top people."

"She is, but enough is enough."

"What do you want me to do?"

"Has the agriturismo heard anything?"

"No. The manager, Monica Lieti, said she was expecting her yesterday. Apparently there was a short period in the early afternoon when there was no one around. They'd all gone to the funeral of one of the gardeners, who she said was a very popular bloke. But firstly Evie had told them she wouldn't arrive until late afternoon, when there certainly was someone here, and secondly, even if she had arrived early, she didn't have wheels, so she couldn't go anywhere once her taxi had left."

"Well, she didn't contact me," said Jane, her voice now tightening with displeasure. "I'll check with the others in the office, but she's not particularly friends with any of them, so I doubt she'd call them."

"She probably wouldn't have been able to call, not on her mobile. There's no signal here."

"They have a landline, don't they?" snapped Jane. "Look, I've just remembered; she was going to call in at our Perugia office. Maybe something came up there. Let me make a few calls and I'll get back to you."

"And in the meantime? I'm supposed to be working and it's your money."

"Perhaps you could recce the place and take what shots you think will be useful for Evie's article."

"OK, that won't be difficult. As you know, the place is a classic Tuscan villa. There's terracotta everywhere, geraniums, and I noticed some sunflowers on the way in near the cypress trees on the drive. I'm spoilt for choice."

"Excellent. And Joe, don't forget the other villa, the abandoned one I told you about. If Evie's delayed for a day or two, it could be an ideal opportunity to take a quiet look at the place."

"Yeah. Four of the six prints you copied and showed me are hanging in the corridor outside my room. I can't help but feel there should be a lot more."

"I agree," said Jane. "There must have been. But whether they still exist is another matter."

"Right, but as far as the old villa is concerned, I want to do a bit of fishing on the subject with Ms Lieti first. See if the official line is still what you said it was."

· · ·

Showered and feeling fresher, Joe returned to the reception to update Monica Lieti.

"She might have been delayed in Perugia, apparently," he told her. "I'll find out later. She's got a bit of a reputation for doing her own thing."

He indicated his camera bag. "Is it OK if I wander around, take a few shots? Those vineyards look pretty smart, and I'm sure there'll be some good shots back towards the villa from among them."

"Of course, Signor Oliver, feel free to go wherever you please and take as many shots as you like. Good photographs are worth a lot in promoting our business, but I should advise you not to venture too far into the forest, certainly not beyond the well-defined paths. If you get too hot, the pool technician has just told me that everything is back to normal, so you can take your swim when you have finished."

"Excellent," said Joe. "Oh yes, I was going to ask. There are some sepia-toned prints hanging on the walls outside my room that look pretty old. Three of them show a rather large building. Was that the original villa?"

He saw a flash of hesitation cross Monica's face before she smiled and came out with the official story.

"Yes, they are of the original villa. The negatives for those photographs were found in a trunk belonging to Salvatore Brocanti, one of the present marchese's ancestors. He was a rather famous artist in his time and, it would seem, something of a photographer."

"Where is the old building? Presumably it still exists?"

Joe noticed Monica's eyes glance down, avoiding his.

"Eh, no, it does not," she replied, her thin smile unconvincing. "It burnt to the ground in a fire well over a hundred years ago. This building we are in was constructed on the site of the old one as a replacement villa for the Brocanti family."

"So they constructed the new one on the same site? Does anything remain of the old one? I ask because old buildings fascinate me. I've quite a portfolio of images I'm hoping will end up as a book one day."

"Sadly no. I believe the old villa was entirely destroyed."

"What about the fourth print on the wall, the one showing the garden that was presumably taken from an upstairs window of the old villa? There's a woman sitting on a bench seat who seems to be reading a book. You can only see the back of her."

"It's thought to be Salvatore Brocanti's first wife, Isabella."

"Really. It's a great shot, very atmospheric."

He paused, watching carefully for her reaction to his next question. "What did you mean just now about advising me not to go too far into the forest? Is it dangerous in some way? This is Tuscany, after all, not the wilds of some jungle."

Monica's laugh sounded rather hollow. "It's quite straightforward, Signor Oliver. The forest is very extensive and it is easy to get lost. For that reason we make it out of bounds to guests. It's for your own safety. A little way into the forest there is a fence. Beyond it, the present marchese has established a breeding area for wild boar so that outside the tourist season, the forest can be used exclusively for hunting."

"I thought wild boar were quite shy animals," said Joe.

"They are, yes. But like all wild animals, if they feel they are cornered or worse, they feel their young are threatened, they can be unpredictable. More than a few hunters have been killed over the years. Boars have very sharp tusks."

"Better to make a lot of noise then?" suggested Joe.

"Better not to go at all," countered Monica, her eyes creasing in amusement. She found herself attracted to this Englishman's openness, his apparent lack of agenda.

From what Jane had told him, Joe knew that at least part of Monica Lieti's account was untrue. For some reason, the family didn't want it to be known that the old villa still existed, which in Joe's mind made it all the more interesting.

An hour later, he had completed his first set of shots of the vines and olive trees and worked out which shots he wanted to repeat the following morning when the sun was in a better position. He worked methodically, finding the angles he wanted before setting up each final shot with his camera on a tripod. He made full use of his favourite telephoto, picking out interesting detail of the villa through the young vine leaves, and he was looking forward to processing everything he had captured on his laptop later that evening. But in the meantime, while there was still enough daylight, he wanted to find the old villa.

Following the path that unbeknown to him Evie Lorrigan had also followed the day before, Joe soon found the way becoming increasingly overgrown. The fence, when he came upon it, was less substantial than he had expected from Monica Lieti's description, but even if the gate in front of him had been locked, climbing over it would hardly have been difficult. Beyond the gate, the path was almost non-existent, although he thought he could see evidence of some flattening of the vegetation. He stopped and listened, wondering how much noise wild boar made as they foraged in the undergrowth.

Feeling increasingly hot as he weaved and ducked his way through the tangled undergrowth, Joe was beginning to wonder if the abandoned villa was a figment of Jane's overactive imagination. He had tried searching for the place on Google Earth, but the forest was dense and the satellite shot of the area was at an angle that teased. There had been a possible roof amongst the trees but it was far from certain.

About to give up, he stopped for a swig of water. As he raised the bottle to his lips, his eyes focussed on a wall through the trees. Having seen it, Joe couldn't believe he'd missed it. It had to be the villa.

As the vegetation thinned slightly closer to the wall ahead of him, Joe could see more of the structure and condition. It was a substantial building, and from the design and position, this was just one end. Glancing briefly at a couple of barred doors largely obscured by creepers and bushes, he headed to the right along the wall. He wanted to see the main aspect of the villa; he could return to the doors later.

His anticlockwise route took him to the rear of the building, the overgrown remains of the old formal garden stretching out in front of him for over thirty metres to where it was bordered by a single-storey projection from the main villa. But Joe's interest was in the condition of the shutters. If one was loose or rotten, he might be able to open it and access a window. He knew from what Jane had said to him back in London that he wouldn't be disturbed and two of the prints she had shown him were a strong motivation for him to indulge in a spot of housebreaking. Which was exactly the reaction Jane had hoped for.

"Anna Riccardi, Ernesto Brocanti's wife, reluctantly showed me these photographs after I badgered her a bit about the old villa," she told Joe when he went to her office to be briefed about the entire two-week project. "Anna's an old friend from uni days, although we've seen less of each other since she married Ernesto and moved back to Italy. I'm not that taken with Ernesto, to be honest, bit up himself. Anyway, I snapped all the photos with my phone when she wasn't looking and printed them out when I got back to my office. These two are apparently of interior walls of the old villa. She swore me to secrecy, said her husband would throw a fit if he knew she had shown them to me. He's adamant that no one should ever go near the place, claims it's cursed and he insists that it must be left over the centuries to rot. Anna agrees with him; they are both strongly religious and very superstitious."

Joe was only half listening, his attention taken by the two prints. "These are amazing," he said. "They appear to be very detailed and convincing trompe l'oeil paintings. It was quite a popular form of decoration in Italy in the eighteen hundreds, earlier too, and as an art form, it's undergone something of a revival recently with people doing some amazingly clever street art. Where did these come from?"

"Anna said they were among a box of possessions belonging to her husband's ancestor, Salvatore Brocanti. There were six in all, the four they've had printed and which are hanging on the walls of the present villa, and these two. They haven't told anyone about them since they don't want there to be any interest in the old villa."

"That's outrageous," objected Joe. "These paintings are exceptional. It's criminal to hide them away."

"I said the same thing to Anna, but she maintains Ernesto is immoveable on the subject. The Brocanti men have a reputation for both extreme stubbornness and fiery tempers, so she doesn't want to rock the boat. She only showed me these two along with the others because I'd been plying her with her own delicious wine. They even deny the existence of the place these days. They tell their clients the original villa burnt down and the present one is built on the same site."

"And you didn't get a chance to snoop around yourself when you were there?" asked Joe, still examining the prints. When Jane didn't answer, he looked up to see her staring at him uncomfortably, her face blushing slightly.

"Er, no," she lied, not able to hold his eyes. "Anna walked me through the forest and I saw the villa through the trees, but she was clearly spooked, even at a distance, and so I couldn't get any closer."

Joe didn't have a lot of time for Jane, considering her to be a hard-nosed and calculating gossip. Normally, the set of her face under her old-fashioned helmet hairstyle was cold and humourless, so when she finished her fiction with an uncharacteristic nervous smile, he was convinced she was hiding something. What did she know about the old villa that she wasn't telling him? For Joe, it didn't matter. He himself wasn't above bending the rules when it came to getting the images he wanted, and on this occasion, his appetite had certainly been whetted by the prints. He wanted to see more of the place, regardless of the position of the Brocanti family.

As Joe made his way along the garden side of the old villa, testing the barred shutters as he went, he noticed a number of broken roof tiles lying in the undergrowth. Looking up, he could see the irregular edge of the roof. He took several steps away from the wall to improve his viewing angle, fitted one of his camera bodies with the longest telephoto lens in his bag and used the camera and lens combination to view the roof more closely.

"They look stable enough," he muttered to himself. "Can't be too careful though; I'll stick as close to the wall as I can."

After testing several securely shuttered and barred windows, Joe came to two larger sets of shutters covering French doors. The first pair resisted his attempts to move them, but the second pair rattled to his touch. He pushed a fingernail into the wood and found it was soft at the edges, rotten from years of rain leaking past a warped panel in the top of the shutter. He pulled a screwdriver from a small pouch of tools in his camera bag and pushed it into the wood at the point where one shutter overlapped the other. The screwdriver blade pushed straight through and made contact with the metal bar locking the shutters together. Joe manoeuvred the screwdriver blade under the metal bar and forced it upwards. It had been more than a hundred years since it last moved, so there was some resistance, but finally it yielded and the shutters opened.

Facing Joe now were two locked French doors. Peering through the glass, he could see a dark curtain obscuring his view of the room, but more importantly, he could see the key was in the door lock on the inside.

He pulled a face as he considered his options.

"Bugger it," he said as he picked up a large piece of roof tile from the ground nearby. "I've got this far, might as well go for it."

Grasping one end of the tile, he hit the glass pane next to the lock battering-ram style and the window broke. Joe froze at the sound of a piece of glass shattering as it hit the ground. But the noise wasn't loud and he doubted the sound would have travelled far in the dense forest.

Joe reached through the broken window and turned the key in the lock. Pushing open the doors, he grabbed a handful of the curtain, only to find that the fabric had all but rotted over the course of more than a century. The entire curtain disintegrated and fell to the ground.

As the light from the open doors flooded into the room, Joe stared in amazement. The room appeared to be some sort of workshop. To his left were benches and racks of tools, ahead of him two large easels, one with a huge canvas on a wooden stretcher painted with the early stages of a pastoral scene, while to his right was a large bellows camera on a massive wooden tripod and a table loaded with piles of sketch pads and loose sheets of sketch paper.

However, interesting as all this was, what quickly caught Joe's attention was the wall opposite the windows. He had been hoping for a trompe l'oeil painting and he was not disappointed. But the one in front of him wasn't just one painting, it was many, each one painted on top of parts of another. It took him a moment to understand that what he was looking at were experimental panels, a wall of subjects partially or fully hidden as a new one was tried out. It had an abstract quality that instantly appealed to Joe's tastes. He was now even more eager to find the others.

Almost without thinking as his eyes soaked up everything in the room, Joe was assembling his camera with the appropriate lens and fitting it on the compact tripod he carried strapped to the outside of his equipment bag. In the following minutes, he systematically recorded the contents of the entire room using exposures of one to two seconds before venturing farther in and capturing closer detail of the huge wall painting.

The bellows camera fascinated him. He had only seen such equipment as props in movies or in museums. Gently, and with great reverence, his hands explored the shutter release, aperture control and plate mounting system.

Below the benchtop, next to where the bellows camera and tripod were standing, were three cupboards. Joe bent to open the first of these, sinking to his knees in excitement when he realised what he had found. The bellows camera formed its images on glass plates of about twenty centimetres by twelve and here in front of him were three boxes each with ten photographic plates bearing negative images. He lifted one from the rack in the first box and held it up to the light. As far as he could tell, the image was a shot of a wall in a house on which were hung a number of paintings in frames. Unlike the older generation of photographers who used film, digital photographers like Joe, who was twenty-eight, had little experience with negatives and he found them hard to interpret. Were they shots from this villa? Were they in fact trompe l'oeil paintings? Joe had to know, but the boxes were too big and cumbersome to carry. He spent the next five minutes removing and carefully wrapping the plates in several lengths of cloth he found on one of the benches, after which he packed them into his equipment bag.

While he was waiting for a long exposure of a wall painting in a dark corner of the room, Joe walked over to a door in a different corner and reached for the handle. To his surprise, his hand grabbed at thin air. The handle wasn't real; it was painted on the wall along with what he had assumed was the wood panelling of the door.

"How do you get out of here?" he mused out loud. "There must be a way in apart from the French doors."

Taking a small torch from his bag, he shone its beam close to the apparent edge of the painted door and found the narrowest of gaps. He tapped on the door. "Wood," he said, and tapped on the wall to its right. "Plaster." He laughed. "Clever stuff. It looks like a door, deceives you into thinking it isn't, but it really is a door all the time. So where's the handle?"

His eyes scanned the surfaces around the door. "It has to be close," he said, as he ran his hands over the wall, which itself was painted to give the impression of being built of rough bricks. Using his torch again, he cast an oblique light onto the wall and found that one of the painted bricks was slightly recessed. He pushed the brick and it moved smoothly into the wall. Moments later the door swung silently open.

Whatever was beyond the door was in total darkness, the light from the open French doors not penetrating more than a few centimetres. He pushed the door open as far as it would go, noticing as he did how perfectly balanced it was, and how it tended to swing slowly back to the closed position. Grabbing a chair, he propped the door open, his intention being to let a little more natural light into the space beyond the door. Shining his torch ahead of him, he walked into the darkness.

The space was a wide corridor leading into the body of the villa, the walls of which were apparently clad in polished wood and hung with paintings. However, closer scrutiny showed this was just an illusion: the walls were all plain and painted like the walls in the workshop. Joe considered photographing the corridor but on checking his watch, decided he should return to the main villa before Monica Lieti began to wonder where he was. But before he did, he wanted to return things to how he found them. He removed the chair holding open the door to the corridor and was once again impressed by the smooth closing mechanism. In the silence that followed, he thought he heard a distant scraping sound. He concentrated hard, but it was on the edge of the limit of his hearing. He shrugged, remembering that woodworm make various noises as they work their way through beams. The chances of an old building such as this being infested must be high.

He closed the French doors, having brushed the broken glass to one side. There wasn't anything he could do about the curtain, but he could carefully put the shutters back in place and with a little effort using the screwdriver, he managed to close the locking bar. To the casual observer, the shutters now looked exactly as they did before Joe set to work on them.

Just as he picked up his bag and turned to walk away, he heard the loud complaining cry of a crow coming from above followed by a faint 'whoosh'. Moments later, a roof tile crashed to the ground just two metres to Joe's left.

"Shit!" he cried. "That was too close to be funny."

Chapter Eight

Twenty-four hours after finding herself trapped with a desiccated dead body, Evie Lorrigan was sitting at the wooden table in the stifling top-floor room, her chin in her hands as her eyes stared up at the dirty skylight. Her head was still thumping with the pulsating pressure that had started to build behind her eyes the day before, while frequent bouts of uncontrollable shivering left her gasping, in spite of her attempts to quell them by wrapping her arms tightly around herself. And try as she may to blank them out, neither the gnawing ache of hunger in her stomach nor the desperate yearning for water would go away. She would never normally go for long without eating something, an hour, tops. It had now been almost a day and her body was screaming at her for nourishment. She cursed herself for finishing all her energy bars and for wasting water back in the forest. What little she still had needed to be rationed. Imprisoned as she was, she was starting to accept it could mean the difference between life and death.

After discovering the body the previous afternoon, Evie had sat motionless for many minutes in disbelief, wondering if for reasons unknown she had actually been lured to the top-floor room and trapped. Finally she stirred, brushed the cobwebs from the chair and pulled it away from the table to increase the distance from the body sitting in the other chair in the alcove. However, as her eyes became accustomed to the dim light, she found them constantly drawn to the figure, as if expecting it to get up and walk over to her.

Hugging her backpack to her chest for solace, she had tried to make sense of her situation. It had to be some sort of stunt, a test perhaps. Surely the door she knew was there, but was such a perfect fit she couldn't see it, would suddenly swing open and some idiot would be pointing and laughing. Or perhaps it was some sort of stupid practical joke. Whatever it was, it hadn't improved her opinion of Villa Brocanti, nor had she forgiven Jane Bawley for sending her there even if the woman hadn't told her about this abandoned villa.

She sneered disdainfully as another unlikely scenario crossed her mind. "Who knows, perhaps I've been set up by the opposition. Maybe there's a long-standing feud between the owners and their neighbours who want to discredit them."

Looking down at the backpack, she pulled irritably at a strap as her hunger gave her gut another twist. "Bollocks to that. I don't give a toss about their feuds. I feel like shit."

She took a deep breath and sat straighter as an idea popped into her head.

"I wonder if I'm being watched," she said, automatically dropping her voice in case someone out there was listening. "I bet there's a webcam capturing everything with some perv getting off on it."

She stood, dropped the backpack and grabbed her phone from where she'd left it on the table.

"Shit!" she cried as she pressed the home button. "Two percent battery left." As she watched, the screen turned black, the tiny gear symbol revolved briefly, and the phone died. "No, you bugger! You can't do this to me!"

Her eyes flickered wildly as she sought inspiration. "I know," she cried, tearing open the backpack. She pulled out her laptop and flipped up the screen.

"Not beaten yet," she muttered defiantly as she opened Word

to a blank white page and enlarged it to fill the screen. She turned the laptop and aimed the screen at the walls. The light from the screen was a poor substitute for the phone's torch, but by holding it close to the wall, she could see enough detail.

A few frustrating minutes later, she slammed the lid shut. Nothing. She had searched every crevice, even braving going closer to the body in the chair than she wanted, but there was no webcam. She wasn't being watched; she was alone.

Tossing the laptop onto the table, Evie sat down heavily on the chair.

"I need a drink," she said, reaching in the backpack for the bottle of water. But as she unscrewed the cap and put the bottle to her mouth, she paused.

"Can't just drink it all," she said, "I don't know how long it's got to last. God, I was stupid pouring most of it over my head in the woods. What a waste."

She took a sip and screwed the cap firmly back in place.

Rifling through the backpack, she pulled out the contents to check if there was anything edible she'd forgotten about, tossing all her things on the floor in frustration when she found nothing.

"Note to self," she muttered. "Always pack more energy bars than even I get through in the average couple of days. You never know when you'll need them. And plenty of water, too."

She looked up at the skylight, wondering if there was any chance of reaching it.

"Why is that bloody thing so high?"

She stood and pulled at the table, wanting to move it so it was directly under the skylight. It was heavier than it looked and she had to pull hard even to move it.

"It may be old, but if the weight's anything to go by, it should be strong enough," she said, leaning against the table and breathing heavily. "Should be OK to support my slender form."

She picked up the chair and positioned it on the table top so the feet were centred. Clambering onto the table and holding the back of the chair, she gingerly climbed onto the seat and, after carefully standing up, reluctantly released her grip. With nothing to hang on to and her headache pounding the inside of her skull, she felt dizzy and horribly vulnerable.

She slowly raised her eyes towards the skylight. "Shit! The damn thing's still bloody miles away."

Yelping as the chair wobbled, she clambered back down to the floor, glaring back up at the yellow glass in frustration.

"I've got to break it, even if there is no chance of getting through it. If I can break it and yell, someone might hear."

She yanked the chair from the table top and angrily sat on it. Snatching up her backpack, she shook it again in case she had missed something.

"Is there nothing of any use in this damn bag?" she cried, glaring at the contents scattered across the floor. She grabbed her washbag, unzipped it and glanced regretfully at the toothpaste. "Not edible and not heavy enough to break a window. Bloody useless."

Another small zipped up bag contained cables. She picked one out. "Jeez, what a dummy! I can charge my phone from the laptop, at least until it goes flat."

She opened the laptop and scrutinised the display. "Sixty-five percent," she read. "Better than nothing."

After plugging in her phone and checking it was charging, she looked around at the contents of the backpack strewn across the floor and noticed a plastic roll-on deodorant stick.

"I wonder if that would be heavy enough?" she said, picking it up and tossing it in her hand.

For the next ten minutes, Evie lobbed, tossed and flung the deodorant stick at the skylight. Mostly she missed and on the occasions she hit the glass, the stick bounced off, the momentum nowhere near enough to break it. She even tried standing on the table to get closer, but the angle was difficult, the result equally disappointing.

"Arghh!" she screamed in frustration as the stick yet again bounced across the room, this time rolling under the other chair and wedging itself between the floor and the boot of the skeletal body.

She went to retrieve it, but thought better of it. The light was starting to fade and she had no desire to touch the body. Instead, she flopped down onto her chair, looking longingly at the plastic bottle with its precious drops of water.

The night had seemed endless, the silence in the room overwhelming whenever she stirred, which felt like every ten minutes. And every time she woke, the aching in her gut and the relentless pounding in her head reminded her of where she was and the hopelessness of her situation. She tried curling herself up in a ball, clutching at her head with her hands to hide her unseeing eyes, but the silence and the darkness were ever-present, conspiring to make her shudder with fear and to whimper like an animal caught in a trap.

The only reason she knew she had actually slept was that she awoke to find daylight filtering into the room through the skylight. The last time she had woken up, the darkness had been complete.

She stretched her aching limbs and stiff back, deciding she was a pampered wimp, that at thirty-four she should be able to get her head around a little adversity. It wasn't as if she had never slept rough. How many times had she camped in the wilds of nowhere when on assignment? Dozens, so why was this so different?

Suddenly she shivered violently and sneezed.

"That's ridiculous," she complained, "this room isn't in the least bit cold."

She touched her forehead; it was burning. "Jeee-sus!" she yelled, immediately regretting it as the noise echoed around her eardrums.

Standing to walk to the chair, a hand reaching for the wall to steady herself, she realised she needed to pee. Taking a wide course around the chair with the body, she made her way to the rear of the alcove in the left corner of the room, the darkest part, farthest from the table and her chair, and relieved herself on the tiles. She wondered if it would be the last time she peed, given how little water there was in the bottle. She had no idea how these things worked.

As she walked back past the body, she plucked up courage to bend and retrieve the deodorant stick from where it had rolled the previous evening. She shuddered as her hand brushed the leather boot containing what she assumed would be a horribly shrivelled foot. Weighing the stick in her hand, she adjusted her position to maximise her throw and hurled it at the skylight. It missed, smacked into the ceiling tiles and bounced across the room. She left it lying there, giving it up as a bad job.

Remembering her phone, she turned it on and checked the charge.

"Plus side," she announced to the room, "the phone is back to fifty per cent; downside, the laptop is dead."

She switched off the phone and tossed it onto the table. "I'll only use the torch when I really need to. Right now, I've got to find something heavier to break that skylight."

Rubbing a hand over the wall, she had an idea. If she could scrape into the space between the stones, she might get far enough to loosen one and pull it out, much as she had done the day before in the small outhouse. She peered around the room. The internal dividing wall was rendered and painted to resemble a stone wall, but the outside wall was just the original stone. However, its stones were large, probably too large. She returned her attention to the dividing wall. Before she could get to the stone or brick used to build it, she would need to remove some of the plaster covering it. It would take time even with a knife, and all Evie had were her fingernails. There was nothing sharp in her bag; it wasn't allowed in hand luggage.

Looking across at the body slumped in the chair, she wondered if men from his era wore belts. A belt would have a buckle. Did she have the nerve to explore?

She took a deep breath and, shrugging with a nonchalance she didn't really feel, she walked over to the figure. First, she had to unfasten the six large buttons securing the substantial coat he was wearing. Each one took some effort, especially as her hands were shaking, but eventually she freed them all and slowly pulled open the coat. Underneath was a waistcoat that covered the top of the man's trousers. Using the extreme ends of her forefinger and thumb, Evie carefully lifted the bottom of the waistcoat.

"Bugger!" she muttered. "The braces are held by buttons. But hang on, there's a chain looping across the waistcoat pockets, a watch chain, and from the bulge in the pocket, there's a watch attached. A watch might be good for scraping."

In her haste to take the watch and chain, Evie pulled more firmly on the waistcoat than she intended and felt the body move. She screamed and jumped backwards as the body sagged, and with nothing to support it, rolled to the floor, ending up face down.

"Shit! Now I've got to turn it," she moaned despairingly.

However, the shrunken body proved to be lighter than she had expected. It was easy enough to turn, once she got over the revulsion of grasping a leg and the upper part of an arm.

Almost gleefully, she returned to her chair to examine the watch and chain. There were no sharp edges, but the winder was protected by a ring narrow enough to double as a scraper. And perhaps, if she could prise the back off the watch, the cover would be thin enough to be an alternative tool.

She decided she might as well be comfortable in her work, that sitting would conserve energy. Grabbing the second chair from next to the body, she positioned it by the wall, sat down and began scraping.

Three hours later, dejection over her progress was undermining Evie's resolve, while her fever had increased along with the headache. She was shivering constantly. The plaster was altogether harder than she had anticipated, and her tools inadequate for the task. She threw the watch to the floor, stood up to stretch and moved to the other chair. She had only made the slightest of progress. She stared up at the skylight, hunger gnawing at her insides and her throat parched.

"Let me out, you bloody bastards! I can't die here. Let me out!"

She clenched her teeth in an attempt to control the shivering, determined to remain strong even as her chin quivered and tears flooded her eyes.

"Please," she whispered.

She was dozing, her mind drifting, her hunger a beast snapping at her insides. She had no idea how much time had passed. She thought about it. There was still daylight coming through the skylight and certainly another night hadn't passed, so it could only be a couple of hours. She was beginning to wonder whether she really cared, what difference it made, when suddenly she thought she heard the very faint sound of glass breaking.

She sat up with a start and squealed as her head pounded in protest.

"Help!" she screamed at what was meant to be the top of her voice. But the top of her voice was no longer working, her high temperature sapping what remained of her energy reserves. What emerged from her mouth was little more than a whisper.

Dejected, she slumped back to the floor, where she sat for some minutes, trying to gather her strength. Finally, she sighed heavily, shaking her head.

"That's not good enough, Evie Lorrigan," she growled through clenched teeth. "Get a grip, for Christ's sake."

Picking up the watch, she continued her feeble attempt at removing some plaster.

She was still scraping sometime later when Joe was preparing to leave the workshop on the ground floor, but from such a distance, the weakness of her efforts was all too easy for him to confuse with woodworm.

Chapter Nine

Half an hour after Joe's close encounter with a roof tile, he was walking back through the Villa Brocanti reception, eager to transfer the files from his camera to his laptop.

"Ah, Signor Oliver, you are back," Monica Lieti called after him as she emerged from the office behind the reception desk. She smiled warmly at him. "Were you successful with your photography?"

"Er, yes, I think so," replied Joe, not wanting to stop. "I'll need to review them all on the computer, but I think there are some good shots."

"May I see?" asked Monica, touching Joe's arm and pointing to his camera bag.

The last thirty or so shots were all of the interior of the old villa; the last thing Joe needed was for Monica Lieti to get sight of them.

"Actually, there are rather a lot," said Joe, stalling. "They'll be much easier to see once I've optimised them. At this stage of the process, digital images are only really half-completed. The rest is all done on the computer."

"Of course," replied Monica graciously. "You are a professional. I am used to just looking at photographs on my phone. Perhaps you will show me later?"

"My pleasure," muttered Joe guiltily, avoiding her eyes. He turned and hurried off to his room.

Before he processed his shots of the workshop, Joe was keen to examine the glass plates. After carefully unwrapping them, he stacked them next to the laptop on the room's small desk. Without the correct light sources, he needed to improvise. He called up a word processing program, opened a new file and switched the image to full screen. His screen was now a large white backlit surface which he tilted back as far as it would go and rested the first glass plate on it. Satisfied the plate was secure, he set up his camera on a tripod so it was exactly at right angles to the plate, worked out the exposure and hit the shutter release. Having checked the image on his camera's screen and accepted it, he repeated the process for all thirty glass plates he had taken from the old villa, after which he carefully wrapped them again and put them away inside his wardrobe.

Ready now for a session in Lightroom and Photoshop, he transferred all the files from his camera to a new folder on his laptop. He called up the first of them and with a few clicks and slides of the tone controls, the image on the screen switched from a negative to a positive. A few more clicks and he had optimised the tone densities. He hit full screen and leaned forward to scrutinise the shot.

He immediately appreciated the care that had been taken in making the original image using the bellows camera. It was a pin-sharp and perfectly exposed general shot of a wall hung with a dozen framed portraits above a large stone fireplace, and it wasn't until Joe magnified the image to almost pixel level that he could see sufficient detail to confirm that everything in the image was painted on the wall. He felt a thrill of anticipation as he saved various versions of the image.

Two hours later, Joe had examined every one of the images from the glass plates. He sat back in his chair, his fingers drumming on the desk. He had uncovered a major set of paintings and he had no idea what to do about it. Before talking to Jane, he had never even heard of Salvatore Brocanti, and even after checking on

Google, he knew little more — his search produced only the briefest summary of the man's life and work. Having now seen the paintings in the villa, it was clear to Joe that the artist was not just underrated, he was hardly considered at all. But before he thought further about what he might do with his discovery, he wanted to process his own shots from the workroom and the corridor beyond it. Given the care Joe had taken in making them and the high quality of his equipment, his images were inevitably even better than those from the glass plates.

As he stared at the computer screen, his external shots of the vineyards and olive groves for the article quite forgotten, he knew he had to go back to the old villa, get inside and find the rooms with the incredible trompe l'oeil paintings. He was tossing around ideas of when he might do this when he was interrupted by an incoming call on his laptop. It was Jane Bawley.

"Hi Jane," said Joe as he hit the 'accept' button. "What's new? Any sightings of Evie?"

"No, there's nothing and I'm beginning to get quite worried. I still can't raise Ronaldo, our agent in Perugia. Honestly, I don't know why we use him; he's never in the office, and his secretary only answers the phone when she feels like it."

"Have you established that Evie even made it to Italy?" said Joe, wondering if perhaps she'd had an accident while still in England.

"Yes, I checked with the airline and they confirmed she was on the flight. It arrived on time at Perugia airport yesterday morning at eleven."

"So where is she? Do you want me to contact the police, see if there's any report of an accident? I could get Monica Lieti to call them."

"God, I don't know. Do you think it's really necessary? I mean, the Italian police …"

"Well, what then?"

"I was wondering, you've got the rental, haven't you? And you're not too far from Perugia. Would you mind popping down there first thing in the morning and checking out the agent's office? The secretary might be more helpful if you show up in person."

Joe wasn't keen on the idea until it occurred to him that by heading off to Perugia, he might have a way to go back to the old villa without Monica Lieti knowing.

"OK, Jane, I could do that. Listen, I've had another thought. I could go to the airport as well and ask the taxi drivers. Maybe one of them brought her straight here."

"Well, if he did, where is she?"

"No idea. Do you have a photo of Evie you could email me? I can show it around, see if it jogs any memories."

"Good idea, I do have one, yes. I'll send it immediately. How did you get on this afternoon? Did you get a chance to look at the old villa?"

Joe paused. Something in his mind was telling him not to let on to Jane about his breaking into the villa. Not yet, anyway.

"No, I didn't have time. I was too busy shooting this villa from every conceivable angle."

He heard a disappointed sigh from Jane. "I guess you'll have to put it on hold until we find Evie," she said.

"I'll keep you posted on progress, Jane."

"Okay. In the meantime, I think I'd better contact the other agriturismos you and Evie were scheduled to visit and tell them there will be a delay."

While they were talking, Joe remembered he'd promised Monica Lieti he would show her the vineyard shots. He hadn't even processed them yet. Pulling a face in frustration, since he was now more than ready for his swim, he scrolled through the images, made a selection of thirty and processed them in detail. Moving the new set into a distinctly separate part of the computer, he disconnected his laptop and went to find the direttrice. He had no intention of showing her anything to do with the glass negatives.

Chapter Ten

The following morning, Joe checked all his camera equipment and stowed it in his camera bag. Regardless of the outcome of his trip to Perugia, he was not intending to return to Villa Brocanti before making another visit to the old villa in the forest. In preparation, he had scrutinised the roads and tracks around the estate on Google Maps and found an old road skirting the estate that came reasonably close to where he now knew the old villa was located. He could drive there on his return and make his way to the villa on foot.

Having Jane send the photograph of Evie Lorrigan proved to be a good move. When Joe arrived at Perugia airport, a group of taxi drivers was waiting for the Stansted flight in the hope of fares and he quickly found several who remembered the demanding English-woman. After conferring and arguing briefly over the exact time and day, two of them pointed through the bar window where one of their colleagues was engrossed in a pink newspaper.

The FT? thought Joe, incredulous at the prospect.

"Franco, signore," said one of the taxi drivers, shrugging in sympathy at the man's misfortune. "He take the English signora."

Joe rushed into the bar, deciding he could do with a coffee. But first he pulled out Evie's photo and held it up to the taxi driver.

"Excuse me, signore," said Joe, his Italian failing him. "Questa signora, was she one of your fares two days ago?"

Franco slowly lifted his eyes from his 'La Gazzetta dello Sport' and settled them on Joe's, saying nothing for sufficiently long for Joe to feel uncomfortable. Finally, he reached out to Joe's hand, turning it slightly to see the photo more clearly.

"Perugia," he said, after another long pause.

"Perugia," repeated Joe. "Just Perugia?"

The man waited for another eternity before shrugging his shoulders and half closing his eyes. "Perugia," he repeated.

With some more imperfect Italian, Joe managed to establish that the driver had taken Evie to the address of the WanderFever office in the old town. All thoughts of coffee now gone, he thanked the man profusely, ran back to his car and headed for Perugia.

Watching him go, the taxi driver shook his head slowly. "Pazzo," he said to no one in particular. *Crazy*.

Not having a resident's permit, Joe couldn't drive into the historic centre of Perugia. Instead, he parked on the outskirts, took a series of escalators and hurried along to the WanderFever office, using his phone to guide him.

Evie's porn star was occupied with painting her nails when she buzzed Joe into the reception.

"Si?" she said through her botox-enhanced pout, languidly raising her eyes to determine whether this specimen of manhood who had had the effrontery to interrupt her was worth the effort.

Joe explained his quest, his Italian faltering as he forced his eyes away from the substantial amount of cleavage revealed by the woman's low-cut top.

After a few seconds of silence while she worked out what Joe was trying to say, the receptionist's face distorted into the closest approximation to a smile her surgery would allow. When the smile was followed by a harsh snort, Joe worried that her face might shatter.

"She go Anghiari, signore. I call the taxi." She paused, her eyes creasing wickedly.

Joe raised his eyebrows in question.

"She your friend?" asked the secretary, testing the waters.

"No, no," said Joe, stumbling over his words. "A … a sort of colleague. Una collega."

She nodded in approval. "Bene. She maleducata. Rude-a. I not like. I find her oldest taxi in Perugia."

Joe laughed. "I'll bet that went down well. Do you have the number? Of the taxi driver, I mean. I wonder if you'd mind calling him and asking exactly where he took her."

The receptionist lifted a telephone receiver in front of her, pressed several numbers and, once the call was answered, launched into fast, heavily accented Italian. After some laughter and questions, she wrote something on a Post-it note and handed it to Joe.

"Villa Brocanti?" read Joe. The woman nodded.

"What time did they arrive?" added Joe.

She fired another question into the phone, nodded, and rang off.

"A leetle after one, signore."

Back in the street, Joe thought about calling Jane to update her. But the same reluctance he had felt over telling her he had broken into the abandoned villa returned. He was sure she was holding back on something. Maybe it would be no bad thing if he did the same.

Of more immediate concern, he remembered Monica Lieti telling him that between one and three, there was no one around at Villa Brocanti. What if Evie had gone wandering and found the old villa? Joe hadn't explored the grounds around the villa, just the area by the garden where he had broken in. Thoughts of falling roof tiles made him wonder if Evie had been hit by one and even now was lying injured in the overgrown garden. Or worse. He certainly wouldn't have seen her without specifically looking for her.

Forty-five minutes later, after pushing the Fiat 500 to its limits along the E45 superstrada north from Perugia to Sansepolcro, Joe was driving along the track he had found earlier on Google Maps. He stopped the car, double-checked his position, and drove on a little farther before pulling off the track. As he automatically turned to lift his camera bag, he paused. The bag was heavy and Evie's fate was more important than photography. He could fetch it later if he still wanted to go ahead with his mission in the villa.

More than ever convinced he was going to find Evie either injured or dead in the undergrowth near the house, he broke into a brisk jog as he followed what he could make out of the old track to the house. It had been almost two days since Evie went missing. Two days in the present heat was a long time without water.

The track was longer and more overgrown than he'd anticipated, quickly reducing his jog to as brisk a walk as he could make it, and it wasn't until fifteen minutes later that he emerged from the forest into the overgrown gardens at the rear of the house. Spotting the shutters he had forced open the previous day, he decided to start his search from there. He had been walking anticlockwise around the villa; he would continue in that direction while checking the grounds in case Evie had been hit and had staggered some way before collapsing.

He quickly came to the single-storey extension separating the two gardens. Walking around the end of it, he saw the smaller garden beyond, and on this side of the extension, two doors and some shuttered windows. The door farther from the main villa was half open. He pushed it and peered inside, but could see little in the darkness apart from it obviously being a storeroom. His torch was in his equipment bag, but a phone torch would help. However, as he felt in his pocket for it, he remembered that it too was in the car. He had tossed it on the passenger seat when he had been checking the map.

Sighing in frustration, he walked into the dark room and stood while his eyes adjusted to the dim light. Once he could see more, he made his way around the room, wanting to check in case Evie had crawled into a corner.

There was a door in one wall that would lead into a room closer to the main villa. He turned the handle and opened it, but the room beyond was even darker. Again he waited until he could see enough to avoid tripping over anything lying on the floor before satisfying himself that Evie wasn't there either. While searching this room, he found another door that had to lead into a room even closer to the villa, but it was locked and resistant to his shaking.

He went back outside and checked the shutters, working out that two of them must cover windows that were in the room closest to the villa. The first shutter swung open when he pulled it, revealing an unlatched window. Joe pushed open the window and pulled the shutter clear of the window space. The sill wasn't high and he could easily peer into the room. It was another store like the first one with shelves on the walls and freestanding shelves in the centre. Since he could see most of the floor space, he felt sure that if Evie had been in there he would be able to see her, and so he decided not to climb in. Instead, he thought it more important to continue his original search of the old gardens and grounds around the house.

Forty minutes later, Joe had completed his circuit of the villa and was back close to the French doors. During his search, he had walked as far as a hundred metres away from the villa, trying to cover the ground in a grid-like way, but there was nothing, no sign of a body or of any disturbance to the vegetation that would indicate someone crawling or dragging themselves along. He sat in the shade of a tree, satisfied now that he had been wrong: Evie had not been injured in the garden.

But there was no doubt she had arrived at Villa Brocanti. So where was she?

He looked up at the trees and thought about the huge forest around him. If Evie had become lost in its vastness, or fallen and been injured in some way, it would take considerable manpower to undertake a search, and even then the chances of her being found would be slim.

As he wondered what to do next, his eyes again fell on the old villa and the outhouse separating the gardens. The shutter on the outhouse wall had been unfastened, as had the window behind it. No, that wasn't right. The shutter wasn't just unfastened, it had been forced. Could Evie have done that? Now he thought about it, there was a substantial length of wood on the ground near the window.

The idea took shape in his mind. Evie could easily have been as inquisitive as he was about the old villa and she might well have broken in. Certainly it needed further investigation, and if it led to an alternative way in, perhaps it would help him in his search for the paintings shown in the glass photographic plates.

Joe jumped to his feet and headed off back to the car to fetch his equipment bag and phone.

Chapter Eleven

Evie's second night was even less comfortable than the first, her hunger and thirst now constant, stabbing discomforts overlaid with a growing terror that gnawed away at her mind. And exacerbating all of these was the infection she had picked up. Every few minutes, she would jolt awake shivering, her teeth chattering, her arms wrapped round herself, her throat and mouth raw for the want of water.

She had put on double layers of clothes in a vain attempt to reduce the extra loss of water resulting from her high temperature. Her remaining clothing, such as it was, was layered as makeshift bedding, anything to relieve her body from the unyielding hardness of the terracotta-tiled floor. She had moved to the extreme end of the room, as far as possible from the body. But somehow the fact that it was also on the floor — and therefore at her level when she lay down in her attempts at sleep — made the body's presence even more disturbing.

Don't be ridiculous, she told herself. It's a body; it's dead, inert. It has no more life in it than the table and chairs.

But it was alive once, a quiet but insistent voice in her head kept reminding her, as alive as you are now.

"Hmmgrh." Her attempt at an angry retort emerged from her mouth as a painful grunt. "That's not saying much since every hour I grow rapidly closer to dying."

. . .

At some time during the night, she had glanced up from where her head was resting on the backpack, her eyes staring in the direction of the body in the total darkness. It didn't matter that she couldn't see it; it was there. She told herself that if she ever got out of this place, if she ever wrote anything else, it wouldn't be bloody travel garbage, it would be something meaningful, something with more permanence than a list of overrated restaurants and bars that were here today, gone tomorrow. She would write about the mental torture of isolation, and about how terrifying it was to be sharing a room with a body that had probably been here for more than a hundred years, callously left to die by some madman or madwoman.

She thought back over her passage through the house. Had she been guided by the succession of tricks and falsehoods presented to her, the smoke and mirrors of trompe l'oeil paintings? Had she been targeted? Or was she the victim of fate, of her own reckless impulsiveness, an unexpected rat caught in a long-forgotten trap?

That thought offered no comfort: if no one had organised or orchestrated her entrapment, no one knew she was there. As far as Villa Brocanti was concerned, with the whole staff absent for some stupid funeral, she was simply a no show. Jane would write her off as unreliable, her opinion of her confirmed.

"Shit!" she screamed into her backpack, immediately regretting the expenditure of energy and the effect on her parched throat.

She turned her back on the body with a petulance she knew was pointless and childish, but it felt good.

"In the morning, we'll get to know each other better, you and I," she hissed.

A wave of shivering hit her. "And that coat of yours is looking very attractive and very warm from here. You are going to be a gentleman and give it to me."

She stopped, her despair rearing up and confronting her once again, her lips quivering as she tried to banish it from her thoughts.

"But until then," she added with a defiance that pleased her, "I'm going to bloody well ignore you. I'm going to get some sleep."

. . .

But she could manage no more than ten or fifteen minutes of continuous rest before one thing or another disturbed her: the hard floor pressing into her bony hips and shoulders, her body screaming for sustenance, the almost constant shivering. During one of the longer periods of semiconsciousness, when the hunger pangs were dancing on her stomach wall, she had idly wondered whether there was any flesh left on the bones of her companion …

As the dawn light slowly made its inadequate way into the room, Evie gave up on trying to sleep, turned and sat up. She dragged the backpack behind her to act as a pad between her spine and the uncompromising hardness of the wall. The effort left her giddy and breathing heavily. She was so cold.

Hunting around in her belongings, she snorted angrily. Why hadn't she packed anything more substantial than a couple of Ts? Because she was in bloody Italy in bloody June, that's why. Because she hadn't anticipated getting intimately acquainted with a dead man in an abandoned villa or catching some filthy bug.

Picking up the water bottle, she congratulated herself on how strong willed she had been in eking out her meagre resources, determined to maximise her chances. Even so, she reckoned of the original half litre, there was little more than one large mouthful left. She unscrewed the lid from the bottle and put her cracked lips to the top, tilting the bottle gently to make sure every drop came her way, that nothing was spilt.

She limited herself to a few drops and quickly screwed the cap back on. The water had hardly moistened her mouth. At least she felt no urge to pee, which she reckoned must mean her body was conserving resources.

Reaching out to where she had left her phone near her on the floor, she pressed the 'on' button and waited for it to boot up. Would there be a signal by some chance? What did the 'emergency calls only' message mean? She had no idea what the emergency services number was in Italy, so she tried a few combinations: 999,

911, 123. Nothing worked. She must be outside the range of any phone service. The things weren't magic; they needed a signal of some description to function.

She glanced at the screen. Forty-three percent. Better to turn it off. As she did, she noted the time: seven forty-three. Was that Italian or UK time? She didn't remember changing it. Did it happen automatically? Did it matter? It certainly didn't impact on the quality of the room service.

Evie sat staring across the room in the gradually increasing light. It was never going to be bright, given the yellowed, dirty skylight, but her eyes were more used to it than on the first day. She was studying the object of her day's goal. The body. She was going to come to terms with the body.

She had seen the TV programmes, the police procedurals; she had watched the post-mortem examinations the actors carried out, ever more convincing in gore and gruesomeness as the technology behind the rubberised dummies improved. Although, according to a medical researcher she'd once dated who was totally disparaging of the TV portrayals, they never got the reaction to the smell right. It was all right for pathologists, he told her, they were used to it, but the one thing about post-mortems that caused police officers, inexperienced crime scene people and other hangers on to pass out or go diving for a sink was the smell. Bodies don't smell nice. Except very old and desiccated ones, like the one in front of her. So she'd been told. And given that the only smell pervading the room was the general mustiness of stale air rather than rotting flesh, it seemed her information was correct.

She thought back to when the body had fallen from the chair. Apart from a cloud of dust, there had been nothing nauseating about it except what was in her mind at the time. Now she'd had longer to think about it, she had rationalised it further. Maybe.

Evie pulled herself to her feet, swayed alarmingly and immediately sat down in the nearest chair. The giddiness must be a result of her hunger, she thought, or the wretched infection. Or both. She shivered. She had to wrap up more.

She lowered herself onto her knees and crawled over to where she had left the body lying on its back after taking the pocket watch.

"Let's see what you're wearing, Alfonso," she croaked.

Leaning over her new friend, she tried to slip an arm inside the coat behind his shoulders, but all she achieved was the release of a cloud of dust that she tried not to breathe in.

Coughing as she sat back on her heels to review the problem, she spluttered, "Turned you once, Alfie, I can turn you again."

She took hold of the body's left arm and left leg and pulled it onto its front, making sure that neither of the arms was trapped.

"Right," she said, tugging at the sleeves, "let's see if we can pull this thing off."

There was some resistance until she caught hold of the coat tails, after which the coat slipped off easily.

Evie slowly stood and leaned against the wall, breathing heavily and holding out the coat as she did. She made her way to what in her mind she was calling the bathroom end of the room and, grasping the coat by the shoulders, gave it a thorough shaking. For good measure, and hoping it wouldn't fall apart, she also beat it against the wall, although in her weakened state, the beating achieved little.

"Hey, that's quite a good fit," she wheezed as she slipped on the coat, coughing as more disturbed dust lifted from the material. "Nice and long too. It should certainly keep me warmer tonight. In fact I'm leaving it on."

She looked down at the coat, enjoying the feeling of security it gave her, but before she buttoned it up, she checked inside the pockets. There were two on the outside and two inside, none of which she had checked the previous day when she had been distracted by the pocket watch.

There was nothing in the outside pockets, but in one of the breast-level inside pockets, there was a single folded sheet of paper. Pulling it out, Evie unfolded it to find what appeared to be a letter on headed writing paper, the font so ornate she had difficulty making out the words.

The letter itself was unintelligible for two reasons. Firstly, she knew no Italian and secondly the writing was as compact and elaborate as the printed address. All she could make out was the first line, which looked like 'Carissima,' and a date 23 v 95. She gulped when she realised that the last two numbers were short for 1895. Her eye fell on the end of the letter where the only word she could discern was 'Ugo'.

"So you're Ugo are you, not Alfonso," she whispered. "Thanks for the loan of your coat, my friend."

Evie glanced at the remaining clothing on Ugo's body, but she hadn't got the energy to do anything about it. She shuffled over to the chair nearer the table, pulled the coat around her, and sat. The other clothing would still be there if she needed it, but for the first time since she had been trapped, she was enjoying feeling warmer.

Chapter Twelve

Joe dropped his equipment bag through the open storeroom window, lifted himself onto the sill and jumped into the room. Pulling his powerful torch from the bag, he directed its beam around the room. At first he could see nothing out of the ordinary, but when he shifted position to the wall opposite the window and looked in the direction of the main villa, he saw a door in the corner. And it was ajar! However, on moving closer and running the torch beam over the door's surface, the three-dimensional illusion was soon lost. To confirm it, Joe reached out to touch the space that was apparently left from the door opening, and found it was part of the painting. And unlike the painting of a door he had found in the workshop, this one had no indentation around it. It was a painting and no more.

Like Evie before him, Joe shone the beam around the wall to the left of the door painting, a wall painted with amazingly realistic brickwork, and found the indentation of the real door.

He laughed. "Variation on a theme here. This time there's a hidden door right next to a fake one. Where's the handle to this one?"

He pointed his torch at the wall running at right angles to the door, immediately spotting the space from where Evie had removed the one real brick. He put his fingers in the space and they closed around the latch bar. The door swung open away from him as he pulled on the bar.

Remembering how the door in the corner of the workshop was perfectly balanced to swing slowly closed, he grabbed a wooden box from the storeroom and pushed it against the open door.

Beyond the door was a dark space that turned out to be a corridor leading off to the left. After grabbing his bag, Joe walked along the corridor, stopping briefly to check an open wooden door that appeared to be designed to close off the corridor. But his attention was taken by dark curtains hanging at the end of the corridor. In the harsh light of his powerful torch beam, they were clearly not real, whereas a large pile of curtain material lying on the floor in front of them clearly was. Not understanding it, he looked to the right of the pile of curtains into the large room beyond and, as he played his torch beam around the walls, he saw the familiar sight of the fireplace with portraits hung above it that had been the subject of one of the glass negatives.

"Yes!" he cried, balling a fist and punching the air. "I wonder if there's any natural light in here." He switched off the torch and the room was plunged into total darkness.

"OK, bad idea," he complained, and switched the torch back on. "Maybe if I …" But his conversation with himself faltered as he looked closer at the curtained windows, windows he quickly worked out, as Evie had done, could not be windows since they weren't anywhere near an outside wall.

He glanced upwards and saw the curved balustrade with the sky above it.

"Brilliant!" he exclaimed. "Abso-bloody-lutely brilliant. This room's a box, plain and simple, and yet, look at it!"

He let his eyes roam the room for a few moments, enjoying the many illusions and wondering how to record them.

"So where do we go from here? Hang on, there's a door in the corner of the fireplace wall that looks real enough."

As he adjusted the equipment bag on his back, he considered setting up a camera and tripod to take some shots. But the light was so low, it would take too long. Instead, he walked over to the door he had just noticed, pulled it open and shone his torch beam into the darkness.

"Another corridor," he said. "Let's see where it leads."

After checking the door wasn't going to close on him, he walked along the corridor to where it turned right and came to the stairs. Stopping only briefly to shine his torch into the gloom, he climbed the stairs, initially as taken in by the balustrade and corridor behind it as Evie had been. But when he moved the beam around and saw no shadow from the balustrade on the wall beyond it, he realised the truth and shook his head again in admiration of the skill involved in the execution of the painting.

Led on, as he was supposed to be, by the corridor to the two doors a short way along it, Joe opened the left door and peered into the room.

"Daylight!" he exclaimed in excitement before the contradiction hit him. "Daylight? From an open shutter? There isn't one! Not one of the shutters I saw outside was open. What's going on?"

As he took a step forward, the edge of his vision caught the painting on the floor. "Whoa!" he cried, jumping back in alarm. But as he shone the torch around the apparent collapse in the floor, he shook his head. "Wow! This bloke was really good. It's better than any street art I've seen."

He looked around the room and was busy taking in the pastoral scenes and portraits he had first seen on the glass photographic plates, when he remembered the window.

"The light," he said, striding over to it. "Where's it coming from?"

He looked over the sill and saw the scene of the woman sitting in the garden reading a book. "I don't believe it!" he cried. "I've got to get this one."

He dropped his equipment bag at his feet and assembled a camera and lens. Having checked and adjusted the camera settings, he took a series of shots.

Fired up with enthusiasm, he was about to start a more methodical record of the room when he again remembered he was supposed to be looking for Evie.

"It'll still be here tomorrow," he muttered, and stowed his equipment back in his bag.

It was while he was doing this that he noticed the room had a second door, this one partly hidden behind a curtain. Opening it, he shone his torch along a short corridor that seemed to turn right after a couple of metres. But as he walked through the door, he paused.

"Can't be too careful," he said, dropping his bag on the floor to keep the door from closing.

As he shone the torch around the walls, the scene was familiar from the glass negatives, but so much better in the flesh. He tried all three of the doors with real handles, but only one opened, one where the surrounding wall was painted to resemble a staircase. The mythical creatures and serpents on the stairs and walls beyond the open door were also familiar from the photographic plates, but he couldn't remember there being any more plates in the series. This meant that whatever was up the stairs was going to be unfamiliar territory.

Shining the torch beam high ahead of him, he climbed the lengthy flight of stairs and stopped in front of a large black door at the top. It was plain and wooden, with no adornments, the first like it he had seen since entering this labyrinth of rooms, corridors and illusions. He turned the handle and pushed open the door — another, he noticed, that felt superbly well balanced — and was immediately surprised by the unusual dimensions of the room he had entered.

It was too wide for its depth and far too high. He shone the torch upwards, noting the ceiling of terracotta tiles and wooden beams over four metres above his head. It was the roof; this was as far as the journey would go.

He moved the torch beam around the room, noticing the lack of decoration, unlike all the other rooms. And yet there was a door in the centre of the wall opposite where he had entered, a panelled wooden door. But was it? Three quick strides took him to it, and just as quickly he jumped back to the doorway he'd just come through. In the corner of his eye, he had noticed the door from the stairs start to move.

He was looking for something he could use to prop the door open when he felt the weight of the torch in his hand.

"Should do the trick," he said, as he placed the torch against the edge of the door and tested it would hold. He left the torch switched on with the beam shining upwards, which gave a general illumination to the entire room.

Remembering the door from the storeroom on the ground floor, Joe ran his fingers around the edge of the painted door. "Thought so," he said, nodding "It's another one."

Before searching for the handle, he stood back and took in the entire room.

"Of course," he said, after puzzling over the geometry for some moments. "It's half a room. Maybe even less than half a room. But why?"

He thought about the villa, the eccentric artist who must have created this maze of rooms, the path he now knew he had been predestined to follow: they all led to this spot. And to the room beyond this door. A room, like this one, on the top floor of the villa, a room most likely to be a dead end.

He thought again about Evie. Had she come this way? Had she followed the same route? Certainly someone had recently broken a shutter, forced a window, removed a brick from a wall in the storeroom to pull a lever that opened a door, and pulled on an ageing and rotting curtain sufficiently hard for its fastenings to fail, letting it fall to the ground.

She had to have come this way. She had even left at least one door open, a door not designed to close automatically, it was true, but it had been open.

He looked up at the painting of the door. Was the final room a trap? Would the door open to let an unsuspecting person in before closing again? Was Evie beyond the door?

"Evie!" Joe yelled, at the top of his voice. "Evie! Are you in there?"

He banged on the door, and was surprised to find it felt more like stone than wood, and he banged on the walls. "Evie!"

"Christ! Where's the latch? I'm coming Evie! Hang on!"

Frantic now, he ran his hands over the wall, up and down,

searching for a removable brick or stone. The wall was painted like the others, he noted, but there was nothing, no proud or recessed edges.

"Shit!" he yelled, kicking at the wall in frustration, his foot connecting just above the junction between the wall and the terra-cotta-tiled floor.

There was a quiet swish as the door swung open into the inner room.

"Evie!" yelled Joe as he ran through the doorway.

Chapter Thirteen

Wrapped in Ugo's coat, Evie managed a two-hour doze that was closer to sleep than any of her tortured naps so far. For a few brief seconds as consciousness returned, she even felt comfortable, but very quickly her mind flooded with the horror of her situation.

As her eyes flickered open, she was hit by her desperate need for water. The fever had left her lifeless and parched, her tongue feeling like a large piece of dried fruit without any of the flavour, while her throat was on fire, as if it had been scraped with sandpaper. She pushed the tip of her tongue onto her cracked lips, trying to ease their discomfort, but her tongue was too dry. She had to drink some of her precious water supply.

She looked across to where she had made the feeble attempt at scraping away the plaster covering what she assumed would be brick. Her goal was to smash the skylight, and to achieve that she needed the energy to continue scraping.

She understood that water alone wouldn't give her energy, but it would help to restore her cells to whatever balance they needed to function efficiently. The science didn't interest her; all she wanted was to stop feeling giddy, and the strength to dig out something from the wall that she could throw.

Turning her body slowly from where she was sitting against the wall, she got onto all fours, not even attempting to stand. She crawled the few paces to where the water bottle was standing on the floor near the table and slumped against the wall next to it. She stared at it longingly for some moments before she sighed reluctantly, and, after unscrewing the cap, lifted the bottle to her lips. This time she tilted it higher, allowing the contents to flow into her mouth. She pressed her lips together, rolling the precious fluid around, slowly and carefully, trying to moisten every cell before she swallowed. Even when she did finally swallow, she tried to make the action as slow as possible, giving her throat a chance to take full advantage of the water flowing through it.

She sat back and closed her eyes. God, that felt good.

After a few seconds, Evie opened her eyes to see how much water was still in the bottle. She estimated there was another half mouthful, less than she had just drunk, but enough to reinforce the effect of her first gulp. She decided to drink it all.

Ten minutes later, she was sitting on the chair she had left by the wall and gently but persistently scraping the plaster at the same spot she had been working on the day before. Her renewed determination, helped by the water, saw her pushing hard on the pocket watch with each stroke. Her progress was infinitesimal, but as the small pile of plaster on the floor below where she was scraping increased in size, she knew her efforts were achieving something.

An hour later, Evie was getting tired, and in spite of there being some progress, she knew there were still hours of work ahead of her. A feeling of hopelessness bubbling up inside her once again; she doubted she had the energy to finish the job, let alone hurl whatever stone or brick she might dig out at the skylight.

She needed a larger tool, something she could grip with both hands to work at the plaster. She looked around. There was nothing in the contents of her rucksack and the only other items in the room were the two chairs and the table. She needed the table to get closer to the skylight, and for the same reason she needed at least one chair. What about the second one? She certainly didn't need two; she wasn't expecting company.

But how easy was it going to be to break up a chair? They were identical to each other and totally different from the modern kitchen junk made from pine, the sort of thing she might possibly have been able to smash against the wall. These chairs were substantial, made from some sort of hardwood; heavy, with thick legs and solid backs. Good sturdy kitchen chairs.

She hauled herself to her feet and turned to grasp the chair back. Her intention was to pick the chair up and swing it hard against the wall, but after two days with no food and water, and with a persistent high fever, her physical strength was compromised. She could hardly lift it. There was no way she would be able to manhandle it sufficiently to break it.

Angrily, she pushed the chair over, kicking at the legs. Her first attempt saw her falling over backwards, and even when she balanced herself better, the chair remained stubbornly resistant to her kicks.

"Bugger!" she rasped. "Buggering bloody bugger!"

She sank to her knees, her head in her hands, her chest heaving with the effort.

As she calmed, she realised she was crying again in her frustration.

"Don't waste water," she told herself angrily, and pulled her fingers under her eyes to catch what she could of her tears, licking the moisture from them.

She looked up and her eyes fell on Ugo's body lying face down a short distance from her. When she had turned him over the night before, she'd shuddered at the thought of him being skeletal. She had wondered if an arm would come away in her hands. Her eyes narrowed as she relived the thought. There was only a little tissue remaining on his skull; was the rest of his body the same? How easy would it be to dismember him? After all, he had no more use for his limbs and a bone would make the perfect tool for digging at the plaster.

Fifteen minutes later, she had removed the rest of Ugo's clothing and tossed it across to where she slept. The trousers she could wear, they would add another layer of insulation and padding when she next attempted sleep; the shirt, waistcoat and underclothes could be balled as a pillow, if nothing else. And as an added bonus, his socks were thick wool while his boots were far more substantial than her cross-trainers.

Rocking back on her heels, she examined the body. Trying to avoid eye to eye socket contact — she was feeling more than a little guilty about stripping him, let alone that she was intending to pull his body apart — she focussed her attention on the torso and legs. She wanted one of the leg bones, something long enough to get some leverage against the plaster. But there was still quite a covering of skin that needed to be removed.

After her efforts in removing Ugo's clothing, the body was now lying on its back. She took hold of the left foot and, gripping it tightly, she stood, balancing herself against the wall with one hand until the dizziness threatening to topple her subsided. She took a deep breath and lifted the foot, the tension against the knee joint keeping the leg straight as the thigh bone moved reluctantly in the hip joint. As the leg came closer to being vertical, she pushed harder against the joint, but as she did, the torso began to roll.

She relaxed the pull on the leg and thought the problem through. She had to keep the torso flat while she levered the leg, tearing whatever remained of the ligaments and tendons attaching the thigh bone to the hip. To achieve this, she needed something heavy to prevent the body from moving, and the heaviest object she had was the table. But by now she was too weak to move it.

Over the following ten minutes, during which she took several breaks, Evie pushed and pulled, pulled and pushed, slowly dragging the body until it was positioned under the table with one table leg pressing hard against the inside of Ugo's upper right thigh while another pinned the torso, preventing it from moving. Grasping the foot of the left leg once again, she pulled the leg outwards, away from the body, an unnatural movement for a leg. There was an initial resistance, as she expected, but by pulling and pushing on the leg, the freedom of movement increased as the top of the thigh bone was forced out of the hip joint. The leg freed with a loud crack, and Evie fell over as the tension was released.

Winded and breathing heavily, she crawled back to inspect her handiwork and was pleased to see that much of the parchment-like skin and tissue beneath it had torn. Having no sharp instrument to cut the leg free, she dug her hands into the remains of the skin and tissue, and tore it apart.

She sat down in one of the chairs to rest, the leg lying across her lap.

"Gross or what?" she croaked. "But," she added with a shrug, "needs must and all that."

Still sitting in the chair, Evie set about tearing what she could of the remaining tissue from the thigh bone. While there was more than she had expected, soon much of the bone was exposed almost down as far as the knee joint. Since she didn't want a large round and smooth joint at both ends, she decided she needed to break the thigh bone just above the knee joint. She thought about laying it across the gap from the table to one of the chairs and hitting the bone at the knee joint with one of Ugo's boots, but in the end, she decided it was probably easier to snap the bone with her foot while angling the bone against the floor, breaking it like a piece of firewood.

The desiccated bone was brittle and, much to Evie's delight, it broke on the first attempt.

Before using her new tool on the wall, she rewarded herself with another short break. Breathing steadily and willing herself to ignore the ever-present hunger and thirst, she looked over at the mutilated body.

"Sorry, Ugo," she whispered, "but my need is greater than yours. And you've got to admit, it's the most exciting thing to happen around here in more than a hundred years."

She paused before adding, "Tell you what, if I ever do get out of here, I'll make sure you get a decent burial."

After an hour of scraping with the sharp end of Ugo's broken leg, Evie had definitely achieved a lot more than she had with the man's watch, but it was far from being enough. There were still many hours of work ahead before she would be able to remove a brick.

The effort, combined with her ever-growing weakness, was making her tired, and increasingly she drifted off to sleep. At times she would jolt awake as the bone slipped from her hands to the floor, or a vivid dream would bring her back to consciousness. It was while her mind was wandering, half-asleep, half-awake, but definitely not alert, that in the deep recesses of her consciousness she thought she heard her name being called.

"I'm here, in here!" she yelled in her dream, but in reality no sound left her parched lips.

"In here!" she yelled again in her head, before slipping back into a deeper sleep.

Chapter Fourteen

Jane Bawley sat drumming her fingers on her desk. Why hadn't Joe Oliver called to update her? He'd promised and it was now early evening in Italy; he should have been back from Perugia hours ago.

Finally, she couldn't stand the waiting any longer. She dialled the number for Villa Brocanti.

"Pronto. Villa Brocanti. In che—"

"Can I speak to Monica Lieti, the direttrice, please?" interrupted Jane.

"Un attimo," came the reply. "One moment."

The finger-drumming on Jane's desk continued while she waited a considerable number of moments. She was beginning to wonder if she had been put on permanent hold when a voice cut into the background static.

"Monica Lieti."

"Ah, Signora Lieti, sorry to bother you. My name is Jane Bawley, from WanderFever. Perhaps Anna Riccardi has mentioned my name. She's an old friend."

"Of course, Signora Bawley. Anna has talked of you."

"Let me get straight to the point," said Jane. "I'm calling about Joe Oliver … and Evie Lorrigan. I take it there has been no news of her."

"Nothing so far, no," said Monica. "Signor Oliver told me he was going to Perugia today at your request to see your agent. Has he made any progress?"

"That's the problem; I don't know. He was supposed to call me immediately he got any more information, good or bad, but there's been nothing. And from what you just said, he clearly hasn't called you either."

"You are right, he has not. I wasn't worried since I assumed you had instructed him to go somewhere else to make his photographs."

"I certainly haven't," snapped Jane, her tone bordering on aggressive. "And further to that, a couple of hours ago, I finally managed to get hold of my agent in Perugia, who informed me that his secretary called a cab for Evie Lorrigan when she arrived there two days ago, and the driver took her to Villa Brocanti."

"That is very puzzling," replied Monica. "You know, I think, that all the staff were briefly absent for a funeral two days ago. Is it possible that when she found no one here she called another taxi and went somewhere else?"

"That's unlikely for two reasons. Firstly Joe told me there's no mobile signal at the villa, so she would have had to use a landline. The other reason is that if she had done that, if I know Evie, she would have been on the phone to me pretty damn quickly moaning about everything under the sun."

Jane paused, wondering how to phrase what she wanted to say, whether she should even go there. But she had to. It was partly out of a feeling of guilt towards the woman she was now talking to that she had readily agreed to the review in WanderFever when Anna had called her.

"Listen," she began. "Anna has told me something of the history of Villa Brocanti, and I know what you tell the guests about the old villa burning down isn't true. Ernesto Brocanti insisted, according to Anna, that this is the story that's told in order to keep anyone from getting too interested in the old villa."

There was another pause while Monica considered her answer.

"It was Anna who told you this?" she said, eventually.

"Yes, we had rather too many glasses of wine one evening when I was there a couple of years ago, and they loosened her tongue. She made me promise not to tell anyone, particularly Ernesto. Said he'd throw a wobbly if he knew."

"Wobbly?"

"Be very angry."

"I see. Yes, he would have been very angry. Like his parents and grandparents before him, he is convinced the old villa is cursed in some way. There were some strange events that occurred there many years ago that have never been explained. The family is genuinely concerned that anyone going too near to the old villa might be affected by the curse."

"And you believe this?"

"It is not for me to say, Signora Bawley, but I must honour the family's wishes."

Jane wasn't satisfied; she was on a mission, or at least she had sent Joe on one, and as far as she was concerned, the reasons were honourable. It was more than time to lay her ghosts to rest.

"You don't think it possible Evie went for a walk around the estate and maybe found the villa, do you?" she asked, trying to make her question sound innocent.

"It is possible, yes, but the area is fenced off and the villa secured, so I believe. So even if your Evie found it, she would not have been able to get inside."

"So you believe?" echoed Jane.

"Yes," replied Monica. "I have only once seen the villa. Anna showed me when I began working here, just so I would know where it is, but I didn't go near, neither of us wanted to. It was certainly very secure at that time and the reports from the estate worker who checks it from time to time say it is still like that."

"OK, but it's still possible she did go there, or perhaps went farther, into the forest. Could she be lost there?"

She heard Monica Lieti take a sharp breath.

"I … I … it is … possible, yes. It wouldn't be the first time."

"No, I'm sure," replied Jane, backing off.

"As I think you must know, Signora Bawley, someone went missing in the forest only two years ago."

"Yes." Jane's voice was suddenly soft. "It happened … while I was there. He was never found?"

"That's right, my brother was never found."

"Your brother?" said Jane, trying to sound as if she didn't know, but the tone of her question sounded unconvincing to her.

"I'm very sorry," she continued.

"Paolo was a wonderful man," said Monica, as if she weren't listening. "After the accident, he was never the same. I mean, he was still kind and very trusting, and although he was strongly built, he wouldn't have hurt anyone, ever."

"Accident?" asked Jane, although she already knew the details; Anna had told her. She had been horrified when she found out.

"He fell into some farm equipment, his brain was damaged and he was horribly scarred. Afterwards, he found people very difficult. He couldn't think fast enough, you see, and everyone thought he was stupid. But he could still communicate if he was given the time. He sometimes wrote poetry. Beautiful, sad poetry. And letters. If he really wanted something from me, or wanted me to do something, he would write it down. It would take him ages, but it worked."

"Signora Lieti, I'm so sorry, that's really terrible, I can't begin to imagine what …" She paused. She didn't want to risk going any farther down this track; it was dangerous territory. She had to move the conversation on.

"Look," she continued, "I hope you can understand that I'm very worried about both Evie and Joe. They seem to have disappeared, one after the other. Joe didn't talk about going into the forest, did he?"

"Signora Bawley, I must apologise, I let my emotions get the better of me. I too am concerned about your colleagues. To answer your question, no, Signor Oliver mentioned nothing about going into the forest. However, I am sure there is a perfectly reasonable explanation. He is, after all, a professional photographer. Maybe he decided to make a detour on the way back, to one of the many hill towns in the Valtiberina, perhaps."

"Then why doesn't he answer his phone?" Jane was back to growling angrily. "I know the signal is bad where you are, but the whole of Italy isn't like that, surely?"

"No, of course not. In most places, the signal is excellent.

Signora, I am afraid I must go. I will call you as soon as I hear anything."

She rang off. There was something about Jane Bawley's tone she didn't fully trust, although she couldn't put a finger on it. Nevertheless, she had to admit, two disappearances in a matter of three days were hard to understand.

A knock on the door interrupted her thoughts. The receptionist, a new girl, put her head around the door.

"I am sorry, Direttrice Lieti," she said, "but it is already six o'clock …"

Monica glanced at her watch. "Oh, Chiara, I lost track of the time. Off you go, I can manage things from here."

The girl looked sheepish. "What is it, Chiara?"

"The maid, Rosanna," she began. "She—"

"Reported sick, I think," interrupted Monica.

"Yes. She asked me to apologise for her. She didn't have time to tidy the Englishman's room. Signor Oliver."

Monica sighed. "Ok, Chiara, thanks for telling me. I'll do it myself."

As she watched the door close, Monica realised she had been handed an opportunity. Joe Oliver had not returned and she now had a perfectly valid reason to enter his room.

Stopping only at the linen store to pick up a change of towels, she quickly made her way to Joe's room and quietly let herself in.

One look at how the room had been left confirmed her thoughts: Joe Oliver had fully intended to return. The room was untidy and his laptop was sitting on the desk.

Concerned now that Joe might return and find her in the room, Monica opened the windows. The room looked out onto the gravelled driveway connecting the main entrance to the villa. If a vehicle were to arrive, she would hear it.

She glanced around the room, wondering where to start, but her eyes kept returning to the laptop. Without moving it, she carefully lifted the lid and the screen sprang to life with a desktop photo of Joe with a pretty twenty-something girl wrapped around him looking content. Monica grunted in disapproval, her automatic reaction being that the girl wasn't good enough for Joe.

Surprised she hadn't been asked for a password, Monica swiped the touchpad and another screen appeared with what looked like a photo-editing program open. One glance at the top left of the screen confirmed her thoughts: Lightroom, and he hadn't closed it.

But what immediately caught her attention was a black-and-white photograph in the centre of the screen. It showed a large trompe l'oeil painting covering an interior wall in a house or villa. She gasped. It was similar to a print Anna Riccardi had once shown her when she was explaining in confidence about Salvatore Brocanti and his work. However, it was not the same photograph. Where had Joe got this one?

Unfamiliar with Lightroom, Monica looked around the screen and saw a strip of images along the bottom, some in black and white and some in colour. One of them was highlighted, which she could see was the one enlarged in the centre of the screen.

Running her fingers over the touchpad, she moved the cursor to the strip of images and clicked on the next one along. The image in the centre of the screen now changed to another wall painting showing the same remarkable trompe l'oeil effect as the first one. And again, it was an image she had never seen before. Quickly, she clicked from one black-and-white image to the next, marvelling at each one. Running her finger along the strip at the bottom of the screen, she counted thirty black-and-white images, the thirty-first being an image in colour. Clicking on it, she was amazed to see a colour shot of a complex trompe l'oeil painting, one that appeared to be several paintings, one on top of the other.

She looked quickly through the other colour shots. They all seemed to be shots from one room, but none of them were colour versions of the black-and-white images she had just looked at. However, it was immediately clear to Monica that Joe had been in the abandoned villa, and to have made the positive set of images, he must have found some more glass plates. Since he hadn't had time to take them back to the old villa, unless he had taken them with him to Perugia, they must be in his room.

Monica looked around and saw the wardrobe door was slightly ajar. She pulled the door open and there on the floor of the wardrobe was an ancient-looking length of cloth that was clearly wrapping something. She lifted the bundle out of the wardrobe, placed it carefully on the bed and removed the top layer of cloth to reveal a glass photographic plate. Holding this up, she thought the image looked like one of the pictures she had seen on the screen.

A few minutes later, she had counted thirty plates, the same number as were now portrayed as pictures on Joe's computer.

As she stood back, trying to work out what Joe's movements might have been, she heard a vehicle on the driveway. She rushed to the window, and was relieved to see it was a French-registered 4x4 belonging to two of the other guests. She needed to get down to reception in case they wanted anything, but Joe's room had to be returned to how she found it. The bed could be made later. She quickly wrapped up the glass plates and placed them back inside the wardrobe, after which she ran over to the laptop, clicked on the photo that had been on the Lightroom screen, swiped the screens back to the desktop image of Joe and his girlfriend, and closed the lid.

Half an hour later, having dealt with the returning French couple, Monica was at the reception desk deep in thought. Nagging at her was the thought that Joe might have gone back to the abandoned villa to find the originals of the images on the glass plates. But if that were the case, why hadn't he returned?

If he was still absent the following morning, she would have to go to the abandoned villa herself and look for any signs of him. She shuddered at the thought. For her and for others who had lived near it, the building seemed to radiate evil. But at least she wouldn't have to walk all the way there through the woods. There was an old unpaved road around the estate she could use to drive to a spot she knew to be closer to the old villa than Villa Brocanti.

It wasn't the ideal solution, but there was no way she could go to the abandoned villa at night. As she sat at the desk, her thoughts drifted to what she knew of Salvatore Brocanti and his family, the wife and three children who had disappeared without trace. What had happened all those years ago to provoke Salvatore's wife into abandoning her husband and her position as a local noblewoman, a marchesa, and running away with her children? For that was what Salvatore had told people had happened. And what, if anything, had her disappearance got to do with Salvatore closing up the villa and declaring it was possessed, full of evil, a place to be avoided at all costs?

She regretted not trying to get more information from Anna Riccardi, if indeed she had any more to tell. Perhaps Anna's husband, Ernesto Brocanti, would be a better source, but his reputation, well deserved in Monica's view, was that he was cast in the same mould as many of the Brocanti men over the years: quick-tempered, secretive, and unsociable. He had always left no doubt that the secrets of the old, abandoned villa would remain secrets. They were not a matter for discussion.

Part Two

1894-95

Chapter Fifteen

A malevolent scowl distorted Salvatore Brocanti's face as he glared through the undergrowth at his wife and her lover. To think he had once loved this woman, the mother of his three children. Would they be infected with her treachery and grow up to be as duplicitous and unfaithful as their mother? The girls almost definitely, he thought, they were so like her. But his son Tommaso, would he too? Surely not. Salvatore could see more of himself each year as the boy grew. Although still only eight years old, he was going to be big like his father, and his introspective moods were likely a precursor to a darker side of his personality in the future. The boy was a true Brocanti.

Salvatore's eyes narrowed as the furrows in his brow deepened. Were the girls even his? How long had his wife been secretly meeting the puny, bespectacled pharmacist? They certainly bore no resemblance to himself that he could see. The elder one, Delfina, was even short-sighted like the pharmacist, whereas Salvatore had the sight of a hawk, and his wife, too, had no need of spectacles.

While these thoughts flashed through an analytical part of his brain, a more combative part was urging him to burst from his hiding place and confront the couple. As the compulsion for action grew, his lips curled into a fearsome snarl and he lowered his head like an enraged bull ready to charge. But something held him back, stopping him in his tracks, his entire frame quivering in a supreme effort of self-control. He choked back a yelp of pain as his finger-nails sliced into the skin of his palms, his fists balled so tightly that his knuckles cracked in protest. And slowly, droplet by persuasive droplet, the swirling mists of anger in his mind coalesced into a single word of action.

Revenge!

Confrontation was not enough; they needed to experience his pain and pay for it. Physically, mentally, and above all, slowly.

Although only a mere twenty metres from Salvatore, the couple remained supremely oblivious of his presence. Thinking themselves secure in a dense thicket of trees and bushes deep in the forest, their world was no larger than themselves, their eyes locked as they faced each other, their fingers intertwined.

The man leaned his head forward to place a tender kiss on the woman's lips. "This is so wonderful, Isabella, and so unexpected. I can't believe we're together again so soon."

Although the man had spoken in little more than a whisper, Salvatore heard his words as clearly as if they were being bellowed from the treetops.

Isabella smiled softly. "Nor I. Salvatore's departure for Rome was a complete surprise, coming so quickly after his return from Naples. I expected at least a month of more crazed behaviour, more mean-spiritedness. But now, magically, I have you in his stead."

She released the man's hands and reached up to fold her fingers behind his head, pulling him towards her. "My dear, wonderful Ugo. Without you, I should go mad. I fear my husband's cruelty towards me is a trial contrived by the devil himself."

Ugo pulled back and pushed on the bridge of his small round spectacles, concern in his eyes. "This is not the first time you have mentioned cruelty. If he were ever to strike you, I should kill him, no matter what the consequences." He put his hands on her shoulders. "You must not protect him. I cannot bear the thought of him even touching you, let alone hurting you."

She smiled at his concern and brushed his cheek with the back of a hand.

"Rest assured, my love, he has never struck me; he is too cunning for physical cruelty." She paused to gather her thoughts. "But I must say, it is a paradox. For a man of so tempestuous a spirit, a man so engulfed in an almost constant rage, you would imagine that violence would be the natural outcome. Strangely, however, I do not think it in his character to be violent physically. I have certainly never seen it."

"A small mercy," nodded Ugo, "but a mercy nevertheless."

Salvatore remained motionless as he watched his wife and her lover, but his mind was still a storm of wild, conflicting plans of action, fragments of notions and half-formed ideas tossing and twisting, all vying for attention.

He clenched his jaw as he thought how flawed Isabella's assessment of him was, how very wrong. If he were to confront them now, he had no doubt he would lose control and kill them both with his bare hands. He was more than capable: his bear-like frame and huge, muscular arms could crush them both with almost no effort.

He had to tear himself away, retreat to the darkness of his private rooms in the villa where no one was aware of his presence. And he had to do it now, immediately, before this treacherous pair's passionate words developed into something more physical. If he were to witness them lying together on the forest floor defiling the very Brocanti estate on which he stood, he would snap their necks.

Chapter Sixteen

THREE DAYS EARLIER

Salvatore Brocanti's apparent departure to Rome so soon after his return from Naples had been a total ruse. He had not even left the estate.

Apprised of her suspicions by the housekeeper, Egidia Galli, Salvatore was immediately blind to anything else. He had to learn the truth.

"The marchesa is not the mouse you think her to be, Marchese," Egidia had wheezed from her sick bed when, after having been told of his housekeeper's illness, Salvatore rushed to see her within minutes of his return. He was shocked: in thirty years of service, he had never known her to be ill.

"She thinks she can take advantage of my being sick, but I'm not the only pair of eyes around here, in spite of your unwillingness to employ enough staff."

Salvatore grunted, ignoring the habitual criticism. As far as he was concerned, the fewer people employed around the villa and getting in the way, the better. Palatial villas like his always employed far too many staff. In his ideal world, a housekeeper, a maid or two living in and rooms in the stables for a groom and coachman were all that was needed. The head groundsman and his two main assistants lived in a cottage nearly three kilometres away in another part of the estate. They were essential for the upkeep of the formal gardens, but other staff needed from time to time could be employed on a casual basis. And now he had partitioned off a huge portion of the villa as his studios for reflection and experimentation, rooms where absolutely no one was allowed to go, not even the trusted Egidia, the requirement for staff had decreased further.

The five-bedroomed apartment, together with a couple of smaller rooms for the live-in staff, that Salvatore had created at one end of the once-grand villa was still spacious, and in his view, more than sufficient for his family's needs. They never entertained, he had forbidden it, and there were no callers. There must be nothing and no one to interrupt his work, and no one to corrupt the minds of his wife and children.

Salvatore maintained that his wife was more than capable of assisting Egidia in cleaning the apartment and of carrying out other domestic chores such as the preparation of food, no matter how much she thought it beneath her. In spite of her own noble heritage, he saw no reason why Isabella should pass her days in idleness like some parasitic pet while others toiled around her.

His own aristocratic ancestry meant even less to him. He had hated his father and grandfather, his memory of both being of severe and unbending men, distant, conceited and haughty, with an inflated sense of their own importance.

For her part, Isabella had so far managed to resist him and, in addition to the housekeeper and the two live-in maids, a cook still arrived daily from Coniglio, but now the living area was so much smaller, their days were numbered.

Head of the Brocanti family he may be, the Marchese Brocanti, no less, but in Salvatore's world everything, without exception, was subordinate to his art. All these aristocrats who considered themselves superior to their fellow men, as if they were an enlightened and more intelligent variety of homo sapiens, meant nothing to him. Almost to a man, he found them superficial and half-witted, often inbred and supremely lazy.

However, his scorn for the aristocracy was one thing, business was another. While the family estates brought in a considerable income, for Salvatore, augmenting that income with profit from the fruits of his own outstanding skills was more than useful; it was his lifeblood. He lived for his painting. And in spite of inheriting the Brocanti hermit gene and fiery temper, Salvatore was by no means averse to leveraging his own aristocratic history.

As an artist to the aristocracy, he was welcomed as one of their own, and regularly gained commissions from many of the noble and supremely wealthy families up and down the country, mostly to paint family portraits but also to create huge landscapes of their rolling estates. And there was always work: children grew, with all stages of their growth requiring an artistic record, after which they became adults, married and had children of their own. Of course, he was more than simply a good artist; he had to be. Being one of them would mean nothing if he were merely some amateur dauber. In reality, he was brilliant, gifted at capturing a likeness and presenting it in the most complimentary way, no matter how plain or even downright ugly the subject.

His clients thought him more than a little eccentric, the thought of soiling their hands with work anathema to them. But at least he understood them, was one of them.

"How did your suspicions arise, Egidia?" Salvatore asked the housekeeper.

"It was her refusal to obey your orders, Marchese," gasped the old woman as she lay in her bed propped against her pillows. "It's always a sign in an individual that something's afoot. Once I became ill, I reminded her that you had forbidden her to go to the village alone. And you were right, Marchese, it was for her own safety. A six-kilometre walk in the country was perilous enough for the two of us, but for a young woman on her own, it is the height of foolishness. A provocation, no less."

"Quite, Egidia, quite." His voice sounded calm but Egidia knew him too well to be fooled. She could detect the signs; she knew the dam holding back the floodwaters of irrational anger could be breached at any moment.

"You mean to tell me that in spite of your reminding her not to leave the estate, she persisted in going on her own? What was the purpose? Did she enlighten you?"

"She seemed intent on constantly visiting the pharmacist, Ugo Gasperini, Marchese. He is a young man, newly qualified."

"The son of Severino Gasperini, the physician?"

"The very same, Marchese."

"Did you ask her why she needed to see him, why she couldn't have sent Rocco?"

"Well, apart from the fact that Rocco is perhaps the stupidest man ever to take on the duties of a groom, which is one of the very few points on which the marchesa and I agree, she insisted that the medicine she required was for a problem of a delicate nature, one she certainly didn't want the groom or anyone else knowing about."

"And before you were sick, when you accompanied the mistress, did she also visit the pharmacist?" Salvatore was now marching up and down the room, running first one hand and then the other through his thick mane of tight salt and pepper curls, unable to keep still as he snapped out the questions.

"She did, Marchese, but only a few times in my presence. After the third visit, I think it was, she always contrived some chore for me to attend to, something I couldn't easily refuse. I'd make haste, always, but I only ever saw her leaving the pharmacy. I never again managed to get there while she was still inside."

"And how often were these visits? How many times did she see Gasperini?"

"She first visited the pharmacy several days after you left, Marchese. After that, I should say she made visits twice a week when I was with her. Then after I became ill and could no longer accompany her, she continued to go to the village in the same routine."

"Twice a week! On her own! By all the gods …"

Egidia crossed herself at what she considered blasphemy.

"There is something else, Marchese."

She paused, wanting to be sure she had his attention.

"Well!" he snapped.

"She has taken to walking in the forest. Alone. It's when I'm feeling well enough to look after the children, so clearly I cannot accompany her. And her walks tend to coincide with when the groom is busy and the maids up to their armpits in washing. There is no one else I can trust to follow her."

When there was no immediate response, the housekeeper lay back against her pillow. "Forgive me, Marchese, I feel so weak. I have never known such a malady. It is as if my body has been drained of energy."

Salvatore's eyes focussed on his housekeeper for the first time in their exchange, his voice calmer. He let out a deep sigh.

"It is I who should apologise, Egidia. I shall let you rest. Thank you for the information. I hope my suspicions are wrong about my wife. I shall take pains to find out the truth. But Egidia, she mustn't know that you've told me anything, do you understand?"

"Of course, Marchese," she replied, taken aback at the unusual civility in her master's tone.

Prior to his return from Naples, it had been three months since Salvatore had seen his wife and their three children. And yet, there was little joy in their reunion when he went to them in the play-room immediately after his interview with Egidia.

The only one who seemed pleased to see him was the youngest, Clara, who, at just three years old, was too young to have been affected by her father's moods and eruptions of temper, too young to have been sent to her room.

"Papa!" she cried, when he burst through the door. He had decided to be as fatherly as he could manage; Isabella should suspect nothing.

"Tesoro!" he beamed, holding out his huge arms to gather the child and whisk her off her feet while at the same time looking across the room at his wife.

"Salvatore," said Isabella, looking up from the novel she was reading. "You have returned."

In spite of her neutral tone, as far as Salvatore was concerned, his wife's eyes had already betrayed her. As an artist, he was a keen observer of expressions, and he could see immediately how ill at ease she was with him standing in front of her. That in itself was nothing new, given his temper, but this was different. There was an underlying coldness he had not witnessed before, a defiance in the way she held her shoulders.

He bowed his head. "Isabella. You are well? And Tommaso and Delfina, you are as fine as this young lady?"

Their elder daughter, Delfina, adjusted her spectacles and looked up from where she was drawing. Her mental image of her father was of a man with little time for her or any of them. She resented her younger sister's display of affection. In the wisdom of her own six years she considered it absurdly babyish.

The boy, Tommaso, now eight, was reluctant even to look up. He had been rebuked too many times by his father, reprimanded vehemently in words he didn't understand for misdemeanours he had no memory of committing. And yet, like all boys, he secretly craved his father's approbation, some sign of recognition that he had a jot of worthiness.

"We are all well, Salvatore," replied Isabella as she stood and gathered her things together. "Come, children, it is time for your supper." She reached out her arms towards her youngest child. "Clara, desist! Your father must be exhausted after his long journey in the carriage."

She took Clara from her husband and walked towards the door, the other two children following at her skirts while looking back at their father. She turned. "You must forgive me, Salvatore, I had no notion of your imminent return and hence I have nothing prepared for you. I shall instruct the cook to make something for you, but I regret you will have to wait an hour or so."

Salvatore stared at the door Isabella had closed behind her, the ire rising once again in his chest. He had been outmanoeuvred and dismissed in his own home by the wife he had now convinced himself was not only a cold-hearted schemer, but also a philandering whore.

Resisting the temptation to march after her and demand an explanation for her visits to the village, behaviour that flew directly in the face of his most specific and unequivocal instructions, he strode instead in the direction of the stairs leading up to the bedrooms. Here, immediately beyond the foot of the stairs, was a heavy door that led into the private part of the villa, the huge number of rooms and corridors that were used by him and him alone. After retrieving the door key from his pocket and opening the door, he marched through, slammed the door and relocked it. From here, he made his way to the large studio on the ground floor, the studio where he experimented with paint mixtures and blends, techniques and styles.

As he threw open the shutters, light flooded the room revealing a bizarre collection of paintings on all the walls. Fragments of vivid landscapes, one painted on top of the other, were interspersed with detailed, half-finished architectural features: steps leading nowhere, half-open doors and ornate balustrades. And seeming to hang at random as if hovering in the sky, were portraits in apparently gilded frames with shadows that defeated the eye and registered as real objects in the brain of any observer.

Ignoring everything in the room, he picked up the nearest chair by its backrest, raised it above his head and proceeded to smash it to pieces against the floor. When all that was left were the remains of the backrest in his hands, he flung the remnants at the nearest wall and threw himself onto a large sofa positioned near some French doors.

Here, over the period of the next two hours, he reflected on everything the housekeeper had told him and what he must do to establish the awful truth. For this was the crux of the matter: if, by some chance, the old housekeeper was mistaken in her assumptions and Isabella's visits to the pharmacy in Coniglio were a necessity borne from a genuine sickness that for some reason his wife wished to keep from him, specific action against the young pharmacist would not only be unnecessary, it would be an injustice.

He suddenly stood up. He had made his decision; he was ready. His scheme was a simple one, but would leave him in no doubt. It helped that he had long since divided the villa into the family apartment and his private space; the maze of rooms were the perfect hiding place.

· · ·

The following morning, he had the carriage harnessed and drove himself into Coniglio where he bought provisions enough to last him a month: preserved and dried goods requiring no cooking, together with cheese and wine. Water he would draw from one of the many wells on the estate during the hours of darkness and keep in lidded pitchers. He stored everything in a first-floor room at the far end of the villa, as far from the apartment as possible, but still he kept the shutters closed. He didn't want some sharp-eyed gardener noticing activity and reporting it to the head grounds-man. As it was he would be spending little time in there during daylight hours; his goal was to watch his wife without her knowing.

Chapter Seventeen

Once his secret preparations in the closed part of the villa were complete — a mere two days after his return from Naples — Salvatore arrived at breakfast waving a letter, one he had, in fact, written himself.

"I have news of a new commission, Isabella, one I have been expecting for some time and one I am obliged to commence as soon as possible. I shall be leaving for Rome immediately."

"You are leaving again so soon, Salvatore?"

His wife still didn't deign to raise her eyes to his, but her tone was enough. To Salvatore's ears, the surprise in Isabella's voice was edged with delight.

He scowled, immediately angered by her indifference to him and her apparent flippancy.

"How long will you be away this time?" she continued.

"How can I possibly say? A month? Two? It all depends on how the sittings go and whether my sponsors develop a desire for additional pieces." He tossed his head in haughty self-importance. "It often happens."

He paused, waiting for her to look in his direction instead of occupying herself by helping the children with their food. When she finally lifted her eyes to him, he continued, his voice slowly rising. "I must, it seems, remind you of my instructions regarding leaving the estate, instructions that are for your benefit and safety as well as the children's, instructions that I expect, no, I insist, are adhered to without fail."

"Salvatore," interrupted Isabella, not attempting to hide her exasperation. "We are so isolated here, the children see no one, speak to no one apart from the staff. They are restless, Tommaso particularly. He needs other boys in his life, and he needs a tutor. There is only so much I can achieve with his education."

She is cunning, thought Salvatore, oh so cunning. Not a word about herself, she uses the children as weapons, as bargaining tools.

"You will obey me, Isabella!" he bellowed, banging his fist on the table. A cup jumped in the air and fell to the floor, smashing. Clara burst into tears.

"This is intolerable!" continued Salvatore, still yelling. "You cannot even keep the children under control. You certainly do not need the further distraction of visits to the village. It will not happen! Do I make myself clear?"

Isabella dropped her eyes, attending to Clara.

"*Do* I?" Salvatore's eyes were on fire.

"Yes, Salvatore," whispered Isabella.

"Good. With Egidia confined to bed with her sickness, all your attention is required here at the house. I have instructed the groom that under no circumstances, none whatsoever, is he to take you anywhere in the carriage nor to allow you access to a horse. If you are spied attempting to leave the estate, he is to bring you back, by force if necessary."

"Salvatore! I—" protested Isabella, but her husband ignored her interruption and continued to shout his commands.

"And finally, let me also remind you that the closed part of the villa will remain entirely out of bounds to you, to the children and to all the staff. No one is to go near it or to attempt to enter it."

With that, he spun on his heels and marched out of the room, slamming the door behind him.

Ten minutes later, Isabella heard the sound of horses pulling the departing carriage, its wheels crunching the gravel on the drive. She stood and walked to the window to watch the carriage disappear, her anger at the intransigence of her husband entirely forgotten as she smiled to herself, thrilled to know she would be seeing her lover again far sooner than she had expected.

Salvatore sat in the carriage, impatiently drumming his fingers on the seat next to him. Some eight kilometres from the borders of the estate, at a high point in the road where he could not only see back across his own substantial forests, but also ahead to where the road could be seen winding south along the Tiber valley for many kilometres, he called to Ignazio, the coachman, to stop.

As the carriage pulled to a halt, he jumped out of the door.

"Is there something wrong, Marchese?" cried the bewildered coachman. "Must we return? Has something been forgotten?"

"There is nothing wrong, Ignazio, nothing at all. This is as far as I intend to go, that is all."

"Marchese?"

"It should be quite simple to understand, Ignazio, even for you. I am getting out here. You will continue to Rome with the carriage and luggage where I shall catch up with you in a few days. I have private matters to attend to that do not require the carriage."

"Surely I should wait, Marchese, until you are ready. You should not be alone here in the countryside; it is not safe."

"It is perfectly safe," snapped Salvatore, his voice rising as his intolerance to the driver's insolence in questioning him started to get the better of him. "Now, go! Do as I say and wait for me in Rome. If I have other instructions for you, I shall send word. Is that quite clear?"

"Of course, Marchese," replied the puzzled coachman, not daring to pursue the matter further. He had been on the short end of his master's tongue too often.

Salvatore watched the carriage drive off and waited deep in the cover of the trees until, about an hour later, it appeared on the road far in the distance, making its way slowly southwards. He wanted to be sure the coachman was following his instructions.

Satisfied, he turned and headed into the forest. It would take longer to return to the villa this way, but in these woods that he knew so well, he was confident he would meet no one.

Almost three hours later, still in the cover of the forest, he was back near the villa, patiently waiting and watching until the light faded and darkness fell. He had not expected to see any development that day, but he wanted to be certain that the groundsmen working in the gardens near the house didn't see him. No one could be aware of his presence.

Late in the afternoon, but earlier than they should, the groundsmen packed up their tools and headed for their cottage on the far side of the estate. Word of my departure must have spread quickly, thought Salvatore, making a mental note to deal with the staff at some later date.

He was about to make his way towards the single-storey storerooms at the rear of the villa that formed a natural barrier between the kitchen garden and the formal gardens, when he heard a door slam at the apartment end of the villa followed by footsteps hurrying along the gravel in the direction of the main gate to the estate.

Staying among the trees, Salvatore walked quietly in the same direction until he could see clearly who was leaving at this time of the evening. He fully expected it to be his wife, so brazen had she now become in his imagination. He was, therefore, almost disappointed when he saw the figure was one of the two maids who lived at the villa, the one called Imperia, whom he had noticed was the one more attentive to his wife.

So now he knew how Isabella sent word to the pharmacist: her faithful little maid. As soon as he had confirmed his suspicions of his wife with his own eyes, the girl would be dismissed and he would ensure she never again worked for anyone in the area.

Knowing that nothing more would be likely to happen that evening, Salvatore quietly made his way to the storerooms from where he let himself into the echoey, empty rooms of the main villa and settled himself comfortably for the night, wondering if perhaps events would play out faster than he had imagined.

Chapter Eighteen

Twenty-four hours later, Salvatore was again in the room in the villa he had prepared for his vigil, sitting on a chaise longue under a closed window, the room lit by several candles. He was staring in the direction of a small, round table on which remained the remnants of a meal of cheese and bread he had taken earlier, but his eyes saw nothing.

In his heart, he had known the outcome of his elaborate preparations to spy on his wife would result in what he had witnessed earlier that afternoon in the forest: the passionate meeting of the two lovers. What shocked him was that it had all happened so quickly, that they had wasted no time in taking advantage of what they thought was his absence.

But beyond the anger, the hair-tearing, fist-pounding fury over his wife's infidelity that consumed him, he could also feel a burgeoning sense of relief that what he saw as a life tortured by the coldness of his calculating wife would soon change for the better.

The day had gone by in a flash, with one event following quickly upon another. He had been up before dawn to position himself in the trees near the villa and watch for activity. About an hour after sunrise, the time it would take to walk at a brisk pace from the village of Coniglio, the maid he had seen leaving the previous evening appeared on the path and made her way into the apartment. Salvatore felt sure she must be carrying a message. Would the traitorous pharmacist be so brazen as to come to the villa itself? Surely not. Did, in fact, everyone know about him, including the children? Had he already supplanted Salvatore in their affections? No, there had been no indication of that. The youngest of them, at least, was guileless enough to have blurted something out. Isabella could not risk that.

Two hours later, a young man on a horse had arrived, greeted almost before the horse had been pulled to a halt by Isabella herself running from the apartment door. The young man retrieved an envelope from a small satchel slung over his head and handed it to Isabella.

"Wait!" Salvatore heard her command. "I may have a reply."

She tore open the letter, which seemed to consist of a single sheet of paper. Salvatore could see her eyes devouring its contents, her face lighting up in delight as she did.

She clutched the letter to her chest and looked up at the young man. "Yes!" she cried, "Just tell him, 'Yes'. He will understand."

The young man nodded. "I shall do as you say, Marchesa," he said, turning his horse, and with a kick of his heels into its flanks, he galloped away.

Almost skipping with joy, exuding a happiness Salvatore could not remember ever witnessing in her, even when he had proposed marriage more than ten years before, Isabella rushed back into the apartment.

Not half an hour later, the groom had brought the light chaise to the apartment, one of the quieter, less skittish mares in harness. Salvatore frowned, thinking his plans would be thwarted. Was Isabella going to the village to visit her lover? It was a possible scenario he had stupidly overlooked. But no, to his surprise and indignation, Isabella appeared at the apartment door with the children and Imperia, fussing as she made them all comfortable within the confines of the chaise. It was small and Clara had to sit on the maid's knee, but she seemed excited by the prospect of the outing. "Signorina Gasperini will meet you, my darlings, near to Coniglio, and you will have a lovely afternoon tea in the woods by a stream."

"Can't you come too, Mamma?" cried Delfina.

"Next time, amore, next time. Mamma has some urgent business this afternoon. Now, off you go and have a wonderful time. Signorina Gasperini is the sweetest person, and I know she will have prepared all sorts of treats for you."

She waved enthusiastically until the chaise was out of sight, after which she hurried back into the apartment.

Salvatore felt as if he were watching scenes from a play, something entirely detached from his own life. His wife and his children were exhibiting such happiness. Was it always like this when he went away?

Some time later, in the early afternoon, he had followed a clearly light-hearted Isabella as she left the apartment and skipped into the trees. After well over a kilometre of walking, during which time he was careful not to be heard or get too close, it became obvious to Salvatore that the pharmacist would be arriving by a circuitous path to avoid being seen by the groundsmen, the same precaution Salvatore himself had taken the previous day.

Chapter Nineteen

Salvatore sat on the chaise longue still staring blankly, his mind's eye replaying everything over and over again: the lovers meeting in the woods, the joy they had expressed over each other's company, the caresses, the whispered affection. What more had happened once he had torn himself away from the scene of betrayal he could only imagine, and for once in his life he hated his gift for imagination, the gift so important to him as an artist that was now mocking him in his darkest hour.

It was the mocking in his mind, the cackling laughter of a swirling mass of hysterical jesters gesticulating at him in the dancing candlelight that saw him focus his thoughts and move towards a resolution of his dilemma. He had been played for a fool. Marchese Salvatore Brocanti, aristocrat and brilliant artist, his work not just admired but revered by so many, was a cuckold, and his wife, a woman who professed so strong a faith in the Church and in God, was a lying whore employed by the devil to torture him. Now his worst fears had been confirmed, Salvatore sat and let the anger and scorn for his wife build along with his contempt for her lover. They would pay, and pay dearly.

Alternating between pacing the room, his huge shadow darting across the walls, and being slumped on the chaise longue, head in hands as he gnawed at his knuckles, he had passed the night considering a thousand alternative ways to exact his revenge.

It was some of his experimental panels on the walls in front of him, lit inadequately by the guttering candle flames, that had finally crystallised his ideas into a workable plan. What better way than to use his expertise as an artist to lure his victims into a web of his own construction? It would take much time, since he would have to make all the preparations himself; no one else could be involved at any stage. He would need to become builder and plasterer, labourer and artisan, but the outcome would be magnificent. And it would all be carried out under his wife's nose until the preparations were complete and he was ready to spring his traps.

Hours later, the room in darkness since the last of the candles had collapsed into a pool of wax, Salvatore finally drifted into a troubled sleep. It was just before dawn, although in the pitch blackness, he had no awareness of the time.

He awoke soon after noon and waited impatiently for the day to pass, not wanting to risk leaving the closed part of the villa through the storage rooms for fear of being seen. He was supposed to be in Rome, and it was to Rome he would now head to pass a week sketching out paintings along with designs for restructuring rooms, walls and corridors.

Leaving the villa at dusk, Salvatore walked into the forest as far as a small, abandoned hut some three kilometres distant where he spent the night. At first light, he took the road west, away from the estate, a road that meandered over the hills towards Arezzo. Even at a brisk pace, the walk took him the whole day and he cursed his impetuosity in sending the carriage to Rome rather than having the coachman wait at one of the villages. However, as he sat on the train from Arezzo to Rome, he knew his actions had guaranteed that no one was aware of his movements, that there had been no gossip from the coachman to any villagers about the strange ways of the marchese.

One week in Rome quickly drifted into two and then three as he set about putting his plans on paper, the rooms in the lodgings he had taken strewn with sketchpads, notebooks and later huge rolls of drawings as his ideas took on flesh. He worked every day from dawn until seven in the evening, when he would march to a nearby tavern for dinner. Later, he would pass two hours making use of the extensive services of an adjacent brothel, known for its dealings with the aristocracy. He had used the place on many occasions, but this time the women found him harsher and more violent as he worked off the rage still consuming him whenever he thought of his wife.

Finally, at the beginning of his fourth week in Rome, Salvatore was ready. He summoned his coachman who loaded the carriage with the mountain of material Salvatore had generated during his stay, leaving barely enough room for his master to sit inside. However, the weather had turned wet and Salvatore certainly wasn't inclined to sit on top next to the coachman.

Hearing a carriage arrive at the Brocanti villa, Isabella ran to the window, her worst fears realised when she saw it was her husband returning. She called her maid as she grabbed a pen and paper to scribble a note.

"Imperia, take this immediately to Dottor Gasperini in the pharmacy at Coniglio," she said to her maid as she sealed the envelope. "It is of the utmost importance. And Imperia, do not let the master see you leave."

"The master, Marchesa?" asked the maid, confused.

"He has just returned. That was his carriage on the drive. Quickly, girl. You must hurry."

The maid scuttled away while Isabella went to the children's playroom to settle herself with them, thinking her husband would burst into their presence within moments. When he didn't, she peered out of the window and was surprised to see him carrying armfuls of papers and leather satchels towards a door that led into the closed part of the villa, waving away the bewildered coachman's attempt to help as he went. It took five trips for Salvatore to empty the carriage, after which he disappeared into the forbidden area for almost two hours.

. . .

By the time her husband finally appeared in the playroom, bursting in as she had expected earlier, Isabella was in a state of extreme agitation, consumed with worry that Imperia had somehow missed Ugo, who had been due to come to the villa that very afternoon.

"Salvatore!" she exclaimed, her voice far shriller than she intended. Her husband immediately noticed the tone, reading all kinds of guilt into it. He scowled around the room, as if expecting to see the pharmacist lurking somewhere in a corner or behind the curtains. The children eyed him suspiciously, making no attempt to greet him. It was as if a stranger had walked into the room.

He took a deep breath, attempting to relax.

"I have returned," he announced. "The commission was a failure, the family charlatans with no money to pay me. I have wasted more than three weeks."

"And will you be … staying?" Isabella's question was hesitant as she hoped against hope that Salvatore would be off again soon, knowing how restless he would become if he had no work, and how it would only deepen his moods.

To her surprise, he smiled and held out his arms, as if expecting to embrace them all. "You will doubtless be delighted to hear, my dear wife, that indeed I *am* staying. I have had enough of roaming the country in the service of people I despise. I have decided to remain here for the foreseeable future to work on a project in the villa."

He paused, noting with pleasure the shock on Isabella's face. He ignored it and held up his hand as if stalling an enquiry about his project. "I cannot tell you what it is, Isabella, and neither must you or the children make any attempt to visit me in the villa when I am working, which will be constantly."

"But Salvatore, your other clients. What will they do?"

"They can wait. My project is more important." He shrugged, attempting nonchalance. "If they really want me, they can pay more for my services, but no matter what they offer, my project will come first. And speaking of which, I have work to do." He gave a stiff little bow, turned and strode out of the room, surprising Isabella once more by not slamming the door.

. . .

"What's a project, Mamma?" asked Clara, looking up from the doll she was playing with.

The question broke into Isabella's thoughts as she stared after her husband.

"It's a … it's work your papa does, amore. When he is away from home producing his wonderful paintings."

"But he said his project is here," countered Delfina, frowning. "In the part of the villa that's forbidden."

"It can be there too, Delfina. His projects can be anywhere. I do not know precisely what the nature of his new project is, and I doubt we shall know until he either shows us or tells us about it. However, you must remember, he does not like questions about his work, so you should not ask him. He is a very clever man and clever men do not like to be distracted. By that I mean we should not bother him with the ordinary things in life."

"What ordinary things?" asked Clara.

"Well, Clara, things like your visits to have tea with Signorina Gasperini. Or when her brother, Dottor Gasperini, visits to help Mamma with her medicine. These are ordinary things your papa really does not need to be bothered with."

She smiled at her children, hoping her message would register. She was all too aware that the risks she had taken during Salvatore's absences were likely to come back and haunt her, especially if innocent little tongues wagged.

"Let's keep it our secret, shall we? And by doing that, we'll be helping Papa with his work."

From the sideways glance the eight-year-old Tommaso gave her, she knew that he, at least, was not convinced by her story. But given Tommaso's caution in dealing with his father, she doubted he would be a risk.

At that moment, the door to the playroom opened and Imperia hurried in. "Marchesa," she said, breathlessly. "Might I speak with you?"

"Of course, Imperia. Let us go into the corridor." She stood and followed Imperia through the door.

As soon as she shut it, she grasped Imperia's arm, her eyes darting around to check they were alone.

"Were you successful?" she whispered. "Did you meet … our friend?"

Imperia smiled. "I did, Marchesa. He had not left the … he had not left."

Isabella sighed, her whole frame relaxing. "Oh, Imperia, that is such a relief, I can't tell you."

Looking around to make her own check there was no one watching them, the maid put a hand into the pocket of her jacket and pulled out a small envelope. She handed it to Isabella.

"He asked me to give you this, Marchesa."

Taking the note, Isabella tore it open and scanned the few lines.

'My darling, your maid has helped us to avoid a catastrophe. I shall await further news. If you consider writing too risky, a verbal message delivered by Imperia would perhaps be safer. My love, always, U.'

Relieved to have weathered at least this potential storm, Isabella was nevertheless distraught. She had become used to meeting with Ugo while Salvatore was in Naples, and their meetings had continued over the three weeks he had been in Rome. Salvatore's declaration that he would be remaining at the villa for an indefinite period was as crushing as it was unexpected, leaving her distracted with despair, wondering how and when she might see Ugo again.

Chapter Twenty

To Isabella's surprise and eventual relief, the pattern of life at the villa quickly established a routine that gave her almost as much freedom as when Salvatore was away on a commission, with negligible risk of her husband randomly deciding to take a walk in the forest and happening across her and Ugo by chance.

Two days after Salvatore's surprise return from Rome, the first of a succession of horse-drawn wagons arrived at the villa bearing sacks of mortar, bricks, sand and large lengths of wood together with the tools for processing them. Isabella wondered if Salvatore was intending to build another house in the garden, or somewhere else on the estate. But the materials all disappeared inside the closed area of the villa, access being granted by Salvatore to the workmen to one room only for them to deposit their loads, the large room next to the storeroom outhouse. And as soon as any worker or pair of workers had dropped their loads, Salvatore would shoo them out before they got a chance to get their bearings in the poor light the candles gave the room.

A few days later, when the deliveries stopped, Salvatore announced to Isabella that since he wanted to be as close to his project as he could, he intended to spend his entire time in the closed part of the villa. He instructed that food should be left for him three times a day on a table he placed outside the door connecting the apartment to the prohibited area. If he needed anything else, he would ring a bell left on the same table. The door would remain locked except when Salvatore wished to pass through it.

To Isabella's further delight, Salvatore even chose to sleep in the closed area. She had been dreading him returning to their bed. His lovemaking had never been gentle and over the last couple of years, it had been increasingly brutal, leaving her bruised and sore for days. The only relief had been that his demands had been far less frequent than in the early days of their marriage. In contrast to the infinite tenderness of her lovemaking in the forest with Ugo, she considered her husband's approach to be nothing more than violation.

What Isabella did not understand was that Salvatore was disgusted by her. The very thought of sharing a bed ever again with a wife soiled by the attentions of another man, especially one as puny as the pharmacist, was anathema to him. He would rather visit any number of whores in Arezzo or Sansepolcro when the need arose.

After only three weeks of feeling her way around the new arrangements, Isabella had dared to send a message to Ugo suggesting they might meet in the forest. They chose a place farther from the villa than before where the trees and undergrowth were particularly dense and where anyone approaching would surely be heard.

The first time they met there, they fell into each other's arms, embracing with a passion that surprised and excited them both. Isabella had never felt so liberated in her life, and any pangs of conscience from her religious beliefs telling her she was sinning were quickly put to one side. She insisted to herself that life was not intended to be a penance, something to be endured in the face of daily adversity; life was for living and she had no doubt she wanted to live the rest of hers with Ugo.

After making love on a bed of leaves on the forest floor, or sometimes on a rug if the ground was a little damp, they would discuss the future.

"What will happen when this project of Salvatore's is finished, my love?" Ugo would ask as he gently stroked her hair. Being a practical, scientific man, he needed his boundaries defined, and while he remained in constant awe of the good fortune that had brought this amazing woman to him, he was also desperately aware that it might all end. "Do you even have any idea what he is doing?"

"Absolutely none. On the few occasions he has gone away for a day, sometimes two, I have crept around the villa looking for a way in, or even for some indication from the outside of what he is up to. But I have learned nothing. Every single access to the villa is completely sealed; there is no way in I can find."

"Do you think he is renovating the villa for family use? Is he mad enough to imagine you will be so overcome with pleasure at using the whole place once again that you will return to being a happy, loving family?"

"Since we have never been a happy, loving family, I hardly think so. He shows no positive feelings towards me whatsoever, only barely disguised disdain. In fact at times he is so dismissive I feel he must know about us."

"But if he did, surely he would act, even if it were to disown you, ruin your reputation."

"Surely," she agreed.

"What about the children?"

"He hardly sees them. I think he has no idea how to treat them. His relationship with his own father was nonexistent and I think he has nothing to draw on for guidance. Certainly he appears to have no natural paternal instincts. Even when the children were babies, apart from the initial wonderment, he had no idea what to do with them or even how to hold them. I thought he would learn, but he never did."

"How terribly sad."

"I wish we could have children of our own, Ugo. I know you would be the most wonderful father. I have seen the way you talk to my children, how they respond to you. Do you think it would ever be possible that we could be a family?"

"Only if Salvatore were to die. And given that he's as strong as an ox and apparently very healthy, barring an accident, I fear that is most unlikely."

When Isabella didn't reply, Ugo moved his head so he could see her face.

Her eyes looked up at his. "Accident …?" she said, raising her eyebrows.

Ugo pursed his lips.

"Surely, Isabella, you are not suggesting …?"

"It worked with Egidia, did it not?"

Chapter Twenty-One

The housekeeper's illness had been carefully calculated. To be successful, poisoning needs to be. The idea had occurred to Isabella soon after her visits to Ugo in his pharmacy became a twice-weekly routine in the early days of Salvatore's long absence in Naples.

Egidia was under strict instructions to accompany Isabella whenever she left the confines of the estate. And to discourage her from even wanting to leave, Salvatore had banned the use of the chaise or the carriage, so Isabella was forced to walk the six kilometres to Coniglio. The arrangement wasn't favoured by either woman, but to make matters worse, during the early visits, Egidia was constantly by Isabella's side, especially in the pharmacy, her attempts at eavesdropping unsubtle. Isabella's solution to avoid this irritation was to send Egidia on tasks around the village that would take at least an hour, but as time went on, keeping the nosey woman occupied became an increasing frustration.

"Ugo, you are a pharmacist, an expert in the compounding and dispensing of medicines. Is there something you could prepare that I could introduce into the tonic Egidia takes every day for her nerves?"

"Isabella!" cried Ugo. "What you're suggesting is completely unethical. Are you thinking of poisoning the woman?"

Isabella feigned innocence as she shook her head. "If by

poisoning you mean the substance would kill her, then most certainly not. I could not be a murderess no matter how much I dislike and distrust the woman. What I had in mind was something that would give her the symptoms of an illness, make her feel sufficiently discomforted not to want to accompany me on the long walk to the village."

Ugo pursed his lips in thought for some moments before he nodded and gave a resigned shrug.

"Well, there are certain plants I know of growing wild in the forest, the berries of which, if crushed for their juice and added carefully to an already noxious tasting tonic that would mask their taste, could bring on excessive drowsiness and fever. Certainly enough to convince a person such as your housekeeper to take to her bed."

Isabella clapped her hands and reached up to kiss him. "Just show me the plants and I'll do the rest, my love. You need play no further part in it. Your reputation and career will remain spotless."

Ugo shook his head. "I think I should give you a demonstration, just to ensure you don't overdo it."

The plan went well and within two weeks, Egidia was forced to report to Isabella one morning that their trip to Coniglio would have to be cancelled owing to her feeling indisposed. Showing all due concern, Isabella complied, but when the hapless housekeeper showed recurring symptoms of illness and an increasing tendency to stay in her room, Isabella informed her she would have no choice but to go to the village alone, such was her need for constant advice from the pharmacist.

Egidia was still exhibiting the same symptoms when Salvatore returned from Naples. Her recovery soon after was attributed to whatever disease had possessed her running its course and being finally defeated by the power of prayer and the earnestness of her confessions.

.   .   .

The suggestion of using a poison on Salvatore was an altogether different proposition and one which immediately filled Ugo with alarm. It would not be sufficient to incapacitate Salvatore, that would serve no purpose. If they were going to poison him, it would be with a view to killing him, and Ugo could not contemplate being party to murder. He could not possibly go ahead with such a plan, but he needed to dissuade Isabella.

"Since your husband doesn't take tonics, the substance would have to be added to his food or perhaps his wine," he suggested as they continued their discussion.

Isabella frowned as she considered this. "As far as I know, his wine comes from a vineyard near Coniglio. It has been that way since the estate stopped producing grapes. But the demijohns are stored in the closed part of the villa; I should not be able to gain access to them."

"Then it would have to be in the food." Ugo paused, allowing Isabella time to mull over the possibilities.

"I could easily add it to the food on his tray after it's left by the door to the closed part of the villa," said Isabella.

"You could," agreed Ugo, "but it would have to be administered in small doses, otherwise he might taste it. And if, as Egidia did, he thinks he is unwell, have you thought what might happen?"

"What do you mean?"

"I mean that your husband is nothing if not bad-tempered, a man who thrives on irritability. If he is incapacitated through apparent illness, would he not become frustrated and even more noxious? Would he perhaps even take to his bed in the apartment and demand your services to nurse him back to health? Would he—"

Isabella held up a hand to stop him. "Enough, Ugo. You have convinced me. Administration of some sort of … poison would be foolhardy and perhaps even dangerous. If he were to discover what had happened to him, he might even suspect you, as the local pharmacist, to be the source. We daren't risk that."

She shook her head. "No, sadly, my dearest, we must trust to providence that some accident befalls him."

She giggled. "How wicked I am to even have such thoughts. Do you think me wicked, Ugo?"

"Irredeemably," he said, shaking his head sadly.

She laughed and tapped him lightly on the arm. "And you, I suppose, are a pillar of virtue."

Nodding, he added, "And of the community, Marchesa."

She took his hand, serious again. "If only I had a fortune of my own. I should leave him, regardless of the scandal. Leave him and move to another part of the country. Now Italy is unified, such a prospect is easier than it used to be. But sadly my brother inherited our parents' estate and wealth, as is the law, and although he has no heirs since he is not married, as far as I know he enjoys excellent health."

"He was not disposed to share the inheritance with you?"

"My brother! Heavens no. He is a good many years older than I. We have never been close and he is a firm believer in the rights of the male of the species. I have received nothing, apart from a meagre selection of my mother's jewellery."

"Then it would appear we must indeed wait and hope that providence smiles favourably on us," said Ugo.

Chapter Twenty-Two

As the months passed, although Salvatore's work in the closed part of the villa progressed apace, his family seldom gave him a second thought. Often not seeing him for days on end, they were reminded of him only when carriages laden with yet more building materials arrived and the contents were carried into the villa. Apart from that, since Isabella no longer worried that her husband might appear unexpectedly in the forest on the occasions when she went to meet Ugo, it was only when the cook asked her about his food that he featured in her mind at all. And even then only briefly. Her often-repeated reply, or variations of it, were the talk of the kitchen.

"Feed him whatever you like, Maria. Feed him horse manure in a pie if you wish."

The situation for Salvatore was altogether different. Even though he gave his full attention to his project, Isabella and her continued liaison with Ugo Gasperini were ever present in his mind. And while the storm of his rage rumbled on through the days, weeks and months, he was at least consoled by the thought that every day brought him closer to exacting his retribution.

As for his children, while he was working, he fantasised about becoming closer to them, particularly Tommaso. He knew that his own short temper had always got the better of him when dealing with the children, that he was dogmatic in his demands and unbending in his requirement for obedience. But his self-delusion was such that he blamed all his shortcomings on his wife's constant provocation and interference. In Salvatore's eyes, it seemed that every time he tried to interact with the children, she would step in and whisk them away on some pretext, deliberately stoking the rage she knew would get the better of him.

However, the time was approaching when all this would change. Isabella would disappear out of their lives forever. When this happened, rather than telling the children their mother had died, he wanted to foster a dislike for her in their minds, a sense of betrayal. He would tell them that their mother's affection had been a lie, that she had abandoned them, run away, deserting them and everything else in her former life. They would be shocked and distressed, but Salvatore was convinced he could fill the void of their mother's absence with his own presence and attention, become a kind and understanding father his children would love and respect, a father completely different from his own.

Once his project in the villa had served its primary purpose of trapping and entombing Isabella and her lover, Salvatore had decided that he would open it up to his children, the only exception being certain rooms on the top floor that would be sealed forever. With its enchanting paintings and maze of rooms and corridors, the villa would become their magical palace, a source of endless fascination and excitement, a tribute to his ingenuity and skill for which they would cherish and love him.

In the meantime, whenever Salvatore heard the children playing outside near the house, he would stop what he was doing and watch them from an upstairs window. The girls, like their mother, seemed to enjoy books, although Clara was at the stage where she was still only looking at pictures. Tommaso, by contrast, was restless, just as Salvatore had been at that age, always on the move, engaging in mock battles with imaginary foes, chasing butterflies, birds, anything that moved, hardly ever stopping. And whenever he did skid to a halt, as if a switch had been thrown, he would invariably turn and stare at the closed part of the villa, his eyes scrutinising the windows and shutters. At these moments, Salvatore would dart back from his vantage point into whichever room he was standing, embarrassed that the boy might have caught sight of him.

One afternoon, while he was watching the children from an upstairs window, Salvatore saw Isabella come into the formal part of the garden and sit on a bench seat. Her back was to the villa and her head leaned forward as she opened a book to read. The scene had an almost ethereal quality as a gentle breeze teased the leaves of the surrounding trees, filtering dancing shafts of light that caught Isabella's hair in ever-changing intensity and colour.

Salvatore quickly grabbed a sketchpad and within minutes he had reproduced the essentials of the scene on paper. Later that night, after many hours of furious work, he completed a large canvas of almost photographic quality, its detail so precise he felt he was viewing a real scene rather than a painting. He smiled to himself; the painting was perfect. By showing Isabella with her back to the villa, symbolising her rejection of him and, by association, their children, it would be a constant reminder to the children of their mother's cold-hearted duplicity. He knew exactly where he would hang the painting, delighted that something unplanned could fit in with everything he was creating elsewhere in the villa.

He also knew that in order to become closer to the children, he would have to change in their eyes. He needed to rebut his wife's provocation, to confound and frustrate her efforts to undermine his relationship with them. It wouldn't be easy, he understood this, but he couldn't wait until Isabella had mysteriously disappeared. He had to start soon, and as he started to plan his tactics, he realised to his delight that any improvement in his dealings with the children would inevitably frustrate and anger his wife, something he would enjoy witnessing. However, it would be difficult in the present environment of the closed villa and the apartment, patterns of behaviour were too well established. But once he had finished the work on the villa's interior, he knew there would be another way. In the meantime, he would have to be patient.

Chapter Twenty-Three

1895

Fifteen months to the day after Salvatore began his secretive work of remodelling and repainting the interior of the closed part of the villa, he stood back from the final painting, the last of dozens that were fundamental to his scheme. His eyes roamed the walls and ceiling of the room, checking the detail.

In the two lower floors of the villa, his work had been made easier by the fact that false ceilings had been added to each room more than a hundred years previously to hide the beams, joists and terracotta tiles that would normally be visible in such a villa. These false ceilings were themselves made of terracotta tiles arranged in a herringbone pattern, the whole ceiling slightly domed and keyed to prevent collapse, and then plastered. All Salvatore had to do when creating his maze of deception was to repaint these ceilings in the same way he repainted the walls, using the trompe l'oeil style of which he was a true master.

While creating his masterpieces throughout the villa, Salvatore had necessarily used as much light as he could to illuminate the walls, throwing open shutters and windows and placing oil lamps everywhere. He was aware that in the glare of daylight or a strong light source, the deception inherent in the paintings wouldn't stand close scrutiny. But that wasn't the point. None of the paintings was intended to be viewed in anything but the light from a single lamp or candle; all the shutters and windows would ultimately be closed to any outside light. The intention was to grab the attention, confuse the senses and lead his intended victims onwards and upwards, teasing them, frightening them, confusing them.

He had done all he could while his family remained close by. It was time to move on to the next phase of his project: specific alterations to a number of windows to be made from outside the villa, for which he needed to be certain no one might accidentally witness what he was doing. It was also time for him to move forward with his plans to improve his relationship with his children while at the same time finally frustrating his wife's efforts to undermine him.

After two days of clearing the rooms of all construction materials and other paraphernalia, Salvatore appeared unexpectedly in the playroom where Isabella was entertaining Clara while Delfina and Tommaso worked at their desks on exercises their mother had set them.

Isabella looked up, startled by the door swinging open and her husband marching in.

"Salvatore," she said, trying to keep the surprise and alarm from her voice. She was intending to meet Ugo later in the forest and even now her lover might be on his way.

She stared at him in surprise. She had hardly set eyes on him for several weeks, and during that time, he had lost weight, the months of hard, manual labour tightening his physique.

"You look … well," she said. "And you are dressed for a journey. Are you leaving?"

Salvatore strode over to the window and threw it open, a blast of cool October air gusting into the room. Isabella pulled her shawl around her. "Salvatore, please, I do not wish the children to catch a chill."

As she was speaking, the sound of the large carriage drifted up from the drive as the coachman brought it round from the stables.

"May I enquire where it is you are going?" she added.

Salvatore turned to look at her, his eyes cold and penetrating. "No, but you may enquire where *we* are going."

"We?"

"Yes, we. All of us. I have decided we should spend some time at our other family estate by Garda. It has been too long and we have neglected it."

"But—"

"But nothing, Isabella. You always used to say how much you preferred the Garda estate, how much you wanted to live there. Well, I have been thinking about it and it is time you had your wish. The children too will benefit from the fresh mountain air."

"We are leaving?" whispered Isabella, the horror evident in her voice. "When?"

"Immediately. I have given instructions to the maids to pack everything we need for the next few days. We shall depart in the carriage for Arezzo within the hour where we shall take the train north to Verona. The carriage will return here to collect our trunks and catch up with us at the Garda estate in a few days time. I have already sent word to the staff there; everything is arranged. This house will be closed up and Egidia, along with the other staff, will follow shortly."

"Salvatore, this is so sudden. What about your project in the villa?"

"It is complete. I have done all I wished to do." He waved a hand dismissively at her. "Come, ready the children. I do not wish to miss the train. Children, gather your books together, you may continue your lessons on the journey. It will be most exciting. You have not seen the mountains. They have a wondrous beauty, especially in the winter. Quickly now."

The three children turned their heads towards their mother in complete bewilderment.

"Mamma!" cried Delfina.

"Do as your father says," said Isabella, rather more sternly than she intended. She felt distracted and confused, the hopelessness of her situation threatening to overwhelm her. Her prime concern was to somehow get word to Ugo, but it seemed clear from the way her husband was standing by the door, a victorious sneer on his face as he watched her every movement, that he had no intention of letting her out of his sight.

Isabella took the girls' hands and signalled to Tommaso to follow. "We must fetch your travelling clothes," she said, heading for the door. Salvatore stood to one side to let them pass. "They are already laid out on their beds," he said.

Turning to follow them, he called after Isabella. "Their bags for the journey are ready, they simply need to put on their coats."

As the group walked along the corridor to the children's bedrooms, Imperia, the only maid Isabella could trust, appeared from the girls' room. Isabella caught her eye and silently mouthed 'Ugo' to her as she walked past. The maid's eyes dropped as she blushed in confusion.

"Ah, yes," boomed Salvatore as he brought up the rear of the group. "Imperia. I forgot to mention it to you, Isabella. Imperia is accompanying us to help you with the children. Hurry now, all of you. The carriage is waiting."

Isabella felt her knees weaken as the reality of the situation hit her. She had been completely outmanoeuvred. For Salvatore to have taken this action in this way, right down to the detail of controlling Imperia's movements, could mean only one thing: he knew about her relationship with Ugo. And if he knew, what was he planning?

Chapter Twenty-Four

Salvatore ignored Isabella during the journey, speaking to her only to issue some instruction or other. In the seclusion of their first-class compartment, he attempted to engage the children in conversation, pointing out interesting features in the countryside as the train trundled north. Not used to any conversation with him, the children responded in monosyllables, shifting uncomfortably in their seats until their eyes drooped and they drifted off to sleep.

For Salvatore, the effort required to control his temper was apparent in the set of his jaw. Isabella knew the signs and was awaiting an eruption. Imperia too, although she was completely preoccupied in coping with the alien situation in which she found herself. Travelling on a train for the first time in her life to a place so far away from her village of Coniglio it might as well have been on the moon, her response was to sit rigidly to attention, not daring to move, her eyes dropped towards her lap and focussed on nothing, her hands tightly clasped.

But the eruption never happened. Salvatore was determined to start laying the groundwork for what he perceived would be his new relationship with his children. Nothing and no one would defeat his newly found self-control. His solution, every time the spectre of fury beckoned, goading him with crushing thoughts of his wife in the arms of the pharmacist, was to turn his thoughts to his work in the villa, to walk his way in his mind's eye through the corridors, passage-ways and rooms, remembering every false doorway, every hidden catch, savouring and checking every painting, every trick he had incorporated into the myriad brushstrokes it had taken to complete his masterpiece. For that was what it was: his villa was a complete entity to be appreciated as a whole. His villa was a masterpiece.

To add to Isabella's frustration and worry about not being able to contact Ugo was the irritation that the children responded posi-tively to their new-found freedom in the enormous house above Lake Garda, surrounded as it was by hundreds of hectares of woodland and farmland sweeping down to a wide, private frontage onto the lake. No longer confined to a few rooms at one end of an otherwise forbidden villa as they had been in Tuscany, they were now free to roam the entire house and the estate, the latter with either a groundsman in tow to ensure they came to no harm, or their father himself. And to add to their pleasure, there was the new motorcar Salvatore had imported from Germany. Tommaso loved the magical vehicle and when they were not driving around the countryside, he would spend hours sitting in it undertaking imagi-nary adventures of his own.

The arrival of the staff from the villa brought Isabella no closer to contacting Ugo. She had hoped the constraints on Imperia's time would ease with the extra maids, the Garda house staff consisting only of an ageing housekeeper, a cook of dubious merit and a supremely lazy maid. However, Egidia didn't arrive with the staff. She had refused point blank to budge from the villa, claiming that at her age, her constitution wouldn't allow it, that she'd prefer to be alone in the villa than move north. But Salvatore wanted nobody in the villa so he rented rooms for her in Coniglio, telling her he'd contact her when he needed her.

Isabella had a letter ready for sending to Ugo, explaining every-thing but with no immediate solution to suggest. However, she found herself virtually imprisoned at the house, and with Imperia having no time to go to the nearest village, the letter remained unposted, hidden in her purse.

Although Salvatore was keen to complete the external part of the project at the villa, he was equally keen to consolidate his improving relationship with his children, which he knew would add to his wife's already visible distress. And given that all the predictions for the winter were that it would be unusually cold, he had no desire to freeze in the villa over the winter months — the previous one had been hardship enough. He therefore delayed his departure until the spring.

His plan worked. During the winter months, his relationship with his children gradually improved owing mainly to his great efforts at self-control. At the same time, his relationship with Isabella deteriorated further, their exchanges becoming little more than the occasional single-word instruction barked by Salvatore.

With no word from Ugo and no way of contacting him, Isabella spent the winter months half-crazy with worry. She dreamed of being set free from the nightmare of her existence, wondering constantly if her dilemma was a punishment by God for her infidelity.

For Salvatore, seeing Isabella's spirits weaken daily was a small and delicious taster of the sweet revenge he would eventually take, and he quietly revelled in it. But as winter turned to spring, the impatience to get moving again began to surface. To his delight, he had enjoyed being with his children, but to complete what he intended to be their transition from their mother's affections to his, he had to get back to the villa in Tuscany, although, as with his previous deceptions, Isabella must not know he was going there.

No sooner had the alpine wildflowers sensed the coming of spring and burst into life in the fields around the house, than Salvatore produced a letter one morning at breakfast, a meal he insisted on the entire family attending every day, even though Isabella's participation was never more than desultory.

"Children," he announced, deliberately excluding his wife, "I have some news you may not like, but which I am obliged to act on. With luck, it won't take too long."

"What is it, Papa?" the girls cried together.

He waved the letter, which like earlier fictions in the same vein, he had written himself. "I have had a request from one of the most important families in Rome, a family whose ancestry goes back many centuries, in fact, some say as far as the days of the Roman Empire. Several years ago, I produced a series of portraits of the present conte and his delightful family" — this part of Salvatore's story was true, at least — "and now the children are growing, they want me to return to paint more portraits."

"How long will you be gone, Papa?" wailed Clara.

"Not long, I hope, no more than a couple of months. I'll be back before you know it."

"A couple of months is forever, Papa," continued the melodramatic Clara, as she burst into tears.

Salvatore pulled her onto his lap, loving the way the child now naturally turned to him rather than her mother. He watched for a reaction in Isabella's face, but her features appeared to be set in stone.

"Mamma will be here to look after your every need, and of course Fabio and his team will take you out around the estate every day on the horses. They love you all nearly as much as I do and they will make sure you are happy all the time."

Before his departure, Salvatore reminded Isabella of his rules: neither she nor the children were allowed to leave the estate, with the exception of Saturday afternoons when Fabio and one of the maids — never Imperia, whom Salvatore didn't trust — would take the children on a trip to the nearest town for cakes and juice, and rides on the carousel that had been set up in the town square for the spring and summer. He warned Fabio that under no circumstances, barring extreme illness, was the marchesa permitted to leave, and she most certainly couldn't go with them on Saturdays. Isabella had become withdrawn and petulant with the staff, and Salvatore had capitalised on this by hinting at a certain mental instability. "You wouldn't want to be responsible for her in the town if she were to lose control, Fabio, would you?"

"Certainly not, Marchese," Fabio readily agreed, and on his own superstitious initiative, spread the word to the rest of the staff of the marchesa's condition, instructing them that if she were found wandering on the estate, she was to be gently but firmly brought back to the house.

Chapter Twenty-Five

Not trusting his motorcar for such a long journey, Salvatore took the train back to Arezzo where he rented a chaise and two horses for two months. Arriving back at the deserted villa, he opened the apartment and stored the provisions he had bought in the pantry next to the kitchen. Eager to revisit his masterpiece, he unlocked the door that led into the closed part of the villa and, carrying a large oil lantern, he made his way through each of the many rooms, soaking up the paintings and the sheer ingenuity of his creation as he went. He was particularly pleased to find the many secret doors with their hidden latch-pulls operated as smoothly as the day he had set them up, each of them closing silently and efficiently as they were designed to do. As he moved from one room to the next, or opened up another hidden stairway, he was careful to prop each door open. He had no desire to be trapped by his own labyrinth.

Satisfied his masterpiece was as brilliant as he remembered, Salvatore went outside to review the state of the gardens and to plan his approach to the completion of the work to the outside of the villa.

Spring growth had not yet taken full hold of the gardens, and after the cold winter, they still looked relatively tidy. He knew that over the next couple of months they would become unkempt and weed-ridden, but their condition would be nothing the gardeners could not put right in due course. In the meantime, he had laid off the entire squad on full pay for a year, the sole condition being that they were not to set foot on the estate during that time. With such a windfall, the men were happy to comply, as was Egidia, who on hearing of his return and contacting him to ask when she should report for duty, was told her services were not yet required.

Free to work uninterrupted and with no fear of being spied on, Salvatore set about his work on the outside of the villa with great vigour. The weather helped — it was a dry spring and he lost little time to storms. His principal task was to set up the false shutters that would appear to be closed from the outside and yet open on the inside owing to the light reflected through a glass and mirror system at the top of each shutter. It took much experimentation and frustration, since he wanted it to continue to function for many years, but finally he hit upon an arrangement that worked perfectly. However, that it eventually survived for well over a century would have amazed even Salvatore.

The pièce de résistance was the creation of the false view in each of the false windows: the painting of Isabella sitting on the bench in the garden. On the day he put the first of these in place, he felt a pride in his work that exceeded even the pride he had felt on completing the villa interior the previous autumn.

Once the last shutter was in place, the final illusion set on the outside of the villa and the locks in place to prevent any random thief easily breaking in, Salvatore had one final task to complete, a task requiring just one day: he weeded and tidied the herb garden.

The work was completed late one Wednesday afternoon and although Salvatore was now at last ready to start exacting the revenge he had dreamed of for so long, he knew he would have to wait until the following Saturday morning before setting his plan in motion.

Thursday and Friday passed slowly, but Salvatore was elated to find that contrary to how he would have reacted in the past with much ill-temper and rage at the delay, his new-found peace with the world saw him uncharacteristically calm, his mood one of eager but controlled anticipation.

Relaxed after a good night's sleep, his whiskers trimmed and hair pomaded, Salvatore set off in the rented chaise at eleven on the Saturday morning for Coniglio. There was a market on the outskirts of the village that attracted most of the inhabitants and the road was busy with horse-drawn carts, pedestrians and even one ambitious young man in a bright red and yellow checked suit who had bought himself a bicycle. Sadly for him, his pride suffered badly when his front wheel found a pothole and the machine stopped abruptly, tossing him over the handlebars into the dust at the feet of the young lady he was hoping to impress. However, battered pride was a small price to pay for her concerned attentions.

The weather was fine and hot with a prediction of a good but not-too-dry summer. The olive trees were in flower and the young grapes on the vines were starting to grow; the villagers could sense a profitable year.

The pharmacy on the one main street through the village was open, as it was every Saturday morning. The ageing portion of the population liked the reassurance of knowing medicinal help was available to them more or less as needed, and the young pharmacist, Ugo Gasperini, was willing to oblige with a great degree of flexibility in his hours, having been brought up well by his equally public-spirited physician father. The father, indeed, was a pillar of the community, and while his son was respected, there were rumours that he had a roving eye, and scandal in a small Tuscan village was ill-tolerated. However, there was nothing proven, and in recent months, although he had seemed quiet — some would even have said withdrawn — he had shown a diligence in his work that had been somewhat lacking the year before.

Pushing open the pharmacy door, Salvatore ducked through the low opening as the bell rang. As he looked around the shop, he was immediately impressed with how clean and tidy everything was.

There were none of the dust-encrusted bottles and mysteriously shaped items of glassware adorning many pharmacies. This pharmacist was clearly happy with his abilities and had no need of the arcane to reinforce his bona fides.

Ugo Gasperini was bent over an elderly woman giving her instructions for how and when to take a medicine he had just handed her.

"Immediately after each meal, signora, not before. The medicine is of far less value if you take it on an empty stomach. Two teaspoonfuls each time, and do remember to shake the bottle."

The old lady looked up at the pharmacist. "Thank you, Dottore. May the Blessed Virgin smile upon you; I shall include you in my prayers," she croaked as he helped her up.

"You are too kind, signora," said Ugo as he turned towards the door to help her on her way.

As he did, he looked up at the customer who had just walked in and the colour drained from his face. Salvatore Brocanti!

Salvatore stood to one side to allow the old lady to pass. Fortunately for him, she was stooped and her eyesight poor; she wouldn't later remember the marchese being in the pharmacy because she simply didn't see him.

Ugo closed the door after the old woman and, adjusting his spectacles to make sure he wasn't seeing things, he turned to face Salvatore.

"Marchese. How may I help you?"

Very cool, thought Salvatore. Butter wouldn't melt in his mouth. Perhaps I should make more room for it by removing his teeth.

Standing tall, so Ugo would be acutely aware of the fifteen-centimetre difference in their height, and pulling back his shoulders to demonstrate the width of his powerful frame, Salvatore smiled, but his eyes radiated a fox-like cunning.

"I am pleased to say I have no need of your medicinal expertise, unlike my wife whom I believe last summer needed to consult you frequently. No, I am in the finest of health, something I attribute to clean living and pure thoughts."

He tilted his head slightly as if to emphasise the point.

Ugo's eyes were fixed on Salvatore's, a half-smile frozen on his lips, the sheer terror he felt in the presence of this man in great danger of setting his features twitching uncontrollably. He had never seriously thought the day would come when he would be standing alone in his pharmacy a mere metre from his lover's husband, a huge man who could snap him over his knee like a length of wood.

Slowly and carefully, he transformed his smile into a questioning frown. "Then how else may I help you, Marchese?"

"It is your herbal expertise I seek, Dottore," said Salvatore, politely using the title applied to Italian professionals, no matter what their expertise.

Alarm bells rang in Ugo's head as he thought of the herbal preparation he had coached Isabella to use on the Brocanti housekeeper. Had the old woman discovered her tonic had been adulterated? He doubted it after so long, and anyway, she had been living back in the village for many months.

"Herbal expertise?" he repeated, hoarsely.

Salvatore smiled at him. "Yes. You may not have heard that I have returned here from my house in Garda ahead of my wife and family to open up the villa. Over the winter, I have been reading about the use of herbs in the formulation of remedies and I have discovered there is a dearth of certain beneficial types available in this country. This necessitates them being imported from abroad, sometimes from as far away as China, thereby making them prohibitively expensive, for the average person, that is. Am I right?"

Ugo's head was reeling. This was a totally unexpected development. Had he and Isabella really been successful in keeping their love a secret? They had certainly been careful enough, but nevertheless, the maid Imperia knew, and therefore possibly others. Had no word reached this man? A sense of relief flowed through him with dizzying force.

"Dottore?"

Ugo took a breath, his voice catching slightly as he pushed nervously at the bridge of his spectacles.

"Eh, yes, Marchese, you are indeed right. The unavailability of some herbs is a severe constraint on what can be made generally available for prescription to … to the populace."

"Precisely!" boomed Salvatore, the volume of his retort making Ugo jump. "Well, it occurred to me it was about time this situation changed. I have heard that in botanic gardens around Europe, all manner of plants may be cultivated if the soil conditions are manipulated or the climate controlled by means of glass houses. I have a huge garden I should be pleased to devote to addressing the problem of availability of these herbs. What do you say?"

"I … I think it is a capital idea, Marchese," replied Ugo hesitantly, hardly able to believe his ears. "In what way do you seek my assistance?"

"You're an expert, man; you can advise me. If you are agreeable, I should like you to assess the garden next to my villa, and if necessary, other locations on my estate, perhaps take samples of the soil, consider where best to construct glass houses. That sort of thing. I know nothing of these matters, but what I can provide is the manpower and financial resources to make it work. It would be my pleasure to do so."

He beamed at the bewildered pharmacist, and although his eyes were still cunning, they had relaxed almost enough to be convincing.

Ugo had a particular interest in herbal medicines and had read widely in his studies of the more exotic ones and their potency. He knew their cultivation away from their natural habitats was fraught with problems, requiring specific climatic and soil conditions. Added to this, the seeds, which were, by necessity, imported, were expensive and hard to come by. His dream was that one day he would have the resources to turn his ambitions into reality. That a way forward for his plans had walked into his pharmacy in the form of Salvatore Brocanti was beyond belief. And yet the marchese appeared to have made the offer in all earnestness with no indication he knew anything of Ugo and Isabella's relationship.

"Well, Dottore, what do you say?" Salvatore enthused, breaking into Ugo's thoughts.

"I … er … I think it is a most generous suggestion, Marchese. I should be delighted to advise you in any way you require. To make some of the more exotic herbs more widely available would be of inestimable value to the community. When do you wish to start this project?"

Salvatore wanted to show he had thought the idea through; it would reinforce the appearance of his proposal being a genuine one.

"Well, some of my ideas would take more than a little time; several months, at least. I'm referring to the glass houses, of course. These things don't just appear, they need planning and time for construction. However, for the part of the project that doesn't need glass houses, for plants that can be safely grown outside, I should have thought there is no time like the present. The season is moving on and if we want to achieve anything this year, I should suggest that the sooner I can make the appropriate arrangements, the better. What do you say?"

Ugo nodded his agreement. "You are right, Marchese. In fact, I suspect we might already be too late for this year. However, before any planting can take place, the condition of the soil would need to be addressed. If all the soil preparation were done this year, and the beds given time to settle and be enriched with the correct fertiliser, then we should be ready next year to take full advantage of the whole season."

For you, pharmacist, thought Salvatore, there won't be a next year.

"I can see already that in you I have found the perfect adviser, Dottore," said Salvatore. "When would it be convenient for you to come to the estate to look at my proposed location and perhaps take some soil samples?"

Ugo took out his pocket watch and checked the time. "The market will be starting to pack up soon, and after that, I do not anticipate much need for the pharmacy to remain open. What about this afternoon, Marchese? Would that be convenient?"

Salvatore clapped his hands. "That would be most kind; I am indebted to you for your positive response to my proposal."

Ugo shook his head. "On the contrary, Marchese, the indebtedness is all mine. I thank you for thinking me worthy of your consideration."

"Shall we say three o'clock?" said Salvatore.

"Perfect," replied Ugo, as he shook Salvatore's outstretched hand.

Salvatore made to turn, but stopped. "There is just one thing that occurs to me, Dottore."

Ugo tilted his head in question, nervous again at what the marchese might say. "There is?"

"Yes. It probably isn't important, but we are discussing a business venture, for want of a better expression, one that could prove to be extremely profitable, for both of us, I mean. It would be unfortunate if someone else heard of our scheme and decided to go ahead with one of their own, wouldn't you agree?"

Ugo frowned. The thought hadn't occurred to him. "I am sure you know far more of business than I, Marchese. What are you suggesting?"

"Oh, simply that we keep this idea to ourselves. Tell no one. I think at this stage it would be far better. Give us peace of mind, so to speak. Probably better too if you weren't seen coming to the estate. If someone were to see you, you'd be surprised how quickly they might put two and two together, maybe even start spying on what we are doing."

Ugo was shocked. "Heavens, are businessmen really so unscrupulous? I had no idea."

"The world of business is a harsh one, Dottore. Always better to make sure any competitors don't get a whiff of what you're doing." He tapped the side of his nose to reinforce the point. "To that end, do you know the rear entrance into the estate, the gate that is set back in the trees on the old farm road from Coniglio?"

Ugo knew it well; he had used that way into the estate whenever he visited Isabella. He rubbed his chin and adjusted his spectacles. "Yes, Marchese. I think I can recall having seen it. Do you think it better I arrive that way?"

"Probably better, yes," said Salvatore with a slight smile. "Can't be too careful, can we?"

. . .

Ugo stared after the marchese as the door to the pharmacy closed, his mind still reeling in confusion and shock. A confidential project in the perfect location for seeing Isabella? When would she be returning? Soon, no doubt, from the way the marchese had spoken. And he, Ugo, would have a completely legitimate reason for being at the villa, indeed to be with her since he knew she had a fondness for the cultivation of plants. After many months of worrying whether he would ever see her again, of having no communication from her and not being able to send her any himself for fear of interception, his world had unexpectedly brightened. Perhaps he and Isabella had a future together after all.

He was, however, puzzled by the marchese. He had only met him a couple of times in the past, and briefly at that. On both occasions he had appeared brooding and distracted, his manner of speaking curt to the point of rudeness. Certainly his experience tallied with Isabella's description of her husband's general demeanour. But on this occasion, the man had seemed most congenial, without a hint of brusqueness or temper. He wondered what had precipitated the change. But he didn't let these thoughts concern him for long; he was far too excited about the prospect of seeing Isabella again.

Chapter Twenty-Six

Two hours later, Ugo set out for the Brocanti estate on foot. He had considered taking his horse, but that might have raised a casual question from the groom at the stables where he kept it. He also made no mention of his destination to his housekeeper, in fact he hadn't even told her he was going out after lunch; he just took his hat and cane and left. The thought of being involved in a secret project excited him, adding a little spice to a life that had been dull and monotonous since Isabella had disappeared so abruptly.

For Ugo, the path through the forest from the rear gate to the estate was one well trodden with happy memories. He passed a number of places where he and Isabella had met and made love, spent blissful hours revelling in each other's presence and yearning for a time when they could be together permanently. He paused at several glades, staring into the undergrowth, idly running his hand along a branch or catching some leaves in his fingers, his heart racing at the thought that he had shared these spots with Isabella.

At one point, he glanced along a narrow track branching from the main path that led to a small hut they had used occasionally in wet weather or on colder days when they had wrapped themselves together in blankets Isabella brought from the villa.

He felt inside his coat for the pocket where he'd put a letter he had written to Isabella that morning after Salvatore had gone, a letter expressing his love and excitement that they would soon be together again. He had no idea what he would do with it; there would be no one at the villa he could leave it with. Perhaps he should hide it in the hut; there was a loose board in the floor where they had sometimes left messages. But no, that would be inviting danger should it be discovered by Salvatore, and he had no wish to compromise either the project itself or the prospect of seeing Isabella regularly again.

Isabella had always teased him about his letters, claiming his handwriting was so small and compact that she had to spend hours deciphering it. "It's only your signature, my love, written with its characteristic flourish, that assures me that it is from you at all and that it's not a copy of some medieval screed written out by an aged monk in his cell by the light of one inadequate candle."

Ugo smiled to himself at the memory, feeling for the letter once more and caressing it with his fingers.

He removed his watch from his waistcoat pocket to check the time. It was five minutes to three; he shouldn't linger in the forest, the marchese would be waiting for him. He walked on, reluctant to leave an area of such fond memories, but he felt sure there would be many more, and as this thought crossed his mind, a spring entered his step.

"Ah, there you are, Dottore," called out Salvatore as soon as Ugo emerged from the trees into the overgrown gardens. "I was concerned you might lose your way; the forest is really quite extensive."

"No, Marchese, although the path meanders a little, it is really quite clear. But you are right, it was farther than I, er, imagined." He gulped to himself; he had nearly said 'remembered.' That would have taken some explaining.

Salvatore laughed as he beckoned Ugo to join him. "Glad I didn't have to send out a search party, since it would have consisted only of one. Me! There's no one else here."

Something in his tone sounded a faint alarm in Ugo's mind. For the first time it occurred to him that he was alone on this vast estate with his lover's husband and not another living soul knew he was here.

Salvatore steered Ugo to where he had cleared part of the herb garden.

"This soil is wonderfully rich, Dottore," he enthused. "Do you think it would be suitable?"

Ugo nodded. "We should need to check its acidity and mineral content, but yes, for certain herbs, a rich soil is ideal. However, for some of the more difficult types to cultivate, a rich soil can overwhelm the plant with too much goodness. That sounds strange, I know, but it's as if some species have become used to having to fight for survival, scouring the earth for every drop of nourishment. It isn't wise to make life too easy for such plants."

Salvatore smiled. "You are clearly well read on the subject, Dottore, I am delighted to have your expertise for my project."

"It will be an interesting challenge, Marchese, and one I look forward to. Tell me, where are you thinking of positioning the glass houses?"

He looked around the extensive garden considering various places. "Not too close to the villa, I think."

Salvatore had given it no thought at all; he wasn't in the least bit interested in glass houses, or even, for that matter, in exotic herbs. But he thought he would humour the pharmacist for a little longer; there was no need to rush matters.

"I have one or two ideas," he lied, "but why don't we take a turn around the garden and see if your ideas agree with mine? I'd like to think some of my notions make sense."

Ugo laughed. "You are too modest, Marchese. Although the garden is rather overgrown at present, I can see its layout and planning have been expertly considered."

He stopped and frowned. "I am, however, rather surprised not to see a squad of gardeners working here. Are they elsewhere on the estate?"

Salvatore could hear a certain tension in the question. The last thing he wanted now, given he was so close to his goal, was to frighten the pharmacist into thinking he was in danger. A simple lie would suffice.

"Exactly so, Dottore, extremely astute of you. I must confess that my being away for so many months has led to neglect in this normally beautiful part of the garden.

"Before I went away, I charged the head groundsman with the task of renovating the extensive vineyards and olive groves on the other side of the estate, some three kilometres from here. They were planted by my father, but to my shame, I failed to give them the attention they required and over the years they have deteriorated.

"My wife has often scolded me over this. You see, her family estates were famous for their vineyards, still are, and she felt that given the quality of the wine for which this region is renowned, and given also that the Brocanti wines were once quite famous, it was remiss of me to let them go. In the end, I saw the wisdom in her advice and I conceived a plan to have them renovated for when she returns. I'm hoping she will be delighted by the surprise.

"However, when I returned, the wretched groundsman was full of apologies, excuses more like, claiming the work had taken far longer than expected and that although the vineyards are now almost up to scratch, he had been unable to give time to the formal gardens and the parts beyond. But he assures me that while this year they will not be as they should, by this time next year, they should be resplendent once again."

This little speech set more alarm bells ringing in Ugo's head. He had discussed the estate on a number of occasions with Isabella and he knew that Salvatore had absolutely no interest in the vines or the olives, considering them a waste of time and money. But worse, Isabella had told him that although her family estate had been extensive in the north of Italy, there were no vines on the property and never had been. As for the account of the apparent harmony and positive discourse between Salvatore and Isabella, that was the worst lie of all: their relationship had been appalling for years and there was no way Salvatore would bother to present his wife with a potential 'delightful surprise'.

From the pharmacist's rather negative reaction to his story,

Salvatore realised that in his enthusiasm to convince, he had over-stated his case. He needed to move quickly on to the real reason he had persuaded the man to come before he panicked and tried to leave.

"Anyway," he beamed, trying to restore some bonhomie into the conversation, "enough of the garden. I think we agree that with a little work and judicious application of your extensive exper-tise, we have a most promising project on our hands."

Ugo tilted his head, attempting to be gracious. "You are too kind," he said, fumbling as he again pulled his watch from his waistcoat. He glanced at it. "Oh, dear me—"

"Dottore," interrupted Salvatore, "I don't want to waste any more of your valuable time, but if you would humour me for a little while longer, there is something I should like to show you. It's a project I have been working on for some time now, many months in fact, and now that it is complete, I am impatient for someone to see it. I should be honoured if that first person were you."

He paused, noting the look of hesitation on Ugo's face. He put his hands together submissively. "Please, Dottore, your opinion on how it has all turned out would mean so much to me."

Against his better judgement, Ugo sighed. "You have made it sound very intriguing, Marchese," he said. "I should indeed be honoured to be the first to see it, whatever it is. Would you be so kind as to enlighten me as to its nature?"

"I should be absolutely delighted to, my dear Dottore," beamed Salvatore. "Please, come this way and I shall explain as we walk."

Chapter Twenty-Seven

With every one of its shutters firmly closed, the villa signalled caution, a forbidding presence that increasingly filled Ugo's vision as the pair approached it. Salvatore led him towards the single-storey storerooms separating the kitchen garden from the formal gardens.

"Rather than go all the way round to the front, there is a convenient entrance here, Dottore, and one that will immediately amuse you." He pulled a set of keys from his pocket, inserted one into one of the doors and pushed it open.

"Let me light a couple of lanterns," he said, reaching over to a shelf and retrieving two oil lamps. He pulled a flint and steel from his pocket and struck them together next to each lantern's wick.

"There," he said, "take a lantern and shine it into the room, towards that door at the far end. You will see, I think, that it is ajar."

Ugo lifted his lantern, glancing around the room as he did. It was a storeroom with freestanding racks of shelves. At the far end a door stood slightly ajar, but the light from his lantern was insufficient to penetrate the darkness of the room beyond.

He turned to see Salvatore also lifting his lantern and pointing towards the door. "Lead on, Dottore, this is the beginning of a fascinating adventure. I cannot wait to see your reaction. But first, why don't you put your hat and cane on this shelf, you will have no need of them in the villa. You can retrieve them when we leave."

After putting down his hat and cane, Ugo crossed the room towards the door and with his free hand, he reached out to push it open. When it didn't move, he initially withdrew his hand as if he had been stung. The door felt strange. He tried again, this time moving his hand over the door's surface.

"This door has the appearance of wood, but its surface feels more like plaster." He tapped it. "And not plaster on wood." He lifted the lantern close to the door to examine the detail. As he moved the light to the gap and what appeared to be the darkness of the room beyond, he laughed.

"Marchese, this is remarkable. It is not a door at all but a painting of one on the wall. And the gap a mere painting too, to make the door appear ajar. But it cannot be ajar since it isn't a door. The whole thing is part of a solid wall."

He turned to see that Salvatore was standing close behind him. "I've seen this effect elsewhere," continued Ugo. "Let me see, yes, it was in Florence at one of the Renaissance palaces. I must say you have executed it remarkably well. It is most convincing."

"Thank you, Dottore, I am pleased you are impressed. Now, if that isn't the door, where is the way into the main villa?"

Ugo turned back to the wall and shone his light carefully over it, tapping at the surface as he went. "Yes," he cried, "I have it! There is a carefully hidden door here. When the surface is tapped, the sound is different from the wall. The door is here, Marchese, but unfortunately there is no handle."

"Indeed there is not!" exclaimed Salvatore, laughing. "At least, not one you can see. This one is rather hard to find and there is much I want to show you, so let me release this particular door myself."

He lifted his lantern to the wall on the left of the door and ran his hand down the rough brickwork. Finding the brick he wanted, he pulled it free from the others and reached inside for a recessed lever and pulled it. The wooden door concealed in the wall swung open in the direction of what Ugo assumed would be a room beyond.

"There," said Salvatore, "the first of my puzzles explained. Please, Dottore, let us move on."

He indicated the doorway and Ugo walked through, only to exclaim immediately that it was a passageway heading off to the left with another door a short distance along it.

"Another illusion, Marchese?" called Ugo as he walked towards the door.

"I wonder," said Salvatore. He waited until Ugo was fully focussed on the door ahead of him before moving a box from the storeroom floor and placing it in front of the door they had just passed through.

"Ah," called Ugo, "this one has a handle that I think … yes, it is real." He turned the handle and pushed the door open, only to be confronted by an extension of the passageway. But instead of another door, a heavy purple curtain was hung across the passageway ahead of him and another along the wall to his right. Ugo walked forward and reached out to pull back the curtain ahead of him. But when his fingers brushed against the wall, he stood back and, raising his lantern, examined it closely.

"Brilliant, Marchese, incredible. May I congratulate you; it is another painting. But is this where our exploration stops? We are confronted by paintings of curtains. There is no way through."

When there was no answer, Ugo turned to see Salvatore's face starkly illuminated by his lantern, a smile of mischief on his lips. He raised his eyebrows and briefly turned his eyes towards the other curtained wall.

Frowning, Ugo reached out to touch what he had assumed was another painting on another wall, but his hand disappeared into the folds.

"Aha!" he cried, pulling at the curtain. When it didn't move, he pulled at it again, and saw that it disappeared behind the wall of the passageway he had walked along. Billowing it out and keeping the material from the lantern, he made his way along the edge of the wall until he reached the end, and found himself walking into the large room it had been hiding.

He lifted his lantern high, letting the limited light illuminate one part after another, his eyes fooled by the imagery in front of him.

He jumped when, without warning, Salvatore's voice sounded close to his ear. "What do you think, Dottore?"

His head shot round to find once again the marchese was directly behind him.

"It's … it's quite outstanding. The decoration is exquisite, and the paintings hanging are …" His voice drifted away as he moved the light around to view the paintings. "Are not real at all," he continued. "At least, they are real, but they are not in frames as it would appear, but for each one, the entire thing, painting and frame, is painted directly onto the wall. Another magnificent illusion, Marchese. I congratulate you once again, these are superb."

In answer, Salvatore smiled and lifted his lantern high. "Look up," he said. "You can see—"

"The sky!" interrupted Ugo. "But of course it cannot be, it is all part of the illusion. But tell me, why do you keep it in the dark? Would it not be better to open one or two of those shutters?" He pointed across the room.

"That would be difficult, Dottore, since they are part of the illusion. The wall on which they are painted is not an outside wall. As for a more natural light, I have still to decide on the best form, since if the light is too strong, the illusions on the walls are less effective. For now, I prefer light from a lantern."

Ugo looked around the room for a way out, but couldn't immediately see one. "There is more?" he asked. "There doesn't appear to be a door."

"Look in the corner, behind the curtain," replied Salvatore.

Ugo shone his lantern in the direction of the curtain, realising as he did that the curtain covered one entire wall of the room.

He strode over to the corner, hoping that another room might offer more light in spite of what the marchese had said. Pulling the curtain to one side, he found the door and was relieved to find it was real, along with a real handle.

He pulled open the door to reveal a short corridor leading to the right, its walls painted black.

"Shall we continue?" Salvatore had again followed him and was standing rather too close for Ugo's liking.

Ugo walked along the corridor to where it turned sharp right. Here, he was surprised to see a flight of stone stairs disappearing upwards into the gloom. He climbed the stairs, a little uneasy at their narrowness. On reaching the top, from the way the light from his lantern was falling onto the walls ahead of him, he could immediately see that what appeared to be a wide corridor running away from him was in part artificial, and that a wooden balustrade apparently separating it from the stairs was entirely so. The walls were plain and painted like the ones in the room below him.

"I am beginning to get used to the idea," he called back to Salvatore. "Even though it looks wide, this corridor is, in reality, quite narrow, but it goes somewhere. Are those two doors I can see of interest? Are they even real?"

Not waiting for an answer, he marched along the corridor and turned the handle of the door to his left. As it opened into the room, Salvatore was again directly behind him, almost whispering into his ear.

"Look at the vaulting," he said, making Ugo jump yet again. "I am particularly pleased with it."

Ugo looked up, and, distracted by the vaulting in the ceiling that appeared to soar away from him, it was a few moments until he noticed there was natural light coming into the room.

Seeing the open window, he took a step towards it.

"Be careful!" warned Salvatore.

Ugo stopped just as a beam in the floor creaked. He looked down and yelled in fright, jumping back as he did.

"By all the saints, what has happened here? I could have fallen to my death! Marchese …"

He stopped, the laughter from his host surprising him. It wasn't the manic laughter of a madman watching him risk his life, it was simply amusement.

"You were in no danger," chuckled Salvatore, and he walked around Ugo and directly into what appeared to be thin air, the space where the floor had apparently collapsed into the room below.

Ugo watched in awe, as if Salvatore were performing some sort of magic trick, levitating above an all-too-real scene several metres below him.

Salvatore threw his head back and laughed. "Come! It is perfectly safe," he cried as he jumped up and down to prove the point.

Ugo took a tentative step towards him, then another. Looking up, he grinned sheepishly. "Incredible, Marchese. Truly incredible. Of course now I have moved to a different spot and the perspective hasn't changed, I can see how the illusion is created, but from near to the door, well, I am in awe of your skills."

"You are too kind, Dottore. Now, do you wish to see more?" He pointed back towards the door through which they had entered.

"I do indeed," said Ugo, "but first, I should like to see the view from this open window. I have become a little disoriented; does it look out onto the gardens we have been discussing?"

By way of answer, Salvatore raised an arm towards the window. "Be my guest," he said. "Perhaps you could tell me what you think the view is."

Puzzled by his remark, Ugo walked over to the window, glancing with almost every step at the floor in case the illusion of a gaping hole suddenly became a reality.

The sill was quite high, although when he was close he could easily see through the glass. As he took in the view, he gasped. There below him in the garden, some twenty metres away, sitting on a bench seat with her back to him was his beloved Isabella. She was quite still and appeared to be reading a book.

Unable to turn his head away, he called to Salvatore.

"I thought you said, Marchese, that your wife and family were still at your estate in Garda, that they would be coming here soon."

When there was no reply, he tore his gaze away and turned to Salvatore, who was still standing in the centre of the room. His face was serious, with no trace of the humour of a few moments before. He nodded slowly. "You are quite correct, Dottore, that is exactly what I said."

"But …" Ugo turned his head again to the window.

"Come," called Salvatore. "I must show you something else. By way of explanation, you understand."

He turned on his heel and strode to the door. When Ugo didn't move, he held out an arm, beckoning him. "I promise you, the floor is as sound as the others, if that is what is still concerning you, Dottore."

With a last glance towards the window, Ugo walked across the room and through the door Salvatore was holding open for him. He crossed the narrow corridor and took hold of the handle of the door facing him, turned it and pushed open the door. As he looked into the room, his focus was firmly on the floor in case there was another trick awaiting him.

But the floor of this room appeared solid enough, and, unlike the other room, this one was furnished with a chaise longue, several chairs and a writing desk. However, none of this registered as strongly to Ugo's eyes as the window on the wall facing him. It was identical to the one in the room opposite, and its shutters, too, were open, letting in a diffuse light.

This one must look out onto the gravelled drive at the front of the villa, thought Ugo, since the other looked onto the garden where Isabella is sitting. The garden … there was something different about it. Of course, it was immaculately tidy, resplendent with flowers and shrubs, and … and the sun had seemed to be far stronger. Had the overcast day he had left behind not too many minutes ago changed so dramatically?

Not waiting for any comments from Salvatore, he marched over to the window and peered through. Not only was the view identical, Isabella was also there sitting on the bench, her head bent forward as she read her book.

Unable to interpret what he was seeing, Ugo turned, expecting Salvatore to be immediately behind once again. But he wasn't. He was standing by the door watching Ugo, his face neither stern nor amused.

He sighed and took a couple of steps forward. "You are puzzled I think, Dottore, are you not?"

Ugo nodded. "I am indeed, Marchese."

By way of explanation, Salvatore swept an outstretched arm

around, indicating the room as a whole. "What do you see, Dottore, on the walls and the ceiling? How is the furniture, if you study it closely? Is the library real? What was the decoration to the room opposite?"

"Library …?" stuttered Ugo, his eyes roaming the room. "I confess I saw no library until now, nor did the decoration to the walls of the other room really register. I am afraid I was preoccupied with the state of the floor and then by the view from the window."

"Ah, yes. My wife. You were preoccupied with my wife."

"No!" protested Ugo, the word coming out as a squeak. "That is not what I meant. What I meant was … I was surprised to find she is here."

"She isn't."

"I … I don't understand."

Salvatore's sigh was one of exasperation. He was beginning to lose patience with the pharmacist. He clenched his jaw in an effort of self-control.

"Tell me, what did you see through this window?"

"I saw the garden once again, even though I think it should not be there, and again, I saw your wife."

"Have you learned nothing from your wanderings through this villa. Surely, you must have; you keep congratulating me on my skill."

Ugo stared at him as the explanation hit him. "You mean to tell me the views from the windows are illusions too? More paintings? But how can that be? You can't paint daylight coming into an otherwise dark room. I am not seeing the painting with the assistance of a lantern as in the rooms downstairs that are in darkness."

Salvatore laughed, but there was now no humour in the sound. "A little trick I devised, nothing more. If it fooled you so easily, think how easily it will fool my wife and children when they see it for the first time."

Ugo was shocked. "Surely you do not intend to let your children roam this house; they will be terrified. The darkness and the illusions, the feeling of being trapped, confined, as on the stairway back there, these things could cause untold damage. They might be permanently affected."

The laugh from Salvatore was this time more genuine. "Don't fret yourself, Dottore, I have no intention of introducing them to the illusions in quite so dramatic a way as I have to you. I shall do it little by little, a room at a time, and with far better light. I can assure you I have no intention of my children coming to any harm, nor indeed of frightening them."

"I am relieved to hear it." Ugo felt admonished. Perhaps he had overreacted. "I am sure you will understand that seeing the views was something of a shock, so effectively are they executed. As I said earlier, your skill in this work is profound." He looked around, taking in the portraits on the walls for the first time.

"Ah," said Salvatore, watching his eyes. "The Brocanti rogues' gallery. Quite a bunch, don't you think? Raving mad, most of them. Now, are you ready to see the rest of what I have prepared?"

"There is more?"

Salvatore smiled. "Oh, yes, Dottore, there is more. Come this way."

He pointed towards a curtain covering part of the wall opposite the door through which they had entered.

"Pull it to one side, it's real enough."

Ugo took hold of the curtain and pulled. It swished effortlessly along its pole revealing a door.

"The door is also real," said Salvatore condescendingly.

Ugo opened it and peered into the darkness. He held up his lantern and could see a corridor that turned to the right after a short distance. As he walked cautiously down it, he could hear Salvatore following him.

Turning the corner, Ugo could see several doors, all of which were real. He tried their handles, only to find the first two were locked. However, the third opened, one with the wall on either side painted to look like a stairway. Raising the lantern, he peered ahead to another set of stairs rising into the gloom. He paused to look at the stairs and walls on either side and was surprised to see they too were painted, the effect jungle-like with roots, vines and many serpents and mythical creatures interwoven, crisscrossing the stairs, almost pulling him upwards.

"Another truly amazing effect, Marchese, I feel that if I step on one of these creatures it might rear its angry head and tear at me with its fangs. Do you still maintain this will not frighten your children?"

"You are right, Dottore," called Salvatore from behind him. "This section of my little creation is perhaps rather more grotesque, but the children will not see it until they are considerably older. However, I see no harm in your witnessing it today."

Ahead, at the top of the stairs, was a heavy black door blocking the way. Ugo reached out for the handle, turned it and pushed the door. It swung effortlessly away from him. The room ahead was also in complete darkness but the light from the lantern quickly showed it to be far smaller than the rooms on the lower floors and, strangely, thought Ugo, far wider than it was long. And there were no paintings: the walls were constructed of stone and there was just a single door in the wall facing him.

He heard Salvatore behind him so he walked into the room, letting the extra light from the second lantern help him to orient himself. Closer now to the walls, he could see that his first impression had been wrong: the room *was* decorated, but differently from the rooms downstairs. To confirm his thoughts he reached out to touch the walls and found the surface wasn't stone, it was painted to look like stone. And the door, like others he had seen, wasn't a door, merely a painting of a door.

He turned to Salvatore to find he was watching him carefully, his eyes now dark and menacing.

"This room is quite different from the others below," said Ugo, holding up his lantern. "It is extremely high, genuinely so, and that looks like the roof of the villa. And yet the room is far wider than deep. Was it once longer and has been divided?"

"Very astute of you, Dottore," said Salvatore. "You are quite right."

Ugo watched him as he placed his lantern by the door at the top of the stairs, preventing it from closing.

"You will be wondering, no doubt, where we go from here," continued Salvatore.

Ugo nodded. "Yes, it had crossed my mind. All we have is a door that is not a door, merely another one of your paintings."

Salvatore smiled mirthlessly. "I shouldn't be quite so sure of that. Feel around the edge of the door."

Ugo followed his instructions. "There appears to be the slightest of depressions, as if there is a well-fitting door. But it doesn't feel like wood."

"That's because it isn't wood; it is a large slab of finely worked stone."

"Where is the handle?"

"Do you not remember the first door we went through, from the storerooms into the passageway that led into the main part of the villa on the ground floor? Let me show you."

He moved to Ugo's left and pushed the toe of his left shoe hard against the lowest part of the wall in the corner. To Ugo's surprise, the stone door swung open to reveal what must once have been the other part of this room, only this part was slightly larger. And unlike its partner, this room was not in total darkness. Ugo looked up to see a small skylight set into the roof tiles, giving the room a dingy, shadowy illumination.

Lifting his lantern, Ugo could see that placed centrally in the room were a table and two upright wooden chairs, while to the left, the room extended about two metres farther into a shallow recess. There were no more doors, painted or real, unless there was one disguised by the painted walls, but he doubted it. This was the end of the road.

He turned towards where Salvatore was standing.

"Marchese—" he began, but got no further, the powerful punch to his face taking him completely by surprise and knocking him off his feet. He tumbled backwards, tripping over one of the chairs to fall clumsily against the far wall, his spectacles flying off into a corner.

Salvatore took a step forward, rubbing the knuckles of his right hand in his left palm. "You cannot imagine how long I have waited to do that, *Dottore*," he growled, his pronunciation of the title now a sneer.

Ugo yelped as he screwed up his eyes, trying to focus. The pain was intense, as if shards of bone were piercing his entire head, and he knew instinctively that his nose was shattered and his mouth damaged. He could taste the blood flowing over his lips.

"Marchese," he repeated, but this time the word was slurred, his mouth now full of saliva and blood. He wiped at it with the back of a hand and felt one of his front teeth detach. He spat it out along with the contents of his mouth.

"Marchese," he tried once more, clearer now. "Why …?"

"Why?" screeched Salvatore, "You ask me *why*? Do you think I am a blind fool? Do you think I don't know what has been going on? You have taken my wife, the mother of my children, as a lover, had numerous assignations with her on this estate, *my* estate, debasing its name and its very ground, taken advantage of my prolonged absences to ingratiate yourself with my children, humiliating me in the process. Your behaviour, signore, has been disgraceful, betraying common decency, and you dare to ask me why!"

The words hit Ugo with a physical force, pounding into his head like more punches. He recoiled and tried to push himself back against the wall. Against all common sense, he wanted to stand.

"I should stay sitting where you are, if I were you," snarled Salvatore. "That first punch was extremely satisfying; do not give me cause to deliver another."

Ugo's body slumped as he forced his mind beyond the pain, trying to make sense of his situation. What was this madman intending?

He winced as he raised his head, lifting his right arm slightly and feebly indicating the room.

"T-these m-months of work, on the villa," he stuttered, pausing every two or three words as he struggled to construct them with his disfigured mouth, "the maze of rooms, the illusions; were they all designed to trap me? Is your hatred so profound?"

Salvatore's laugh was a coarse bark. "Not just you, you fool, not just you. You are not the only one who must pay. My wife will also be suffering the consequences of her infidelity. You see, I had been suspicious of her for some time and when I discovered the two of you in the forest, my first instinct was to kill you both there and then. I could easily have hidden your bodies, buried them somewhere remote; they would never have been found.

"But as I watched the two of you and your disgusting behaviour, I saw that a quick death would be too easy, too good for you. I decided the only right and proper punishment for both of you would be a lingering death where every moment is a torture of anguish, knowing you have no chance of escape or rescue, and knowing death will come upon you so very slowly."

Ugo spat more saliva and blood from his mouth, but this time more to register his contempt.

"You are completely insane, Brocanti, like your ancestors before you. Your entire family is cursed with madness. Surely you are not intending to trap your wife here as well as me. She is the mother of your children."

"Sadly, she is, but the sooner her influence over them is removed, the better their lives will be, as will mine. And her influence *will* be removed, I can assure you. I have every intention of showing her this masterpiece of a villa in much the same way as I have shown you. Like you, she will be confined here forever and like you, she will starve to death, losing her mind in fear and regret as her body fails her."

"You intend for us to die here together? I am amazed you would allow that."

Salvatore laughed scornfully.

"Most definitely not. No, by the time Isabella meets her fate, you will be a rotting corpse."

Ugo knew he had one chance to escape, one slim chance to overcome this man who was many times stronger than he. As Salvatore was goading him with his intentions, Ugo slowly shifted his weight and pulled his feet back to give himself some leverage when he sprang. But to be successful, he must be closer, which meant enticing Salvatore to approach him.

Screwing up his eyes in an attempt to focus them without his spectacles, he chose his moment as Salvatore's eyes left him briefly while he made some point. He leaned back hard against the wall, the movement designed to catch Salvatore's attention.

"I told you—" began Salvatore, as he took a step forward.

Ugo pushed against his feet with all his strength, launching his body at Salvatore's legs, grabbing at his ankles and pulling sharply. It worked, and a surprised Salvatore tumbled backwards. Ignoring the sickening jolts of pain searing through his head, Ugo released Salvatore's legs and sprang to his feet. The door, like the others Salvatore had quietly propped open, was very close. If he could get through it and pull it closed after him, trapping the madman inside, he would have all the time in the world to find his way out of the villa and report Salvatore to the authorities. Or would he simply leave him there?

As the thought flashed across his mind, he took one step, then another, then …

But the third step never happened. A huge hand flashed out of nowhere and clamped itself onto his leg just above the ankle. The powerful arm to which the hand was attached folded at the elbow and Ugo found himself falling sideways. Even as his body hit the floor, he was being yanked sideways like a rag doll as he was flung back against the far wall.

Salvatore stood, his eyes watching the slumped body carefully for any sign of a further attack.

"A worthy effort, Gasperini, and I applaud you for it," he panted. "However, given the difference in our size and strength, it was inevitably doomed to failure."

He took a step back to the doorway and picked up the lantern he had left on the floor to prop open the door. He was about to leave when a thought struck him.

"Ah, leaving you with your lantern would not be a good idea. The oil won't last long but a light shining through the skylight at night, however weak and however unlikely to be seen, would not be in my best interests."

He picked up Ugo's lantern and walked through the doorway into the outer room, watching as the finely balanced door slowly closed after him. He stopped it with his foot.

"I should point out that these walls are far thicker than the others. Sound won't travel from here, so screaming will do you no good. Your dungeon is secure and cut off from the world."

He heard a grunting noise from Ugo's body.

"What was that, Gasperini?"

"May you rot in hell," slurred Ugo.

"I probably shall," laughed Salvatore, "but I shall have the satisfaction of knowing both you and my unfaithful wife will have rotted there long before I do."

He lifted his foot and watched as the door clicked into place. Ugo Gasperini's fate was sealed.

Chapter Twenty-Eight

Retracing his steps through the villa, Salvatore checked each room, removed the objects he had used to prop open the doors and finally left by the stout door to the single-storey storeroom, locking it after him. Everything was effectively in place for when he took Isabella through the villa, but that would not be for a few weeks. In the interim, he wanted to be certain that Gasperini had starved to death. Given there was no water in the room he doubted this would take longer than a week, but he would give it a wide margin of error.

After checking the apartment was in order, Salvatore took his rented chaise and horse back to Arezzo, but before returning it to the stables, he stopped off at an inn frequented by the dregs of the city, men whose physical strength and brutality were easily bought. After talking to several, he chose four. He needed them to follow his instructions without question, but he also needed them to be superstitious men with a healthy respect for the ways of the devil, men with no wish to cross paths with him or his agents.

Their brief was simple. "You patrol the estate, ensuring only those to whom I have given authority to deliver food are allowed in, no one else. Once my wife and children return to the estate, they must not be allowed to leave. If they try, they must be escorted back. My wife is of a delicate disposition, you understand, and cannot be subjected to the stresses of ordinary people. But you are not to enter the villa, nor to stay in sight of it for too long. It may seem benign, but a terrible tragedy occurred within its walls some years ago and spirits from that tragedy still linger there."

It was enough for the four men Salvatore recruited, and it was only because he paid them well they considered taking on the task at all.

During the first few weeks that Salvatore was away from Garda, Isabella's feeling of hopelessness at her situation intensified as each day passed. How long would her husband keep her imprisoned like this? What would happen as the children grew?

And then, with no prior warning, her situation changed dramatically for the better. Suddenly there was hope for a future she had never dared dream of, a future with her children and her lover, a new start far away from her despicable husband.

The news came one morning at breakfast. A letter addressed to Isabella, an event so unusual she thought at first it must be a mistake. Nobody wrote to her. She studied the writing on the envelope, but it offered her no clues. Flipping it over to tear it open she saw the expensive crest of her family's lawyer embossed on the flap. She nearly stopped there since all previous correspondence from the lawyer had been to inform her that her brother had enacted yet another way to restrict her access to anything to do with the family fortune. In her present mood, the last thing Isabella needed was more bad news. But she tore it open and read it anyway, resigned to accepting whatever new measure had been taken.

As her eyes scanned the lines of flowery script, they widened, and widened again.

"Oh my," she gasped, clutching the letter to her chest. "Oh my."

What surprised her immediately on reading and rereading the letter was that she felt no sadness, no loss and certainly no guilt. In a completely matter of fact way, the letter stated that with the greatest regret the writer must inform her that her brother had died unexpectedly following a short illness, so short there had been no time to get word to her of his condition. There had already been a funeral since the illness to which he had succumbed was thought to be a contagious one and medical advice was that the burial should go ahead with all haste.

The final two paragraphs left Isabella staring in disbelief. Given that her brother had never married, she read, it was the writer's duty to inform her that she had, therefore, inherited the entire family fortune. It finished by telling Isabella there would be a second letter within two days to give her more details of the estate and advice on how she might best wish to manage it.

Isabella sat back, her breakfast entirely forgotten. She was rich! Rich in her own right, independently of Salvatore, rich enough to leave him and start a new life. But given the law and the rights of husbands over wives, it was imperative Salvatore knew nothing of her good fortune.

Two days later, two days Isabella spent in a knot of anticipation, the second letter from the lawyer arrived, this one written in a far less formal tone. After reading hastily through it, she reread it several times, each time leaving her more incredulous, more tearful and more wracked with guilt. She had completely misjudged her brother. The lawyer informed her that the reason for her brother's distant behaviour over the years was that he had always intensely disliked and distrusted Salvatore, considering him a most unsuitable husband for his sister. However, she had chosen to marry the man, and his opinions were therefore of no importance. Nevertheless, he had undertaken to keep any money out of what he considered to be Salvatore's grasping hands. He had placed a cleverly worded document in his will leaving his fortune to Tommaso, Delfina and Clara, his only nephew and nieces, in a trust to be administered by Isabella alone, effectively giving her full and free access to the fortune with no rights for Salvatore.

Full of remorse for her response to her brother's apparent coldness over the years, Isabella now yearned to visit his grave to make some sort of peace with him. However, for the past ten years he had lived near the Spanish border in Southwest France, a difficult journey requiring several days. She was still considering how to make the journey when Salvatore arrived, unannounced and unexpected, at the Garda house with the news that he had finished his commission in Rome rather more quickly than anticipated and that the family would be returning to Tuscany immediately.

Knowing there could be no discussion with Salvatore over the matter, and since she had no valid reason she could give him for not complying, Isabella had no choice but to revise her plans.

At least returning to Tuscany would mean she would be closer to Ugo. As soon as they arrived, she would contrive a way to get a message to him, arrange a meeting and give him the good news. They would then make plans to run away with the children and make a fresh start in a new country. On their way, they would visit her brother's grave, after which they would perhaps cross the Atlantic and go to America. Thousands of people did that and now she was rich, they would want for nothing and be entirely beyond Salvatore's reach. It was a good plan.

However, once they arrived back at the villa and Isabella learned of the new arrangements Salvatore had put into place, arrangements far more restrictive than ever, she had a dark sense of foreboding. Why had he tightened the screw? Had he found out about her relationship with Ugo? She still didn't think it was possible since a man with Salvatore's temperament would not have been capable of containing himself. He would have exploded with rage.

It was a stark homecoming. There were no estate staff and no housekeeper. The only maid was the incredibly shy Imperia who had returned with them from Garda and who literally shook whenever she was in Salvatore's presence. However, even Salvatore couldn't object to Imperia going to Coniglio; it was where she came from and she had family there she hadn't seen for months. Imperia would be able to get a message to Ugo.

The day after their return, in the quiet of her room while Salvatore was out somewhere in the grounds, Isabella wrote a brief note to Ugo, intending to give it to Imperia. She read it through, tore it up and wrote another which she also tore up, and then a third and a fourth. Why, she thought, am I so nervous? It is only a note. Ugo will understand why it cannot be a full expression of my love.

It was as she was composing the note for the fifth time that she realised what was wrong, what was tormenting her: a note in physical form could be intercepted, could fall into Salvatore's hands. She immediately burnt all the torn up notes and went to find Imperia in the kitchen.

Seeing the fear in the girl's face, she sought to reassure her. "I need you to carry no message, Imperia, neither as a note nor anything verbal. All I need you to do is go to the pharmacy to fetch some medicine. Dottor Gasperini will doubtless be pleased to see you, ask after my health and casually ask of my location. Telling him we have returned will be message enough. I shall leave all other arrangements in his capable hands. But if he asks you to carry any message, you may tell him I have forbidden it on the grounds that it could put you at risk."

Imperia nodded furiously, grateful to be relieved of any responsibility.

"What tasks have you for the rest of the day, Imperia?"

"I have only to finish preparing the dinner, Marchesa."

Isabella shook her head. "I want you to go to Coniglio, I am in need of a supply of the dottore's tonic. Perhaps I shall finish the dinner preparations while you go to the village. I should have no objection if, while you are there, you were to call in briefly to see your family. Would you like that, Imperia?"

The girl looked up from the duster she had been twisting nervously in her hands, her eyes filled with tears. "Very much, Marchesa. Thank you, thank you very much."

Isabella smiled at her. "Good. Off you go then, fetch your coat. I shall expect you back before nightfall."

An hour later, Isabella was still busy in the kitchen when Salvatore marched through the door.

"Isabella! Whatever are you doing?"

"I should have thought it obvious, Salvatore, but since you ask,

I am preparing these vegetables prior to cooking them as part of our dinner."

"You are what? I employ a maid to do that. Where is she?"

"Yes, Salvatore, you employ a maid. One maid. A girl who shakes in fear in your presence, so intimidating does she find you. One maid is simply not enough; there is too much for her to do, so I have decided to help her in this simple task, at least."

Salvatore was taken aback by his wife's tone. He had never heard her speak so forthrightly to him.

"What is she doing that prevents her from preparing the dinner?" he barked.

"I have sent her to Coniglio to the pharmacy. I am in urgent need of the tonic Dottor Gasperini prepares for me. Since you will not allow me to go there myself, I had no option but to send Imperia." She paused, waiting for him to look at her. When he did, she continued, her tone loaded with sarcasm. "I trust that meets with your approval?"

The flash of fury that crossed Salvatore's face was so strong Isabella thought he might strike her. Instead, he grunted, turned on his heel and left the room.

Chapter Twenty-Nine

By four, Isabella was back in her room, having checked on the girls in the day room and looked through the window at Tommaso who was working off his energy charging around the formal garden, the only part of the grounds where Salvatore would currently allow him to play. Her mind was preoccupied with thoughts of a future thousands of kilometres from this prison, a future that couldn't come soon enough.

The brief knock on the door surprised her, especially when she recognised it as coming from Imperia's hesitant hand.

"Come in, Imperia," she called, puzzled that the girl was back so soon. She had hardly had time to reach the pharmacy and return; she could not possibly have also seen her family. As Imperia entered the room, her eyes on the floor and her hands shaking, Isabella's stomach twisted immediately into ropes of anguish, the dreadful foreboding she had tried to put to the back of her mind gripping her once again.

"What is it, Imperia? What has happened?"

She stood up from her writing desk and walked quickly over to her maid, putting an arm around her shoulders.

"You're shaking all over. Sit here and tell me what it is that ails you."

Imperia allowed herself to be guided to a chaise longue where Isabella eased her down and sat next to her.

Isabella's first thought was that Imperia had been attacked, violated. She had taken one look at the so-called estate patrol Salvatore had employed and forbidden the children from having anything to do with them. But she knew they lurked in the forest, just out of view. For once, she didn't want Salvatore to go away again and leave her at their mercy.

Imperia was still shuddering. "It's the dottore, Marchesa," she said, looking up at Isabella. "He's disappeared."

This was the last thing Isabella had expected to hear. "Disappeared? What do you mean?"

Imperia sniffed and rubbed her nose furiously with her forefinger. "I went to the pharmacy, just as you instructed, Marchesa, only to find it was locked and bolted. It's never like that normally so I rang the bell, but there was no answer. As I think you know, next to the pharmacy is a small haberdashery, run by Signora Foschini, the sister of my aunt's husband, the aunt being on my mother's side."

"Yes, yes," said Isabella, not too interested in the family connections.

"Signora Foschini was quite surprised to see me, thinking I was still in Garda, but after I'd briefly told her my news, I asked about the pharmacy and she told me Dottor Gasperini had gone missing about four weeks ago."

"Four *weeks* ago! What did she mean, 'gone missing'?"

"She said it was on a market day, a Saturday. The village was busy even though the weather had turned overcast and the day was rather cool. The dottore had been in his shop that morning, Signora Foschini herself had been there to collect some medicine from him. He closed up the shop around lunchtime and went home for his lunch. His housekeeper didn't hear him leave again and he said nothing about where he might be going. She knows he left because the overcoat he wears for walks together with his hat and cane were all gone."

"And there has been no sign of him? What does his father, the physician, say?"

"He knows no more than anyone else. He has organised searches in the woods and forests, in case the dottore had an accident and was unable to walk. Groups of villagers scoured the woodland for many kilometres, including going onto the Brocanti estate and the other, smaller one beyond it towards Arezzo."

"Did your aunt, or whatever she is, did she say how the dottore seemed that Saturday morning? Was he different in any way? Preoccupied? Did he mention any plans?"

"Signora Foschini remembers nothing out of the ordinary, no. And neither does the dottore's housekeeper. It is a complete mystery and still the talk of the village. The Gasperini family are beside themselves with worry."

Isabella sat back, her hands in her lap. She felt as if she had been struck, but beneath the shock, her mind was working out times and dates. Four weeks ago. Salvatore had still been in Rome, or at least, that's where he said he was. He had been different when he returned and ordered their immediate departure for Tuscany, more like his old distracted self with less time for the children. When they forced their attentions upon him on the train, something he had encouraged them to do when they first went north to the Garda house, his response seemed less natural, as if he were preoccupied and acting a part.

His attitude towards Isabella herself had not changed at all; he was as distant as ever, but if anything his mood was darker, his face folding into a scowl whenever he was near her. But, unusually, he had been monosyllabic in his responses about the commission in Rome. Normally he would at least sing his own praises for a while; this time there was almost nothing. Again, she questioned whether he had been to Rome at all. But if he hadn't, where had he been? Had he been undertaking more work on the villa? She hadn't been outside since their return, perhaps she should take a look.

After thanking Imperia for returning so quickly, Isabella fetched a shawl, made her way downstairs and walked out onto the gravelled driveway. She turned to look up at the main part of the villa where Salvatore had spent so many months sequestered away undertaking heaven knew what.

It didn't appear to be any different; the shutters were all closed tight against the walls, forbidding and cold. She walked onto a lawn, farther from the villa so she could get a more general view.

She sighed. It was potentially such a lovely building, grand with a fine entrance, all unused. It was a terrible waste.

"What are you doing, Isabella?"

She jumped; she hadn't heard him approaching across the grass.

"Salvatore. You gave me a fright."

"I asked you what you were doing."

She sighed, sick of his petulance. "I heard you. I should have thought it was obvious, I am taking some air. I've been cooped up in the apartment all day either in my room or in the kitchen doing the maid's work."

Salvatore shrugged. "That is your own fault; you are the one who sent her on an errand."

"Yes, it is. And what a tale she returned with."

"I shouldn't expect a maid to return with anything else but village gossip; it's what they thrive on."

"This is more than gossip, Salvatore, this is a cause for great concern. Dottor Gasperini, the pharmacist, has gone missing."

"Gone missing? What is that supposed to mean?"

"It means he walked out of his house one day after lunch, with his coat, hat and cane, and has never been seen again."

As she looked up into her husband's eyes to watch his reaction, she thought she saw a flash of concern fly fleetingly across his face, but it didn't seem to be concern for the pharmacist, rather his focus moved distinctly to the villa.

He shrugged, affecting a nonchalance Isabella had seldom seen in him.

"Have they searched the forests? If a man had an accident deep in these woods, the chances are he'd never be found. Too many animals around for a start. Haven't you heard the wolves at night?"

"Salvatore! That's a terrible thing to say."

Another shrug. "He wouldn't be the first, that's all I mean. Now, I really don't think it's a good idea for you to be wandering around this part of the garden. It's rather unkempt at present."

"That's hardly surprising since you laid off all the garden staff. The oafs you have on patrol aren't the types to lift a spade."

"They are necessary," he snapped. "There have been burglaries, robberies. Worse. I don't want you to worry your head with them, Isabella, and certainly the children mustn't know, but having these oafs, as you call them, is for your own good."

"What robberies have there been? Nothing has happened here, has it? While we've been away?"

Salvatore was becoming edgy, distracted. He wanted her gone. He'd forgotten all about Ugo's hat and cane. They were still in the storeroom at the back of the house where he'd left them. The doors were locked, but they couldn't remain there. He needed to retrieve them and dispose of them.

"As I said, Isabella, it isn't a good idea for you to be wandering in this part of the garden, and certainly not at the back. I was there earlier and I saw two snakes in two separate places. Vipers. A child can die from a viper bite. An adult too."

"You have seen poisonous snakes in the garden? Salvatore, Tommaso has been playing there all day. What are you thinking of?"

His lie had caught him out. "No, not that part, the other part. I saw them in the other part, the old kitchen garden. Tommaso isn't allowed to go there."

"Tommaso is an adventurous boy with a mind of his own. And you know how it is with children and their imaginations. His flights of fancy when he is playing could easily lead him to stray beyond his boundaries."

"Then perhaps he should remain in the apartment. Yes, that would be better."

Isabella was shocked. "No, Salvatore! That would be most unfair. You have encouraged him to expand his horizons in all your activities with him at Garda, you surely can't confine him to the apartment here, he would become impossible."

She watched her husband draw himself up, the tension of his anger starting to get the better of him. She waited for the explosion, knowing her defiance and replies to him were more than he would normally tolerate. But with the news of Ugo's disappearance at the forefront of her mind, together with Salvatore's apparent indifference to it, she was in no mood herself to be submissive.

But the explosion didn't come. Instead, Salvatore turned to walk away.

"Perhaps you are right," he said, looking back over his shoulder. "However, for now, today, please return to the apartment. I myself shall make a thorough search of the gardens near the house for any snakes and remove them. After that, it will be safe for Tommaso to play there. The girls too, for that matter."

With that, he strode away purposefully towards the far end of the villa and climbed the ornamental steps leading to the rear.

Isabella watched him go. Although she was confused by their conversation, she had lost interest in his strange ways and anyway, she wouldn't have to tolerate them for much longer. But as the implications of Ugo's disappearance on her plans wormed their way back into her thoughts she knew she couldn't proceed without her lover; she couldn't possibly succeed alone. And yet she couldn't stay here with Salvatore.

Her shoulders sagging with the despair that had swept away her happiness, she dragged herself back to her room in the apartment. Alone at last, she burst into tears as she threw herself onto the bed, her arms beating the pillows in anger and frustration.

Chapter Thirty

Salvatore had expected Isabella would hear the news of the pharmacist's disappearance within a few days, but that it came so quickly surprised him. Now it had, he was eager to complete the sordid business of her removal from his life.

His plan was simple and he could see no reason why it should fail. He was particularly looking forward to the part where Isabella would become aware that the rotting body of the pharmacist was nearby, but beyond her reach.

However, there were arrangements to be made. Firstly he would announce he was going to Naples for another commission. And this time he really was going south, although only as far as Rome and not for any commission. He was a man, powerful and vital, and since he no longer found Isabella remotely desirable, her body sullied by the despicable pharmacist, he needed to find satisfaction elsewhere. With the intense work of the past few months and the need to become closer to his children, there had been no opportunities for him. Two weeks with his favourite courtesans in Rome would more than fulfil his needs, after which he would spend the following two weeks back at the Garda house ensuring everything was perfect for the children. He would have their rooms redecorated, employ governesses to attend to their education, perhaps even buy three ponies so they could all ride the estate together. He knew they would miss their mother to start with, it was inevitable, but he planned to occupy their lives to the full, leaving no time for sadness. They would soon forget about her, especially when they discovered she had deserted them.

During his four weeks away, he knew Isabella would be beside herself with anguish over the missing pharmacist. With no news of her lover's fate, and no opportunity to leave the estate, she would be frustrated and distracted, unable to make rational decisions. By the time he returned, she would be putty in his hands.

At that point he would need an excuse for sending the children ahead to Garda. He still hadn't finalised how he was going to do this, but he had a notion to summon the new governesses to introduce them, after which they would return to Garda with the children while he remained at the villa with Isabella. Perhaps he would pretend renewed affections for his faithless wife, suggest they needed to spend some time alone together, maybe a trip to an island in the Tyrrhenian Sea. It was pure fantasy, of course. Once the children had departed, he would waste no time entrapping Isabella and leaving her to her fate.

But first, there was one more thing to do before he could guarantee they would be alone in the villa.

The morning after Isabella learned of Ugo's disappearance, Salvatore was deliberately a little late for his breakfast. Entering the dining room, he found his wife in a state of confusion as she alternated between setting the table and ringing the bell for Imperia.

"Where is the wretched girl? Delfina, will you please go to Imperia's room and knock politely. She might be ill. No, perhaps I should go myself. Why don't you cut some fruit for your sister." She looked up. "Ah, Salvatore, you will have to wait for your breakfast, it seems Imperia is indisposed."

Salvatore sat at the head of the table and watched her fussing, saying nothing for a few minutes. Finally he coughed to attract her attention.

"She is not indisposed, Isabella," he said, "she is no longer in my employ. I have dismissed her with two weeks' wages in lieu of notice. Most generous, I should say. She left late last night."

Isabella froze, the hand that had been reaching for a plate now stationary in midair.

"You did *what?*" she screeched, not even trying to moderate her tone. "Have you gone completely mad? How are we going to cope with no staff at all? Do you expect me to carry out *all* the household chores? Cook the meals? Clean the rooms? Change the bed linen? Empty the chamberpots?"

Salvatore shrugged, the action infuriating Isabella further. "It is only for a month, after which we shall be returning to Garda where the full complement of staff remains awaiting your every whim."

"So why didn't you wait until we leave? Why dismiss her now?"

"It's quite simple, Isabella. She was an insolent girl who did not know her place. She answered me back once too often."

"That, Salvatore, is egregious nonsense. Imperia found it hard even to look at you, let alone speak. The very thought of her being insolent is laughable. Why are you doing this to me? You are making my life intolerable."

Salvatore stood and pushed his chair back. "Are you telling me you are incapable of looking after yourself and your three children? What kind of mother are you?"

Isabella bristled; she was within a whisker of losing control, but she wouldn't give her husband the satisfaction. "I am perfectly capable of looking after them, and myself. As long as your oafs arrange for the food that is delivered to the gate to be taken to the kitchen, I shall prepare our meals. *Our* meals, Salvatore, not yours. If you want breakfast, luncheon or dinner, you can prepare them yourself."

Salvatore's smile was supercilious. "I shall have no need to do that. I am leaving today for Naples. When I return in four weeks' time, we shall depart immediately for Garda. The children will be far happier there. Coming back here was a mistake."

He turned his back on her and walked out of the room. As the door closed, Isabella picked up a glass from the table and threw it at the door with all the force she could muster. "Tyrant!" she screeched, and sagged to the floor. For one brief moment, she was pleased there were no staff. There was no one apart from the shocked children to witness her outburst.

An hour later, Isabella watched from the window as Salvatore drove off in the chaise. With the large carriage still in Garda, there was now no transportation available to her apart from walking, but with four brutish men posted as guards to deter her, walking far would require some planning.

Later, having fed the children their lunch, she acceded to Tommaso's pleas to play outside. "You may, Tommaso, but go no farther than the garden. You must not enter the forest, is that clear?"

"Yes, Mamma. Don't worry, I know my way around."

She smiled at him. To look at, he was a miniature Salvatore, but in temperament, he couldn't be more different. She hoped he would remain so as he grew.

With the girls drawing in the playroom, Isabella paced her own room devising a way of escaping the guards and getting to the village. She had to get more information about Ugo, and she had to find Imperia to see what had happened.

The children were still tired after their journey from Garda and over an early dinner, Isabella casually asked Tommaso about the guards.

"Do they watch you while you are playing? They must be bored patrolling the forest. Nothing ever happens. I should have thought they would enjoy watching your games; it would be a distraction for them."

Tommaso had a mischievous grin on his face. "They do watch me, Mamma, and they think they are so clever. They don't know I am also watching them."

He giggled to himself.

"Tommaso, what have you been up to?" Isabella laughed along with him.

The boy sat back in his chair and folded his arms, just as his father did when he was explaining something.

"I played a trick on them this afternoon. First, I waited until I knew they were there."

"How many of them, Tommaso? All of them?"

"No, Mamma, just two of them. The other two were at the gatehouse by the main gate. They never leave it; they are very lazy."

"What did you do?"

"When I knew they were watching, I walked slowly to the edge of the forest, and then I ran among the trees, zigzagging everywhere. I could hear them shouting to each other and running after me. I can run without making any noise, but then I hid under a fallen tree trunk and watched them looking for me. They were searching everywhere. At one point, I threw a small branch and they chased off in the direction of where they heard it hit the ground. It was very funny. Then, when they couldn't see me, I quickly ran back to the garden and carried on with my game. About ten minutes later they came rushing out of the trees, and then stopped, pretending that nothing had happened."

Giggling loudly at their brother's story, Delfina and Clara ran around the room pretending to be the guards, hiding behind the chairs and yelling "Boo!" as they jumped out.

Isabella smiled, a plan forming in her head. "Tommaso, my darling," she said. "You know how much Mamma needs to go to Coniglio, I have a number of things to get there, my medicine particularly, but Papa has said I mustn't go. He thinks it is dangerous, but I know the way very well and I know I shall be safe. Now, if I can avoid those oafish guards, I think I can get there and back without their even knowing. But I need your help."

"What about us?" cried the girls. "Can we play too?"

Isabella looked at them. They were too small to walk the six kilometres into Coniglio and even if they could make the journey, they would slow her down.

She smiled. "It's too far for you to go to Coniglio, my sweethearts, but there's something important you can do."

She waited until she had their full attention.

"While Tommaso is teasing the guards, I want you to watch, and every time you see Tommaso come back into the garden, I want you to yell his name as loudly as you can. When he hears you, he will run off again in another direction, and of course the guards will hear you and come running back through the trees. It will be great fun and they will get so confused. But you must stay indoors; I don't want you out in the garden as well while I am not here. It's all right for Tommaso, he can run very fast, easily faster than those fat guards, but you two are still too little."

Chapter Thirty-One

The following morning they were all ready. The girls were so excited that Isabella had to cajole them into eating their breakfast.

"I might well be away the whole day, my darlings, and although I am leaving you food for your lunch, it would be better for you to have a proper meal now. You are going to need lots of energy."

While they were eating, Isabella ran over the girls' roles with them again. Tommaso needed no reminders; he knew exactly what he was doing.

Isabella was surprised how easy it was to slip away while the guards were occupied with following Tommaso. She watched him in action for several minutes as he charged around the garden, after which he drew the guards away from the villa in the opposite direction from the one she was about to take. She couldn't help laughing to herself; Tommaso was in complete control of the situation, like a sheepdog herding its flock.

She waited several more endless minutes to allow Tommaso to lead the guards farther from the villa, after which she slipped quietly out of the door and hurried across the garden to the edge of the forest. The path was one she knew well, having followed it many times to meet Ugo, and a little over thirty minutes later she passed through the rear gate of the estate and turned towards Coniglio.

The hours Isabella spent in Coniglio were frustrating and ultimately unrewarding. Having located a distraught Imperia, she attempted to calm her with the news that, if she wished, she would soon be able to work again for Isabella under far better circumstances, as long as she was prepared to travel. But Imperia wouldn't be calmed. She didn't want to travel, and even if she did, going out of Italy as Isabella suggested they might was unthinkable. However, her prospects for employment locally had been shattered by her unceremonious dismissal, and although Isabella would provide a reference for her, it would not be the same as a full reference from her master, the marchese. It wasn't until Isabella suddenly giggled and exclaimed, "I have it, Imperia! I'll forge a reference from Salvatore. I have the crested notepaper and the official seal, and his signature is easy," that the girl relaxed a little.

With Imperia mollified, Isabella could concentrate on her main task of finding out more about Ugo's disappearance. But there was no more, and worse, when Imperia led her to Ugo's parents' house in a quiet lane in the smarter end of the village, she was treated rudely by the maid who answered the door. On hearing Isabella's name, the girl left her standing there while she fetched Ugo's father, the physician. Isabella had only met him once, a passing but formal introduction in Ugo's pharmacy. The man now blocking her way seemed to have aged ten years since that meeting, his whole frame shrunken with the experience of losing his only son. His tone was frosty, almost accusatory, as he told Isabella curtly he had no more news.

"I regret that I have been forced to accept that my son has been the victim of some dreadful accident in the forest."

"Dottore," pleaded Isabella, reaching out a hand to touch the physician's arm, "I—"

But she got no further. Gasperini recoiled from her touch, as if it would contaminate him in some way.

"There is nothing more to say, Marchesa. I bid you good day."

As the door closed in Isabella's face, she felt dirty, her affair with Ugo clearly common knowledge. She thought she had detected a few mutterings behind raised hands as she walked through the village. Now she knew. She was the woman, the *married* woman, a member of the aristocracy no less, who had wantonly led the hapless Ugo Gasperini astray and been indirectly responsible for his death. For dead they assumed he was. After all, if he had run off with her, firstly, she wouldn't be here now looking for him, and secondly, no matter how disgraceful running off with her would be, he would surely have had the decency to write to his parents and his sister to assure them of his safety.

A dispirited Isabella trudged heavily back to where Imperia was waiting for her on the lane.

"Is there no one else I can turn to for information?" she asked imploringly.

Imperia shook her head. "I don't think so, Marchesa. I heard that the dottore's father checked the records in the pharmacy to find the names of everyone who had bought anything on the day the dottore disappeared. Apparently no one thought he was anything but his normal quiet and professional self."

She paused, hesitating. Isabella picked up on her discomfort. "What is it, Imperia?"

The girl averted her eyes from Isabella's. "I didn't want to tell you, Marchesa, but there have been rumours in the village."

"Rumours?"

"Yes, rumours. Rumours about you and the dottore. I think the dottore's mother has been spreading them. She's a highly religious woman and the thought of scandal besmirching her husband's family's name is more than she can bear."

"So why is she spreading rumours?"

"To put all the blame on you, Marchesa. In her account, her son is a blameless victim."

Isabella shuddered. "If that's the case, I think there is nothing else for me in this village. I'd best leave before the priest starts running after me down the street threatening eternal damnation. I know I am not blameless, but—"

"I understand, Marchesa," said Imperia, touching Isabella's

arm. She paused, hesitant again. "Marchesa. I … I have been thinking about my future and I think it would be better if I do not travel to France with you. I hope you understand."

"Of course, Imperia. Do what you think is best. When I return to the villa, I shall produce the references you need. I'll leave them under the stone by the rear gate to the estate, the one we've used in the past for messages from Ugo. However, I don't think references from either me or my husband will be of much value to you in Coniglio. Maybe you should try farther afield. Anghiari, perhaps, or Sansepolcro."

"Thank you, Marchesa."

"No, Imperia, thank you. You have been a loyal maid; I shall miss you terribly. I hope one day we shall meet in happier circumstances, perhaps when you have met someone of your own."

She laughed as Imperia blushed. "Smile for me, Imperia. I want to remember you smiling."

She held out her arms and hugged the girl, taking her by surprise, and then, as quickly as she had done it, she turned on her heel and walked away.

In spite of walking as fast as she could, it still took Isabella the better part of two hours to get back to the villa. There was less than an hour of daylight left, but it didn't concern her. She was expecting to find the three children ready to regale her with tales of Tommaso and his antics with the guards, and thoughts of this helped to lighten her mood.

When she finally arrived, she was initially surprised to find the apartment was completely silent, but, she thought to herself, perhaps the day has exhausted the children: they are probably all asleep in the playroom.

She was partly right. As she gently pushed open the playroom door, she could see both girls stretched out on cushions on the floor. But there was no sign of Tommaso. She tiptoed along to his bedroom, but clearly he hadn't been back there since that morning. More concerned now, she hurried to the other rooms in the apartment, but there was no sign anywhere of her son.

Returning to the playroom, she gently shook Delfina from her sleep.

"Mamma," said Delfina, as she stretched, yawned and reached for her spectacles. "Why have you been so long?"

"Delfina, where is Tommaso? Is he hiding somewhere, playing one of his games?"

Delfina frowned. "I don't think so. I haven't seen him for ages."

"What do you mean, you haven't seen him for ages?" Isabella's voice had risen without her intending it to.

"Mamma, you're shouting," said Delfina through pouted lips.

"Mamma?" Clara was now awake and immediately moved across to where Isabella had knelt on the floor. She threw her arms around her mother.

"Listen, girls," said Isabella, her voice now calmer. "Does either of you know where Tommaso is? It's important. It will be getting dark soon. Is he still outside?"

The girls looked guiltily at each other as if Tommaso not being there was somehow their fault.

"He was teasing the guards," said Delfina, quickly adding as a defence for Tommaso, "like you told him to do, Mamma. It was very funny because the guards didn't know where he was and even when they saw him, it was only for a moment, and he was gone. Then one of the guards called to the other one. They stood together talking for a bit and then walked off around the side of the villa where we can't see."

"What about Tommaso? Could you see him while they were talking?"

"Oh yes," said Delfina. "I saw him hiding behind a tree, watching them. When they walked away, Tommaso looked up to us, pointed into the forest and waved. Then he walked off into the trees."

"And what happened next? Did he come back?"

"No, Mamma," chimed in Clara before Delfina could continue. She wanted to give her version of the story.

"No?"

"No. We waited here by the window for ages looking for him, but he didn't come back to the garden. Then we got hungry and went to the kitchen for some food. Delfi thought Tommaso might be there, but he wasn't."

Isabella hurried over to the window with the best view of the garden and looked out.

Turning to her daughters, she said, "It's starting to get dark so I'm going to fetch a lantern and go into the garden to look for Tommaso. He must be hiding somewhere, silly boy. He's probably fallen asleep."

Out of nowhere, a memory of Salvatore's talk of vipers crashed into her mind. She gasped. Perhaps he had been bitten and was lying injured. She had to search.

"Can we come too, Mamma?" wailed both the girls.

"I don't think so. It would be better if you stayed here."

"But Mamma," objected Delfina, "you've been out all day. We don't want to be alone any more. Please let us come with you."

Isabella sighed. "Oh, very well. But quickly now, get a shawl, both of you, it's cooling down. I'll go to the kitchen and light three lanterns, one for each of us. There are some smaller ones you'll be able to carry."

Five minutes later, they were in the garden. Isabella put down her lantern and cupped her hands to her mouth. "Tommaso!" she called, as loudly as she could, but the sound hardly seemed to travel before it was soaked up by the darkening forest. "Tommaso!"

"Tommaso! Where are you?" screamed both girls, after which Delfina added, "Come out from where you're hiding. You mustn't frighten Mamma."

"Right, girls, pick up your lanterns and walk close behind me. We're going to go a little way into the forest. Maybe it will help to be in amongst the trees, I don't know, but we'll try from there, shall we?"

They walked about a hundred metres into the trees, stopping in a small clearing. Isabella was both surprised and concerned how much darker it was now the sky couldn't be seen. All three called Tommaso's name loud and long, but each time the sound faded to nothing and they were left with no more than a squawk or two from disturbed birds and the background chatter of summer insects.

"Tommaso! Tesoro, please!" yelled Isabella again, this time the panic sounding in her voice.

She sighed. "Listen, girls, I think Mamma should go and ask the guards if they have seen Tommaso. Maybe after all his antics, he's actually made friends with them and he's at their hut by the main gate."

"We're coming too, Mamma," insisted Delfina, her tone indicating there was no choice in the matter.

Making their way around the apartment end of the villa, they followed the tree-lined gravelled drive that curved its way to the estate's main gate some six hundred metres away. There, a small single-storey building, originally designed as a head groundsman's lodge, served as shelter for the four guards. Owing to both the distance and the many trees bordering the drive, the villa could not be seen from the guardhouse.

The girls both wanted to hold Isabella's hand but it was impossible whilst carrying the lanterns. Instead, their mother told them to hold onto her skirt, one child on either side of her as she held up her lantern in the encroaching darkness.

In the gloom, with a backdrop of trees, there was nothing to be seen of the guardhouse but candlelight flickering in the windows. As they approached, the muffled sound of voices became louder, and Isabella heard a sudden belch and a roar of laughter from inside.

She paused and dropped to her knees by the girls. "Delfina, Clara, I think it would be better if you both stayed here by the edge of the gravel. The guards are coarse men whose manners leave much to be desired. I doubt they would know how to behave correctly in the presence of noble young ladies. You need not be frightened, I have no intention of entering that building. I am going to speak to the guards from the doorway where you will be able to see me the whole time."

The girls nodded obediently and walked to the edge of the drive.

"Put your lanterns on the ground so you don't get tired from carrying them, but don't let go of the handles."

"Yes, Mamma," whispered the girls in unison.

Isabella hurried to the guardhouse and knocked on the partly open door.

"Hello?" she called out. "May I speak with one of you?"

Four heads shot round at the sound of the voice.

"What the …? Who are you? Where did you come from? This is private property, you can't go in." One of the men stood and took a couple of steps towards her.

In the flickering, shadow-filled light, he was a gruesome sight. Tall and well-built, but overweight with the patchy, reddened complexion of a heavy drinker, rheumy eyes and a bulbous, misshapen nose latticed with tortured veins, he towered over Isabella. A sneer of recognition slowly distorted one side of his face.

"The marchese said you might come, try to sweet talk us. Surprised it's taken so long seeing what a fine bunch of stallions we is."

There was a snigger from somewhere behind him and the sound of a chair scraping as one of the other guards made to stand up. But the man held out one arm to his left, stopping whichever of his colleagues was thinking of joining him.

"I'll deal with this," he growled.

Isabella swallowed her fear and looked the man in the eye. "Since you appear to be in charge and you know who I am, I'll get straight to the point. I need—"

"The point, your *highness*," interrupted the man, the mockery in his voice chilling, "is we ain't permitted to talk to you. About nuffin'. Don't matter what you say, the marchese's told us, no matter what, we ain't to converse."

"But—"

"But nuffin. I told yer, we're guarding the villa, guarding you, but we have to guard ourselves too. The marchese said we keeps our distance, said that if we talk to you, you'll likely put a spell on us. Lure us, that was the word, *lure* us with your sweet talk, con us into doing whatever you wanted. Said if he found out we'd spoken to you, we would get no bonus, might not even get paid at all. And that wouldn't do, would it, boys?"

"Too right," replied one of them. "Tell the bitch to get her fancy arse back to the villa before I picks her up and carries her there. And if I do, I might just be tempted to stroke that fancy arse and whatever else I find under that skirt. The marchese didn't say nuffin about not doing that."

Ignoring him and the sniggers from the others, Isabella tried to get through their resistance, appeal to their better nature, if such a thing existed.

"You don't understand! My son Tommaso, he's gone missing. One of you must have seen—"

The chief guard was shaking his head. "What is it about you aristos? Don't you listen? Didn't you hear what I just said? We. Won't. Talk. To. You."

He spat out each word, emphasising each one by pointing an index finger at Isabella as he said it.

As he said 'You!' he continued pointing past Isabella towards the villa. "Now, get back to the villa! That's our instructions. Keep you in the villa, using force if necessary."

Isabella took a step backwards, and then another.

"He's lost!" she cried.

"Not my business," growled the man. "Now go before I let Marco have his way."

There was more scraping of chairs on floorboards. Isabella turned and hurried back to the girls.

"Come, girls, we have to go back to the villa," she said, her voice urgent. It wasn't herself she was afraid for, but her daughters must not be put in harm's way.

As they hurried away, the man's voice called out from the doorway of the guardhouse.

"Ran into the woods. Hours ago. We ain't seen him since."

Isabella stopped and turned, hoping he might have changed his mind, but as she did, the door slammed and all she heard was some more muffled laughter.

By the time they reached the main door to the apartment, the darkness was complete. Isabella paused as she held up the light to the door and turned towards the garden and forest beyond.

"Tommaso!" she yelled, as loudly as she could. The girls joined in, Clara's effort more of a screech than a name. The sound died in the darkness along with their hopes of finding him that night.

"We shall have to wait until the morning," said Isabella. "We'd become hopelessly lost if we continued searching now. I am sure your brother is safely curled up under a bush somewhere, so fast asleep he can't hear us."

She hoped the girls were too young to hear the lack of conviction in her voice.

"Let's do the same, shall we?" she added as brightly as she could. "We'll have something to eat and then go to bed. As soon as it's light in the morning, we'll get into the forest and find him."

Clara pulled at Isabella's skirt. "Mamma? Can we …?"

"Yes, amore," answered Isabella, anticipating the question. "You can both sleep in Mamma's bed. If we're together, we won't be frightened."

The girls were soon asleep, but, lying between them, Isabella lay awake for hours, her mind an agitated jumble of worry about Tommaso and anger at Salvatore for creating the nightmare situation that was now potentially risking their son's life. Finally, the disconnected thoughts became the random, illogical and fragmented imagery of semiconsciousness, although the sleep that followed was anything but restful.

Chapter Thirty-Two

Aware of a sudden silence after the torture of her dreams, Isabella snapped awake, the peace of her bedroom and the sleeping forms of the girls beside her filling her with a welcome contentment for a fraction of a second before the memory of the previous day exploded in her mind and left her gasping for breath.

"Tommaso," she whimpered, swallowing the word so as not to wake the girls.

The soft, grey, first light of dawn was making its way into the room. Isabella lifted herself carefully from the bed, trying to avoid disturbing her daughters, and hurried to the kitchen.

The three of them would need breakfast and they would need food for later if their search proved to be a long one. Water too, since it would be thirsty work, and Tommaso, when they found him, would be parched.

Retrieving two large flat loaves Imperia had made two days before, she prepared a platter of cold meats and cheeses for their breakfast, after which she wrapped a generous supply of the same in a clean cloth which she put in a small bag she could sling over her shoulder. Filling flasks with water, she caught sight of the remains of a piece of hard crust from one of the loaves. Is it really only two days since Imperia was here? she thought in horror. It seems a lifetime ago.

. . .

With the light intensity increasing by the minute, Isabella was impatient to get on with the search. When she returned to her bedroom, the girls were still fast asleep, but there was no way she could leave them. She was disinclined to let them out of her sight ever again.

Rousing them gently, she wiped the sleepiness from their eyes with a damp cloth, dressed them in suitably rugged clothes for trudging through the forest and found their sturdiest walking shoes.

"Let's hurry, my darlings. We'll have something to eat quickly before we go, otherwise we'll have no energy to keep searching for Tommaso." She tried to keep her tone light; she knew the search would be made all the more difficult with the girls in tow, but there was simply no choice.

"I won't need food, Mamma," insisted Delfina, lifting her chin as a challenge to the world. "I'm going to search and search for Tommaso all day until we find him."

"That's very brave of you, amore, but a little food now will help you a lot later on, believe me."

"How long will it take?" asked Clara.

Isabella sighed. How long indeed?

"I hope not too long, tesoro, Tommaso hasn't eaten since his breakfast yesterday. He will be ravenous, and thirsty too," She smiled at the girls, still wanting to lighten the situation for them. "If we stand in the forest making no noise at all, we might even hear his tummy rumbling."

As the three of them crossed the garden in the direction of the forest, Isabella felt the immensity of the task pressing down on her. If Tommaso was lying injured somewhere, he might not have the strength to answer their calls; they would have to search every last corner of a huge area. She quietly cursed the Brocanti family. What was the point of owning hundreds of hectares of forest when no one ever entered them? They might look for weeks and find nothing. Dottor Gasperini had sent a team of people to search for Ugo and had not been able to find him. They, on the other hand, were one adult and two small children who would quickly tire.

Fighting to dismiss the enormous difficulties they faced, she stopped and turned to the girls. "I've been thinking, my darlings, this forest is big and we don't want to waste time. The trees all look identical after a while so we must be careful not to search the same place twice. Tell me, did Tommaso ever say whether he had a favourite place he liked to go to? A camp he'd made, perhaps, or a bush he liked to hide under?"

The girls wrinkled their brows, trying to think of any secrets Tommaso had told them. He had, of course, boasted of many exploits in the forest, exaggerated stories about the wild and dangerous animals he had seen and chased off, the vast lakes he had swum to save an injured bird. They gave Isabella garbled versions of what they could remember, but she quickly saw they were of little value. But not wanting to dampen their spirits, she suggested they keep their eyes peeled in case they saw anything that looked like the things Tommaso had described.

"And perhaps while we're doing that, we should look to see if there are any pathways Tommaso has made by going the same way many times, any patches of grass he has trodden down. Shall we do that to start with?"

It seemed a good idea, and initially, close to the garden, they found a number of places where the grass was flattened. They followed each of these paths, but none of them led anywhere of value, each of them fading the farther they walked into the forest until the path disappeared.

It was frustrating and tiring, and by mid-morning, the girls were too exhausted to carry on. But Isabella couldn't stop; there were still many hours of daylight left. Finding a clearing, she sat the girls down and said she needed to carry on alone while they had a rest.

"What I'm going to do, my sweethearts, is walk off in that direction," she said, pointing roughly in the direction of the sun. "Every minute or so, I'm going to call out to you. When you hear me, I want you to call back. Then I'll know where you are and that you are all right. When I call and I don't hear you answer, I'll turn round and come back. Then I'll head off in another direction and we'll do the same, calling to each other. Before long,

I'll have searched quite a big area and you will have had a nice rest."

As a plan, it worked. Refreshed after an hour's rest, the girls joined Isabella once again to widen the search. But no matter which direction they took, nor how systematic they were, there were no signs that either Tommaso or anyone else had been in the forest.

Isabella was aware how easy it would be for them to become disoriented and lose their way in such a large area. She had no desire to spend a night lost in the forest with or without the girls, and she tried where possible to take note of the more recognisable glades and clearings they came across, tying pieces of ribbon to trees at the points where they entered and exited to help retrace their steps.

By mid-afternoon, the girls were running out of energy. Not wanting to carry a sleepy Clara, Isabella reluctantly turned round to head back to the villa. As they walked, they all continued to called out Tommaso's name, but to their disappointment, they neither found nor heard anything to indicate they were on the right track.

As they got closer to the villa, Isabella was relieved to find that she recognised various glades and stands of trees, and when the path leading from the villa to the rear gate of the estate appeared in front of them, she breathed a sigh of relief.

Back in the apartment, she helped the girls to wash and change into fresh clothes, and she was just able to feed them before they were both sound asleep on cushions on the floor of the playroom. Not wanting to disturb them, she fetched blankets and quilts to cover them, and made herself comfortable on the chaise longue.

By the end of two more days of searching, Isabella was becoming desperate. Tommaso had been missing for a total of four days. If he were lying in the forest, and she could think of nowhere else he might be, the situation would by now be critical for him. The guards were nowhere to be seen, although she suspected at least two of them kept an eye on her when she was near the house. As for when she and the girls went farther into the forest, the guards would know they couldn't go far, the girls were too young.

She contemplated going to Coniglio to seek help. If no one else, Imperia would volunteer. But it was too far for the girls to go. Their energy was decreasing each day, and since Tommaso had disappeared during her last trip there, she couldn't risk leaving them alone in the apartment.

On the morning of the fifth day since Tommaso's disappearance, the girls were fractious, their tiredness from the endless walking through the forest, their constant shouting of their brother's name and their fear of what might have happened to him all conspiring to dampen their spirits. At breakfast, an argument broke out between them over which boiled egg belonged to whom and when Isabella, herself on a short fuse, intervened, Delfina stormed out of the room. From the hallway outside the kitchen she yelled that she hated her sister and that she intended to break all her dolls.

"Delfina!" yelled Isabella.

"Mamma, she can't!" screamed Clara and hared off after her sister.

As Isabella stood wearily, intending to follow and wondering what she could do to restore peace, there was another scream from farther along the hallway. "Mamma! Quickly, Mamma!"

Thinking one or more of the guards had had the temerity to disobey Salvatore's instructions and enter the apartment, Isabella dashed into the hallway. Looking along it she saw the door at the end beyond the foot of the stairs was wide open, the door leading into the closed part of the villa, the door Salvatore always kept locked, the key always with him.

"Mamma!" It was Delfina's voice coming from the darkness beyond the doorway. "I've hurt my leg. Quickly, Mamma!"

Clara appeared from the darkness. "Delfi's hurt her leg, Mamma."

Isabella rushed through the doorway and now, with the light behind her, she could see Delfina sitting on the floor rubbing her shin. It was clear the injury was a minor one, the shock of it happening unexpectedly frightening the girl, her angry state amplifying her reaction.

"Delfina! What happened?"

Delfina looked up accusingly at her mother as if what had happened was all her fault. "Clara was chasing me and as I turned to run up the stairs, I tripped. I reached out to stop myself falling and my hands grabbed the door handle. I didn't know it would open; it's always locked. Why did you unlock it? I hurt my leg as I fell through it."

Isabella knelt to console her, looking along the corridor into the darkness as she did.

"I didn't unlock the door, amore. I don't have a key. Only Papa has a key."

"So why is it unlocked?"

"I don't know, amore. I don't know."

Chapter Thirty-Three

Tommaso was a confused and resentful eight-year-old. Confused because his overbearing father was inconsistent in his behaviour towards him and his sisters — one day he would be kind and thoughtful, paying them much attention, while other days, most days, he would act as if they were nothing but an irritation to him, snapping at them constantly or ignoring them completely. And resentful because Papa was always so nasty to Mamma, his words hurtful and unkind.

Like many children in that situation, Tommaso wondered in his heart whether his father's behaviour was the result of anything he had done. Was it his fault?

But whatever was behind his father's behaviour, Tommaso still yearned for his affection. The time they had spent recently in Garda had been special for him. Papa had been full of fun, taking him and the girls out sledging, horse riding and hiking, and to wonderful cafés in the town that were full of amazing cakes. The only sad part was that Mamma never came with them.

Tommaso had also been delighted when he was finally allowed to go outside to play in the garden at the villa in Tuscany. Like his father, he had a vivid imagination and in his games, the garden and forest became magical kingdoms packed with excitement, dream-like places from another world.

He was also fascinated by his father's skills as an artist and he wondered if he might be the same when he grew up. He could certainly draw quite well although he had never dared to show Papa his efforts. Before he did that, he wanted Papa to show him how he painted, how he created the incredibly lifelike images of people on his canvases. But Papa always seemed too busy, too distracted.

On the occasions when Salvatore returned to the apartment during the months when he was creating one trompe l'oeil after another, Tommaso devised ways of following him. He would watch him from the shadows, particularly when he took the key from his pocket and opened the door to the forbidden part of the villa. The key was large, not on a ring with others, but kept separately in one of Salvatore's trouser pockets. Did he keep it somewhere in his room, the one Mamma no longer visited, or did he take it with him when he went out or went to Garda? To Tommaso, taking it to Garda seemed illogical. After all, he might lose it. Suppose there was no other key? Papa would have to break down the door. No, it was far more likely that he hid it somewhere.

Once Tommaso had convinced himself of this, he was determined to find out where the key was hidden. Whenever he could, he would follow his father around the apartment, keeping his distance so his father remained unaware of his presence. He would listen at his father's door when he went to his room, listening for sounds of drawers or cupboards being opened.

One day, his father even left the door to his room ajar and from the gloom of the corridor outside, Tommaso held his breath and watched him moving about his room. His spying was soon rewarded. Salvatore's habit when entering his room was to empty the contents of his pockets onto the top of his desk, and included among the assortment of nails, screws, a small notebook and pencils was the key.

After what seemed an eternity of watching, one day he finally saw his father take the key and place it inside a book he pulled from a long shelf full of books. The book was called *Republic* by someone called *Plato*. It looked new. Perhaps Papa hasn't yet read it, thought Tommaso.

The yearning to see inside the closed part of the villa grew in Tommaso like a creeper taking over his body. He knew instinctively he would be rewarded by seeing many fine paintings created by his father; all he needed now was the opportunity. However, Mamma would never allow it since Papa had given her strict instructions, instructions Tommaso had heard him repeat on many occasions.

"Under no circumstances, Isabella, are you or the children to set foot inside the area in which I have been working. There are still construction materials there, items that might fall or collapse. I don't want anybody to be injured."

His mother always nodded her head, but she did reply on more than one occasion that since the place was locked up and she had no key, she didn't see how she might achieve what he was forbidding anyway.

Tommaso remembered that when she spoke to Papa in this way, cross words would follow and Papa would storm out of the room.

On the day his mother announced she was going to defy Papa and walk to Coniglio while Tommaso distracted the guards, Tommaso saw his opportunity. He knew that once Mamma had gone and he had lain low for half an hour, the guards would get bored and go back to the guardhouse by the main gate. After that, he would have several hours in which to explore the villa. The only concern he had was that his sisters might see him and either make a fuss or insist on going with him. Neither option was acceptable to him. He was on a secret mission, he didn't want silly baby girls in the way. Therefore, once he emerged from his hiding place in the forest, he made his way quickly and silently to the apartment and crept upstairs to check on his sisters. The apartment was quiet, which puzzled him, but when he carefully opened the playroom door and peered in, he saw that both girls had fallen asleep where they had been playing.

The next part of his plan made him feel more guilty than he

had ever felt in his life. He was about to defy Papa by entering his room without permission and taking the key from the book.

He crept into Salvatore's room, his movements exaggerated and overly cautious since even though he knew his father was hundreds of kilometres away, he couldn't shake off the feeling that his angry voice would suddenly boom across the room, demanding to know what he was doing.

The bookshelf was higher than he thought and he had to fetch a chair to stand on to reach it. And when he did finally pull the leather-bound book from the shelf, it was so heavy he nearly dropped it. His hands were still shaking from the effort as he placed it on the desk.

When he pulled the stiff cover open and found there was no key inside, he almost burst into tears. Frantically, he turned more pages, and it still wasn't there. His young brow puckered; he was sure it was the right book. He checked the title once again. Perhaps Papa had put it in another book the last time he had hidden it. Tommaso looked up to the long row of books. It would be hard work checking inside each one, most of them were bigger than the one he had taken down.

He sighed and stood back on the chair, peering as he did into the gap left by the book by Plato. And there it was. The key. Papa hadn't put it in the book, he had put it behind it.

Reaching into the gap, he took hold of the key and put it in his pocket, carefully replacing the Plato book so nothing looked disturbed. He was pleased with himself. In his mind, he was a spy collecting secrets, leaving behind no trace of his actions.

After putting the chair back in its place, Tommaso tiptoed down the stairs to the door leading into the forbidden part of the villa. Making sure he made no noise, he cautiously put the key into the keyhole and turned it, after which he pushed down on the handle and gently opened the door. To his delight, it moved silently. However, beyond the doorway, all he could see was the beginning of a corridor that disappeared quickly into darkness. If he shut the door after him, he wouldn't be able to see a thing, and yet he couldn't risk leaving the door open.

He ran to the cupboard in the kitchen where the lanterns were stored. Choosing one that wasn't too heavy, he checked the level of oil, lit the lamp and returned to the dark corridor. He thought about locking the door after him but decided against it. He didn't know what he was going to find and if he wanted to leave in a hurry, he didn't want to waste time fumbling for a key. Instead, he pocketed the key and closed the door. The girls would never dare even to touch the door or its handle, so whether it was locked or unlocked didn't matter.

The corridor he entered ran for several metres until it reached a flight of steep steps leading downwards. He held the lantern up high and took the steps slowly to the bottom where there was a closed door. Remembering other keys he had seen his father pull from his pocket, he prayed the door would be unlocked since he didn't want to waste time searching his father's room for more keys. To his huge relief, when he turned the door handle and pushed, the door swung open.

Ahead of him now was a huge room with a vaulted ceiling that, although empty, Tommaso knew must be one of the cantinas, the cellars beneath the entire villa that would have been used for storing wine, olive oil and all manner of produce in the days when the estate was fully productive.

He looked around the cantina, wondering where to go from here. He shone the light from the lantern onto the walls, looking for another door that might lead him somewhere. Not seeing one immediately, he walked several steps into the room, looking left and right. The door through which he had come entered the cellar about half way along its length, so part of it must run under the apartment. To his left, at the far end, he could see a door, but since he was sure it would lead to the outside, he decided to turn right.

He made his way through the shadowy silence until he reached a wall beyond the various empty racks that had once carried wine barrels, and there he saw two doors much like the one he'd come through from the stairs. He tried the one to the right and found it too was unlocked and when he opened it, he saw a flight of stairs beyond it leading upwards. He felt a surge of excitement: this was the right direction.

At the top of the stairs, there was a door immediately to the right and a corridor disappearing into the darkness. To his delight, he found the door wasn't locked, and on pushing it open he found himself in a large room. Looking around with the light from the lantern, he could see a thick curtain covering almost all of the wall facing him, while smaller curtains appeared to cover windows on the wall to his left and a fireplace was centrally placed on the wall to his right. Many paintings hung on the wall over the fireplace and on the wall above the door through which he had entered.

He peered at the paintings, wondering if they were his father's creations. Some were portraits while others were scenes of the countryside. He looked up and to his surprise, he could see a wooden balustrade running around the room up where the ceiling should be and above it, the sky.

He frowned. That didn't make sense. It was daytime outside and if that really was the sky, he should be able to see daylight. He lifted the lantern and, moving it around, he could see he was looking at a painting of the sky, not the real thing. Not only that, the wooden balustrade wasn't real either; it was another painting.

Tommaso walked closer to the wall with the fireplace and lifted his lantern again to look up at some of the paintings hanging above it. With the light this close, he could now see that everything about them — pictures, canvases and frames — was painted directly onto the wall. His eyes dropped to the fireplace, and now he was standing close to it, he could see it too was a painting on a plain wall. Uneasy now, he took a few steps back, but the farther he moved from the fireplace, the more realistic it looked.

He turned towards the curtained windows, thinking he would open one to get a better light than the lantern could produce. However, as he reached out to the curtains to pull one of them, he saw they were also painted on the wall. Nothing in the room he had seen so far was real; it was all painted.

Were all these paintings created by Papa? They were very clever, but what was the purpose? A painted fireplace wouldn't warm the room. Tommaso decided he had seen enough. No doubt there were other rooms like this, but he couldn't work out any reason for them, and if he was being honest with himself, he would have to admit he found it all rather too frightening. He would go back to the apartment, lock the corridor door and put the key back in Papa's study, his curiosity satisfied.

Feeling a sudden urgency to leave, he ran back across the room to where he knew he had entered through the door. But the door had closed and he could no longer see where it was. The wall where the door had been also appeared to be hung with many pictures in ornate frames, but like the ones above the fake fireplace, they were painted directly onto the wall, and below them, there was nothing. Tommaso didn't like it; he was scared. Where was the door? When he held the lantern up close to the wall where he thought the door should be, he could just see a faint line that must be the door's edge. He reached out and touched it. On one side of the line, the surface felt like a wall, while on the other side it felt wooden. But there was no handle, no way to open the door.

Agitated, he held up the lantern to take another look at the room. He hadn't yet looked at the wall opposite, the one that appeared to be completely covered in a curtain. Was this one real? Afraid to cross the open space of the room, Tommaso kept to the walls, following the one to his right that took him past the painting of the fireplace. Arriving at the corner of the room, he reached out and was relieved to find this curtain at least was real. He pulled it to one side and there behind it in the corner was a large ornately carved wooden door.

The handle seemed to beckon him to try it. Hoping it wasn't another painting, he held out his hand and felt an immediate sense of relief as his fingers closed over the handle. It was real! Maybe this was the way out.

As well as being real with a real handle, the door wasn't locked. Tommaso pulled it open and saw a dark corridor leading off to his right. Holding the lantern out in front of him, he started along the corridor, only to find that it quickly turned right again. Here, in the gloom at the edge of the reach of the lantern's light, another stairway led upwards. He peered into the darkness, holding his lantern ahead of him. The stairway seemed to narrow slightly, but at the top was another wooden balustrade.

He climbed the stairs, looking ahead as best he could. At the top, he reached out to take the handrail of the wooden balustrade, only to find it was a painting. Feeling frightened again, he moved his hand around the walls and found that although a corridor ahead of him was real, it was far narrower than it looked. And all the paintings and their frames were painted directly on the wall too, like the ones in the room below.

Along the corridor, he could see two doors, one to the left and one to the right. Beyond them, the corridor appeared to continue, but as he approached the doors, he saw that the rest of the corridor was simply another painting.

Taking hold of the handle of the left door, he pushed it open and was immediately relieved to find the room beyond wasn't in darkness but lit by an unshuttered window on the far wall. If there was a window, perhaps he would be able to open it and climb out. But as he walked into the room, he stopped short. The floor ahead of him had collapsed into a large room below.

Or had it?

The false collapse had been painted by Salvatore with the intention of being viewed by an adult standing on its apparent edge. Tommaso was an eight-year-old child and he was standing by the doorway, his angle of view therefore giving the painting on the floor a rather different perspective from the one intended. Not convinced by what his eyes were trying to tell him was real, Tommaso took a step forward, and then another. He knelt down and when he reached out into the hole, he found his suspicions were correct. It wasn't a hole, it was another painting.

Having discovered that the hole in the floor wasn't real, Tommaso was no longer interested in it. There was light coming through an unshuttered window; it must be a way out. He ran over to the window, but the sill was above his head height: he was too short to see anything through the glass except the clear blue sky. He looked around for some furniture to climb on, but there was none, the room was empty with not even a chair in the corner.

Tommaso stood back a little from the window. He could see

that the glass was set back from the edge of the sill, and on reaching up, he felt a ledge about ten centimetres deep. He was young and agile, and from his days spent playing in the woods, a ten-centimetre ledge just above his head height shouldn't pose much of a problem. He had certainly made more difficult climbs when trying to reach the first large branches of a tree.

Gripping the sill tightly with both hands, he pulled himself upward while swinging his right foot at the corner of the frame to wedge it and give himself some purchase. He nearly made it on the first attempt but his foot slipped at the last moment and he fell. Undismayed, he tried again and on this attempt he managed to throw his body upwards and swing his bottom onto the flat of the sill. It was a precarious position, but at least he could now see through the window. And when he did look through, he was stunned to see Mamma sitting on a bench in the garden below him, her back to him and her head bent over as she read a book.

"Mamma," he gasped before screaming, "Mamma! Mamma!" He banged on the glass with his fists, the force of the blows nearly toppling him backwards from the sill. But he somehow stayed on and kept shouting and banging. But there was no response from Mamma. Nothing. How could she not hear him?

Frantic now to get his mother's attention, he looked around the window frame, hoping to find a way to open it. But there was nothing. The window wasn't the usual type that opened, it was a single pane of glass. It didn't slide and it wasn't hinged. It was an immovable fixture in the wooden frame.

"Mamma!" Tommaso yelled again, banging his fists as hard as he could on the glass. But she still didn't hear. Tearful now with frustration, he banged at it one more time, but he had shifted his body slightly, relaxed the pressure on his foot, and he slipped from the sill, landing awkwardly on his right foot. A jolt of pain shot up through his ankle and he yelled in shock.

He sat up and reached out to rub his ankle. The pain quickly subsided — he had fallen out of trees in the forest and his ankles had hurt far more. He got to his knees and with one hand on the wall, stood on his good leg as he gingerly put his right foot down. It hurt, and he lifted it. After hobbling around on it for a couple of minutes, it felt considerably better, but he knew that hauling himself back onto the sill was now out of the question.

He looked around the room for something he could use to break the window. If he could do that, then Mamma would hear, and even if he couldn't get onto the sill, she would be able to work out a way of rescuing him. But there was nothing in the room, just the stupid painting on the floor. He was wondering if the room on the other side of the corridor would have anything he could use when he noticed a curtain hanging from a rail in the corner of the room, the corner away from the window side. Hobbling over to it, he pulled the curtain aside and found another ornate wooden door like the one that had led him up to this floor. The handle on this one was also real and when he turned it and pulled, the door opened towards him.

Picking up his lantern, he looked through the doorway to find a short corridor that turned sharply to the right after about two metres. He walked along it and turned the corner. Ahead, he could see three doors that looked real on the left wall of the corridor, and others that might be paintings. He tried the handles of the first two doors, and although they were real, the doors were locked. As he moved on to the third door, he saw that the wall was painted on either side of the frame with a painting of stairs climbing away from him. Puzzled, he tried the door handle and the door opened into the darkness beyond.

A few steps beyond the doorway, Tommaso could see yet another flight of stairs ahead of him. Remembering the stairs painted on the wall in the corridor, he walked backwards far enough to see the paintings of stairs on the corridor wall and the real stairs beyond through the door. At a certain point, the image of stairs and the real ones appeared to merge as one large staircase, the sort he had seen portrayed in books about grand houses and theatres. Again, he could think of no reason why anyone should want to paint something like that in a place where they couldn't possibly be real.

With no sign of any furniture he could drag to the large living room, he was about to turn back to try his luck elsewhere when he noticed that the stairs and walls ahead of him weren't plain but brilliantly painted with three-headed serpents, rearing unicorns and tangles of creepers. Thinking these decorated stairs might lead to a room with some furniture on the floor above, Tommaso decided to go up and take a look. And even though he knew the snakes and creepers on each step weren't real, he still took care to avoid treading on them.

At the top of the stairs was a large, black wooden door. Turning its handle and pushing it open, Tommaso found himself walking into a wide room that was at least as high as the rooms on the lower floors but not very deep. And unlike the other rooms he had passed through on the lower floors, this one was quite plain, its wall made up of large stones. Centrally placed on the wall directly opposite where he was standing was one large wooden door mounted in a stone frame, but there was no door handle, not even a fake one. As he walked forward to touch the door and its surround, Tommaso realised none of it was real. The whole facade was painted: the door, the stone surround and the stones making up the walls.

Tommaso was still staring at the painted door when he heard a quiet swish from behind him. He spun around in horror, holding up his lantern in time to see the door from the stairs close back into its frame with a soft click.

"Mamma!" he yelled instinctively, even though he knew that seated in the garden she wouldn't be able to hear him. "Mamma!" he wailed again.

There was no light in the room apart from the flickering flame of the lantern. There weren't even any windows or shutters, just plain walls painted to look different from what they really were.

Tommaso stumbled backwards into the wall opposite the doorway and slid slowly down it until he was sitting. Putting the lantern down in front of him, he banged his fists on the floor. He didn't know what to do and the all-consuming fear he had managed to suppress earlier was returning. He slumped farther and rolled onto his front, banging his fists on the floor and against the wall a few centimetres above floor level. Suddenly something in the wall moved slightly and he saw that one of the stones that looked painted like the others was actually a real stone. Another swish sounded, but this time from the fake door painted on the inner wall.

Tommaso scrambled to his feet and snatched up the lantern, holding it out in the direction of the sound. What he saw gave him hope: the painted door was a real door that had opened into another room, but better than that, there was light coming from somewhere in the room.

He ran through the door, his eyes darting everywhere before he looked up and saw a skylight set in the roof. It was an impossible distance above him, but at least he was no longer in darkness. Without thinking, he put the lantern down on a small wooden table in the middle of the room and looked around. This room was a little larger than the one he had just come from, although it was still a strange shape.

The flickering lantern flame caught his attention and he realised he didn't need its light; there was sufficient daylight streaming in through the skylight for him to see. He had a flint and stone in his pocket, he would turn the light out and relight it later, unless Mamma had already found him by then.

As he concentrated on the lantern wick, another swish from behind took him by surprise. For the second time in a few minutes, he turned to see the door to the room he was in close quietly back into place with the faintest of clicks.

Somehow, although he knew he was trapped, this time it didn't feel so bad. At least he could see by the light from the skylight. It was the thought of total darkness that had been so frightening before. He sat on a wooden chair next to a table in the middle of the room and peered into every corner, but there was nothing apart from one more wooden chair on the other side of the table.

Tired now, he put his arms out on the table top and rested his head on them. The hunger was still there, and he was starting to feel thirsty, but at least he knew that Mamma wasn't far away, and once she knew he was missing, she would come looking. As he drifted off to sleep, he thought about the door from the apartment that led into this part of the villa. He shifted his head onto one arm and with the free arm, he reached down to touch his jacket pocket.

The key was still there. He was pleased he hadn't locked the door after he had come through it.

As the daylight faded, Tommaso remained asleep and it wasn't until dawn the following morning that he lifted his head, wondering where he was. In the dream coursing through his mind moments before, he had been running through the forest back to the house. But each time he seemed to get closer, there would be a loud swishing sound and the trees and bushes would close ahead of him, trapping him and forcing him to go another way. And then it would happen again, and a third time. Round and round he went, but he never got any closer to the house.

His eyes focussed and the memory of the previous afternoon returned. He sat up and his head spun. His stomach was aching with hunger and he was thirstier than he could ever remember, but more than anything, he needed to pee. He wondered if there was a chamber pot he had overlooked, but when he stood and looked around, he saw there were only the chairs and the table. Swaying slightly, he went to the nearest wall and followed it around the room to the far corner, his hand pressed against the stonework for support. Feeling rather embarrassed that he was peeing against a wall inside the house, he nevertheless felt slightly better once he had finished. But he was still shaky so he returned to his chair and sat down.

After a while, he summoned up the energy to explore the walls in more detail. Was there really only one door in the room or were there others cleverly concealed by the plaster and paintwork? He had to know, and he had to check for hidden door releases like the one he had accidentally discovered in the room outside.

For the next hour, Tommaso searched the walls meticulously, only to discover there were no other doors and no hidden door release. He had pushed, hit and kicked everywhere, but the room remained sound. The only thing changing was the intensity of the light as the morning wore on, together with his hunger, which had developed into a painful gnawing.

Where was Mamma? Why was it taking so long for her to find him? If she could find time to sit on a seat in the garden and read, she had time to look for him. He hoped she wasn't wasting time looking for him in the forest. She must know he'd be getting hungry. If he were in the forest, he would have come home. Surely she realised that!

Rejecting the table and chairs, Tommaso curled up in a ball in the corner of the room, as far as he could from the spot he had chosen to relieve himself. The floor was hard, harder than the forest floor when he took naps there, but he didn't care. All he wanted to do was sleep until Mamma found him. If he could sleep, the hunger wouldn't feel so bad.

And sleeping in the corner was where Isabella and the girls found him three days later.

Chapter Thirty-Four

It took Isabella and the girls the better part of three hours to work their way through the same rooms Tommaso had found. Initially this was because the girls hated the darkness — the lanterns they were carrying doing little to illuminate large areas, the darkness behind them being as frightening as the darkness in front. To reassure them that they were safe, Isabella returned to the apartment three times with the girls to carry as many lanterns as they could, leaving them lit and carefully placed in the rooms and corridors they passed through. But as they progressed, the girls became more and more frightened and Isabella had to keep pausing to cuddle and reassure them as she tried to absorb what she increasingly saw as her husband's madness adorning the walls.

Why had he done this? Who was it for? Why the hidden doors and stairways? Was it all some sort of huge and silly game? She doubted it; there was nothing light-hearted about it, just as there was nothing light-hearted about Salvatore himself. On the contrary, its overall air was sinister and threatening, designed to frighten.

Isabella hadn't trusted any of the doors not to close, especially once she found the first one with a handle on only one side. If their purpose was to trap, she wasn't going to let it happen. She had, therefore, made sure to prop open each door they passed through with anything substantial she could find. With that and a series of lanterns lighting their route, if they felt they needed to leave in a hurry, they would be able to.

When they entered the room with the trompe l'oeil of the collapsed floor, the girls had gaped at it in horror, clinging to their mother's skirts. Isabella had seen through it in seconds and, to the objections of the girls, had run into the middle of the room and jumped up and down, spinning around and laughing, trying to relieve the tension. It worked, and for a few minutes they all played, pretending to fly above the room below.

When Isabella investigated the window that was apparently letting in light, the implications of seeing herself in the garden outside terrified her, even though she knew it was just another painting.

"What can you see, Mamma?" asked Delfina, tugging at Isabella's arm. "Can you show me?"

"It's just the garden, sweetheart," replied her mother, not wanting the complication of trying to explain the painting. "There's nothing much to see."

"I *want* to see, Mamma," cried Clara holding up both arms. "I want to see the garden. Please!"

Isabella sighed in resignation and lifted her younger daughter.

Clara spotted the person in the garden immediately. "Who's that sitting there? It looks like you, Mamma," she said, frowning.

Isabella thought her laugh sounded absurdly hollow. "You are right, Clara, it does. But it can't be, can it? After all I'm here and she's there, and I can't be in two places at once."

As she spoke, she could feel Delfina still tugging at her. "Show me too, Mamma, I want to see."

Delfina was more perceptive. "She's not moving, Mamma," she said once Isabella had hoisted her up to the sill. "Are you sure she's real?"

"She must be," laughed Isabella. "Unless someone has left a dressmaker's mannequin there. No, she must be someone from the village who's come to see me."

Delfina wasn't convinced. "No one ever comes to see you."

"Well, she can wait," said Clara. "We haven't found Tommaso yet."

"You are quite right, amore," said Isabella. "We must continue our search. At least the light from the window helps. Look, there's an open door over there, where the curtain has been pulled back. I wonder if Tommaso went that way. Let's take a look, shall we?"

After the relatively well-lit room, the girls took some persuading to go into the darkness of the corridor beyond the door, and far more to climb the serpent-and-creeper-covered stairs once they had found the one door that opened.

"Like many things in this strange house, my darlings, those snakes and vines are only paintings. They're not real and so they can't hurt you. Come on, there isn't much farther to go; these stairs go up to the top floor."

The total darkness of the room beyond the already sinister blackness of the door at the top of the stairs was a shock to Isabella. There were no windows, not even a pretence at windows, simply a strange-looking door in the centre of the wall facing her that seemed to be false. Yet another painting, she assumed.

She turned to check the door they had come through, a sixth sense telling her that it posed some sort of danger, the feeling confirmed when she found there was no handle on the room side. She needed to prop it open, prevent it from closing, but the room was empty.

"Delfina," she said, softly. "Amore, I'm going to need your lantern for a moment to place against the door. We don't want it closing on us, do we?"

"But, Mamma," said Delfina, pouting, "I won't be able to see without my lantern. Can't you use Clara's?"

"Yours is a bit bigger and heavier, amore, it will hold the door better. You'll still be able to see; all three lanterns are lit and this room isn't very big."

Delfina handed Isabella her lantern and stomped off into the corner. She turned round, leaned her back against the wall and slid down it.

As Isabella did her best to secure the lantern against the door,

Clara wandered over to her sister and held out her lantern. "Here, Delfi, you can have mine," she said.

"I don't want yours," snapped Delfina, "I want mine!"

She ignored the proffered lantern and banged both fists on the wall behind her. When the door painted on the wall along from her opened with a quiet swish, she jumped. "Mamma!" she yelled.

Isabella had seen it. "How did you do that?" she said as she rushed to the doorway, holding up her lantern ahead of her.

Tommaso's dehydration had reached a critical level, his semiconscious, delirious mind a whirl of fragmented, unconnected images. He no longer knew where he was; he just knew he was dying, and he didn't want to die alone. He wanted Mamma.

When the arms enveloped him, lifting his shoulders and face into the familiar smell of his mother's clothes and her warmth, he initially had no real perception of what was happening to him. But slowly Mamma's voice permeated his mind. Faint at first, distant, before it grew stronger and clearer.

"Tommaso! Oh, Tommaso, my sweet child, we've found you! Everything is going to be all right. You're safe, my darling, you're safe."

There were other voices too, voices he recognised. Who was there with Mamma? The voices were disembodied, echoing inside his head, competing with each other. His sister's voices. Were they his sister's voices? They were! They were Delfina and Clara's voices! They had come with Mamma to find him.

A wave of relief surged through him. He had dreamed of Mamma appearing in the room, but only Mamma, he hadn't thought his sisters would be there. Was this all a dream too? Was Mamma real?

"Tommaso, sweetheart."

It *was* Mamma. She was real; she was there in the room with him.

"Can you hear me? Can you open your eyes?"

He could feel something wiping gently at his eyelids, wiping away the salt from his tears, the stickiness that had made his eyes so hard to open.

He took a deep breath and his whole frame shuddered with the effort. As his eyes slowly opened, the light was blinding, painful, but as they slowly focussed, he could see three faces peering at him, three wonderfully familiar faces, each of them crying and laughing.

"Tommaso," said Isabella again. "We have found you. You were trapped but we have found you. You are going to be fine. You are …"

His mother's words blurred one into the other as they echoed around Tommaso's head, but out of the jumbled cacophony, one word emerged, one terrifying word that slowly and insistently became clearer as it repeated and repeated, getting louder and louder until it was booming, deafening, drowning out all the others.

Trapped! She had said trapped. Was he still trapped? He couldn't be, surely. Mamma was there. Mamma and his sisters. But did they know?

"Mamma." His voice was hardly audible, the muscles in his throat too parched to work, too parched to make the sound he knew he had to make.

He wriggled in his mother's arms, cold terror now overwhelming the warmer relief, crushing it. But her arms were firm, supporting him, caressing him. He wriggled more, he had to free a hand, he had to warn them.

"It's all right, Tommaso." He could hear Mamma's soothing tones, trying to comfort him.

"No," he croaked, and fought harder against his mother's grip, twisting and turning. "No!"

He turned again and an arm came free from his mother's grasp. Breathing heavily with the effort, his head shaking in desperation, he struggled to raise his arm, the effort of working his wasted muscles almost too much.

"Door," he said, finally pointing his outstretched fingers in the direction he wanted. "Door."

Isabella's head shot up. In the relief of seeing her son when the light from her lantern filled the room, all thoughts of securing the door had evaporated, her only concern being Tommaso and whether he was alive. She hadn't thought … she had rushed to him and the girls had rushed in after her … she hadn't stopped them … she hadn't told them to put a lantern against the door … she hadn't …

Her scream of anguish reverberated around the room, bouncing from the roof, filling the space with a wild terror so intense that the girls automatically screamed with her, not knowing why.

But Tommaso knew. As his body slumped in his mother's arms, the will to live now ebbing fast, the effort of the last few moments defeating what few defences remained in his emaciated body, he knew.

He knew what his eyes hadn't had the power to see but what his mother had seen. The door to the room had quietly closed while she was cradling him.

They were all trapped.

Chapter Thirty-Five

Salvatore Brocanti pulled on the reins of the chaise to stop it at the gatehouse. He was tired and irritable after his journey from Garda. The train had been delayed after the breakdown of an earlier one, and every carriage was packed with people, even in first class. A group of nuns with third-class tickets had descended on his compartment, oblivious to his sense of outrage that his privileged space had been invaded. They had ignored the dark, menacing glare in his eyes while silently praying for his tortured soul. When he eventually fell asleep and slumped in his seat, his knees pressing firmly against the horrified nun next to him, she had promptly awoken him with a sharp elbow in his ribs. This had done nothing to improve his humour.

"Vito!" called Salvatore from the chaise. Where was the idiot? Was he deaf? Hadn't he heard the carriage? "Vito!"

The door to the guardhouse opened hesitantly and a wary head poked around it, its eyes widening in horror.

"Marchese! I wasn't … I didn't …"

"What? You didn't expect me? What does that matter? You are supposed to be protecting this estate, you and your squad. That doesn't mean sleeping in the guardhouse in the middle of the day.

Where are the others? I hope they are on patrol and not asleep in there with you."

"No, Marchese, they are not here."

"Well, at least that's something. They are on patrol, yes?"

"No, Marchese, they are not."

Salvatore's short fuse got the better of him. "What!" he bellowed. "What do you mean they are not? Where the devil are they?"

"They may well have been taken by the devil, Marchese; I hope they have. But they are not here. They have gone. Quit. I am the only one left."

"Why? When?"

"A week, Marchese, ten days perhaps. They were frightened."

"Frightened! Of what? You and your gang of ruffians were hired because you don't get frightened. You frighten other people."

The guard Vito said nothing, his own fear obvious.

"Well, Vito! Explain yourself."

Vito hung his head. "They were frightened of you, Marchese. What you would say. That you would demand the money you paid us to be returned."

"Why would I do that? What has happened, man?"

"It's the marchesa, Marchese, and the children. They seem … they seem to have disappeared. All of them."

"Disappeared! How? Weren't you watching them as instructed?"

"We were, Marchese, very carefully. Every day." His eyes dropped, sheepishly. "All day," he added, compounding the lie. "One day they were here, with your son playing in the garden, the next there was no one." He wasn't inclined to tell the angry marchese about Isabella's visit to the guardhouse and his refusal to help her look for Tommaso. Lying was easier.

"I think they must have crept away in the night, Marchese, through the forest to the rear gate."

"Damn you!" screamed Salvatore. "You incompetent idiots. What did they take? They must have had luggage. They must have had help from someone in the village. It'll be that damn maid,

Imperia. Have you checked the apartment to see what they have taken?"

"No, Marchese. You forbade us from going inside. I have only approached as far as the kitchen door to leave food supplies from the market, as instructed. And those supplies have not been touched for three weeks."

"Three weeks! They have been missing for three weeks and you have done nothing!"

"I called from the kitchen door, Marchese. I called loudly for the marchesa every time I went. But there was no reply."

"Of course there wasn't if they'd left, you moron!"

Salvatore cracked his whip on the horse's backside. The surprised animal sprung into life and the carriage lurched off towards the villa.

"Stay there!" he yelled to Vito. "I haven't finished with you yet. Leave at your peril!"

The carriage skidded to a halt outside the apartment entrance. Salvatore ran to the door, cursing when he found it was locked. His keys were buried in one of his bags; it would be quicker to run round to the kitchen entrance, which the guard had said was open. It was, and the scene inside surprised him. Dishes from what appeared to be breakfast were still on the table, even a loaf of now mouldy bread.

Puzzled, given Isabella's insistence on order and tidiness, he ran from the kitchen to the stairs leading up to the day rooms. Here too he found a scene hardly consistent with an orderly departure. In the playroom, the girls' toys were scattered around, including a doll Salvatore knew Clara would never leave behind if she were departing for good.

What clothes had they taken? What bags? How would they manage hauling bags through the forest in the dead of night? Nothing made any sense.

Angry now at his incomprehension of the scene confronting him, Salvatore strode purposefully into the hallway in the direction of the stairs to the bedrooms. And at the end of the hallway, when he saw the open door that led into the rest of the villa, the reality of what must have happened hit him with the force of a hurricane.

"No! Please, God, no!"

The cry of anguish was strangled as he ran to the door and peered into the darkness. He knew every inch of that darkness, every room, but even he needed light to navigate his way around. Sprinting to the kitchen, he went to the cupboard where the lanterns were kept, and was surprised to find it almost empty. Puzzled, he grabbed the largest, checked the base for oil, lit it and ran back to the doorway leading into the main part of the villa.

Running along the familiar passageway to the steps leading down to the cellar, Salvatore had his fears reinforced. A lantern, long since burnt out when its oil reservoir emptied, was on the ground at the foot of the stairs, just inside the cellar. Another was propping open a door at the far end of the cellar that led onto stairs going up into the villa.

He ran up the stairs to find that the door into the large room with the trompe l'oeil paintings and frames, the false fireplace and the false curtains over false windows was also propped open with a lantern. This at least gave him some sort of hope. If Isabella — and it could only be Isabella — had come through here, she had been wary of the doors. Rightly so, thought Salvatore, remembering the effort he had gone to in achieving a perfect balance in certain of his doors to ensure they would slowly but surely swing closed, leaving them hardly discernible on the wall they slotted into and no obvious handle to open them.

But where were the children when Isabella was exploring? Surely she hadn't brought them with her, the rooms would be far too frightening for the girls, and even Tommaso's bravado might have deserted him. However, if she left them behind and became trapped, the children would never find their way through this maze on their own, and since they weren't in the apartment, they must have gone with her.

Three weeks. Vito's words flashed across Salvatore's mind. *Three weeks!* That was far longer than he had expected the pharmacist to live without food and water. Surely they couldn't be …

Frantic now, Salvatore ran through the door revealed by the

drawn-aside curtain — he remembered he hadn't left it that way after he trapped the pharmacist — and hurried along the short corridor to the stairs. Not even glancing at the paintings at the top — the deception of the balustrade and the false effects of the paintings on the corridor walls — he ran to the end of the short corridor and flung open the left door. His eyes flashed around the room. Which route had they taken? Another lantern propped open the wooden door in the corner of the room; this must be it.

The door to the stairway of serpents and creepers was also propped open, confirming he had chosen the right route. He ran up the stairs and found an unlit lantern holding open the large black door at the top. But the door in the wall opposite him, so artfully concealed in a wall of faux stone, was closed.

"No," Salvatore mumbled, his head starting to shake in rejection of what was in front of his eyes. "No! It can't be. They can't be in there."

He walked to the corner of the room and kicked at the wall near floor level. He had been proud of the concealed door release, proud of the craftsmanship involved in constructing it and in concealing it. His intention had been to make it deliberately obscure, difficult to find so that a person wouldn't accidentally gain access to the room beyond. When the concealed door in the wall started to move, he wondered if he had been wrong in his assumption. Perhaps it was easy to find.

As the door opened and he lifted the lantern, the foetid stench of decay hit him even before he saw the bodies. And when his eyes focussed on the remains of his family, he sank to his knees in the doorway, his mouth working but no sound emerging, his heart pounding as he gulped for air.

Laid out in a macabre tableau in front of him were Isabella, her back to a wall and her head drooping forward; Tommaso, his body stretched out to Isabella's left, his head in the crook of her left arm; and the two girls, who lay side by side on their mother's right, Delfina's head resting in her right arm and Clara's on her lap.

While a scene of total horror, it was also a scene of peace, one that in no way reflected the awfulness of the deaths that had occurred here. From the arrangement of the bodies, it was clear that Isabella must have been the last to die, hanging on to comfort her children before laying out their bodies and succumbing to her fate herself.

As he knelt, his eyes transfixed by the bodies of his family, the door to the room followed its predetermined path and started to close. But Salvatore was in the way, blocking it. As it gently nudged against his right arm, he jolted, realising what was happening. He pushed it away in anger, grabbed the lantern and blocked it open. He was shocked to think that if he had taken two steps into the room before sinking to his knees, he too would have been trapped. The thought flashed through his mind that perhaps that would have been for the best, but he immediately rejected it. If he chose that path, the villa and its secrets would soon be discovered, perhaps by the idiot Vito, or perhaps by others Vito informed. Salvatore certainly didn't want that. He didn't want the body of the pharmacist to be discovered, nor even the bodies of his family. He had to make arrangements, ensure that no one would come here. And to do that he must stay alive.

Staring at his wife's body, and with thoughts of the pharmacist that were now inextricably linked with Isabella, his eyes hardened. This was all her fault. If she hadn't encouraged the man with her whore-like ways, he wouldn't have had the nerve to start an affair, not with the wife of a marchese. If she had remained the dutiful wife she was supposed to be, this wouldn't have happened.

However, it had happened and it had ruined his plans for the final retribution on his adulterous wife and her lover. His plan had been for her to end up in this room alone, where she would die slowly in the most dreadful anguish, knowing, because he would have told her, that her lover was lying dead only a short distance away beyond the walls confining her.

But nowhere in his wildest nightmares did Salvatore imagine his children, particularly his beloved son Tommaso, would die in this room. That it had happened was entirely his wife's fault. He glared at the peaceful scene again. She may have died with them but her body wouldn't rot and crumble to dust with the bodies of her children. She didn't deserve it. He wouldn't let it happen.

Still on his knees, Salvatore crawled over to Tommaso's body and gently put one arm around his shoulders, the other under his legs. Gently lifting his almost weightless son, he crawled across the room and laid the body carefully on the floor, straightening it out as best he could and pulling his arms up to cross his hands on his emaciated chest.

Satisfied the boy looked comfortable, he crawled back across the room and lifted Delfina's body and finally Clara's, placing them gently alongside their brother. As an afterthought, he linked one of Delfina's hands with Clara's, and her other hand with Tommaso's. The tears now flowing freely, he fussed over the arrangement of their clothes, straightening and tidying, making sure they were comfortable.

After some time, he stood and turned to Isabella, his features hardening. With the removal of the children, her arms had fallen to her sides and Salvatore could now see she had a folded piece of paper clutched in her hand. Snatching it from her grasp, Salvatore opened it to find a brief message.

'How could you be so inhuman? What has your madness done? You have killed our children.

Rebuffed by your idiot guards, after days of frantic searching for Tommaso, I tracked him here. But I was too late, he was within moments of death. And now my precious daughters are also dead from the starvation you have inflicted upon them.

I can only assume too that the disappearance of Ugo is your doing, that he is somewhere in this accursed villa, also dead from starvation.

I am now very weak and will soon die as well unless you happen to return and find me here. But I don't want you to, not now you have murdered my chil-dren. I should rather die alongside them.

You are a monster. May you live the rest of your life in a torture of anguish, plagued by the images of the death masks of your children, and may you spend eternity in the flames of hell.'

He shook his head, rejecting the words in front of his eyes, unable to face the truth of the situation. It was *not* his fault; Isabella was wrong. It was her carelessness in looking after the children, her …

The reality of what was written in the note hit him like a slap to the face. Tommaso had gone missing, which meant he had found his way into the villa alone, followed the labyrinthine path through the rooms and become trapped. Alone.

Dropping the note, Salvatore fell to his knees in front of the body of his son. "Tommaso, my child, this was never meant to be. I can't …" But his words were lost as he sagged in dejection, his body wracked with huge, shuddering sobs as he once again took hold of the boy's emaciated hand and gently held it.

When eventually his sobbing subsided, he wiped his face on his sleeves and looked around him, wondering how Isabella had managed to write a note. Then, partially hidden by Isabella's clothing, he saw Delfina's leather satchel, the one she carried everywhere that contained what she maintained was everything she needed to survive, including sheets of paper and a number of pencils. Sadly, her survival kit included neither food nor water.

Picking up the note, he glanced at it again before screwing it into a ball and flinging it to the floor.

"No, Isabella, this is all your fault, all your doing," he shouted, pointing at his wife's body. "It was your unfaithfulness that set everything in motion. Did you expect me to sit back and watch you fornicate with another man? Did you? And in your final act of irresponsibility you brought my daughters with you when searching for my son. You were not fit to be the children's mother, and you won't spend eternity clutching their bodies or even be close to them."

Roughly, he hooked his arms under his wife's shoulders and half carried, half dragged her across the room so she would be as far away as possible from the children. He let the body sag to the floor and made no attempt to straighten it.

Making his way back to the doorway, he picked up the lantern and held it high, the light giving him one final view of the scene.

"Arrivederci, my little ones," he said, softly. "I will return and be with you. Not for a while, but I will come and we shall be together forever."

Removing his foot from where he had placed it against the door after picking up the lantern, he backed out through the doorway and watched as the room resealed itself.

He remained standing there for a moment, staring at the closed door. While he blamed the deaths of his children completely on his wife, there were others who could have helped to prevent them. Sooner or later, all of them would pay, the first almost immediately.

Chapter Thirty-Six

"Vito!" barked Salvatore as he jumped from the chaise and marched towards the guardhouse door. "Vito! Out here, now! I need your help with something."

The door opened a little way and the guard's head peered around it.

"Is everything all right, Marchese? At the villa, I mean."

Salvatore was still reeling with the shock of finding his children dead; he was in no mood for small talk with one of the men who could have saved them.

He stopped and turned back towards the chaise, his head down. He didn't want the guard to see his grief-stricken, haunted face, his eyes still red raw from several bouts of uncontrollable weeping that had stopped him as he made his way back through the villa to the apartment. He had collected several of the lanterns left by Isabella as he went, others he kicked at angrily, but at each point, images of his children standing in the same spot took over his mind with such vivid clarity that he could have been convinced they were real, had he not known their bodies were lying only a short distance away.

"Follow me," he ordered, ignoring the man's question. "To the house."

Vito did not take orders from many people. He was large and well built, used to using his fists and feet or, preferably, a weapon.

But the marchese was different. A large man himself, he radiated an air of threatening authority. He also paid well, very well, and Vito didn't want to jeopardise the large sum he was due.

He followed the chaise, half walking, half running, and when he arrived at the door to the kitchen, Salvatore was standing by it, arms folded, waiting.

"There's a box in the cantina that's very heavy," he said. "It will take two of us to carry it." He pointed through the doorway into the kitchen. "It's this way."

Not giving the still-panting Vito time to recover, Salvatore disappeared into the kitchen. Vito sighed, rolled his shoulders, and followed.

"Up these stairs," he heard Salvatore call.

When he caught up with the voice, Vito saw there were two glowing lanterns on the floor next to a door leading into what appeared to be an unlit room. Salvatore picked them up and handed one to him.

"Mind the stairs at the end of this corridor," he said. "They are rather steep."

He marched off. Vito watched the light bobbing down the corridor before disappearing abruptly as Salvatore turned and walked down the stairs.

"Don't have much choice really, do I?" he mumbled. He turned up the flame in his lantern and set off down the corridor.

Arriving in the cantina, his first impression was of its size. With high, vaulted, brick ceilings, it must have stretched under half the villa, with the potential to store huge quantities of produce from the estate. But its heyday was over and now there were no barrels, presses or any other equipment, let alone bottles or jars for storage. Just a massive semi-underground space.

When Salvatore first made his plans for the rooms on the villa's main floors, he realised it was imperative for him to develop his skills as a builder: he was a fine artist, not a labourer. His plans would require a great deal of time and expertise, not only for the construction of extra internal walls but also of doorways with doors that were finely balanced to close with extreme precision, their release mechanisms hidden in a nearby wall. Not wanting to waste time honing his technique while immersed in the main project, he decided to practise with prototype rooms, walls and doors in a section of the cellar until he was satisfied he could produce the required result every time. As a consequence, there were two doors at the far end of the cantina. One led onto the stairs that Isabella had taken with the girls and Tommaso had also taken four days before them, while the other led into a passageway that went nowhere, a passageway created by Salvatore when building his prototype rooms.

It was to this door and passageway that Salvatore was now heading.

"The items I need removing are in here," he said to Vito, pointing to the left door of the two at the far end of the cantina. He opened the door and beckoned to the guard to follow him.

The passageway they entered was about two metres wide and ten metres long with a ceiling over three metres above the floor. The walls along both sides and at the end were unrendered brick.

Salvatore stayed by the door, letting Vito pass him.

The guard turned to Salvatore, puzzled. "There's nothing in here, Marchese. What is it you want removing?"

Salvatore's laugh was menacing. "Oh, there's more here than meets the eye. Let me show you."

He turned to the wall on his left and raised his lantern so the light fell onto a course of bricks. Reaching out, he pushed the end of one of the bricks and to Vito's surprise, it pivoted along with three others above it, opening a space into which Salvatore was now inserting his hand.

A soft sound behind him made Vito turn and what he saw was a considerably greater surprise. Near the end of the corridor where he had thought there was a continuous brick wall, a section of the wall on the left side had opened like a door into what must be another room.

"A clever piece of engineering, don't you think?" said Salvatore.

"This whole wall is not what it seems. Run your hand over it, you'll see what I mean."

The guard frowned. He was beginning to think he should have cut his losses and fled with the others. Nevertheless, he did as instructed, only to find the brick wall was an illusion. There were no bricks, simply a plain wall painted to look as if it were made of bricks.

He turned to Salvatore. "I don't understand, Marchese."

Salvatore shrugged. "Nothing to understand, Vito, just a little project of mine. Now, the items I need moving are in that room, the one down there where the door is now open. I'll come with you. When you go in, you'll need to raise your lantern to see to the far end. There's a door there that opens into a store."

As Vito walked to the open door and into the room, Salvatore followed, watching the man's reactions.

"Can you see it, the door at the other end?" he said. "It isn't locked; you just need to turn the handle."

The guard walked towards the door, but when he was two steps from it, Salvatore called out to him.

"Vito, before you open the door, there's something I want to mention."

The guard stopped and turned, dropping the arm he had just outstretched to grasp the handle.

"I wanted to ask you," continued Salvatore, "if you know how long a man can survive without food and water, in the desert, shall we say, or maybe trapped somewhere that he can't escape from. A cell, if you like. Do you know that, Vito?"

"Eh, no, Marchese, I don't know how long. But without water, I should think it would be maybe … a week?"

Salvatore shook his head. "A little ambitious, Vito. A week is a long time without water. Food yes, you can live off the fat in your body for quite a while, but water …" He paused to make sure he had the guard's full attention.

"I wonder how long my wife and children lasted," he continued. "They had no water. Did you know that? Imagine the children, trapped, crying in fear, wasting water in the process. I don't think they would have lasted more than a couple of days, do you?

Oh, but of course, you didn't know, did you. You didn't know because you and the idiots with you sat in your guardhouse doing nothing while my family got themselves trapped and they died. Why did you do nothing, Vito, why?"

"We, I, we didn't do nothing, Marchese. You told us not to speak to them, to the marchesa, you said we mustn't."

"But she came to you asking for help, didn't she? What did she want?"

Vito said nothing, trying to calculate if he could rush at the marchese and overpower him.

"Tell me!" yelled Salvatore. "What did she want?"

"She said she couldn't find the boy, your son, that he'd gone into the woods and she couldn't find him."

"And what did you do? Refuse to help?"

"That's what you said we should do, Marchese."

"I said nothing of the sort. I said you weren't to listen to any entreaties from her to help her and the children to get away. That's all. If she or one of the children were hurt, how could you possibly refuse to help? What kind of monster are you?"

"I didn't mean no—"

"She's dead, you idiot! Dead! And so are the children! My children are dead because you wouldn't help. You have killed them."

"No, Marchese, I wouldn't—"

"Well, you have. And now you are going to pay. As will the rest of those cowards when I catch up with them. They will pay too, sooner or later. But for you, Vito, it's sooner. You are going to find out how long a man can last without water."

"What do you mean, Marchese?"

"Try the door handle behind you, Vito. Go on, try it!"

The guard turned and reached out to grasp the handle, but there was no handle.

"There's nothing, Marchese," he said, "it's just painted on the wall, like the bricks in the corridor outside."

"Exactly," said Salvatore with a sneer. "It's painted on the wall. Like everything else in this room and the rooms outside. Like most of the rooms in this villa. It's an illusion, designed to fool you and trap you so you can pay for what you've done."

As he was talking, Salvatore had slowly edged backwards into the doorway, expecting the guard to rush him at any moment.

Taking hold of the edge of the door, he looked triumphantly at the bewildered guard. "Once this door closes, Vito, it cannot be opened from the inside. You will be in a sealed box, and once the oil in your lantern runs out, you will be in total darkness. As you are dying, remember my children. What they suffered is what you will be suffering."

With a flick of his arm, he slammed the door shut, just as the guard finally reacted. But for Vito it was too late.

Chapter Thirty-Seven

Salvatore felt no satisfaction from entombing Vito; he simply knew it had to be done. If the man had possessed an iota of common sense or decency, he would have listened to Isabella, helped her. As it was, Vito and the guards who had deserted were as responsible for the children's deaths as Isabella was.

However, his thoughts of retribution on the other guards were hazy and ill-formed as he made his way to the sitting room in the apartment, stumbling and weaving like a drunk, no longer in command of his senses. He collapsed onto a sofa, burying his head first in one cushion, then two, and then another, trying to deaden the screaming, swirling, cacophony of anguish filling his head, a maelstrom threatening to burst it open. Not once in the months of planning, preparation and construction of his project of revenge had it occurred to him that his children might also fall victim to his scheme. He knew there would be dangers for them if they wandered into the villa, but he had expressly forbidden that, carefully hidden the key when he was away, made the villa impregnable.

The key. Where was the key? He hadn't checked but since there was only one, it must have been found. He hadn't looked in his children's clothing for it, or Isabella's; it hadn't crossed his mind. But the thought of returning to the room to check was more than he could bear. And what did it matter now? There was no longer any need to shut off the villa from the apartment. There was no need for any of it any more.

With no warning, the deafening screeching in his head stopped. One by one he threw away the cushions and sat up. In a moment of clarity prompted by the silence, he knew what he must do. His plans had been shattered, his schemes for bricking up access to the top-floor rooms and opening the rest of the villa as a bright, airy, fairytale castle of fantasy-filled adventure for his children's delight now amounted to nothing. Instead, the villa had become a tomb for his children. He knew he could no longer spend another night in the place; it was cursed. No, he would close up the entire villa; it would be a mausoleum for his loved ones, and in due course he would join them. He didn't care that the mausoleum would also contain the bodies of the two people he had hated most in the world. The pharmacist was rotting in his own chamber, forgotten, while his wife was nothing more than a jumble of clothing tossed aside from her children.

His eyes were now alert once more, wild and flashing with the thoughts of what needed to be done. He would board up the villa, seal it off from the world, freeze it in time while it slowly rotted and crumbled to dust. That would take centuries, but it didn't matter, the estate was huge and if he constructed the right legal documents, it would remain unsaleable and untouchable in perpetuity.

But to ensure that, there had to be a good reason for no one to want to go near it, to avoid it at all costs. It must be thought of as cursed, haunted, possessed. He quickly realised that it wouldn't take much. Once he had boarded it up and spread stories to the gullible in Coniglio, the tale would take on a life of its own, like Chinese whispers. The local people were nothing if not God-fearing, steeped in superstitious claptrap reinforced at every turn by priests anxious to maintain control of their minds and lives. An ordinary man might find it a difficult task, but Salvatore was no ordinary man. He was a marchese, an aristocrat, a member of the nobility. His reputation for wild behaviour and eccentric ways was already considered more than unsavoury by many in the community; they would relish knowing he was suffering for whatever practices he had been following in the mysterious villa, that he had fallen foul of the devil as well as the true path.

He would announce that his wife and children were gone with no likelihood of returning. Like him, they could no longer cope with whatever cursed the villa. He would fabricate stories of noises in the night, foul mists emanating from the very essence of the building, an environment too hell-ridden for any mortal. Some would say he should raze it, burn it to the ground, but he would point out that the ground on which the building stood was cursed along with the land for a hundred metres around it, a site of evil dating back millennia. The only solution, according to Brocanti family lore, was that when whatever possessed the building became uncontainable, it should be isolated from the world and left to rot; to decay to dust. Only by letting that decay fall back into the ground would the evil be neutralised. It would take far longer than any man's lifetime, but he, Salvatore Brocanti, must take the responsibility for ensuring it happened.

He sat back and looked around the room. It *was* evil to him now, threatening, as if constructing a tale of what the building might be had already made it start to happen. He couldn't bear the thought of spending another night in the apartment, or anywhere in the villa. Tomorrow he would begin boarding it up, but in the meantime, there was an old gardener's cottage about three kilometres across the estate where he would go. It hadn't been lived in for some years, but the last time he had looked at it, it was sound enough. He would base himself there. Once he had sealed off the villa and ensured no one would go near it, he would consider what to do next.

He hurried from the room to gather the clothes and possessions he needed before packing food from the kitchen. As he did, a second moment of clarity flashed across his mind. Another villa. A new one constructed elsewhere on the estate. More modest than the present building, which was far too large, but nevertheless large enough to be a comfortable home for him, with space to continue his work. Leaving the estate behind was now unthinkable to him. His children were here; he needed to feel their presence, and he couldn't do that from hundreds of kilometres away.

. . .

The next few weeks saw a frenzy of activity from Salvatore. Hardly pausing to eat, he set about sealing the villa. He slept only when the tiredness in his aching body beat him into submission and he had no choice but to collapse wherever he was working into a world of troubled, tortured dreams, his arms thrashing unconsciously as if to ward off demons. Every doorway and window was locked and barred, with extra wooden planks hammered into place to reinforce them and to act as a deterrent to anyone from attempting to gain entry. Only one heavily chained door remained unbarred, a door to the cantina half hidden by thickets of weeds and bushes growing at the apartment end of the villa. The padlock for the chains was substantial and Salvatore kept the key attached to his belt at all times.

Salvatore was certain that sooner or later the three guards who fled would come looking for Vito. He was right and when they arrived, he was more than ready.

He heard them before he saw them, so useless were they, and they followed the route he had prepared.

Seeing the ground-level kitchen door to the apartment wide open, it was only natural the men would look inside.

"The place looks different," said one of them as they approached on foot along the driveway. "Don't remember all those windows being boarded up."

"Never really noticed," said another. "I think some were like that."

"Don't look like no one's around," said the third. "I reckon Vito's inside helping himself to all the marchese's wines, thinking he's a marchese himself."

"Better have left some for us," muttered the first guard. "Maybe he's helping himself to the marchesa as well," he added with a grin.

"Shut yer mouths," whispered the third guard, "the marchesa might be around, still looking for that brat of hers."

"Yeah, she might be," agreed the second, with a leer.

"Looks dark in there," said the first guard, peering through the open door. "I don't remember it being that dark when we delivered food to the place."

The second guard walked into the darkness of the kitchen.

"There's a shelf on the left with some lanterns on, just inside the door," he called. "I'll fetch a couple and then we can see what we're—"

A screech of pain replaced what he was saying as a large animal trap Salvatore had bolted to the kitchen floor and set near the shelves snapped shut, breaking the man's leg halfway up the shin.

"Christ, help me!" screamed the guard, the weight of his collapsing body twisting his leg and almost severing it.

"Maurizio, what happened?" yelled the first guard, half in fear of the unearthly screech and half in fear of what might be lurking in the darkness. He ran in to where he could just see his companion in the gloom, stepping around him as the man writhed in agony on the floor.

"Maurizio!" he cried again. He took a step backwards and immediately filled the room with his own agonising scream as a second animal trap found its mark.

"That looks painful," said Salvatore from behind the third guard. The man spun around and as he did, a large wooden club smashed into his face, knocking out several of his teeth and destroying his nose. He stumbled backwards into the room and collapsed unconscious.

Salvatore picked up a lantern he had put on the ground and walked into the kitchen. Holding the light up high he surveyed the damage. The first guard to be injured had lost consciousness with the pain while the other was trying vainly to open the jaws of the trap gripping his shattered leg.

"Ouch!" said Salvatore with detached nonchalance as he knocked him out with a vicious blow to his head from the club.

Turning to the unconscious guard whose face he had destroyed, he grabbed the man by his jacket collar, dragged him outside and started along a path that led to the hidden doorway to the cantina. Deciding this was too awkward, he released the jacket, and instead picked up the man's legs by the ankles. As he dragged him feet first through the cantina, the man's head bounced heavily on the rough stone floor. On reaching the door by the stairs at the far end, Salvatore opened it, pivoted the flap in the wall hiding the door release and opened the door to the cell in which he had left Vito.

"Four weeks," he said to himself. "It's been four weeks. There's no chance he's still alive."

He smiled towards the body of the man he was dragging to the same cell. "You're going to get quite a fright when you grope around in the darkness and find the body of your old friend. Never mind, you'll soon be joining him in hell."

As he dumped the body in the cell, he saw Vito's body curled up at the far end. The rank smell in the room was all it took to confirm that the guard was dead.

Over the next ten minutes, Salvatore dragged the other two unconscious guards to the same cell and for the final time, closed the door on them.

"I wonder how long it will be before you are discovered," he said, facing the door. "A hundred years? Two hundred? It will be quite a mystery."

The villa sealed and the guards accounted for, Salvatore's final solo efforts were directed towards surrounding the abandoned villa with a new fence, sealing the main gates and establishing a new entrance to the estate three kilometres away, near to where he was intending to build the new villa. With the original villa now isolated and surrounded by forest that would grow ever more substantial over the years, untroubled by human intervention, the focus of the estate would shift to the new villa. For this, Salvatore accepted that he needed manual labour if it were to be completed in a reasonable time. The workers were local, wary of dealing with the imposing marchese and his mercurial moods. But the wages he offered were too good to refuse.

Salvatore saw that having local men on the estate would work to his advantage. He wouldn't need to circulate rumours of the possessed villa in the village, the men would do it for him, and they were bound to embellish the stories he would relate to them, carefully constructed with gaps for elaboration.

Accordingly, word got out of the mysterious disappearance of the four guards at about the same time that the marchese's wife had absconded with his three children. It was quickly established as irrefutable that his wife had been insane. That she was never seen again only reinforced her reputation for evil and for snaring unsuspecting men, among them the four guards she must have lured to their deaths.

Salvatore also hinted strongly to the workers that the old villa was possessed. He claimed to have discovered it was built on the site of an ancient pagan burial ground and that spirits now haunted the rooms.

It was more than enough to ensure none of the local residents, young and daring or old and wary, would venture anywhere near the place. None of them even wanted to set eyes on the villa in case that alone might curse them.

In gathering together his possessions from the old villa, Salvatore included a box containing several glass photographic plates, monochrome negatives he had shot using a large and unwieldy camera with a lightproof bellows system to focus the image on the plate. On learning the techniques of photography while on a commission in Rome, he had become quite interested in it for a while, seeing it as a way of archiving copies of his work. He set up a darkroom next to his studio on the ground floor, intending to catalogue the trompe l'oeil paintings in the villa. However, although he had some success, he found that for many of the shots the lighting was too difficult to control and, as with many of the peripheral projects that attracted Salvatore from time to time, photography had its moment, after which he lost interest. Ultimately it was his art that satisfied his creative energy. Hence, when clearing his studio, he only brought a small selection of the plates; the rest he left in the old villa to succumb to the ravages of time.

. . .

The new villa took nearly two years to complete. Salvatore remained on site, directing operations for the first six months, ensuring the builders followed his instructions to the letter. They soon learned that short cuts, both imagined and real, were given no quarter and increasingly Salvatore's strict attention became unnecessary. He wanted to get away, he had been on the site continuously for too long, accepting no commissions since the death of his children. His biggest fear in leaving was that someone might snoop around the old villa in spite of the folklore that had grown up around it so quickly. While he didn't want to hurt anyone who snooped — they weren't to be despised like the guards rotting in the cantina — he nevertheless needed to know if anyone had been there. He therefore designed a series of trip cords in the forest on the paths leading to the villa, some of which were not yet overgrown. The trips were cotton and difficult to detect, but to prevent them from being snagged by animals, they had to be more than a metre from the ground. He spent several days setting them up and cataloguing their exact location so he could check them easily when he returned.

Not announcing when he would be back — the element of surprise would help to keep the workers on their guard — Salvatore left one spring morning for Garda and stayed away for two months. On his return, after scrutinising his workers' achievements during his time away and declaring them satisfactory, he hurried to the forest and the old villa. Notebook in hand, he moved from one trap to the next, and, apart from one that appeared to have become detached owing to damage to the tree it had been tied to, all the others were as he had left them. Delighted that the old villa was now firmly established as a no-go area, Salvatore felt more confident that its awful secret was unlikely to be discovered.

Chapter Thirty-Eight

1925

Costanza di Lauriatis sat on the sheltered semicircular balcony of Villa Brocanti di Garda flicking through the newspaper, pausing occasionally to dip into her light breakfast. As she pushed a fork into a delicately rolled piece of prosciutto or a sliver of pecorino, she would lift her eyes to gaze at the peaceful waters of Lake Garda spread out before her, a view she had enjoyed for more than twenty years and never once tired of.

Looking back at the newspaper, she had only read two lines of a gossipy story from Verona when a maid came onto the terrace carrying a small silver tray.

"Excuse me, Marchesa," she said, curtseying nervously. "A telegram has just arrived for you."

"A telegram, Lucia?" snapped Costanza, irritated by the interruption. "Do we know who it's from?"

"The postman said it is from Signor Niccolò, Marchesa."

"Niccolò? It's unusual for my son to send me a telegram, in fact I'm not sure he has ever sent me one. What the devil does he want?"

The maid remained silent, knowing the volatile marchesa was not expecting an answer. She had made the mistake of trying to respond to such rhetorical questions before and received the rough end of the marchesa's tongue.

"Here, girl, give it to me."

The maid proffered the tray to her mistress. Costanza snatched the telegram and ripped it open.

Scanning the brief text, she sighed in exasperation and tossed the offending sheet onto the table.

"I suppose that means I shall have to go to Tuscany. Wretched place. Why does he always make life difficult when I'm busy?"

"Marchesa?" said the maid, wondering if she was supposed to understand.

"It's my husband, Lucia. According to Niccolò, he's disappeared again. Hasn't been seen for a week. Not the first time, of course, he's getting quite senile. But he's never been gone for as long as that. Is the postman waiting?"

"He is, Marchesa."

"Good. Tell him to reply that I'll come as soon as I can. Damn it, girl! I'll have to cancel my trip to Venice. The Contessa will not be pleased; she's been prettying up that hideous child of hers so I can paint her portrait. Most inconvenient." She glanced at Lucia. "What's the matter, girl?"

Lucia had flushed a deep crimson at her mistress' language. She curtseyed awkwardly. "Nothing, Marchesa."

"Hmph!" harrumphed Costanza, "Then you can call the chauffeur. Tell him I need him to drive me to the Tuscany villa. I'll use the English motorcar. What's it called?"

"The Rolls Royce, Marchesa?"

"Yes, that's the one. And you'd better pack for me. I've no idea how long I shall be. Pack enough for two weeks. If I need any more, I'll send the car back."

"Yes, Marchesa." The maid turned and hurried from the balcony.

Costanza sighed again and reached out for the telegram to reread its irritating message.

'Mamma. Papa missing now for a week. All usual places in the forest searched but no sign. I fear for him. He has not been himself lately. Foresters continuing the search. Niccolò.'

·   ·   ·

She sat back in her chair, her fingers flicking at the telegram.

"By all the saints, Salvatore, what are you up to now, you old fool?"

Costanza di Lauriatis had been just nineteen years old in 1899 when she married Salvatore Brocanti. Taking a husband thirty years her senior was not what she had imagined for herself, in fact she had little interest in marrying at all. She was far more disposed to follow the life of an artist like her father, the brilliant but struggling Vincenzo Gianpietro di Lauriatis.

However, when the offer came from her father's old friend — Vincenzo was one of the few artists Salvatore respected — it seemed too good to pass up. The man was rich with two large estates, he was from a noble family that went back generations and was a famous artist himself. And unusual for the nobility, instead of his painting being an amusing diversion to pass otherwise boring days, he pursued it with a passion.

Or at least he had until his first wife and children mysteriously disappeared. Rumour was that Isabella, the wife, had absconded with a lover, taking the children with her, and since then, the previously wild and unpredictable Salvatore Brocanti had been somewhat less volatile.

Costanza herself was no meek lamb, rather she could match Salvatore's vesuvian outbursts and tantrums blow by verbal blow. For Salvatore, who had known her since she was a young child, this was part of her attraction. A sparring partner with stunning beauty, and skill as a portraitist that matched his own.

He was also desperate for more children. More than anything in the world, he felt it was his duty to continue the Brocanti line, and now his beloved son Tommaso was dead at the hand of his unfaithful late wife, a new family was a necessity.

Costanza had one concern. "Papa," she asked her father, "I know Salvatore's wife has disappeared, but is he not technically still married? How can he take another wife? The Church would surely object."

Her father nodded. "First question I asked him when he came

to me seeking your hand. He's had the marriage annulled. As far as the Church is concerned, it never happened."

"And his children?"

"Born out of wedlock. Not entitled to anything. No, Costanza, marry the man, give him a couple of children and he'll be happy. He's not in the greatest of health. You could find yourself an extremely rich widow while you're still quite young. Those estates are worth a fortune."

Although Costanza was a good foot shorter than her husband, what she lacked in height she made up for in spirit. After the wedding, she reluctantly moved into the substantial new villa Salvatore had designed and built, but she was never happy in it. She regarded Tuscany as too far south to be civilised and found the summer weather oppressively hot. Their relationship was every bit as tempestuous as two capricious spirits could make it, their rows monumental, their clashes gladiatorial, although mercifully only in terms of verbal combat, never physical.

She was as different from Isabella as was possible, but for Salvatore, this was a bonus. He wanted nothing to remind him of the woman. He succumbed to many of Costanza's demands with a willingness that had been entirely absent in his first marriage, and when their first-born child was a son, he was ecstatic.

"With Niccolò as my heir, I shall die a contented man," he told Costanza.

"You'd better not die yet, Salvatore, I want at least two more children."

In the end, it was three: a girl, Maria, born eighteen months after Niccolò, and twin girls, Abriana and Adelina two years later.

Costanza fully intended to continue with her portraiture for the rest of her life, but in spite of her independent spirit, she was rigid in her faith, and the children were brought up with the strong guidance of the Church. This side of her pleased Salvatore enormously since it made keeping the myth surrounding the old villa alive and threatening far easier. Costanza only once let her curiosity get the better of her when, without Salvatore's knowledge, she slipped into the forest and followed the overgrown tracks until the old villa loomed up out of the trees. She stopped and shivered, even though it was midsummer. Salvatore had woven his tales well, embellishing them frequently. To those convinced of the evil surrounding the villa, merely looking at it was dangerous.

She had intended checking the doors and windows in the hope that she might get a chance to see inside, but in the event, she lost her normally iron-willed nerve and ran the three kilometres back to the new villa, vowing she would never go near the place again.

Costanza wanted to leave the Tuscany estate and move to the one by Lake Garda, and with the children growing, she realised she could use the old villa as a weapon to get her way.

She chose her moment well, waiting until one of the many bouts of rheumatism that increasingly plagued Salvatore was distracting him, making him want to avoid complex arguments.

"I really don't think the climate here in Tuscany is doing my health any good, Salvatore. Or the children's. But it isn't simply the climate, this whole estate has an air about it, as if the evil in that old villa is seeping through the ground and polluting everything near it. Even at this distance I can feel it. I worry about the children, Niccolò particularly. He is a most adventurous boy. As he grows it will be difficult to keep watch on him when he plays outside."

It was enough for Salvatore. The mere thought of losing Niccolò had him wringing his hands in anguish, the loss of Tommaso still a raw wound.

"You are right, my dear," he agreed. "I think you should all move to Garda as soon as possible. I shall remain here for most of the time since there are matters on the estate that require my constant attention. And since most of the small number of commissions I have these days are in or around Rome, I prefer the shorter journey. Garda is such a long way."

· · ·

For Costanza the arrangement was perfect. She had the independence she wanted, the children were safe, and her husband, already old beyond his advancing years, was more than three hundred kilometres away for most of the time.

By the time he was eighteen, Niccolò had decided what he wanted from life. He had been too young to participate in the terrible war that had ravaged Europe for the past four years, and anyway he had no interest in the military or in fighting. He wanted to work the land on the Tuscan estate, restore the vines and olives to at least their former glory, and preferably well beyond it. He wanted the name Brocanti to be not simply a mark of nobility, he wanted it associated once more with fine wine and excellent olive oil the way it had been in his grandfather's day.

Salvatore could see that although his son had inherited none of his parents' artistic talents, his business acumen was good. And he certainly had the strong will and intransigence of the Brocanti men. He happily gave the young man the responsibility of running and developing the estate, the added bonus being that his son lived with him in the new villa.

And while Niccolò laboured long hours, Salvatore took to wandering the forest as he had nearly seventy years before as a boy. Some days when Niccolò returned at dusk, tired and hungry, the housekeeper would report that his father hadn't been seen since he took his breakfast. Wearily, Niccolò would round up various estate workers, equip them with lanterns, and the search would begin. At times it would take up to three hours to find the old man, who often as not was sound asleep at the foot of a tree.

"Papa, you can't keep doing this, it isn't fair on the staff; they have already worked a long day, and it's dangerous. There are still many wild creatures in the forest: boar, snakes, even wolves. As you have told me many times, more than a few people have disappeared without trace here. There was the local pharmacist from Coniglio many years ago, and then a number of guards who had once worked for you. It could even be that your first wife and your dear children by her suffered the same fate. The woods are huge and nature doesn't discriminate between animals and humans when it comes to the sick and wounded. For the same reason we seldom see the bodies of animals here, I doubt the remains of humans would last long either."

Salvatore did his best to look shamefaced. "I am sorry, Niccolò, I am old and forgetful. As you know, I love these woods, I have loved them all my life. It is natural to me to wander amongst them, but unfortunately I lose sense of time and place." He patted his son on the arm. "I shall do my best to inconvenience you less."

His behaviour towards his family was all part of Salvatore's grand plan. It wasn't that he didn't care for them, he loved his son and heir Niccolò, his daughters and, in a way, his wife.

But they no longer had much need for him. His wife was still a relatively young woman who had achieved fame in her own right, Niccolò was successful, while his three daughters were gifted artists and apparently following in their parents' footsteps. Salvatore himself had long since lost his passion for painting, the trips to Rome he described to Costanza merely excuses to meet up with the few old friends there who were still alive. But his body was failing him, he could feel it almost daily. It was time to stop.

With his wandering in the forest, he had successfully established a pattern of behaviour that would leave people in no doubt that when he did disappear, he was somewhere in the hundreds of hectares of wilderness. He had been careful to make no mention of the old villa for many a year, and he knew that both Niccolò and the rest of the family were as much in fear of the place as they had ever been.

On the morning he decided to go, he had breakfast with his son, they talked inconsequentially about matters on the estate and they bid each other farewell. After retrieving the hidden key for the cantina door, Salvatore took a last look around the villa he had built nearly thirty years before, told the housekeeper he would take a late lunch, and set off for the forest. In case anyone was watching him go, he chose a path that didn't lead towards the villa, but once he was in the cover of the trees, he changed direction.

He had often visited the old villa over the years, but he had never gone inside, knowing that to do so would inevitably draw him towards the rooms on the top floor. The cantina door was almost entirely covered by vegetation encroaching from the forest. Disturbing the tangle of brambles and creepers as little as possible, he unlocked the door and slipped inside. As he closed it, he made sure the vegetation all fell back into place. Having locked the door, Salvatore walked through the cantina, holding high a lantern he had hidden months previously in a dry recess by the cantina door. He ignored the left door at the end that led to the long-sealed room containing the bodies of the four guards. Instead, he opened the right door, climbed the stairs and let himself into the first large ground-floor room, letting the door to it close behind him. He was now prevented from returning to the cantina and was, therefore, already trapped inside his own labyrinth.

He was pleased to find the condition of the paintings had not changed. In the limited light from the lantern they seemed as they had been when he created them thirty years before. He walked on, up the deceptive stairs and into the room with the trompe l'oeil floor. Ignoring the painting, and still able to see well in the room owing to the special window he had created, he walked over to the window and peered through. The scene was the same — how could it possibly have changed? There was Isabella, frozen in time, sitting on the garden seat reading her book, her back to him.

He turned and looked around the room, impressed with himself for all the detail he had created in the illusions adorning the walls, ceiling and floor, but at the same time sad that although the primary objective of his project had been achieved, it had ulti-mately all gone so terribly wrong.

As he walked up the final flight of stairs to the top floor, he found himself panting with the effort and stopping for breath, something that had never happened during all the frenetic activity there when he was thirty years younger. He sighed. It was definitely time to go.

He opened the black door at the top of the stairs, walked into the first shallow but wide room and waited for the door to close itself behind him. That it did so quietly and efficiently gave him great satisfaction. He walked over to the wall dividing the original room and moved along to the left corner, firmly pressing his foot against the lower part next to the floor. The door to the inner room opened silently, and, unlike the last time, there was no stench of death or decay, just a dry mustiness.

He faltered at the threshold to the room, suddenly anxious at seeing his children again. It had been thirty years. What fine adults they would have been by now, with families of their own. But instead, thanks to the selfish self-indulgence of the woman whose remains lay tossed in the corner to his left, the bodies of his beloved children lay here in this room, frozen in time, frozen in their childhood.

He looked down at the bodies he had lined up all those years ago and was almost surprised to find they were exactly as he had left them. Deliberately walking clear of the door, he stopped, waiting for it to close, waiting for that final quiet movement followed by the slightest of clicks.

He smiled as he knelt to look at his children. He wouldn't disturb them yet; it would take a while until he was too weak to move, until he was ready to sit with them and arrange them in his arms. He didn't know quite how long it would take, but he assumed it would be a couple of days.

Now the door was closed and there was no going back, he felt an unexpected sense of relief, a comfort in knowing he was at peace and soon to join his children. Not for one moment did it occur to him that none of his victims, intended or otherwise, had felt that peace as they faced the certainty of their deaths.

Part Three

Chapter Thirty-Nine

2018

"Evie!"

Joe Oliver skidded to a halt in the doorway of the top-floor room, but only an eerie silence greeted him.

He had left his torch propping open the door from the stairs, but since the beam was shining upwards, its light hardly penetrated the room beyond the doorway. However, Joe immediately saw the room was dimly lit from another source. Looking up, he saw a small skylight set in the tiles of the roof, its glass smeared with over a hundred years of dirt.

Very aware that the door to the inner room he had just opened might quietly swing closed any second, he remained by the doorway and let his eyes adjust to the gloom. Which was when he saw the chair and table straight ahead of him.

"Perfect!" he cried as he glanced towards the door, trying to gauge how long he had to retrieve the chair.

"Two steps should do it," he said. "Grab the chair and haul it back to the doorway."

As he moved forward and reached out for the chair, something on the edge of his vision to his right registered and he instinctively turned his head to see what it was.

"Jesus!" he yelped, stopping in his tracks, his flailing arm missing the chair back. "What the hell …?"

Sitting on the floor and leaning against the wall some three metres away was the body of a man, his head slumped onto his chest and his arms curled around what appeared to be other bodies.

But before he had time to take in more of the scene, Joe saw the door start to move.

"Bugger!" he yelled as he spun on his heel and dived for the doorway, his arms reaching out for the door and blocking it.

"Bloody hell, that was close!" he muttered, one hand now firmly on the door. He waited until his heart stopped threatening to burst through his chest before turning his head back to look at the bodies. Was one of them Evie? Couldn't be, surely.

"Evie, are you there? You must be. Just hang on, I'll move that chair and then get the torch."

Again there was nothing but a cold silence as his words died in the gloom.

"Right," he said. "Let's be scientific about this. Just how much time do I have until this sodding door closes?"

He pushed the door open to its maximum and let go. For two seconds it seemed to remain still, after which it slowly began to move, gradually picking up speed. He waited until it was at right angles to the frame before he reached out to stop it.

"Five to six seconds," he muttered to himself. "Should be enough time to grab the chair."

He pushed the door back to its wide-open position, took a breath and launched himself towards the chair. His fingers folded around the top rail of the backrest and he pulled hard. The chair was heavier than he expected and he stumbled slightly as he changed direction, but within less than three seconds, he was back in the doorway.

"OK," he said, panting in relief, "next step."

He pushed the inner door wide open again, quickly pulling the chair across the outer room to where the torch was propping open the outer door. Again, within a few seconds, he was back in the doorway, this time with the torch in hand and confident the outer door from the stairs was now securely propped open by the chair.

Turning the torch beam onto the macabre scene to the right of the doorway, he could now make out four bodies: the man he had first seen, and three smaller bodies that could only be children.

He gulped with emotion at the scene's sadness, the deliberate way the bodies had been arranged around and across the man's lap, the clothing on each of them smoothed and tidy.

"The children must have all been dead when he did that," he said, quietly. "Or someone else arranged all four of them. I wonder how long …"

He moved the beam over the clothing, studying the detail. He gasped, a sinking feeling hitting his gut as he worked it out. "This clothing is ancient," he whispered. "Nobody has worn stuff like that for about a hundred years. Christ, have they really been here that long?"

Almost reluctantly, he moved the torch beam to the left of the doorway, away from the bodies, and what he saw in the harsh illumination made him recoil into the door frame.

"Bloody hell, another one!"

This body was different from the others. Curled up into a tight foetal position, its back facing Joe, its story was clearly nothing like that of the grim tableau across the room.

"He's wearing jeans," said Joe in amazement, "and a modern jacket. Is he actually dead, or …?"

Looking more closely, he registered the slackness of the jeans, the skeletal frame under the clothing that appeared to be draped rather than worn.

He shook his head. "Poor bastard starved to death like this lot, but much more recently. He must have found a way in, like I did. I wonder who he is. Perhaps he's got some ID."

He had already taken a step towards the body when he saw the movement of the door in the corner of his eye.

"Shit," he said, in annoyance, as for the second time he stepped back to the doorway and blocked the door from closing. "I've got to find something to prop this thing open. Maybe the table, unless there's something a bit lighter."

Moving the torch beam around the room, letting it seek out the recesses to the far left of the doorway, he saw what appeared to be a pile of clothing dumped unceremoniously against the far left wall. But when he looked more closely, he realised there was yet another body, a woman.

"Evie!" he cried. "I forgot … bloody hell, Evie!"

In the harsh shadows of the beam, he could see the body was lying awkwardly, not arranged deliberately like the man and the children, and not in a pose of dejection like the man curled up on the floor, his back to the world as if attempting to reject his fate to the bitter end. The woman had one hand stretched out ahead of her, above her head, while her face was hidden by her clothing, which had ridden up to cover it.

As he continued to stare at the woman, in the mixture of shadows, clothing and light from the torch beam, Joe thought he saw movement.

"Evie!" he yelled again, and his caution forgotten, he rushed across the room.

"Evie!" He reached for the woman's outstretched hand. "Are you …?" But when he felt the dry, parchment of tissue stretched thinly across the projecting bones, he knew it couldn't be Evie. This woman had been dead for decades. What he thought might be some sort of modern jacket that had moved to cover the woman's face was in fact a full silk blouse, as old in its style as the children's clothing and the man's.

"So where's Evie?" said Joe, raising the torch again to explore the hidden corners of the room.

As if in answer, there was the slightest of swishes as the door to the inner room closed back to its resting position and the lock secured it with a soft click.

Joe turned the beam back towards where he had entered the room, staring in horror as he saw how good the fit was of the door into its frame.

"No! Fuck! NO!" he yelled, as he sprang to his feet and rushed over to the door. He banged and kicked at it, which was when he learned that not only was it made of stone rather than wood, but also it was as immoveable as the wall.

He turned and, leaning his back against the door, he slid down it into a sitting position on the floor, his mind now aware of one thing. He was trapped, like the others in the room had been trapped. At various times over the last hundred years or more, they must all have searched for a way out and failed, while slowly, minute by minute, they had succumbed to thirst and starvation.

Chapter Forty

Anger didn't come close to describing what Joe was feeling. More than simply wild with himself, he was fuming, seething with rage at his stupidity. Sitting against the wall, he pounded his forehead with his balled fists to emphasise every word of self-criticism, each word getting louder until he was screaming.

"Jesus, Joe Oliver! How could you be so fucking STUPID? You! Supreme! Dickhead!"

Panting breathlessly, he stood and kicked at the wall. When this produced no result, he knelt, his eyes searching every imperfection in the plaster, his hands frantically probing every inch.

"There has to be a hidden mechanism, surely. The lunatic who set up this whole madness must have left himself the option of escaping, in case he was dumb enough to do what I just did."

For the next thirty minutes, he frantically scrutinised the room's walls, pushing them and kicking them until he was once again effervescent with frustration.

"Bollocks!" he screamed, kicking out at the table. "Bloody, buggering bollocks!"

The table was heavy and it moved only a few reluctant centimetres, but it was enough to reveal the letter Salvatore had screwed up in anger and tossed away from him. It had come to rest behind a table leg.

Joe snatched up the letter, hoping it might reveal he was the victim of some practical joke, that it would give him the key he was searching for. He opened it, flattened it out as best he could, and shone the torchlight onto it.

"Shit," he said. "It's in Italian and the writing's really hard to read."

After a while, the words began to make sense and Joe slowly worked out what had probably happened. Distracted from his own dilemma, he became immersed in the tragedy that had played out in the room more than a century before.

"So that poor desiccated creature in the corner was the children's mother and the bastard holding the children their father. The mother and children must have got trapped here and all starved to death. Then mad bollocks must have somehow found them and decided to top himself in the same way."

He stared at Isabella's body. "I'll bet she wasn't like that when he found them. More likely, she was holding the children. So why has she been tossed into the corner like a rag doll?"

He walked over to Isabella's body and knelt beside it. Gingerly at first, he pulled at the clothing covering her face, and although he knew she had been dead for more than a hundred years, he was still shocked to see the skeletal remains of her head. Her long hair was still largely attached to her scalp, but most of her features had disappeared.

"You poor woman," said Joe, "you deserve better than this."

He leaned forward with a view to turning the body, which was when he remembered he had his phone in his pocket. Taking it out, he checked the signal, but there was nothing. "But it still has a working camera," he said, "and if I don't get out of here there should be a record of how I found things."

He stood up, turned on the phone's flash, and took several shots of the room in general together with details of the bodies. He also took a shot of the letter he had found.

Once satisfied he had enough shots, he checked the battery level. "Eighty-three per cent," he read out and turned off the phone. "Don't want to waste it; I might be dictating a brief account of what's happened along with my last will and testament."

Turning his attention back to Isabella's body, Joe gently lifted her and turned her onto her back, carefully straightening her clothing as he did. Her right arm, still stretched out, now seemed unnatural and he wondered if he could position it better without it coming off in his hands.

Initially, as he pulled on the arm, there was a resistance from the remains of the tissue holding Isabella's skeleton together, but the resistance faded and Joe managed to turn the arm so it sat as he thought it should.

He looked across the room to Salvatore's body leaning in a sitting position against the wall.

"I'll bet you were like that when he found you, princess. And I'll bet anything you were cradling your children. Let's see if we can get you back into that position and then you can have them close to you again. In my book, that bastard doesn't deserve to be holding them a moment longer."

Joe bent over Isabella's body and put his arms around her so he could lift her. He was surprised how little she weighed and how, with a little persuasion, her body folded into a sitting position as he leaned her against the wall.

"There we are, that seems about right. Let's fetch the kids, shall we?"

Over the following minutes, Joe retrieved the bodies of the three children and with the greatest of care laid them so they were once again in Isabella's arms. Satisfied he had completed the task as best he could, he switched on his phone and took another couple of shots of the family group.

The light was now fading fast, the afternoon long past, the dirty skylight serving only to deepen the gloom. However, aware of the need to conserve resources, Joe resisted turning on the torch; he would save the battery for essential purposes only.

With just enough light, he turned his attention to the other body. "Where did you come from, my friend? And how long have you been here?"

He knelt alongside the man, who was dressed in jeans and a light jacket over a plaid cotton shirt. The decay of this body was far less marked than that of the other bodies in the room, and when he rolled it onto one side to get a better look at him, Joe could clearly make out the deep scars running down the man's face.

He winced, "I wonder what caused that," he said. "Must have been one hell of an accident."

As the last of the light faded, tiredness washed over Joe as the pressures of his ordeal caught up with him. He had to rest.

He turned on the torch and shone it around the room. "Think I'll sleep in the west wing, along with the princess and the children," he said. "There has to be a way out of this place, but I'll need a bit of daylight to find it."

Doing his best to ignore the hunger starting to gnaw at his gut, and the thirst pulling at his dry throat, he curled up on the floor near Isabella and switched off the torch.

Chapter Forty-One

At eight the following morning, once the day staff had arrived and breakfast was being prepared for the six guests staying at Villa Brocanti, Monica was in her office checking the items she had put together in her backpack.

Not being the most practical of people, and certainly not used to pioneering in any sense, she wondered if the two powerful torches, the small hammer and the sheathed knife were sufficient. Somehow, they looked rather inadequate in the bottom of the bag, as if she were missing something. It was only when she lifted her espresso cup to down the contents that she thought clearly. Water! And something to eat. Joe had only been missing since the day before, but Evie Lorrigan had not been seen for nearly three days. If she really were trapped in the abandoned villa, by now her situation would be desperate.

After walking through to the bar and picking up two one-litre bottles of water, some pastries and wafer bars, Monica shouldered the backpack and headed out through reception.

"I'm going out for a while, Chiara," she called. "I should be back by lunchtime. Please take any messages in case my phone is out of range."

Chiari watched her go, wondering what all the secrecy was about and surprised to see her boss dressed as if she were about to go on a serious hike. She hoped the smart boots were lightweight; if not, Monica would boil once the day warmed up.

Monica had no intention of doing much hiking. By turning left out of the main gates in her car, she would come to the old track that had bordered the original estate. Although the driving distance was nearly three times the direct route through the forest, at least she was driving rather than walking, and the place where she intended to leave the car only about one kilometre from the abandoned villa rather than the three from Villa Brocanti.

The track was more overgrown than she remembered from the last time she had driven it, but it was still well defined and from the flattening of the vegetation, it had been driven along recently. She was beginning to think she had missed the clearing she was looking for when she saw Joe's car through the trees. Her heart thumped, his car being here more or less confirming that he had gone back to the old villa. What could have happened? Thoughts of the abandoned villa and its reputation as an evil place forced themselves into her mind, refusing to go away.

Pulling up near Joe's car, she got out and tried the driver's door. To her surprise, it opened, but apart from a map of Umbria on the passenger seat that included the area of Tuscany where she was now standing, there was nothing of interest.

She returned to her car and slipped her arms through the backpack's straps, thinking that perhaps she should have sought help, or at least told Chiara where she was going. Rather too late in the day for that, she thought as she remembered again how long it was since Evie had been seen.

Taking a deep breath, she stood up straight and turned in the direction of the abandoned villa. 'It's only a house,' she told herself, 'all the rest of the hype is just superstitious nonsense.'

Another deep breath saw her take her first step along the narrow path that led from the clearing, and soon she was deep amongst the trees. The dense undergrowth with its tangle of roots, fallen branches and huge clumps of bramble made it impossible to run. Even walking as fast as she could and hacking at the obstructions with her knife, it took her almost twenty minutes to reach the overgrown garden at the rear of the abandoned villa, twenty long minutes during which she increasingly felt the grasping claustrophobia of the forest. It was therefore a relief to be in the relatively clearer space of the old garden, even if the view of that side of the villa was unfamiliar to her. On her previous visit to the villa with Anna Riccardi, she hadn't walked far around this side.

As she studied the villa more closely, Monica saw the single-storey outhouse projecting from the main building and decided it would be an obvious place to start her search. Seeing no windows on the formal garden side of the outhouse, she traced the path to the other side and she was encouraged to see an open door that appeared to have been forced. As she peered into the darkness of the interior, she pulled a torch from her backpack and shone the light into the room. A door inside the room was also open but another in the room it led into was firmly locked.

Monica went back outside where she saw the shutter Evie had forced to access the room closest to the main house. Standing on tiptoes to lean as far across the sill as she could, she shone the torch beam into the room and immediately caught sight of the open door in the wall that would lead into the main house. Like Joe before her, Monica dropped her backpack through the window, pulled herself up onto the windowsill and jumped into the room. Interested only in the open door, she was surprised to find it was propped open with a wooden crate. Puzzled, she shone her torch beam up and down the door.

"There's no handle on this door," she blurted out, "not on this side or the other. I wonder if …"

She glanced at the wall near the door and saw the space where the brick covering the door lever had been removed. She bent over to shine the torch into the space and saw the lever.

Straightening up, she tried to make sense of everything.

"First you'd have to find the latch in the wall," she mused as she absently reached for her backpack and slipped it round her shoulders. "Then if the door closed, you'd have to find the lever on the inside to reopen it. Assuming there is one."

Hesitantly, she peered through the doorway into the darkness of the corridor beyond and played the torch beam up and down the nearby wall, but she couldn't see an obvious lever. Looking again at the door, she put her foot against it while she picked up the crate, and then took her foot away. Within a couple of seconds, the door began to move.

Shocked at the complexity of the trap, she hurriedly put the crate back in place to ensure the door could no longer close.

She now turned her attention to the corridor, shining the powerful beam of her torch along its length. Another open door caught her eye. In contrast to the one next to her, this one wasn't propped open in any way and it had handles on both sides. As she walked past it, she checked the handles to satisfy herself they worked.

Walking on, she hardly noticed the painted curtain as she almost tripped over the pile of real curtain now lying on the floor. What had caught her eye, as had happened with both Evie and Joe, were the paintings on the walls of the room she now entered.

Initially, Monica was as taken in by the paintings as anyone else seeing them for the first time, even though she recognised some as the paintings in the black and white images on Joe's computer that he had processed from the glass photographic plates. And even when the trompe l'oeil effect was lost in the harsh torch beam, she stood staring for several moments at everything in the room, impressed by the sheer quality of the portraits on the walls and the balustrade at ceiling level with the false sky above it.

Another flash of the torch beam around the room and she saw the door in one corner. It was open and, like the one in the corridor, it had handles.

"And there's nothing propping it open," she said as she swung the door back and forth to satisfy herself she wasn't walking into a trap.

She thought back to the images she had seen on Joe's computer. His photographs had clearly not been taken in this room, but at least one of the images from the glass plates was. And from the way at least one door was propped open and others left open, it looked increasingly as if Joe had indeed returned to find the sources of the images on the glass plates.

She shone the torch beam through the door and saw the corridor leading away to the right. Following it, she came to the stairs. Confident now she was on the right track, and also that she had a way out, she climbed the stairs, directing the beam onto the walls. In its stark light, the trompe l'oeil effect was far less obvious and she was taken in only momentarily by the balustrade and the corridor at the top of the stairs.

She hurried along the corridor as far as it went to the two doors facing each other, the left one of which was ajar. Pushing it open, she was surprised to find there was natural light shining into the room from a window on the far wall. Distracted, she was drawn to walk into the room, her attention on the open window. After two steps, her foot found the board set up to fool her and when it creaked she looked down and gasped in shock at the apparent hole in the floor.

Her attention now fully on the scene of the room below, she was backing slowly away from the danger when a crash to her right made her jump in fright. Something large and heavy had hit the floor only about half a metre from her, fragments of plaster, terracotta tiles and clouds of dust billowing up from the point of impact.

As she took another step backwards, there was a second crash directly in front of her, followed by a third to her left.

Convinced the roof was collapsing and smashing through the floor she was standing on, she dived for the relative safety of the doorway, hoping the entire villa wasn't about to be reduced to rubble.

As the dust began to settle, Monica was surprised to see that rather than the gaping hole in the floor being much larger, it was instead covered in debris. The implications of this had only just started to register in her mind when another section of the ceiling crashed to the floor in the centre of the room. But what startled Monica more was the cry of "Yes!" from somewhere above her.

She looked up from the doorway, shielding her head in case more tiles fell in her direction and saw a foot and the lower part of a leg protruding through the ceiling.

"Signor Oliver?" she cried. "Joe?"

"Monica? Is that you?"

Monica shone the torch beam upwards at the foot and saw that the remains of the vaulted ceiling around it was part of the illusion of the room. The real ceiling was far lower than the painting of the vaulting made it appear, but it was still close to five metres above the floor.

"Yes, it is," she called out. "Be careful, it's quite a drop."

"I will, thanks, and I think you'd better stand clear. I don't know how much of this ceiling is going to collapse when I kick it again. I'm hanging on to the beams above it, so if it all crashes down, it won't affect me, but you'd better mind your head."

"I'm already in the doorway, so don't worry," she called, but she instinctively took a couple more steps back to the security of the corridor.

"Right," called Joe, "Let's give it a go."

There was another loud crash as a number of tiles shattered on the floor, filling the room with even more dust. Putting one hand over her nose and mouth, Monica peered upwards and saw Joe hanging from a beam, a hole around it in the real terracotta ceiling above where the false painted terracotta ceiling had been.

"How far to the floor?" cried Joe. "I can't see much with all the dust."

"Your feet are about three metres above the floor," she replied. "It's quite a drop. Do be careful."

A moment later, Joe was standing in the debris next to Monica. "Well, at least that hole in the floor isn't real, or it would have been much further," he said.

"Oh, Joe!" cried Monica and flung her arms around him. "I'm so pleased to see you. Are you all right?"

Joe held her out from him and nodded. "I think so, and believe me, I'm ecstatic to see you."

He paused, puffed his cheeks and breathed out heavily. "Actually," he continued, "I'm parched. Do you have any water?"

"Oh, sorry, of course I do." She pulled open her backpack and handed him a bottle.

"Bliss," he said, taking two huge gulps. "Thank you, that's a true life saver. You haven't got anything to eat in there, have you?"

Monica pulled out one of the pastries and handed it to him, laughing as he devoured it.

After another pastry and another huge gulp of water, Joe sighed deeply and looked around him, as if seeing the room for the first time. As he turned back to Monica, she realised he was shaking.

"Joe," she said, folding her arms around him. "It's all right. You're safe."

Not able to support his weight as he leaned into her, she gently guided him into the doorway, away from the danger of any more tiles that might fall, and sat him down, cradling his head to her.

"I thought …" he began.

"Shh," she whispered, stroking his hair.

"No, I have to tell you. I thought … I thought I was going to die. I …"

She held him tighter as spasms of shuddering convulsed his body and he wept into her shoulder.

"I'm sorry," he said, after several minutes.

"Don't apologise, Joe, you need to let it out, it's important."

He nodded slowly, sniffing now and wiping his eyes with his sleeve.

"I've soaked your shirt," he said.

She smiled. "Just stay here until you feel completely calm. You're perfectly safe now. I made sure on the way in that every door is open. We can walk out of here."

She held him until she was sure the shaking had stopped. "Would you like some more water?"

He nodded and took the bottle. "Thanks," he said. "Sorry about that."

"Joe," she said and took his face in both of her hands. "I'd be far more concerned if you hadn't let it all out. You can't just ignore emotion like that."

He smiled softly. "Yeah, you're right. Can I give you another hug? It really helps."

"Give me as many as you like," she said, her own voice now cracking with emotion.

After a few minutes when neither of them said anything, Joe

sighed and sat up. "That was some twenty-four hours," he said. "I thought for a while I was going to suffer the same fate as the others."

Monica took his hands. "Others?"

Joe looked down at their intertwined hands and lifted his eyes to hers. "It was horrible, Monica. Horrible. That bastard. What he put them through."

"I don't understand."

Joe nodded across the room to a door. "That door leads to a corridor that has several doors in it. Only one is unlocked and that leads to some stairs that go up to the top floor. At the top of the stairs there's a heavy door, one that closes automatically, like the one downstairs. It leads into a weird-shaped room where there's another door in a wall with a hidden lever to open it. Basically, you kick the wall at floor level and it opens.

"Anyway, I did that. I'd been careful and propped open the outer door at the top of the stairs, first with my torch and then with a chair. The inner door to the final room is another that closes automatically, and there is no means to open it from the inside. It's a trap, a cell, where once you're in it, you will die."

"Is that what you mean by the others? Were there other people in there?"

"Yes. There were six bodies. The first one I saw was a man I now know was Salvatore Brocanti, the madman who created all this. He had three children in his arms, all of whom I think died long before he did. The fifth person was his wife, Isabella, who was lying in another corner of the room, almost as if she had been tossed aside. I thought it was Evie, which is how I got trapped. I rushed over to her, forgot about the door and it closed on me. That took some getting used to, believe me."

A nervous smile flickered on his lips, but his eyes still showed his tension. Monica squeezed his hands.

"You've worked out a lot of detail."

Joe nodded. "There was a letter, from Isabella to her husband. My Italian's not brilliant so it took me a while to work out what it said. But I did, eventually, and it's heartbreaking. Look."

He felt in his jeans pocket, pulled out the letter and handed it to Monica.

She held it towards the light and read it through several times.

"Oh, Joe," she said, chewing hard on her lip. "How terrible. What she and the children must have suffered. I can't begin to imagine it."

"Don't even try," said Joe. "It would be a horrible way to die. Yet Salvatore chose to take that path as well."

"It would have been many years later," said Monica. "He married again after the disappearance of Isabella and the children, and had more children. He suddenly vanished as an old man in the nineteen twenties."

"I reckon when he found them, probably soon after they died, he separated the bodies so that Isabella wouldn't be holding them. I've changed that, put her with her children again, given her some peace."

Monica looked up from the letter into Joe's eyes. "You're a kind man, Joe Oliver," she said, reaching out to stroke his cheek. "But, tell me, how did you escape?"

"I was wracking my brains, wondering how I could knock down a wall. I even tried but I just got a sore foot. Then, early this morning, when it was just getting light, I had to pee. I went over to one corner of the room, away from the bodies, and as I peed, I saw that the pee wasn't so much forming a puddle on the tiles as soaking into the gaps between the tiles. That's when I remembered about the construction of these old buildings. The ceilings and of course the floors above the ceilings are constructed of huge beams of something like chestnut which have narrower beams crossing them at right angles. The narrower ones are called joists in English."

Monica nodded. "Travetti," she said, "and the big chestnut ones are called travi."

"Right," said Joe. "Now, the joists are always the length of a tile apart, and the final part of the ceiling is a layer of terracotta tiles laid across the joists, the travetti, and then a layer of dry mortar follows, above which a floor of more terracotta tiles is laid to form the floors of the rooms above.

"Over the years, the dry mortar sets hard, although it retains some flexibility, which is why in old houses the floors can be so uneven. But I guess over centuries, there's a lot of settling. These days, of course, a slab of cement would be sandwiched in between, but not in old buildings. So when I peed, the pee soaked through the gaps in the tiles into the dry mortar. I figured if I could lift enough tiles and mortar, I'd get to the lower layer of tiles, which would be the ceiling of the room below. Remove some of those and I'd be on the wooden beams.

"So since first light this morning, that's what I've been doing. But once I got through, I discovered that below the ceiling was another layer of terracotta tiles in a herringbone pattern, a false ceiling several inches below the real one." He pointed upwards. "And on this side, the false ceiling was plastered and decorated with these amazing paintings. Given the weight of terracotta tiles, I should imagine that the false ceiling is domed slightly like an arch to give it strength, otherwise it would collapse. Of course, it still isn't very strong, so when I kicked at it, my foot went through it, taking several tiles with it. It was lucky you weren't standing right underneath when I did."

Monica made a face. "I nearly was."

"Talk about timing," said Joe as he gently rubbed the top of her head. "It would have hurt."

"More than hurt, I think. But anyway it didn't because they missed me."

She paused, her face clouding over as her features became serious.

"Joe. You said there were six bodies up there. Who … who was the sixth?"

Chapter Forty-Two

"The sixth body?" repeated Joe. "You know, it was really strange. He was curled up tightly in a ball, like he was rejecting everything, or just wanting to die quietly. But the thing is, he hasn't been in that room for a hundred years or more like the others, he's only been there for a few years. His clothing is modern. Jeans, shirt and a jacket."

Joe had been staring across the room while he was talking. When Monica said nothing, he shifted his focus to her face. She had gone white.

"Did … did he have any ID?" she whispered.

Joe frowned and slowly shook his head. "I don't know, I didn't look. I really felt it would be wrong to disturb him. He was so, well, so curled up that it didn't seem right. It would have been like a violation. So I didn't go through his pockets or straighten him out or anything. But I did roll him slightly to look at his face."

"And …?"

"Poor chap had a helluva scar, from close to his hairline right down to his jaw." He pointed to the area on his own face. "And it wasn't just a flesh scar, it—"

"It was far deeper, causing a severe brain injury," said Monica, interrupting him.

"Yes, possibly," said Joe, puzzled. "How do you know that?"

Monica sat back from where she had still been holding Joe's

hands and made to stand. "I've got to see him. Joe, I must see him. Can you show me the way? Please?"

Joe stood quickly and reached out for Monica's hands. "Of course, if that's what you want. But I have to warn you it's pretty spooky in there."

He pulled softly on her arm, turning her towards him. "Why do you need to see him? Do you think you might know him?"

"Monica?"

Monica was nodding her head slowly. She let go of Joe's hands and wrapped her arms around herself, her breathing heavy, her eyes staring wildly.

She began to turn away but Joe put his hand on her shoulder. "Monica, what is it? Who is he?"

Slowly Monica lifted her head, her eyes now filled with tears.

"He's my brother," she said, her voice thick. "My brother, Paolo. He has to be, with that scar. He's been missing for over two years, missing in this forest."

Joe put his arms around her. "Monica, I'm so sorry. I didn't know."

"Don't be sorry, Joe," she said, sobbing quietly into his chest. "You found him. You've solved the mystery of his disappearance. I've wondered and worried about him every day for the last two years. It's a good thing, a wonderful thing. I have found Paolo at last."

She took a step back. "I must see him."

"Of course. We need to go through that door, the one propped open with my camera bag," said Joe, pointing towards the corner of the room. "We must make sure all the doors are securely jammed open; I don't fancy coming through that ceiling again."

He took her hand and they walked over to the door. As they reached it, Joe stopped. "You haven't got another torch in your bag, have you? I left mine up there."

"I have, yes," replied Monica. "My bag's over by the other door. I'll fetch it, in case we need something else to hold the doors."

· · ·

With Joe leading, they walked along the short corridor to the door that led up to the top floor.

"These paintings are grotesque," said Monica, as they climbed the stairs that appeared to be covered in creepers.

"Yeah," agreed Joe. "It's like something's going to reach out and bite you. I found myself trying to tread between the branches."

The door to the room at the top of the stairs was still propped open with the chair Joe had dragged from the inner room. He checked it was firmly in place before walking over to the left corner of the room and kicking at the wall just above floor level. The door to the inner room opened with a soft swish.

"Here," said Joe, reaching out a hand. "Let me have your bag. It looks heavy enough to stop the door from closing."

"Yes," agreed Monica, "it still has a bottle of water in it, and a few other things. It should be heavy enough."

Joe pushed the bag against the door and tested it to make sure it would keep the door from closing before picking up the larger torch he had left in the room.

"This torch has a much more powerful beam than yours," he said as he turned it on. "I deliberately didn't use it last night. I wanted to conserve it; I didn't know how long I was going to be here."

Monica wasn't paying attention. She had shone her own torch onto the body lying a few feet away from her, her brother's body. She wanted to go over to him, but her feet felt rooted to the spot.

Joe watched her, sensing her dilemma.

"Would you like me to turn him so you can see his face?" he said.

Monica nodded as she chewed her lip.

Kneeling down, Joe gently rolled the body until the face was clearly visible.

"There," he said.

Monica knelt on the other side of her brother's body from Joe and shone her torch onto his head.

"Oh, Paolo," she whispered, stroking his face. "You poor darling. You must have been so frightened."

Joe continued to hold the body. After several minutes, Monica looked up at Joe.

"Do you think we could remove him from here? Carry him out, to another place? This isn't where he belongs."

"Certainly. He no longer weighs much, it won't be difficult."

She smiled. "Thank you Joe, it would make a huge difference."

She stood and looked around the room, shining her torch beam onto the group of Isabella and her three children.

"Oh, Joe, they look so peaceful. It's wonderful that you have put the children back with their mother."

She put her hand to her lips and gasped. "Joe, did you look closely at Isabella's clothing? It's just like what the woman in the old photograph on the wall at Villa Brocanti was wearing, the woman sitting in the garden reading a book."

"Wow! You're right," said Joe, surprised. "I didn't make the connection. The original painting is in the room downstairs, the one through there." He pointed to the hole in the floor that marked his escape route. "I don't think you got a chance to see it. I'll show you when we go back down there."

Monica nodded. "That painting, and all these others in this house of madness must have been painted by Salvatore Brocanti for the sole purpose of trapping his wife. He must have really hated her."

"Yes," agreed Joe, "and her lover. But it all backfired on him, didn't it? I'm sure he had no intention of killing his children."

"Is that him, over there?" said Monica. Her voice was lower now, full of bitterness. "Is that the bastard who's responsible for all this misery? The one whose lunacy helped to trap my brother?"

"That's him," said Joe, not registering Monica's change of tone. "It's interesting he chose the same fate for himself."

Monica stood and marched over to the body still propped against the far wall, now well away from the others.

"He deserved far worse. I hope every moment of his time in hell is filled with pain and torture," she said, her voice rising. She took another step closer to the body and lashed out with a foot, kicking it hard in the chest. The body slowly rolled to the floor.

"Monica, I ..." said Joe, but she ignored him. Now Salvatore's body was lying on the floor, he made an easier target. Monica launched several hard kicks at his head and chest. "Bastardo!" she yelled. "Maledetto bastardo!"

Joe rushed over to her and pulled her back, her arms flailing as she tried to resist him. "Monica, you shouldn't—"

"I want to destroy him, crush him to powder," she screamed.

Joe tightened his grip. "It's really not a good idea, Monica. Desecration of the dead and all that. I'm sure your priest won't like it."

He looked worriedly over at the now battered body, ribbons of dust rising above it from the impact of boot on desiccated bone.

"I don't care what he likes. I don't care if I suffer eternal damnation. Think about Paolo, think what he suffered because of this man's insanity." She was still writhing in his grip.

"Monica. Stop!" yelled Joe. "Stop, please. Let's get out of here, take Paolo with us and leave."

She sagged in his arms, taking him by surprise and nearly knocking him over.

"I hate him," she wailed as together they sank to the floor. "I hate him."

"I know," said Joe. "He deserves your hatred as much as he deserves mine. After all, he might have killed me too."

Monica looked up, her head shaking. "No, if you hadn't found your way out, I think I would have found you. After all, I had made it as far as the room downstairs. If I'd come up here, to the other side of that wall, we would have heard each other."

"I hadn't thought of that," said Joe.

"Oh my God!" yelled Monica, sitting up and straining against Joe's arms. He tightened his grip, thinking she was about to launch herself in another attack on Salvatore's body.

"Joe! Where's your friend? Where's Evie?"

"Evie?"

"Yes, you came here looking for her, didn't you? She was the reason you broke into the villa. To look for her."

"Of course, and I followed the trail up through the house as far as this room, as far as it goes, but she's not here. She wasn't trapped like I thought she was. If she'd followed the same route up through the house, she'd be here, and she isn't."

Monica was shaking her head. "Joe, this villa is enormous. Suppose there are other rooms like this. Suppose that madman created two, or three, or even more with different routes leading to them. It's quite possible. She might be trapped in one of them. We should search the whole place. It's been three days now. If she hasn't got any food or water, she might already be dead. Joe, we have to look."

Joe stood up. "Christ, you're right. Being trapped and shit-scared in a room with six bodies in it, and then discovering one of them was your brother, I'd completely forgotten about Evie. Look, let's at least take Paolo's body down to the room below, where there's some light, and from there we can make a systematic search."

He clenched his fists. "Do you honestly believe there are other rooms like this? If there are and Evie's trapped in one, I'll come back here and finish what you started with Salvatore's body. I'll grind the bastard to dust."

Chapter Forty-Three

Joe bent over Paolo's body and carefully slipped his arms under him. The balled position made him difficult to lift, even though the body weighed so little, but he didn't want to disturb him more than necessary.

Monica took all three torches and was about to pick up her bag when she stopped.

"I think it would be better to leave this door propped open, don't you?" she asked.

"Yes," agreed Joe. He looked around the room. "Try the table. I was going to use it before, when I got trapped, but it looked a bit heavy. I was looking for something else when I thought I saw Evie and, yeah, well … Mind you don't fall through the hole in the floor."

After dragging the table over to block the door, Monica put away her two torches and lit the way back down the stairs with Joe's brighter torch, turning it off once they reached the room lit with the fake window.

"I'll put Paolo over here in the corner," said Joe. "Away from the ceiling debris."

Monica had been following closely and once Joe had lain the body on the floor, she bent over it, fussing with the arms and hands.

"I'm just straightening him a little," she said, but Joe was already heading for the door.

"I've just remembered," he called. "When I came along the corridor, I took the left door into this room, as you did. I don't know why, I just did. But there was another door which also had a handle. Perhaps Evie went that way."

Monica caught up with him as he tried the handle to the door across the corridor.

"It's not locked," he said, and pushed it open.

They both stood in the doorway, surprised at how similar the room appeared to the one behind them.

"It's about the same size as the other one," said Joe. "And it's lit by an identical window."

He looked around the room. "The decoration's different though, and there's no trompe l'oeil painting on the floor to make you think the floor's collapsed."

"Why do you think there's a chair lying on its side in the middle of the floor?" asked Monica as she stepped into the room. She looked around. "It matches these two others near the door. It's as if it has been thrown from about here."

"Testing the floor?" suggested Joe. "Maybe Evie went into the other room first, got spooked by the floor and came in here. Perhaps she wanted to be sure the floor was real. I think I would. After all, not much else in here is. Look at this desk. It appears to be quite fancy, but all the ornate bits are painted on. None of it is real."

"What about the window?" said Monica, walking over to where the shutters were apparently open and letting in light.

Joe followed her and peered out.

"Bloody hell! It's exactly the same painting. The one of the woman sitting in the garden reading. You didn't see the one across the way, but it's the same. He's put the same painting in both rooms."

Joe turned his attention to the ceiling. "That vaulting effect is the same. Let's see …"

He turned and thought through the orientation of the room across the corridor. "From the way the stairs run, the rear of the room I was trapped in would be over the corridor outside. Given this room is pretty much a mirror image of the one over the way, there could be another similar pair of rooms above us."

"There's a curtain over there," said Monica, pointing to the corner of the room on the wall opposite the window. "It's been pulled aside and look, there's a door just like the one in the room opposite, and it's open!"

They both walked quickly over to the door and Joe shone his torch into the darkness.

"Look at that!" he said, shining his torch along the corridor now ahead of him. "It's exactly like the other one. This could be it, Monica."

He lifted his head and shouted. "Hold on, Evie, maybe we really have found you this time."

Having made sure the door from the large room was securely propped open with a chair, they both hurried along the corridor, ignoring the first two door handles and instead, trying the third.

"Bingo!" yelled Joe. "This has to be it. Look it's got the same crazy serpent paintings and the mixture of fake and real stairs."

They took the stairs two at a time to the dark, plain door at the top.

"This is one that will close, given half a chance," said Joe. "Let's use your bag to prop it open."

"Evie!" yelled Monica as she handed Joe the bag. "Can you hear us?"

"Evie!" shouted Joe, even more loudly, but there was no reply, no sound from the other side of the wall facing them.

"The hidden catch must be the same," said Joe. "Let's kick it … about here."

He gave the wall a firm kick just above floor level, but nothing happened.

"Strange," he said, bending to examine the wall.

"Look!" said Monica, pointing to the left of where he had kicked the wall. "There's a mark there. I think you were trying too far over. Try that spot."

Joe moved in front of where Monica was pointing and kicked again. This time, the wall gave a little and to their right, in the centre of the wall, there was a soft click followed by a swish as a hidden door opened into the room beyond where they were standing.

"There's a chair," cried Monica, pointing her torch ahead of her. "Grab that and block the door with it."

Joe did as she suggested, ensuring the door could no longer move before turning back to where Monica was now shining her torch.

"What the …?" he said as he moved his torch beam over Ugo's torn and shredded remains. "This was a body, but it's been stripped of clothing and torn apart."

They stared in horror at the body, trying to make sense of the grotesque distortion of the limbs.

"It's not Evie," said Monica, finally. "Look at it, there's not a lot left, but that was a man."

Joe shone his torch around the room. "There's another body over there," he said, pointing with his torch. "Look, a man in a large old-fashioned coat. He's wearing trousers too, and boots. Perhaps one of them was Isabella's lover. He certainly wasn't in the room where I was trapped."

"There's a pile of clothing under him too," said Monica. "It's almost as if it's been arranged like bedding."

"Looks long dead," said Joe as he turned his torch to examine the rest of the room. "So where the hell is Evie? I was convin—"

The rest of his sentence was drowned by a piercing scream from Monica.

"Joe!"

Joe swung round to see she was pointing at the body.

"Joe! It moved!"

For the past twenty-four hours, Evie had been semi-delirious, drifting in and out of consciousness as every cell in her body began to succumb to the effects of ever-worsening dehydration. Her mind increasingly wandered out of control in a churning sea of visions, most of which made no sense. The many places she had visited as a travel journalist throughout her career merged and distorted into tumbling, weaving, rippling images, always just out of reach, always full of crystal-clear water flowing freely across her feet, splashing onto her hands, rushing and gurgling all around her but never reaching her mouth, no matter how hard she strained to push her face into it.

Every now and then her mind would snap back into reality, the dismal surroundings of the room in sharp focus for a few seconds, the musty, dry smell of Ugo's coat wrapped around her forcing its way into every parched cell in her nose and mouth.

In those all-too-brief moments of lucidity, she was aware she was no longer cold, that her fever had passed. The layers of Ugo's clothing had done their work; she had even covered her face with the dead man's shirt, reasoning it would help her conserve what little water she had left in her body.

She had heard no more sounds from outside, what she had thought were voices now no more than a fragment of memory on the edge of her reason. They had merged with other imaginary sounds: water rushing, winds howling, traffic zooming by like a succession of bullets popping from the cavernous barrel of an unseen rifle, children screaming complete gibberish in unrecognisable languages, their voices too alien to be of human origin. Occasionally, very occasionally, there was a word she almost recognised. One word, one short word repeated as if it had significance, a profoundness that was now beyond her comprehension, repeated and repeated. Sometimes stretched, low and distorted, sometimes compressed so it was hardly more than a cry, but it was the same word. She knew she should understand it, it had been with her all her life. She waited, hoping it would be repeated in the same moment the world briefly stopped spinning and that she might understand it.

"Ev…" "E…" "EeeeeVeeee."

"Evie!"

It was her name! Something was making a noise that sounded like her name. No. Some*one* was saying her name.

She tried to reply but her throat no longer worked. Could they see her? Did they know she was there? She had to show them, they mustn't go. Please, oh please, they mustn't go. She needed to wave to them, make them see her. And she did. As her confused mind slipped back towards delirium, her left arm twitched, a movement she registered as her arms waving frantically.

Now there were other words. She didn't know what they meant but she felt they were good.

"Joe!"

"It moved!"

Suddenly the cover of Ugo's shirt was pulled from her face but her eyes wouldn't focus. She felt a hand move gently under her head, lifting it up. The torrent of water that had been cascading around her out of reach now crashed into her mouth. Water!

"Not too much, Joe, I don't think too much at once will be good for her."

Evie didn't recognise the voice but she wanted to argue. You can't have too much water. I want to drown in it. Please, just keep it coming.

But Joe also knew too much too quickly was dangerous and he kept the supply to dribbles to moisten Evie's parched and cracked lips.

"What's her pulse like?"

A pause.

"Weak. Very weak. We've got to get her out of here, get her to hospital."

"Can you lift her?"

"Shouldn't be difficult, she's pretty small," said Joe, as he carefully pushed one hand under Evie's knees and the other around her back. "The only heavy thing about her is the coat. You light the way, let me see the stairs."

Walls flashed past Evie's eyes too quickly for her to focus, but she didn't care. Another human being had burst into her life and a few precious drops of water had been given to her. Perhaps she wasn't going to die after all.

. . .

"Did you come through the window?" Joe had followed Monica back into the storeroom in the single-storey building at the rear of the villa and he was now desperately looking for how they would get out into the garden.

"Yes. There was a door in an outer room but it was locked," said Monica. "It would be where those shelves are," she added, pointing into a dark corner of the room.

"Pull them out of the way, perhaps there's a key in the lock. I really don't want to manhandle Evie through the window."

"Stand back, Joe."

Monica swept baskets and flower pots from the shelves with her arms and hauled on the uprights of the frame. After an initial resistance, it collapsed with a crash.

"Got it!" she cried. "And there *is* a key!"

As they ran into the garden, Monica turned to Joe.

"It's quite a way to the cars, but I think I should run ahead as quickly as I can and drive mine back onto the road. There's a very weak signal up there but it should be enough to contact the emergency services. I'm going to insist on a helicopter ambulance. It will save time and they can give Evie emergency treatment on the way. I'll come straight back for you. Are you sure you can find your way?"

"Of course I can, Monica. Just go!"

Progress through the woods was slower than Joe wanted, but he was constantly aware of the need to be gentle with Evie and to avoid the thorns ripping at them both. He had no idea how fragile she was, but he couldn't afford to take chances. And even though she was small and slim, she was a dead weight, forcing him to stop frequently for breath.

He had just emerged into the clearing where he had left his car when Monica's car screeched back along the track.

"They're on the way," she called as she ran from the car. "Let me help you lie her on the rear seat. Are you all right, Joe?"

Joe had stopped next to her car and was struggling to remain upright.

"Let's just get her in the car. I'll be fine. Where are we going?"

"There's a field just outside the main entrance to Villa Brocanti. We are in luck, the medevac helicopter was out on exercises and in the area. They'll probably be there before we are."

As Monica sped along the road leading back to Villa Brocanti, Joe became aware of an increasing whumping in the air as a helicopter descended towards the designated landing spot. Two paramedics jumped from it almost before it touched down and ran towards where Monica stopped the car. She flung open the door and began issuing instructions in rapid-fire Italian that was way too fast for Joe to follow.

The paramedics, a man and a woman, nodded, returned a couple of equally fast sentences and while the woman retrieved a stretcher from the helicopter, the man leaned into the car and carefully lifted Evie out.

"I told them you are both in need of treatment, but, of course, that Evie's is a matter of life and death. They said I can't go with you, there isn't room and anyway, my presence is unnecessary. I told them I'll follow in the car, but first I'll let Chiara know what's happened. I imagine the Carabinieri will be arriving in force before long, too."

"Where are we going?" asked Joe.

"Arezzo. San Donato hospital. I'll get there as soon as I can."

She reached out to touch Joe's arm as one of the paramedics came over to usher him on board. "She'll be all right, Joe. I know it. They've already set up a drip, look." She nodded her head towards the helicopter.

There was no more time. The paramedic threw a blanket around Joe's shoulders and pushed him towards the helicopter. Within seconds of the door closing, the whumping started again as the pilot increased the rotor speed and they were on their way.

Watching the helicopter fade into the distance, Monica suddenly realised how tired she was. She turned towards her car, almost having to drag her feet to get back to it. She slumped into the driver's seat and put her head in her hands. Her heart was still racing as the events of the afternoon flashed through her mind.

She had found her brother, found Paolo. She sat up and her hands gripped the steering wheel as she stared across the fields to the peaceful expanse of vines and olive trees. She wondered what she should do with Paolo's body, what she should tell the police. And what she should tell Ernesto Brocanti. He was going to be furious that the sanctity of the abandoned villa had been violated. She would probably be fired, but that would be a small price to pay for finding her brother.

As these and other thoughts rolled around her head, she hardly noticed the Vespa motor scooter approach and stop near her car. It was only when Chiara tapped on the window that she jolted back to reality.

"Direttrice, what has happened? Has there been an accident?" asked Chiara as Monica let down the window.

Monica looked up and sighed as she focussed her eyes on the girl.

"Quite a lot has happened, Chiara. I'll follow you back to the Villa and explain there."

"Was it the Englishwoman, Direttrice?" Chiara was frowning earnestly. It had been drummed into her that the wellbeing of guests was paramount.

Monica nodded. "It was, yes."

"Has she been injured?" continued Chiara, crossing herself. "I was worried about her. She seemed extremely concerned. She wanted to know if you were at the abandoned villa. I told her there is no abandoned villa, that the old villa burnt down, that—"

"Just a moment, Chiara. You spoke to the Englishwoman?"

"Yes, Direttrice."

"When?"

"About two hours ago. She arrived in a rental car. She said she had flown into Pisa last night and driven down this morning."

"Chiara, that doesn't make any … Wait a moment, did she give you her name?"

"Her name is Jane Bawley. She said she was here to find the other Englishwoman who was supposed to arrive a few days ago."

"Where is she now?"

"She said she was going to look in the forest, that she knew where to go."

"She went into the forest to look for her?"

"Yes. She was most insistent."

"OK, Chiara, I'll take it from here. I think I might know where she's gone. Go back to the villa and if the police or anyone else from the authorities arrive, please tell them I'll be along shortly."

Monica watched Chiara drive away, but instead of starting her car, she drummed her fingers on the steering wheel. Something was nagging at her mind, something she had forgotten.

She thought through what she knew about Jane Bawley. The woman knew about the abandoned villa, she had admitted it on the phone the evening before, and she had been keen on the idea that Evie might have gone there. Was Evie in fact briefed to go there? Was Joe? He'd lost little time after his arrival in finding the old villa and breaking in. He'd even found the glass photographic plates. If Jane had instructed one or both of them to search the abandoned villa, what was her motive? Did she know of its secrets? Was she trying to trap them?

Her fingers continued drumming. What was it? What had she forgotten? She stared across the fields to the lush vineyards, desperate for inspiration. Jane had been there before, was that it? She had been staying at Villa Brocanti when Paolo went missing. Until now, it had always been thought he died in the forest, but Monica now knew Paolo had somehow found his way into the old villa and become trapped in the maze Salvatore Brocanti had set up so many years before. Jane must know something else about Paolo's disappearance, why else would she be so interested in the abandoned villa? So interested, in fact, that she had followed up on their phone conversation by flying immediately out to Italy and coming to the villa. Monica had to find her and confront her.

She suddenly sat bolt upright. "Oh my God, the ball of paper!" she cried out loud as her hand dived for the pocket of her jeans.

The screwed-up sheet of paper had been clenched tightly in Paolo's fist and it was only when Monica separated his hands after Joe had carried the body down from the top floor that she had seen it. Some sixth sense had stopped her from telling Joe about it, as if Paolo had hidden it in his hand for her and only her to find. She had quickly put it in her jeans' pocket and in the aftermath of all the events that followed, she had forgotten about it.

After carefully smoothing out the ball of paper over her thighs, she held it up to the daylight. It was covered in wild, untidy writing.

Chapter Forty-Four

'*My dearest Nica,*

I am going to die. I know it even though I feel more alive, more my old self, than I have felt since the accident. How can that be?

Nica, I am so sorry that I frightened the Englishwoman. I meant her no harm. I panicked and she thought I was going to hurt her. But instead she hurt me. She hit me with her torch. Which is why I followed her, I wanted to explain. I followed her into the old villa and ran after her along corridors and up stairs until I caught up with her here in this room. She seemed to know the way.

And, oh Nica, how sad this room is. The little children. It must be Salvatore Brocanti and his family. I wonder what happened that made them trapped like I have been.

I thought that when the Englishwoman hit me again in here with her torch and the door shut, she would come back, that she wouldn't punish me for long. But she isn't coming back, I know that now. There is no way out of this room and I am going to die.

I am getting very weak, it won't be much longer. But perhaps it is for the best. My life since the accident has been worth little, even with all your kindness.

I love you, Nica, my beloved sister.'

.   .   .

Monica stared in disbelief at the words on the paper. Jane Bawley had been responsible for Paolo's death? She had let the door shut on him and left him to die in that terrible room? And for the last two years she had known about the secrets of the abandoned villa and done nothing about it?

"Paolo!" she wailed, her voice cracking, tears flooding down her cheeks.

Fighting to control her shaking hands, she gripped the note tightly as if it were Paolo himself and she thought of the supreme effort it must have taken for her brother to have written it. Each letter was deliberately and carefully formed, some capitals, some small, hardly any of them joined. But it was lucid, oh, so lucid. Not the Paolo the world had known since the accident but the old Paolo, trapped behind so many lost motor skills that he was thought to be a simpleton. But he wasn't; he simply needed more time to communicate than most people were prepared to give him.

Monica clenched her jaw. She had to find Jane and demand to know what she was planning. Stop her from whatever it was. She frowned. What *was* she planning? Had she sent Evie to check Paolo's body was still there? Or was she working through some grudge against Evie, and perhaps Joe? Once they were both trapped inside the villa, was she intending to kill them as well? The bitch, she had sounded so plausible on the phone only last night, when all along she knew Paolo had been lying dead in the villa for more than two years.

"And," Monica whispered to herself incredulously, "she must have known Paolo was my brother; Anna Riccardi would have told her. She'd known all along and lied to me on the phone about it. She's one big lie from start to finish."

From the whirlwind of conflicting ideas and anger spinning through her mind, one terrifying thought emerged: perhaps if Jane thought she had both Evie and Joe trapped inside the villa, she intended to destroy it along with all the bodies inside it. Burn it to the ground. That's what the Brocanti family had always insisted had happened. But it couldn't be allowed to happen. Paolo was in there. Jane mustn't destroy his body, nor any of the others. The awful truth of what had happened in the villa, the insane creations of Salvatore Brocanti and all that had happened as a consequence of his madness, must not be lost or destroyed. The truth had to come out and Jane Bawley had to be made accountable for her part in the villa's shocking secrets.

After carefully folding her brother's letter and putting it in her breast pocket, Monica turned the key in the ignition and slipped her car into gear.

As her car bounced back along the rough track to where she had parked early the same morning, Monica puzzled over why she and Joe hadn't crossed paths with Jane. The woman was at least two hours behind them but they should have seen her either inside the villa or in the grounds outside. Unless …

Unless, thought Monica, unless what she and Joe had talked about earlier was true. Unless the labyrinthine maze of tricks, stairways and rooms was far more elaborate and widespread than they themselves had realised. Both she and Joe, and, it would appear, Evie, had found the same way into the villa. But on the day he arrived, Joe must have found another way when he found the glass photographic plates. Suppose that way in led to a different path through the villa. Jane could have followed the same route, or perhaps she knew of yet another way in that led to a different corner of Salvatore Brocanti's madness. How many avenues of deception had the lunatic created? How many top-floor rooms designed to trap people were there? And, if there were more, how many more bodies might they contain? She had to find out, and find out quickly before Jane had the opportunity to destroy everything.

She skidded to a halt near Joe's car, grabbed her backpack that still contained one of her torches along with a full bottle of water, and raced off in the direction of the old villa.

Bursting from the forest about fifteen minutes later, she stopped, her body bent over, hands on knees as she gasped for breath after her second sprint through the forest in less than an hour. Her face and hands were scratched and bleeding from where she had charged through the undergrowth, but she hardly noticed.

As she sucked in air, she considered the best way forward. There was no point in going back in through the storerooms at the rear of the villa, she had to look for another entrance, the one Jane had discovered two years before and probably used again that morning. It must have been well concealed or it would have been found before now.

Knowing Jane would have approached the villa on the track that led from Villa Brocanti, Monica ran along the rear, past the doors where Joe had broken in and round to one side to the point where she was sure Jane would have emerged from the forest. Here she expected to find one or more heavily barred doors that accessed the original cantinas.

She ran down the slightly sloping land at the side of the villa, her eyes searching for any signs of disturbance to the extensive growth of creepers that were clinging to and climbing up the walls. She didn't have to search for long.

"Yes!" she cried as she saw it.

About halfway along the wall, the tangle of undergrowth had been pulled to one side to reveal one of the entrances to the cantina, a recessed door that was now open. Monica stopped in front of it and immediately saw that the brickwork and cement where the hinges had been bolted to the wall had crumbled, making pulling the door open from the hinged side a relatively easy task, one that bypassed the lock. But if those bolts were carefully pushed back into place in the wall, the door would look intact, and if the greenery were also dragged back to cover the door, it would be hidden.

The present disturbance was recent and it seemed clear to Monica that Jane Bawley must have entered the villa this way. And if the door was ajar, that could only mean she was still inside.

Monica took the torch from her backpack, turned it on and shone the light through the doorway into the darkness beyond.

Her eyes were fully adapted to the strong sunlight outside the villa and in the several moments they took to adjust, the torch beam seemed to make little impression on the opaque void of the cantina. She paused, waiting until the space in front of her resolved sufficiently for her to find her way through.

The cantina was larger than she had expected, extending for well over half the footprint of the villa. And unlike in the rooms above, its vaulted ceilings were genuine, while its racks, shelves and alcoves, its stained brickwork and its oily, slightly acidic air were all evidence of the long-past activity of a once vibrant estate. Now only unclaimed memories hung in the air, waiting patiently for oblivion.

While her eyes took in more of the vastness of the cantina, Monica listened carefully for any sounds that might indicate where Jane had gone. But there was only distant birdsong and the chatter of crickets from the forest behind her on the other side of the door.

Confident that she could now pass quickly and quietly through the cantina, she directed the torch beam out in front of her and ran the length of the uneven, stone-slabbed floor. In her haste, she missed the door that opened onto the stairs leading to the old apartment, but even if she had stopped to try it, she would have found it locked.

What did catch her eye as she approached the far end were two doors, one of which was open. Not wanting to miss anything, in case Jane was trying to trick her, she tried the handle of the closed door and found it was unlocked. Peering through, she saw that beyond was a corridor that was bricked up at the far end. She closed the door again; that way didn't look promising.

By contrast, the other door, the one already open, offered a more exciting prospect: a set of stairs leading upwards towards the ground floor of the main villa.

Monica ran quickly up the stairs. At the top, there was a door to her right while ahead of her, a passageway continued into the darkness. She lifted her torch and in the distance, some way along the passageway, another door was caught in the beam, and that door appeared to be open.

She stopped, wondering which way to choose. Again, wary of any tricks, she turned the handle of the door to her right and pushed. As the door opened, she could feel the same balance and movement she had felt earlier in the doors designed to close automatically. Remaining in the doorway so the door couldn't trap her, she shone the torch beam around the room and immediately recognised it as the one with the large painted fireplace she had entered via the single-storey storeroom at the rear of the villa. And as if to confirm her thoughts, in the centre of the room she could see one of the boots Evie had been wearing when they found her. It had fallen off as Joe was carrying her out and they hadn't bothered to retrieve it; Evie's rescue was too urgent.

Monica shone the torch beam around the room. Something wasn't right. She had come into this room earlier that day, as Joe had the previous day, and she had followed the corridor beyond the door in the corner to the upper floor where there had been just two ways to go. The first led into the room with the trompe l'oeil painting of the hole in the floor, from where another door led up to the top-floor room where Paolo had met his fate along with Salvatore, Isabella and their children. The second route had been through the room opposite the one with the fake hole, from where an almost identical stairway led up to the second top-floor room where they had found Evie and the torn-apart remains of another body.

There were no other doors and no other routes. So why hadn't they encountered Jane? She was clearly still in the building, unless she had left and not bothered to replace the camouflage to the cantina door, which seemed unlikely.

Monica backed out through the doorway into the passageway. She needed to check the door at the far end. As she ran towards it, she wondered why the door was open. Why hadn't it self-closed if it was the same as the others? It was only as she neared the door that she saw a chair had been pulled against it, preventing it from moving. She smiled grimly to herself, more confident that now she was on the right track.

When she shone the torch beam onto the walls of the room, Monica stopped in her tracks, her brain not believing what her eyes were telling her. The room was identical to the one she had just left with only one exception: the large curtain was still in place. All other features were identical: the fireplace, the pictures above it, the curtains over the windows, everything, and all of them fake, all of them paintings designed to fool the eye.

She quickly reasoned that if the room was the same, there would be a door in the corner behind the curtain that would lead to the upper floor. Running to the corner, she pulled on the curtain, and there it was, a door with a handle on both sides, one that wasn't designed to close automatically. And beyond that, a short corridor and some stairs.

Quickly now, but as quietly as she could, Monica ran up the stairs and came to the same fake balustrade at the top and the same narrow corridor that looked wider than it was. At the end there were, as she now expected, two doors, one to the left and one to the right.

Stopping outside them, she thought back to the parallel setup farther back in the villa. The way to the room where Paolo had been trapped had been to the left, via the room with the fake hole in the floor. If Jane was looking for Paolo and had taken the wrong route from the cantina, that was the door she would go through. She pushed open the left door, knowing this was also one that wouldn't close on her, and there in front of her was an identical painting of a floor with a huge hole. The room was also lit from a fake window, and Monica couldn't resist running over to it, her suspicions confirmed when she saw yet another version of the painting of the woman sitting in the garden.

She stopped, sensing she was nearing the end of her hunt for Jane, that she would find her in the room above, either examining it or trapped in it. She wondered if she would just leave her if she were trapped. The temptation was certainly there.

"It's all the bitch deserves," she muttered, although the phrase she used in Italian for 'bitch' was far more descriptively vivid and foul-mouthed. She blushed at the thought she had actually said it.

The door to the short corridor leading to the stairs to the top floor was exactly where she expected. She opened it and walked through, cautious now. The farthest of the doors with handles was open and the serpent and creeper covered stairs ran upwards to a large dark wooden door at the top that Monica could see was open.

Something has to be blocking the door to prevent it from closing, she thought.

She walked quietly up the stairs and as she neared the top, she could hear someone muttering indistinctly. She turned off the torch and tiptoed into the room. Directly opposite, she could see the door to the inner room was also open, and kneeling on the ground beyond the door was a woman who appeared to be closely examining something. The light from the same type of skylight she had seen in the other top-floor rooms was diffuse, but less so. She glanced up at the skylight and saw it was broken, a gaping hole in its centre.

Monica stopped by the doorway, trying to see what the woman was doing, and when it became clear she had to suppress a gasp.

Lying on the ground near the woman was the body of a man in military uniform, and the woman appeared to be going through his pockets. Farther away, propped against the far wall, was a second body, its head slumped forward and a gun in its right hand.

"What the hell do you think you are doing?" said Monica, her voice louder than she meant.

The woman jerked backwards and screamed.

"What the …? Fuck, you gave me a start. You could kill someone like that."

"You are Jane. I recognise your voice."

Jane glared at her, putting two and two together and not liking the result.

"Monica Lieti?" she asked.

Monica nodded curtly. "Yes, and you haven't answered my question."

"Question?"

"What do you think you are doing?"

Jane looked guiltily at the body of the man whose pockets she had been searching. "I was just … just checking out who they are."

"They look like German soldiers from the second world war," said Monica as she ran her eyes over the bodies and recognised the uniforms. "And you were stealing things from them."

She nodded towards a small collection of items on the ground next to Jane. A wallet, ID card, coins, a medal, two watches. "Or were you collecting those for their descendants?" she added, her voice loaded with sarcasm.

"They're long dead," said Jane, with a shrug. "What difference does it make?"

"It's theft and you have no right," snapped Monica. She paused and looked around the room. "What are you doing in the villa? Why did you come here?"

Jane looked down at her hands. She was still kneeling on the floor and showed no sign of wanting to move. "I was—"

"You were looking for Paolo, weren't you? Paolo's body, I mean. He died here in this villa because of you."

Jane's quiet reply was defiant. "He was going to rape me. I had to get away."

"Paolo wasn't capable of raping anyone," said Monica disdainfully. "He meant you no harm."

"He was a man," snarled Jane. "He was capable of rape if he put his mind to it."

"No," said Monica, "he wasn't. His mind was a mess because of an accident, but he was a gentle, kind man who wouldn't have hurt a fly."

"Then why did he stop me in the forest, knock me to the ground?"

"I doubt he knocked you to the ground on purpose. It was either accidental or you just tripped. He would have been trying to help you."

'Posso aiutarti?'

The words echoed in Jane's mind.

"You speak Italian, don't you?" asked Monica, her voice breaking into Jane's thoughts.

"*Was* he trying to help you?"

"How was I to know?" protested Jane. "He came out of nowhere. And he looked—"

"Terrible? Ugly? Deformed? A madman?"

"I tried to get away, but he chased me. Chased me here."

"He only wanted to explain. He felt guilty."

"How the hell do you know that? Do you speak to the dead?"

"As a matter of fact, I do," replied Monica, as she removed

Paolo's letter from her shirt pocket. "Do you read Italian as well as speak it?"

"Of course."

"Then read this," she said, thrusting the letter under Jane's nose.

Jane took the letter and read through it. Handing it back, she sat on her heels and exhaled deeply. "Shit, I'm so sorry."

Monica studied Jane's eyes, not convinced by her apology. Her whole attitude was too flippant. "I can understand … just … why you left him trapped in the room. You were genuinely concerned he might hurt you. But then you left him here to die. You murdered him. That is totally unforgivable. Why did you do it?"

Jane looked down at her hands again.

"You have to understand," she said, defensively, "I was raped … in London. Some years ago. When Paolo appeared, I thought it was going to happen again. And anyway, I didn't mean to leave him. I had every intention of coming back the next day and releasing him. I knew how to from when I explored the villa and found the other bodies."

"Yes, of course, you found the bodies of Salvatore Brocanti and his family, and yet you told no one. Why?"

"I'd broken into this villa against all of Ernesto Brocanti's specific and forcefully articulated instructions, and Anna's, for that matter. Ernesto's an intimidating man and I felt as if I'd committed high treason. But I had to do it. I'd seen some of the images of the trompe l'oeil paintings, which I thought were amazing, and I just had to see more. Anna Riccardi told me all the stories about the villa being haunted or whatever, which I thought was a load of crap. And as I said, both she and Ernesto, particularly Ernesto, absolutely forbade me from coming anywhere near."

She shrugged. "I'm a journalist. Being told that was like a red rag to a bull. I had to get inside the place, see what all the fuss was about for myself. The first door I passed through was one of the self-closing ones designed to trap someone, but I spotted it and prevented it from closing. After that, I blocked open all the others I passed through as I worked my way through the villa. The paint-ings were pretty mind-blowing, as you know, and I wanted to see as many of them as I could. Finding the bodies was a massive surprise. I was pretty sure none of the family knew about them, they couldn't possibly have and kept it quiet. But having found them, I fully intended to tell the Brocantis, even with the risk of Ernesto blowing a gasket. I left all of the doors blocked open and I was on the way back to Villa Brocanti to tell them about the bodies when Paolo accost… when I met your brother. Then it all, I don't know, it got out of hand."

Monica shook her head. "I'm sorry you were raped in London. It must have been dreadful. But I still don't understand why you left him to die."

She paused, frowning. "You said you intended to come back and release him?"

"Look," said Jane, "I'd got it all worked out. The next day, Anna and Ernesto were leaving early, heading for Rome, while I was going in the other direction in a cab. I had at least a couple of hours when I would be at the villa on my own, more than enough time to come back here and release your brother. But then they changed their minds. Said they were going north and could give me a lift to the airport. I could hardly refuse."

"So you left him! You left Paolo and told no one!" Monica's voice was rising.

"You murdered him!" she cried. "I don't think you had any intention of coming back to release my brother. If you had, you would have left all the internal doors blocked open when you left the second time, and none of them was. That's why Evie and Joe were trapped. They had no idea about the doors until it was too late."

Jane was shaking her head in denial. "No, it wasn't like that. When I ran from the villa after trapping Paolo, I automatically shut the doors behind me without thinking. Don't forget he had chased me through the villa. I was afraid and at that moment I wanted plenty of barriers between him and me."

The sneer on Monica's face was one of total contempt. "I don't believe one word of that. I think you deliberately left Paolo here to die the most horrible death. Do you know what it was like? Have you any idea?"

Jane continued looking downwards, her eyes drifting towards the two bodies next to her. Monica watched and snorted scornfully.

"Don't think it was the same as for these two. Once they accepted that no one was going to find them, they took the quick way out. They shot themselves."

She glanced up at the skylight. "Presumably they shot out the window and yelled their lungs out, but deep in this forest, there was no one to hear them. Having broken into this place, they too fell foul of Salvatore Brocanti's madness and were trapped."

Jane shrugged. "Perhaps someone lured them into the villa. They were part of the occupying forces, after all."

Monica nodded. "I remember my grandfather telling me that during the war, two soldiers from a squad based in Coniglio went missing. It was assumed by the Germans they had been murdered and so they extracted their usual revenge on the local population: a ten for one reprisal. They dragged out twenty villagers from Coniglio and shot them."

"Then I have no compunction about taking what I've removed," said Jane, tossing her head with a nonchalance that angered Monica.

"Well you should!" she barked. "Don't you think you've done enough damage here? You have no right to take anything." She paused, trying to calm down.

"You still haven't told me why you are here. Were you checking that Evie and Joe were trapped? Were you hoping they would suffer the same fate as Paolo?"

"Don't be so bloody stupid," spat Jane. "I had suggested — *suggested*, mind, not instructed — to Joe that he might like to check out the trompe l'oeil paintings, knowing he would be fascinated. I rather hoped his curiosity would take him through the villa and he would find the bodies, including Paolo's, especially since I found out Paolo was your brother. I thought Joe would be bound to tell you, that you would have closure. I had no idea Evie would stick her stupid nose in."

"You expect me to believe that?" yelled Monica. "Believe that after two years you suddenly had pangs of conscience and decided to do the right thing?"

Her eyes narrowed. "But, of course," she added, her tone once again heavy with sarcasm, "do it in such a way that no blame for Paolo's death would fall on you. What do you want? That I should be grateful to you?"

She felt like punching Jane hard in the face. She paused in an attempt to control her anger before continuing.

"Well, your idea nearly backfired. When we found Evie, she was close to death. She might still die and you'll have another death on your hands. Joe would have too if he hadn't been so resourceful."

"Joe was trapped and escaped? How?"

"Maybe you should spend some time pondering the problem," said Monica as she stepped back into the doorway.

Jane had guessed what was coming and she jumped to her feet. But instead of rushing at her as Monica thought she would, Jane raised her hand, levelling a pistol at her, one she had found lying next to the dead soldier.

"You know," said Jane, her eyes now cold and calculating, "I don't think the police will have too much trouble believing you were fiercely trying to defend what you did two years ago when you imprisoned your simpleton brother and left him to die, that you panicked when I discovered you here and grabbed a gun from one of these two. I'll tell them you intended to trap me here, to leave me to rot."

"What the hell are you talking about? Do you honestly think the police would believe that nonsense? You forget I am known around here. They would take my word over yours."

"That's the point, you idiot." Jane's voice was even colder as she extended her arm to take aim. "You won't be in a position to give them your version."

"Jane!" screamed Monica, her eyes fixed on Jane's finger as it squeezed the trigger.

But the trigger resisted. Jane lifted her other hand, closing one index finger over the other, and still the gun failed to fire, the mechanism corroded after seventy-five years.

"Damn!" she said. She tossed the gun aside and reached

towards the second soldier, whose gun was still resting in his right hand.

Taking the second gun in both her hands, Jane swung round to point it at Monica, but instead of her intended target, she found herself staring at the closed door and the backpack Monica had left behind on the floor.

The sound of Jane's scream was muted by the thick stone door, but as Monica stood by the doorway to the stairs, it was still clear enough.

"Monica! You bitch! You can't leave me here. You'll be as guilty as I was. They'll find me; you'll go to prison. Monica!"

Monica waited, torn between opening the door now or leaving Jane to stew in her terror for a few hours.

"I wasn't really going to shoot you!" yelled Jane. "You have to believe me. I knew these guns were jammed, that they wouldn't fire. I was only trying to frighten you."

Monica was still waiting, still torn, when the silence of the villa was shattered by the sound of gunfire. One shot, followed quickly by another from inside the closed room.

She lifted her chin in defiance towards the door. "Jammed, you say?"

In the inner room, Jane took aim a third time, but she had used the last round. The gun's hammer clicked harmlessly.

"Bitch!" she yelled. "How did Joe get out? What did he know that the others didn't?"

It wasn't so much the answer to her question that frightened Jane, but the increasing faintness of Monica's voice as she walked back down the stairs.

"Work it out," she called. "Work it out."

____

Chapter Forty-Five

Jane Bawley hurled the useless gun at the door.

"Monica!" she screamed at the top of her voice, but all her yelling achieved was to disturb a few birds in nearby trees, the sound carrying through the broken skylight window.

She turned and took aim at the nearest dead soldier with her foot, kicking him hard in the thigh.

"Ow!" she yelled as her toe connected with bone, her trainers offering her foot little protection. "Bastard!" she screamed, kicking him again.

Suddenly repulsed by the thought of being trapped with two long-dead bodies, she folded her arms around herself, backing away until she was leaning against a wall. Her jaw set in anger, she let herself slide down the wall until she was sitting on the hard floor of terracotta tiles.

But although she had put a couple of metres between herself and the bodies, she found she couldn't take her eyes off them. They had been trapped here during the second world war and shot themselves rather than die from the horrifying ordeal of starvation and dehydration.

The other bodies, the ones she had discovered in a different but almost identical room two years before, the room she had intended to return to today but she had taken the wrong door in the cantina and been fooled by Salvatore's tricks, those bodies hadn't had that choice. They had been forced to endure the gradually failing consciousness, the torture of agonising dreams as their faculties and strength failed them. She shuddered in a fit of guilt when she remembered that she herself had inflicted that torture on Monica's brother.

And she shuddered again when she remembered that what the Brocantis, the soldiers and Monica's brother all had in common was they died in their captivity. None of them had found a way out.

So how had Joe? Perhaps the door to the room hadn't closed properly and he had managed to force it open.

'*Work it out,*' Monica had said. What did she mean?

Jane jumped up and turned to where the door closed tightly into its frame. She could hardly get a fingernail into the seam, so close a fit was it. There was no question of it not closing properly, so it couldn't be that.

'*Work it out.*'

Jane sat back down again and explored the walls and roof with her eyes. She shook her head. That's exactly what these two idiots would have done, she thought, so would Brocanti and his family, and perhaps even Paolo. And, of course, Evie, and she hadn't worked it out either. In fact she had nearly died, according to Monica.

She frowned. How come all the Brocantis had died here? Salvatore Brocanti had created the entire nightmare. If there was any way out to be found, he should know it.

Her thoughts kept coming back to Joe. He had worked it out. She pursed her lips. In Jane's book, Joe might be a good photographer, but he wasn't the brightest kid on the block. And yet …

Jane prided herself on her intellect. She had a high IQ, very high, which mainly meant she was good at solving problems. Finding the right box from a set of alternatives. Given a closed gate, she would never assume it was locked and climb over it; she would always try it first. It was an obvious move. That was the point about problems; they were solutions in disguise. Some prat of a maths teacher had once told her that, although he seemed to think the solution to all his problems lay in trying to get inside her underwear, the bastard.

Having eyeballed the entire room, she stood and explored it at close quarters. Which is what the soldiers would have done. And Joe. What had Joe discovered in the process that the others had missed?

'*Work it out.*'

As she turned in the far corner from the door and looked back across the room, Jane saw the backpack that Monica had left behind. She frowned. Why would she do that? It must have been a deliberate action since the pack had been slung across her back. What was inside it? The key to getting out? Had Monica left her the means to escape, or at least, a clue as to how to achieve it?

She hurried over to the bag and pulled open the flap, only to find that all it contained was a one-litre plastic bottle of water.

"That's it?" she cried. "A crappy bottle of water? OK, thanks, Monica, big deal. Is that supposed to add to my life expectancy and improve the chances of someone finding me alive? Or did you leave it so my agony would stretch out further? So instead of four or five days of shitting myself in fear, it might go on to be six, or even seven. Bitch."

She looked across at the soldiers. "No sign of water canteens of any sort. You guys didn't come too prepared, did you? I wonder how long you lasted without water before you decided to end it all. Was it a joint decision or did Fritz 1 get pissed off with Fritz 2's whining and whingeing and shoot him? And then, full of remorse, did he do the honourable thing himself?"

'*Work it out.*'

Monica's three words echoed constantly around her head.

"What the hell did you mean, Monica?" she said as she unscrewed the bottle to take a sip of water.

Bringing the bottle to her lips, she paused. "I s'pose I should ration this carefully," she said. "Mustn't waste it. What do you think, Fritz 1?"

She held up the bottle to the body of the soldier closer to her.

"Or are you Fritz 2? Actually, what are your names? It would be nice to know who I'm sharing this sepulchre with. I was getting there when mad Monica arrived."

She stood and took a step towards the body, but as she did, her foot caught in the straps of the backpack, making her stumble. As she groped for the wall in an attempt to stop herself from falling, the bottle of water slipped from her grasp, its contents flooding from it as it hit the floor and rolled away from her.

"Bollocks! No!" she cried.

She dived for the water bottle, grabbing its neck and lifting it up to eye level to check how much she had lost.

"Sod it!" she yelled. "What a waste! Maybe I can lick it up."

She looked down at the floor to where the puddle of water should be, but all she could see was a couple of damp tiles.

"Are terracotta tiles really that absorbent?" she said, frowning.

She continued to stare at the tiles, convinced they were telling her something. After about ten seconds, she sat back on her heels and punched the air.

"Yes!"

She had worked it out.

An hour later, with the aid of one of the gun stocks used as a hammer to break tiles and a gun barrel to gouge at the mortar below, Jane had cleared a roughly circular area of nearly fifty centimetres in diameter. Her digging had been frantic, but all the time she had been grinning in self-satisfaction, impressed with her powers of deduction.

"I wonder what your eureka moment was Joe? I bet I worked it out faster."

She shook her head. "You crafty cow, Monica. A bottle of water? It should have had 'Pour me' on the label. Anyway, thanks for the tip. Jeez, I'm glad the bloody gun I pointed at you didn't go off. That would have taken some explaining."

Using a boot from one of the soldiers, she scooped away the mortar until she could see the terracotta tiles of the ceiling below. However, on removing several of those, she was surprised, as Joe had been, to see another row of terracotta tiles arranged in a herringbone pattern. Not really understanding it, she reached into the hole and struck the lower course of tiles with the gun stock, knocking some away and squealing with delight as she peered into the room below.

After hammering at the false terracotta ceiling to make a big enough hole for her body to pass through, Jane grasped one of the exposed joists and carefully lowered herself so she was hanging in the air, her feet still over three metres above the floor.

"Fingers crossed," she cried, and let go. She landed cat-like and sprang to an upright position.

"Perfect," she exclaimed. "Right, Monica, I can't wait to see your face when I show up at Villa Brocanti. You called me a murderer. If I hadn't worked it out, you'd be one too."

The room was lit by the fake window, but the stairs leading to the room below and the way through the cantina would be in darkness.

"Shit," muttered Jane when she remembered she had left her torch in the top-floor room. Then she patted her jeans pocket. "My phone!" she yelled, exultantly.

The light from the phone's torch was enough to guide her down the stairs and across the room below to the door that led to the corridor from the cantina. After running along the corridor, she hurried down the stairs and now she could see light at the far end of the cantina coming through the open door.

"The bitch left it open for me," she said. "How kind."

Treading carefully, but still wanting to get to the freedom of the outside world as quickly as possible, Jane hurried through the cantina and stepped through the door. She wondered whether to close it and hide it from view, but given that Monica would no doubt soon be back, there didn't seem to be much point.

She walked out into the sunshine and sucked in a huge lungful of air. She had been in the abandoned villa a total of just three hours, but it seemed like a lifetime.

Pumping her arms in the air, she let out a massive screech of delight. "Wahoo!" she whooped. "Up yours, Monica Lieti! Game set and match to Jane Bawley!"

. . .

Directly above her, on the roof, a pair of crows had been padding around looking for insects and grubs. They were cautious; claws had been bumped and crushed before in this weird environment of loose, wobbly and crumbling tiles.

Startled by the sudden cries from below, the pair squawked their complaints in unison as each of them pushed down on the tile it was standing on to assist the jump for its launch. As they flew away, still complaining to each other, one of the tiles disturbed by the launch began to slide. It collided with another that also began sliding, which in turn collided with others. Moments later, a minor avalanche of five heavy terracotta roof tiles slipped over the edge of the roof and accelerated towards the ground twenty metres below. In their path was a jubilant woman still punching the air in delight at her escape from death.

Afterword

I hope very much that you enjoyed reading *An Imperfect Revenge*. If you did, I should be extremely grateful if you could spend a few moments posting a review on Amazon or Goodreads (or both!). It needn't be long; one word will do — preferably a favourable one! Genuine reviews, however short, are worth a lot.

And equally as important, please recommend *An Imperfect Revenge* to your relatives, friends and colleagues. While word of mouth is very helpful to the cause of any author, it is particularly so for self-published authors for whom marketing is that much harder. If you tell a few people about this book or any of my other books, and they in turn tell others, the word will spread.

You can find more information about all my books and other book-related stuff on my website at davidgeorgeclarke.com. If you are on FaceBook, Instagram, Twitter and/or Goodreads, I'm there too:

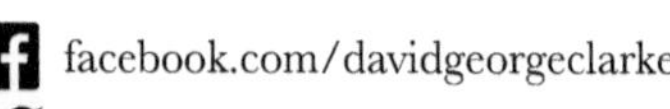

facebook.com/davidgeorgeclarkeauthor

twitter.com/clarkefiction

instagram.com/clarkefiction

goodreads.com/davidgeorgeclarke

If you would like to listen to a free audiobook version of An Imperfect Revenge read by the author, scanning the QR code above with the camera on your phone will take you to a link to sign up to the clarkeFiction newsletter and download the file. You will also be guided to the BookFunnel app for listening to the book.

Enjoy!

Acknowledgments

This novel could not have been completed without the help and encouragement of many people.

First and foremost, I could not have continued down my novel-writing journey without the constant support and encouragement of my wife Gail. She is always there as a sounding board for ideas, a critical and constructive reviewer of drafts, and an enthusiastic supporter of the project. More than anyone, this book is dedicated to her, with love.

In addition, I should like to thank Susanna Moles, Linda Davy, Luci de Nordwall Cornish and Simon O'Reilly for their invaluable help, advice and criticism, together with their expert editing and proofreading.

I should also like to thank my friend and architect Mauro Paci of Studio Associato Paci, Arezzo, for his advice and suggestions with regards to the largely lost art of creating false ceilings using terracotta tiles.

The original idea for this novel came out of a visit I made some years ago to a large villa under restoration in the Chianti hills, although its delightful trompe l'oeil walls most certainly were not created for nefarious purposes. My thanks go to art restorer Laura Salvadori for letting me tag along.

About the Author

After more than thirty years as a forensic scientist, most of which were spent in Hong Kong, David Clarke retired to the more bucolic pastures of Tuscany where, after dabbling in art restoration, he took up full-time novel writing. Drawing on his experiences in the scientific investigation of numerous serious crimes, he has written The Dust of Centuries series, the Cotton & Silk crime thriller series and this stand-alone novel

He now shares his time between Tuscany, Italy and Phuket, Thailand.

A Final Word

Do you have kids or grandchildren, a favourite godson or goddaughter, a class of kids you teach or support in some way? My wife Gail is an author and illustrator who has published ten beautifully illustrated children's books. They are written in rhyme that children from 4–9 years just love reading or having read to them.

Patrick's Birthday Message
Searching for Skye — An Arctic Tern Adventure
Cosmos the Curious Whale
The Chameleon Who Couldn't Change Colour
Sharks — Our Ocean Guardians
[The Shark Guardian Series Book 1]
Jed's Big Adventure
[The Shark Guardian Series Book 2]
Ndotto — An Elephant Rescue Story
Mischief at the Waterhole
Dormouse Snoremouse
Meerkat's Exciting Adventure

You can find more details on Gail's website and YouTube channel:

www.gailclarkeauthor.com
www.youtube.com/c/gailclarkeauthor